Praise f

Set in Stone

'Stela Brinzeanu weaves an engrossing tale of superstition, rebellion and love. A richly rewarding read.'

ESTHER FREUD, bestselling author of *Hideous Kinky*

'*Set in Stone* is a lush page-turner about two women, Mira and Elina, who fight for their futures in a patriarchal society. They stole my heart, and I enjoyed every minute spent in medieval Moldova – from the adventure and romance to the chilling moment when I grasped the meaning of the title. This timely folktale will resonate with readers.'

JANET SKESLIEN CHARLES, award-winning author of *Moonlight in Odessa* and *The Paris Library*

'Forget your damsels in distress – *Set in Stone* weaves together the paths of two bright and fierce young women who are determined to fight for the lives and love they deserve. A memorable debut that brings medieval Moldova to life with vivid colour, this is storytelling at its best.'

ELLEN KEITH, author of *The Dutch Wife*

STELA BRINZEANU

Legend Press Ltd, 51 Gower Street, London, WC1E 6HJ
info@legendpress.co.uk | www.legendpress.co.uk

 British Library Cataloguing in Publication Data available.

Print ISBN 978-1-915054-586
Ebook ISBN 978-1-91505-4-593
Set in Times. Printing managed by Jellyfish Solutions Ltd
Cover design by Rose Cooper | www.rosecooper.com

Printed and bound by CPI Group (UK) Ltd, Croydon CR0 4YY

Stela Brinzeanu was born in Moldova and moved to London where she completed a BA in Media Studies at the University of Westminster before training at the BBC and setting up a community magazine. Stela's work is an expression of her background – a 'cultural crossbreed', whose writing revolves around issues of identity and belonging, gender roles, our interconnectedness with nature and the conflict of organised religion versus spirituality.

AUTHOR NOTE

I've been fascinated by folk stories and legends from a young age, first by listening to them as they were recounted by our elders, and later by reading them myself.

There's one in particular, renowned in Eastern Europe and throughout the Balkans, which has baffled and unsettled me ever since I first read it. As a child, I would cry at the fate of the woman in the story; later, as a teenager in a post-communist country, fearful of authority – I quietly questioned it in my diaries; as a young woman I was enraged by it; and now, as an adult, it makes me consider the role that women have played across history, and their often unknown, unacknowledged contributions to the world we live in.

Perhaps, most importantly, it makes me think about the kind of world we could be living in, had women been able to play an equal role alongside their male counterparts.

Set In Stone is a reimagining of this legend in which I seek to give a voice to the women who have been silenced.

In the interest of authenticity, and out of respect for the place and time the story is set, I have used Romanian words where there was no direct English translation. For those of you who love a glossary – you will find one at the end of this book.

This is a work of fiction, despite its source inspiration. Certain things mentioned in this book have happened at some point in the history of Moldova or the former Romanian Principalities, and this ambiguity is intended to suit the convenience of the story.

The Romanian words sprinkled throughout the novel have been used in their basic form for consistency and ease of reading for non-Romanian speakers.

DOWRY

If only she had hit the Little Owl – that harbinger of death who sang its song of doom on their roof – well, maybe her mother would still be alive.

Unable to forgive herself that fateful slip of the hand, Elina spends most of her time in the woods beyond their manor, practising her archery over and over. Today, her father, Boyar Constantin, the landowner of Pasareasca village, has joined her.

'There! A plump one ready for the picking.' Her father aims at the pheasant in the tree.

'Mine!' Elina releases her arrow, but it misses and the bird flies over the bare, tinkling woods.

'You don't point *exactly* at it, my angel. You've got to aim somewhat away from it.'

'You don't always hit your target yourself.'

'Because I don't like to show off.'

Her father sounds sincere, but Elina knows it's not true. She counts his misses to herself each time.

Still, between them they kill three pheasants and injure a hare. It's more than they need but just as well, for as they approach the manor, they spot her uncle, Bogdan, grinning at them from afar. He has taken to visiting them a lot more often since her mother died, and Elina suspects it's because he wants to work on her father about marrying her to his son, who is also her first cousin. Mihnea is a good-looking young man, but his breath and skin smell perpetually of garlic, and each time her father mentions him as a potential suitor, Elina scrunches her nose.

She does that now, when they are still far enough away that her uncle doesn't see it.

'Say what you may, young lady, but blood is thicker than water,' her father says and spurs his horse into a trot ahead of her.

She can't keep up with him, perched awkwardly in her side-saddle. It's an uncomfortable device for both the rider and the horse. When she's alone in the woods, Elina hides the cumbersome seat and rides bareback, like her mother taught her. She remembers how excited she was the first time she rode astride, and how she ran to tell her father all about it, but her mother caught her arm, stopping her so briskly that her elbow popped out of place. Rozalia, her mother's maid, pushed it back in no time, but the searing pain had etched her mother's warning deep into her skull: 'Don't tell anyone – not your father, not even the priest at confession. It's not a sin, but a skill, which – like so many other skills – is only allowed for our men. Let's be smart about it, shall we, sweetheart?'

It was Elina's first secret.

Her father and uncle have already exchanged greetings by the time she reaches them.

'You look like a famished peasant,' Bogdan says.

'Good day to you too, Uncle.' Elina does a little bow, keeping her distance from her uncle, whose face shines with sweat like it's smeared in lanolin.

Eager to get away, she makes her excuses and takes the horses to the stable at the back of the manor.

Old Neculai, her father's steward and fletcher, whistles a song under his breath as he waxes his master's arrows in the backyard. Elina squats next to him, watching his steady movements.

'A bowman is only ever as good as the arrow he uses,' the

old man mumbles, without taking his eyes off his work. 'Too light or too heavy and you lose your game.'

Elina inspects the bag of feathers by Neculai's feet – pheasant, grouse and goose. When he starts fletching the waxed arrows, he chooses the feathers carefully.

'Not only do they have to come from the same bird,' he says, 'but they have got to be from the same wing, miss. Feathers on the right wing curve in the opposite direction to the ones on the left.'

Seeing how serious he is, Elina can't help the urge to tease him. 'What happens if you mix them?'

Neculai looks at her, blinking. 'The wildlife will be happy, miss. But you'll go hungry.'

'Can I have a go?'

The old man hesitates, but she's his master's daughter and reluctantly he agrees.

Elina starts by inspecting each feather – their curvature and length of barbs – but matching them perfectly isn't as easy as it sounds. It's a tedious task, but then it's not as if she's in a hurry to do anything else.

With Neculai's guidance, Elina has just about managed to fletch the second arrow when she hears the sound that makes the blood in her veins go cold.

The hoot of the Little Owl.

She looks up. The bird is perched high on the roof of their manor. Wasn't the death of her mother enough? Whose death is the Little Owl calling for now?

Neculai shoos the bird away, but it traces a wide loop in the mournful sky and returns to their roof, singing its doom anew.

Elina runs to pick up her bow and chooses one of the arrows she's just fletched.

Neculai steps behind her as if to check her position. 'The arrow you've picked has been crafted with too little strength. This means it'll shoot out to the right of the mark,' he says.

Elina rearranges her aim.

'Hold it for a moment, then – very important, miss – release the arrow ahead of your breath.'

Elina follows his exact instructions, and the owl drops to the ground mid-hoot.

Neculai praises her performance, seeming happier that she listened to his counsel than the fact that Elina has stopped the bird's wicked call, thus averting another death in their family. If only she'd killed it that first time…

Florica, the cook, rings a bell to announce dinner is ready, but her father and uncle are nowhere to be seen.

'They're in the cellar, miss,' Florica says.

Two things strike Elina. First, that servants always know everything about their masters; and second, it's odd that her father took his guest to the cellar, when he'd usually have the servants fetch the wine to the dining room.

Unless it's not wine they're in the cellar for, she thinks and sneaks towards the lower ground floor.

The men speak in low voices, but the bare stone walls carry their words all the way up to the top of the stairs where Elina halts.

'Don't you worry, brother, I keep telling you. I'll make sure she gets a good dowry. You have my word.'

'So you keep saying.'

'We're family. Don't you trust me?'

'These are important affairs we're talking about. I want the best for my boy, just like you do for your daughter.'

'You want to know what the marriage settlement is?'

'Proposition. It's not a settlement until we agree on it.'

Her father laughs. 'Alright then. But one thing. Do you think you could feed your boy less garlic?'

Elina cringes. He wasn't supposed to tell her uncle that.

'Why?' Bogdan asks.

'You know women. Sensitive nerves, sensitive noses.'

'I see what you're doing here. But I won't allow for any distractions—'

'Alright, alright. Are you ready? Here we go: two apiaries,

seventy-five hectares of vineyards and an apple orchard, one mill, livestock, silk robes, jewellery, a well-bred horse and nine gypsies. How's that?'

'Such a skinflint. Why don't you throw in a couple of fleas off your dog while you're at it?'

'You're the same greedy hound as always, chasing everything I own, just like when we were children. Alright, I tell you what, I'll add one more horse, but no more – they're too dear – and a dozen more gypsies.'

'Six horses and a coach, twenty bulls for the ploughing and two hundred sheep. Deal?' Bogdan spits in his hand, ready to shake his brother's hand in agreement.

'Father,' Elina calls from the top of the stairs. 'Dinner is ready.'

'Give us a moment,' Bogdan says, scowling at her.

Instead of leaving, Elina descends the stairs towards them.

'I'm terribly hungry, Uncle. And I don't want to look any more of a famished peasant.' Then she tilts her head at her father. 'It's lonely sitting at the dinner table by myself. Will you come join me? Please?'

Her father nods and stands up, but the two men are slow in climbing the stairs and Elina doesn't wait for them.

When they fail to join her in the dining room, she thinks they've stopped to close their deal, but her worry is dispelled as soon as the men walk in, her father beaming at her. 'I've just spoken to Neculai. He's shown me the dead scoundrel. Spiked right through its throat. I'm very proud of you.'

Elina shrugs. 'Blind luck.'

'Doesn't mean you can't be proud of it. It all counts in life. Especially luck,' her father says, and after a brief prayer to bless the food, he fills up two goblets of wine, handing one to his brother.

'Useless skill for a woman, if you ask me.' Bogdan downs half of the wine in one breath.

'A little harmless fun. Women get bored easily.' Her father tucks into the meat platter. 'Aren't you hungry?' He looks at

Elina, who is picking half-heartedly at a piece of cheese. Her earlier hunger has suddenly vanished. 'That won't be enough.' Her father shakes his head. 'You must eat properly, or the wind will blow you away. Just look at you. A pile of bones.'

'A healthy woman is a fleshy woman,' Bogdan says and belches.

'Not so fleshy as to struggle for breath.' Elina shoots a glance at her uncle's paunch. Her uncle, in turn, looks disapprovingly at her father.

'You haven't learned from your mistakes, little brother. You're losing your grip on your daughter like you did with your wife.'

Her father chews on a wing of fried pheasant, pretending he hasn't felt the sting of Bogdan's words. But the tightness in his jaws tells Elina he has been hurt.

Perhaps knowing he's crossed the line, Bogdan changes subject. 'How's the building of the church coming along?'

'It's not,' her father says. 'The second mason we've hired has given up too. Just like the previous attempts, whatever is built during the day crumbles at night. Both masons have claimed the land is cursed.'

'You don't believe that nonsense, do you? It's probably their way of squeezing more coins out of you.'

'I offered, but they wouldn't take it.'

Bogdan shifts in his seat. 'So what are you going to do?'

All three of them know how important the building of this church is. The voivode – the supreme ruler of the country himself – had ordered it, following a hunting party on their estate. He'd shot an arrow to choose the spot where a new church would be built in his honour. In exchange, the voivode would grant Boyar Constantin's request for Elina's legislative change of status from daughter to son. In the absence of any male siblings, Elina would be entitled to the whole inheritance, should anything happen to her father, instead of it being appropriated by the Court, as is the case with so many other heirless boyars.

Elina looks expectantly at her father, hoping he has the answer. Being granted the right of inheritance means that if he dies suddenly, she won't end up a pauper, or at the nunnery, or at the mercy of some man who marries her out of pity. She will be rich and independent enough to choose her own suitor. That's why her uncle has been pushing for her to marry his son before she's granted this right. To stop her from marrying someone else.

'I've had talks with this master mason – Barbu from up north – who has built abbeys all over the country,' her father says, holding Elina's gaze. 'He tells me he can do the job. Plan is for him and his men to come here in spring.'

'We might even have a wedding by then.' Bogdan grins and empties his cup.

'Will you excuse me, please?' Elina stands down from the table. 'I feel a headache coming. Goodnight,' she says and walks out of the room, the layers of her skirt hissing across the floor.

When Bogdan gets ready to leave the following day, he makes the customary goodbye by kissing Elina's hand. This leaves a wet trace on her skin as if she's been licked by a dog. A little shudder runs through her body, and she rubs her hand on the back of her dress.

She follows Bogdan's coach in secret, riding at a distance and hiding behind trees. She wants to ensure her uncle doesn't change his mind and come back. Only when he's finally over the hill is she reassured enough to take a deep breath and turn back. But she doesn't want to return to the manor straight away. Something troubles her and she can't tell what it is.

Too many things.

She misses her mother so much that she gets a twinge in her chest every time she thinks of her. She loves her father and she's certain he loves her too. She knows that if they locked horns over it, he wouldn't force her to marry her cousin. So what's bothering her?

Perhaps spending some time in the woods will help her

feel better. She hides her side-saddle, keeping only the reins. 'Let's get out of here, Fulger.' She pets her horse, who responds immediately by breaking into a canter towards her favourite place – the bit of the river which twists around a well-hidden glade.

When the wind has plucked the worries out of her head, she draws her bow to see if she's still blessed with the luck she had with the Little Owl the previous day. Unwilling to injure any wildlife unnecessarily, she aims at acorns and pine cones. The more she misses, the more determined she becomes, because she knows she can do it. But it's not happening today, and her arms grow heavy and weak.

A twig snaps and Elina startles, swinging around and raising her bow at the same time, convinced her uncle has come back.

'You're on edge,' the voice says.

It's Rozalia, her late mother's maid. She's standing right behind Elina. How did she get so close without making a sound? But then again, she was always the best beater at her father's hunting parties.

'You show good skills, but there's room for improvement,' the old woman says. 'Your hand and eye are fine. It's your breath that's letting you down. Too laboured for so fine a task.'

'Can't be. We've been walking slowly. Fulger and I.'

'Your body might be calm. But is your mind?'

Elina has no answer to that, for even if she could put a finger on what was unsettling her, she wouldn't reveal it to a peasant, one with whom she already has an axe to grind.

'If you slow your breath down, you'll find it easier to hit your marks.'

Elina has to think about this for a moment. 'Breath does its own thing,' she says. 'How can anyone fiddle with that?'

'There are a few tricks.'

'And you are willing to share them?'

'Who said anything about that?'

'You wouldn't have mentioned it otherwise,' Elina says,

trying not to blink as she looks at the woman who was the last person to see her mother alive.

She will never forget that day – her mother's still body on the floor, her face a pale blue, and a feverish Rozalia kissing her on the mouth and pressing on her chest. She had charged at Rozalia, shoving and kicking her and shouting at her to stop hurting her mother, when the old woman clamped her bony hand on Elina's mouth. 'Keep quiet! I'm trying to lend some of my breath to your unconscious mother. And I'm running out of time.'

Lending some breath? The absurdity of such claim convinced Elina that the crone was insane, but before she could say anything, Rozalia pointed to a half-chewed piece of meat on the floor.

'I've dislodged it from her throat, but she's not coming round.'

Due to her mother's frequent headaches, she often had her meals in her room. Sometimes she wouldn't come out for days at a time, the door to her room jammed from the inside with a broom run through the handle. During this time, only Rozalia was allowed in, bringing with her medicine in small bundles.

None of Rozalia's efforts that day succeeded in reviving her mother. With sweat pouring down her face and out of breath, she said, 'I found her too late. I'm very sorry.'

'You were in her room earlier,' Elina said. She hated Rozalia because her mother often chose to spend time with this coarse old maid instead of her own daughter.

'Yes, I'd brought her medicine for her headache.'

'You were the last to see her alive and the first to find her… What did you do to her? What did you—'

Rozalia grabbed Elina by her shoulders, shaking her. 'If you utter your nonsense to anyone, they'll hang me for something I didn't do. My death won't bring her back. It was an unfortunate accident and I'm devastated I didn't find her in time. Your mother was such an extraordinary… Maybe I'll tell you the truth about your mother's life one day.'

'What do you mean?'

But Rozalia buttoned up then. All she said was: 'I'll tell you when the time is right. But if you go spreading rumours, and I die because of it, the answer dies with me. Do you understand?'

Elina gulped and nodded, saying she'd keep her mouth shut. And she has. So far.

Her second secret.

Now a half smile flutters on Rozalia's face. 'Why don't you come visit me some time? I'll brew your favourite acorn drink. You must be missing it.'

There's an edge of self-assurance in Rozalia's voice, as though she *knows* Elina will visit her sooner or later. And how could she not? This woman knows something about her mother which Elina would do anything to find out. Rozalia could be lying, of course – Elina knows how devious peasants can be – but what if she's telling the truth?

This small doubt is all that's been keeping Elina's mouth shut, and Rozalia alive.

THE GIFT

Mira hurries to finish grinding the rye while her father is out, careful not to catch her fingers between the stones or he'll know she's disobeyed him. The last time she made flour, she ended up with a swollen thumb for days.

'A potter's hands are his bread. You've got to keep them safe, Mira,' her father had said.

But she's sick of eating gruel. So sick she ends up rolling it around her mouth to avoid having to swallow it, which of course makes it worse. The thought of having a stone-baked *turtă* today makes her mouth water. She'll just say she has borrowed the flour from the neighbours.

Her father has only gone down the road to take a new pitcher to the priest, but he's being delayed by the high snow that's caught them unaware this year. The winter has barely set in, and already the lake at the edge of the village has turned to ice.

When she hears heavy stomping in the courtyard – her father must be shaking the snow off his feet – she removes the *turtă* from the baking stones and serves it with some beetroot broth as soon as he comes in. He doesn't seem to notice he's eating *turtă* and, though she's glad of it, Mira knows this oversight means he has something on his mind.

'Did the priest like the pitcher?' she asks.

Her father nods.

'Paid you anything for it?'

'I wouldn't take it even if he had,' he grumbles with his mouth full. 'The church is about virtue and faith and charity… Don't bring money into it, I've told you before.'

'We pay our tithes. Even if it's a struggle.'

The drought last summer has slowed down their trade. Who needs pots when there's hardly anything to cook in them?

'I met with Boyar Constantin at the church earlier,' her father says. 'He wanted to know when the present for his daughter would be ready.'

'But it is ready,' Mira says, and they both look at the vessel in the far corner of the hut.

Her father chews the *turtă* as if it's full of fish bones. 'It's so gaudy it looks ridiculous,' he says.

Mira has observed the boyar's daughter enough to know of her love of colour, and because of this, she has cooked a strong dye by crushing more beetroot and using more onion peel than usual.

'Elina has a way of matching her dresses with seasonal flowers and I thought—'

'Batty. Like her mother, may her soul rest in peace.'

'What do you mean?'

'Word is, that woman didn't see the sunlight for days. Stayed locked up in her room. Can't be right for the head. And you know what they say, the apple doesn't fall far from the tree.' Her father wipes his mouth with the back of his hand and makes the sign of the cross, 'Praise be to the Lord for our meal,' and turns away from his empty bowl.

Mira is still chewing her last mouthful, her throat too tight to swallow the food.

Her father stretches on the fresh layer of straw on his side of the hut. 'The boyar saw the pitcher I made for the priest and said he hoped his daughter's gift would be just as beautiful. But look at yours! How can I deliver this laughing stock?'

Mira startles and a piece of *turtă* gets stuck in her windpipe.

She's grateful for this cough – it justifies her blushing and the change in her voice. She thought she'd be the one to deliver the jug to Elina. She wanted to see the boyar's daughter up close, get to hear her voice. She'd been watching the noble young woman in church every Sunday, and when she rode through their village wearing colourful dresses and crowns of dahlias, or peonies, perched high on her head.

'Don't worry, Father,' she says when her coughing stops. 'I can do it first thing in the morning. I'll carry it on the sledge, the quicker to get there. Handy, this snow.' She doesn't look up, lest her father marks the burning in her eyes.

'You'll have to pass by the witch's house on the way to the manor. I won't put you in peril's way. She's a wicked woman.'

'I'm not afraid of Rozalia.' Mira hopes she sounds assured. 'And if she tries anything, she'll have to catch me first.'

'She's of the devil. And she is fast.'

Mira knows the rumours about the childless widow living at the edge of their village – that she's a witch, a heathen. Because she's turned her back on the church, the people shun her.

But Mira won't let this hinder her plans.

'She's just a poor soul living on her own,' she says. 'Save for her goat.'

'She's made her bed. Let her lie in it.'

Mira changes the subject. 'I'm thinking... what if the boyar's daughter doesn't like the gift after all? Unlike you, I've no reputation to tarnish if she turns it down. I'm still an apprentice...'

Her father falls silent and Mira dares hope his brooding bears promise.

She wakes up to a heavy fog hanging outside the windows. It's as if their hut has been uprooted overnight and they are floating in the clouds.

Mira is fretting about how best to ask the question that's itching the tip of her tongue and is relieved when her father beats her to it.

'It's best you go to the manor before the fog lifts. It'll make for a safer passage when you reach the witch's hovel. Or perhaps I should come with you.'

'I'm not a child.' Mira pretends to be offended as she bundles the jug into a shawl. 'I'll be back before you know it,' she says, strapping the *opinci* tight around her socks and reaching for her sheepskin coat.

As soon as she's out of the house, she wants to skip with excitement, but Mira waits until she turns the corner down the road. Trudging through snow while pulling on a sledge doesn't allow for much skipping, but she gives it a go nonetheless.

In her head, she rehearses what she's going to say to Elina. *Good morning, miss! How are you, miss? 'Tis a special vessel for you, miss…* What else does one say to a boyar's daughter? Is she meant to bob? But Elina is hardly older than her. She is taller, but that's because of all that tasty food they must eat at the manor.

Mira stops for a short break when she reaches the lake, swathed in morning mists as though it were a living, breathing beast. The manor house sits atop the hill on the other side, which she cannot see for the fog, but first she must pass by Rozalia's hut. An idea crosses her mind, and she touches the frozen lake with the tip of her foot. Solid ice. She stretches her arms for balance as she shifts her full weight onto the frozen water. Hard as a rock. She performs a jump. Small at first, then a bigger one. Not a crack. She ponders her idea some more. It would help her avoid passing by the witch's house, but then Mira decides it would be a foolish thing to do, given she's carrying Elina's vessel and the ice could be tricking her. The fog is starting to lift, but the world is still all smudge and shadow and, if she hurries, she may yet walk by unnoticed.

The dark outline in front of Mira is the thatched roof of Rozalia's hut. There's a skin-tingling silence all around. What if the witch is dead and the villagers don't know it? It's not like anyone would miss her, apart from her goat, which would be bleating its lungs out if no one fed it. But then, the animal could also be dead if the witch hasn't been around to feed it. Such a possibility heartens Mira, and she treads with purpose past Rozalia's house, pulling the rope of the sledge close to her body.

She has a funny feeling she's being watched. She pricks up her ears for any sound, but all she can hear is her own heartbeat and she turns to look over her shoulder. Of course there's no one there. Just the snow-laden trees swaying in the morning breeze and the crows hanging out about their boughs, laughing at her foolish fear.

How silly to work herself into such a fright over nothing. What would Elina think? Surely she doesn't believe in witches. Mira takes a deep breath and starts climbing the hill towards the manor. The pathway is well trodden – what with all the serfs working for Boyar Constantin and his horse-drawn sleigh – coiling around the slope steadily like a snake around its prey.

The manor is hidden behind a wall, six-brick wide, which wraps around the house so it resembles a fortress. Only the clapboard roof is visible and the chimney puffing a relentless smoke.

Above the heavy-looking oak gate, there's a little scaffold for the watchman, but there's nobody there now. Mira slams the gate's brass knocker. The wicket opens and a pair of tired eyes scowl at her. A snappy woman's voice – 'No pedlars allowed. Go away.'

'I'm delivering a vessel for the boyar's daughter.'

The maid draws the bolt and, as she swings the gate open, a dog the size of a calf makes to charge at Mira. Its maw is all jagged teeth and slobber, and Mira stumbles, falling on her backside. The maid pushes the beast back and closes the gate behind her.

'Where's the vessel? I'll take it,' she says, reaching for the bundle on the sledge.

Mira jumps to her feet and bars her way. 'It's for the miss… such is my father's bidding.'

'Don't be silly,' the maid scoffs. They do a little dance in the snow as she tries to bypass Mira to get to the sledge. 'I don't have time for games.' She tries to shove Mira aside, but her feet are planted firmly on the ground. 'A trickster, that's what you are. Go away or I'll set the dogs on you.'

Dogs? Is there more than one? There must be, if the barking behind the gates is anything to go by. Mira's knees grow weak at the threat, but her heart won't budge. She's waited so long for this moment… She can't let this haughty maid spoil it for her.

A throaty voice emerges from behind Mira.

'What's all this clamour?'

Mira looks around for the young man who has surely spoken, but all she sees is Elina herself, draped in a robe heavy with furs. She feels a little warmer just looking at them. But it's not the robe that takes her speech away. Mira is bewildered how such a deep voice could ever come from Elina's slender body.

The maid accuses Mira of trespassing, but Elina waves her away.

'I know you,' Elina says, stepping towards Mira. 'From church. You're often watching me when you should be paying attention to the service.'

Mira wishes the ground would split and swallow her. Her cheeks burn as she thinks of all those Sundays spent attending morning service, not least to see Elina, always wondering what it's like to be the daughter of a nobleman, to wear a different dress each day, and to never hear your belly rumble. Of course, she'll never find out, but it feels good to look at someone who does know.

'Cat got your tongue?' Elina asks.

'I'm the potter's daughter,' Mira says, struggling to remember the words she has rehearsed all the way here. 'I have a gift for you.' She unties the shawl and hands the vessel to Elina.

'Oh my! It's… unusual.' Elina turns it on all sides. 'Magnificent!'

Mira's heart shrinks at the sound of the unknown word. Does that mean she likes it, or not? She's reassured by what Elina says next. 'I love the colours. Thank your father for me.'

'I made it myself.'

Elina looks at Mira as though deciding whether to believe her. 'What's your name?'

'Mira.'

'Thank you, Mira,' she says, fishing out a shiny coin from her beaded purse. Mira stares at her open hand, so delicate and soft-looking.

'Take it, or I may change my mind.'

Mira grabs the coin before the rich young woman can notice her cracked and callused palms.

'Thank you, miss.' Mira knows she should turn around and leave, but she can't move. She's never seen Elina so close up before and can't help but gape at what a sheltered face looks like – no chapped lips or weather-beaten skin like everyone else she knows.

Elina wrinkles her nose as she looks about her. 'I can smell smoke or something.'

Mira steps back, squirming. It's the *tizic*, the cow-dung bricks they sometimes burn to keep warm in winter. Though she can't smell it any more, the stench has clung not only to her clothes but also to her skin, following Mira everywhere she goes.

To distract Elina, Mira says the first thing that comes to mind. 'Miss, I… I was sorry to hear about your mother.' But as soon as she blurts it, she knows it's a mistake, seeing Elina's face cloud over. Mira hurries to add: 'My mother died too, at my birth…' But as usual, instead of saving a situation, she's just made things worse.

Silent and frowning, Elina turns away and disappears behind the manor's tall gate, her glorious robe sweeping the snow over her footprints. Mira wants to call after her and apologise, but her lips won't speak. She wishes she'd lost her tongue earlier, before she said the wrong thing.

She walks backwards until she can no longer see the manor house and then clambers onto her sledge, belly first, the better to steer her way downhill. It's not very ladylike, but there's no one around to see her, save for the crows mocking her blunder. The wind makes her eyes water as she plunges down the slope.

The speed of the sledge doesn't allow her to stop as she shoots out of the woods, and she flies over a knoll, landing onto the frozen lake below with a thud, which the wooden sledge just about absorbs, although some of the force still jolts her in the chest. All thoughts of Elina jump out of her head, and she hunches over to relieve the pain.

Mira catches a movement to her right. The witch herself is right there, standing on the shore of the lake, looking just as startled. A sack hangs heavy on her back, twigs sticking out of it. Judging by the direction she has come from, it looks like she has been stealing firewood from the boyar's hunting grounds.

She is, no doubt, worried that Mira will expose her to the boyar. If the old woman didn't have a reason to hurt her before, she certainly does now. Mira picks up the rope of her sledge, hotfooting it across the ice of the lake.

'It's not safe,' Rozalia calls out. 'Come back.'

Mira pretends not to hear as she dashes for the other side, going so fast she thinks she can hear her feet crackling. Then there's a louder crack and Mira looks over her shoulder, half expecting to see the witch at her heels, but she's still on the shore, the bundle of firewood discarded at her feet. Is she getting ready for a chase?

'Lie down.' Rozalia waves her hands to reinforce her words.

As if she's going to make it easy for the witch to lay her hands on her. She's no fool—

What's that?

A mesh of white lines spreads out from under her feet. Clearly, there's no way forward. But she won't lie down either. Mira decides to walk back and meet the witch standing.

She dares not take a breath, hoping to make her step as light as possible, but the ice squeaks again, and she stops.

'Lie on your sledge to spread the weight and sweep your way back with your hands.' Rozalia's instructions are urgent and firm.

Mira stares at the ice floor, all laced with cracks as though she's been trapped in the web of a giant spider.

'Do as I say.' Rozalia's voice is angry now.

Mira has no choice but to follow the advice, thinking now she'd rather deal with the witch than take her chances on this precarious surface. She squats down and just before she can reach her sledge, there's a crash and the ice gives way.

Her scream is choked by a gush of water that feels boiling and freezing at once, and her eyes sting as though she's fallen face first onto a thistle bush. She tries clutching at the edge of the ice, but her fingers slip, and she's swept away. She kicks her legs to come back to the hole she's fallen through but can no longer tell where it is. A blurred shadow looms above the ice and Mira wonders if it's Lady Death spreading her wing over the lake. Her lungs are burning with spent breath, and she starts to punch at the ice ceiling. The water's pull steals her strength and softens the blows. Wriggling out of her sheepskin, she keeps going until there's a muffled snap. The contrasting colour in the ice above her means she has punched through, but something dark flows from her right hand and the water turns cloudy. She grabs on to the edge of ice with her other hand and comes up for air.

Someone is shouting at her, 'Take the rope.'

Mira narrows her burning eyes to see Rozalia lying on her sledge, coming close, but not close enough to help her out of the water.

'Your right hand, grab on to the rope.' Rozalia uses a twig to push the rope right under Mira's nose, but she doesn't want to let go of the edge of the ice.

Her right hand. Where's her right hand? She can't feel it. No more splashes… Has she stopped kicking? Her feet, trapped in the *opinci*, are growing heavy, pulling her under.

Someone's yelling: 'Kick your legs, push out.'

But the world turns into a dizzying blur and a heavy darkness wraps around her. A throbbing lull.

A FRUIT DOESN'T RIPEN IN A DAY

When Mira opens her eyes, the world is still spinning, but she's dry and warm under a pile of sheepskins. What is this place? She's not at home. A fire burns in the hearth, throwing long shadows over walls crammed with shelves: small pots and bundles everywhere. And the smell here, like her nose is rubbed in the upturned soil where a skunk has died.

She doesn't remember much. It all happened so quickly – the crack in the ice, the fall, the fright – and then all that solid darkness. She knew what was happening until she no longer knew.

The witch!

No, surely, she's not… Mira rolls her head to the other side of the hut and flinches. The witch is right there, squatting by her side.

'I've sewn your wrist, but I can't promise you a strong hand. Besides…' the old woman hesitates, 'you've lost your forefinger.'

Despite her right hand being wrapped in strips of linen, Mira can still feel the finger. Rozalia is lying, probably to scare her, to teach her a lesson. As a potter, she can't be missing a finger. The first words she'd ever heard from her father were: 'A potter's hands are his bread. Keep 'em safe.'

However, finding herself in the witch's hut is more worrying than anything else at the moment, and Mira glances about the dank room, searching for the door.

'People talk badly about me, avoid me, but when pain and illness strike them, or their loved ones, they make a beeline for my hut.'

Mira's lips are frozen. Is it the icy lake still gripping her flesh?

'You were fortunate I was around. And don't worry, your father knows what's happened. I told him he could take you home and pray for you like he'd prayed for your mother, or he could leave you to my herbs and potions. And as you are still here, maybe I'm not as bad as he has made me out to be.'

'My mother?' The words stumble out. It's not often that she says them.

'You're shivering. This will make it better.' Rozalia hands her a cup with something green and viscous.

This is what she could smell when she woke up that made her think of dead skunks. She turns her head away, but the urgency in Rozalia's voice forces her to take a sip.

'Here you are. Down in one go. And if you throw it up, I'll just give you a double portion.'

Immediately after Mira downs the silty drink, Rozalia brings a jar of lard. Surely the witch is not going to make her eat this too.

'Badger's balm and beeswax,' Rozalia says.

'No, no, I'm not hungry—'

Rozalia laughs and, pulling aside the sheepskins, starts rubbing Mira's forehead, underarms and her belly with it.

'They don't hurt. It's only my hand.'

'Pain has a wisdom of its own.' Rozalia hums under her breath as she pinches Mira's flesh, presses and pulls it with no regard to the trail of red marks this leaves on her skin.

The walls start to close in on Mira, and the ceiling spins

above like a potter's wheel. All pain drains from her injured arm, leaving her light as a dandelion tuft.

Mira doesn't hear anyone knocking on the door or calling for Rozalia, yet she sees a young man in a long cloak, with the hood over half his face, walk into the hut.

'You look cold. Come closer to the fire,' Rozalia says, as though she's been expecting him.

'A gift for you.' He hands Rozalia a small jar. 'I know how much you like honey.'

Though his hoarse voice sounds familiar, Mira can't recall where she's heard it before. The young man steps towards the hearth and when he pushes his hood back, a long dark braid snakes to his waist.

It's the boyar's daughter.

Mira wants to prop herself up on her elbow to check that she's not seeing things, but hard as she tries, her body disobeys.

Elina also looks uneasy, but unlike Mira, she's come here of her own free will. And with a gift for the witch too. Mira wonders what it is that's brought someone like her to this place.

Elina's eyes sweep the hut and when they fall on Mira, she jumps in surprise. 'I know her,' she says. 'The potter's daughter, right? She brought me a beautiful jug a few days back. What's happened to her?'

A few days back? Mira thought she had only been in the witch's hut overnight.

'Tried crossing the frozen lake and fell through the ice,' Rozalia says. 'She's lucky to be alive.'

When Mira realises Elina is coming her way, she snaps her eyes shut, pretending to be asleep. Elina touches her cheek.

'She's burning, poor thing,' Elina says and cups Mira's face with both her hands – cool and soft, like no other hands Mira has ever known.

'The worst has passed. She'll live,' Rozalia says and

invites Elina to sit on a sheepskin. 'I'm glad you came. I'll cook you your favourite acorn drink.'

As soon as Rozalia starts grinding the nuts, Mira gains courage to open half an eye. Elina is kneading her hands and biting her lips as she watches the fire crackling in the hearth.

'I've been thinking, you can't be that great a healer. All that medicine you gave my mama, it never cured her headaches.'

Rozalia carries on with her work, seemingly unaffected by the hurtful words. 'Your mother never suffered from headaches,' she says without looking up.

'My mama used to stay locked up in her room for days. We all knew about her dizzy spells and… Why, you brought her medicine every day, you were the only one allowed to see her, how can you say—'

'Exactly! And I'm telling you – it wasn't headaches your mother suffered from. Her ailment was of a different nature.'

'So, I'm not the only one keeping secrets.' Elina raises her eyebrows at Rozalia as if the old woman knows what she's talking about. Rozalia must do, seeing how she looks away, and Mira feels left out of their private exchange.

'Everyone has secrets,' Rozalia says. 'And the bigger the secret, the higher the danger and greater the loss if you're found out. But, sometimes, it's worth it.'

'What exactly did my mother have to hide?'

'Born ahead of her time, she was.'

'How do you mean?'

'She possessed an extraordinary gift which she couldn't tell people about.'

'I still don't understand.'

'I'll tell you everything one day, when you're ready.'

'What do I have to do to be ready?' Elina stands up to face Rozalia.

'Spend some time with me. I'll get you there.'

'I'm in no rush to go home.'

'I don't mean just today. A fruit doesn't ripen in a day, no matter how strong the sun.'

Elina scowls and her hands scrunch the sides of her cloak, but Rozalia doesn't seem to notice it. 'It won't be much longer now,' the old woman says, her voice soft, at ease.

Mira wonders if she means the drink she's preparing, or Elina's readiness to hear whatever she knows about her mother.

But before Mira can decide which one it is, her eyes catch a blur as Elina scurries out of the hut so quickly she may as well have slipped through the wall.

THE BALL

Seven sleighs are lined up in the courtyard. It's at times like these that their manor can justify its size. There are candles flickering in each room and this is one of the very few occasions when the house is totally theirs. The rest of the time it belongs to the servants. The hours and the days it takes them to clean and maintain the house, the servants end up living in it more than Elina and her father.

Last week, a Court messenger brought the voivode's decision – the ruler has granted the legislative change of Elina's status, making her a 'son' on paper, so that in the absence of any male siblings, she is able to inherit her father's estate.

'He's a cunning man, our voivode,' her father told Elina when they received the news. 'He's given us what we want so that if we don't keep our end of the deal, it's more painful when he takes away what he has so easily granted. It's more important than ever that we build that church now.'

The servants have been cleaning the house for days, preparing it for this special night to celebrate the news. Elina can't help wondering how such filthy hands can make everything so spotless. The stone floor has been thoroughly polished, and silverware reflects the fire from the hearthside like a hundred mirrors.

As they descend the stairs to greet their guests, her father whispers in her ear: 'Let me know if any of the young boyars you meet tonight take your fancy.'

'Have you changed your mind about marrying me to my cousin?'

'This news we're celebrating; it has greatly increased your marriage prospects. Dowry is one thing, but inheritance is a totally different matter. Many people will have their eyes on you tonight.'

Elina is introduced to noble families from up and down the country. She smiles and bows and speaks very little, for the mark of a well-bred woman is never to speak her mind in front of strangers.

The guests, each holding a crystal goblet filled with ruby wine, marvel at the hunting trophies flaunted all around the reception hall. The head of a wild boar grins from the wall, bearskins sprawl wide on the floor and two fierce wolves guard the crystal collection which goes unused, save for days like today when they have guests.

The one trophy which Elina can't get used to is the stuffed bird with amber eyes: the Little Owl she'd killed on their roof. Though she had objected to it – 'It's ugly and scary,' she'd said – her father had perched the dead bird in a cornice of the grand room, and now it spooks her every time she sees it.

None of the guests share her aversion to it though. The men praise the preservation of its magnificent poise, while the women make comments about the quality of the amber used for its eyes.

The door suddenly swings open, and a servant announces the arrival of the priest, who struts in, wearing a peacock brocade whose golden thread catches the candlelight whichever way he turns. The clergyman stretches his arm towards Elina and her father for the customary kiss of his hand.

'May the Lord help you overcome your grief soon,' the priest tells her father. 'There's a new manuscript awaiting your attention. As soon as you're ready.'

Elina has always been proud of her father's gift for illustrating church books.

'Yes... absolutely... soon,' her father stammers and starts picking at his beard. 'May the Lord hear you, Holy Father.' He performs a deep bow and waves at a servant to bring a glass of red for the priest.

Why is her father so flustered all of a sudden? Elina can tell his moods by how he treats his beard. He strokes it most of the time, and picks at it when he's worried or upset. She often teases him about the bald spot growing bigger and looking at odds with his otherwise fluffy beard.

'The *lăutari* are coming,' her father announces when loud music is heard soaring from beyond the courtyard.

Three men – a fiddler, a pan-flute player and the Old Cobzar – walk through the gate, onto the porch and then into the reception hall, without once breaking their music. Elina has never met the Old Cobzar, as he's known, but she's heard many stories about him. One such story is that when he played for Boyar Dimitri once, the host was so touched by his music that he removed his mantle trimmed with precious stones and sable fur and was about to give it to him when his wife slapped the boyar hard in the face to bring him to his senses.

The guests take their seats at two long tables already laden with food and wine. More platters with roast meats, cheese and pies are brought out regularly, stacked on top of empty plates.

The *lăutari* play at the end of the room, with the fiddler squeezing between the tables to bow to certain guests and thus earn his *bacșiș*.

'You'll get your reward later,' Boyar Constantin shouts at him over the music.

'Our arrangement is why we came. The *bacșiș* is why we play,' the fiddler replies, grinning widely.

Elina has a queue of *coconi* asking her to dance and she indulges most of them, but none of the young boyars catch her interest. Despite the music and the people, there's a cold emptiness swirling about her.

She feels his gaze on her before she sees it. The Old Cobzar watches her with a look that seeks to comb her soul for its darkest secret. She turns her face away, wondering why they call him old. His swarthy skin looks coarse and weather-beaten, but he's not a wrinkled elder. Maybe a little older than her father, yet half his size. Elina guesses it may be because of the hoary-white curls reaching to his shoulders. They sit at odds with his otherwise still youthful appearance, reminding her of an untimely frost.

The *lăutari* sing of love and sorrow, of curses and joy, of life and war and death. The Old Cobzar – with his eyes closed as though the world is an unwelcome intrusion – sets the mood with his tunes, taking the boyars from happy laughter to tears, and then back to good cheer and lively dancing like a fire has been lit under their feet. He has reversed the roles so that he is the true master and the boyars are his slaves, following him blindly to all the highs and lows his music takes them to.

When the *lăutari* take a break, the guests call for more.

'Whoever wants to hear more, let 'em open their purse,' the Old Cobzar says with a smile, revealing two round dimples in his cheeks.

And the boyars pay. They even seem happy to do it.

Her father rings the bell, and a hush descends into the room. 'Dear guests,' he says, 'I'd like you all to raise your glasses to my daughter's good fortune, and to our voivode's grace, of course, for bestowing such honour on my family.'

The guests give out a loud shout of approval and clink their glasses, and as the music starts playing again, Boyar Constantin raises his hand.

'My daughter isn't just fortunate but gifted too. Let's see what the best *cobzar* in the country thinks of her playing.'

Elina wishes she could blink everyone away, wake up from this nightmare in which her father has just thrown her. But he gives an impatient nod, and a servant approaches her with his arms stretched, offering her the *cobză*.

There aren't many things she likes doing more than playing her mother's *cobză*, but certainly not in front of a master.

However, defying her father in public is worse than making a fool of herself, and she takes the tear-shaped instrument. Her face burns as though an invisible candle is held close to her cheeks, and her mouth is so sticky she struggles to swallow. The dining room falls silent, only the odd belch audible in the room, as she starts playing the shortest song her mother had taught her. Even so, an eternity passes by the time she finishes it. The praise is overly exaggerated, which tells her exactly what they thought of her performance. She does a clumsy curtsy and walks out, hungry for fresh air.

The celebration lasts well into the night and it's not until most of the guests are slumped in their seats or over the tables that the *lăutari* stop playing.

'The secret is to know when to leave,' the Old Cobzar says when one of the guests protests. 'So you can invite us again soon.'

She follows the *lăutari* out. It has started snowing again. The men's sheepskins are held together by pieces of rope and their *ițari* are thinned by the wind and rain of many years. She grabs a couple of her father's broadcloth mantles and catches up with the three men as they're about to walk out of the courtyard.

The Old Cobzar laughs. 'The cold and the hunger are our oldest friends. They stopped bothering us a long time ago. And we have our music. Keeps us warm.'

'Thank you for tonight. I enjoyed listening to you.'

'I could tell. It runs in your blood.'

'What does?'

'I was your grandfather's slave once. He was the one who encouraged me to play and later sent me to be tutored by an Ottoman master. Paid the Turk dearly for it too. In gold, horses and a silver flask. A fine man, your grandfather was.'

Though her grandparents died before she was born, Elina has heard all about them from her mother. Sure, they were kind and generous, but they were no fools. Educate a gypsy? What nonsense.

'Thanks to your grandfather, I'm a free man now. Hardly any gypsies are. He gifted me with his name too – Pogor. I'm Tudorache Pogor, but everyone calls me the Old Cobzar. Such decent people your grandparents were… didn't deserve what…' He pauses as though wondering if he's said too much.

'I know about the injustice and betrayal they suffered at the hand of the previous ruler,' she says a little impatiently, hoping to make it clear that she has no intention of discussing this any further.

There is a moment of silence and, as the moon gleams briefly out of the thick clouds, Elina can see he's watching her with the same searching look he had earlier, a wistful smile enhancing his dimples.

'Lord, you look so much like her.'

'I'm sorry?'

'Like your mother, when I first met her.'

'You knew her?'

'I taught her how to play the *cobză*.'

Beyond the gate, the fiddler and the flute player – probably bored with waiting – start playing a cheerful song.

'She was a great woman, your mother was…' His voice trails off. 'Don't believe anything else anyone tells you about her. And by the way, you play the *cobză* as well as she did. By gift of the ear and the whisper of the heart.' He tips his hat and turns for the gate, joining in with his friends' singing. Elina watches the three figures melt away into the falling snow, their merry voices trailing behind them.

Her father is on the porch when she returns to the house wrapped in his mantles to avoid being asked about them.

'So the gypsies have gone,' he says. 'I'll tell Neculai he can bolt the gate now.'

'They are *lăutari* when they arrive and gypsies when they leave? I thought you appreciated their music.'

'Ah.' Her father waves his hand as if shooing a fly. 'Great flair. What a shame it's been wasted on a flock of crows. You better head in before you catch a cold. Sleep well, my angel.'

Elina walks through the reception hall to find the guests slumped on tables, snoring and dribbling over spilled food and wine. A shudder goes through her as she recalls the story of how her grandfather and uncle died. The two of them had been invited for a feast at the royal Court, along with other boyars, during the rule of the previous voivode. At the end of the night – when most of the guests were tired, drunk or asleep – the cunning ruler had ordered his men to behead the boyars to punish them for plotting against his throne. Their chopped heads had been displayed on the outside walls of the Court for all to see. Following the death of her husband and son, her grandmother died of a broken heart. Elina's mother was the only family survivor.

It's well past midnight, but the chat with the Old Cobzar has shaken off her tiredness, and instead of heading to her bedroom, Elina slips out through the back door into the garden, which is now swaddled in a new layer of snow.

She thinks of the *lăutari*, probably still singing as they ride in the dark of night. In an urge to taste their freedom, she runs towards the orchard stretching out beyond the garden, and – catching snowflakes with her tongue – she weaves and darts through the trees, laughing for no reason. It feels good not to care for once, to let go of the stiff front of a boyar's daughter – sensible, obedient, quiet.

So many rules. They feel tighter and more unforgiving than the girdle she's wearing and which she unties from her waist and throws to the ground. So much better without it as she dances in the darkness, her breath deep and strong, not like the shallow flutter she has to live with most of the time.

'Big news we've been celebrating this evening. I see you're quite pleased about it.' The words come out of nowhere, startling Elina. She can't see him, but his voice is unmistakable.

'No more pleased than you must be, dear Uncle.'

'We had an agreement, your father and I.' Her uncle raises the oil lamp and steps towards her. His eyes remind her of the wild dogs her father tells her to keep well away from when she goes riding in the woods. She steps back.

'But your father is changing his tune now, given your improved status. He has always believed he's the smarter one—'

'There is no need to get upset, Uncle. I'm sure—' But the rest of her words trip in her throat as Bogdan lunges forward, dropping the oil lamp and grabbing her by the arm. She digs her heels into the earth, trying to pull away, but it's slippery and his grip is firm.

'I hear m'boy is too stinky for you. That right?'

'Let go. You're hurting me.'

'I know what a spoilt, double-faced hussy you are. Just like your mother. Apples really don't fall far, do they? You've got her in you. Her madness lurks in your eyes too.'

Elina opens her mouth, but her cry is snuffed by the lardy paw clamped on her face.

'Someone might hear you and then what? Your word against mine. And who will they believe, do you think?' His breath smells of dripping and stale wine.

He holds her waist with one hand and her head with the other. Elina tries to wriggle out of his grip, but he's strong as a bull and turns her around, pinning her against a tree.

'I don't even want to do this, but I have to. It's the only way to make sure you marry m'boy, for no one else will want you after this.'

He grunts as he lifts her gown, his hand eager to cup and squeeze her flesh. The world starts to sway in front of her eyes as she's trapped between her uncle's clammy body and the coarse bark of the plum tree.

The same tree her swing was roped to until last summer.

Her fingers trace the grooves in the trunk from all those times when the edge of the swing grazed the bark as her father pushed her higher and higher into the sky.

How she hates that happy child now. And this plum tree, for its treachery.

WILD PEONIES

Mira doesn't know how many days she's been in Rozalia's hut, but one morning she wakes up and the pain has gone. The heavy fog has lifted from her head and if it wasn't for the ugly gap in her hand, she would have thought it was all a bad dream. The time has come for her to leave and because Rozalia – who is busy crushing strips of bark with a stone – hasn't said anything, Mira decides to ask the question outright.

'Will I still be able to make pots? It's the only thing I know…'

'It will take some time to get used to it.'

Get used to working the clay again, or get used to being maimed and useless? The old woman is answering her questions like she did with Elina's – by not answering them at all.

'Sorry about all the trouble, and thank you for saving my life,' she says and gets up to make for the door.

'It's your father you should thank. He has certainly learned from his mistakes.'

'How's that?'

'I guess losing his wife has given the old fool enough wits to avoid losing his daughter too.'

'My mother died giving life to me. I was the one who—'

'The meadows were awash with wild peonies that day,

their royal red spilling whichever way you looked. I was in the midst of a special rite, but I couldn't focus because your mother's cries filled the air. I turned up on your doorstep with a bunch of herbs to help her get through it quicker, but your father wouldn't let me. He said Lord Jesus Christ would soothe and protect his wife.' Rozalia has finished crushing the bark and is scooping the coarse flour into a pot. 'Don't judge your father too harshly. He loved your mother. It's just that he prayed for a miracle instead of accepting my help. You know what people think of me.'

'He should've asked my mother and let her decide.' The words catch in Mira's throat. 'Did you know her? What was she like?'

'You have her looks – same green eyes, grain-coloured hair, even the tiny mole above your lips. And you have her fire too. I used to meet her in the woods often, when she gathered pinewood for your father's kiln. Tiny yet feisty, she was. Her bargaining with Boyar Constantin for the price of wood was legendary. Without her, your father wouldn't be the potter he is today. Here, take this with you.' Rozalia hands Mira a beet she's fished out from the edge of the hearth. 'To keep your hands warm until you get home.'

Stepping out of the hut into the whiteness of fresh snow makes Mira's eyes burn and she narrows them to a slit. Maybe it's the layer of powder concealing the packed ice underneath, or maybe it's the prolonged rest, but her feet are fearful and slow and the slippery calfskin *opinci* aren't helping. She loses her footing and though she recovers in time, her flailing arms make her lose the hot beet. Unable to trace it in the snow drifts around her, Mira shuffles on, blowing into her hands. How can a missing finger hurt so much? She stops often to look at the gap in her hand and remind her brain there's nothing there now.

Their chimney is puffing and despite wishing for warmth, Mira isn't so keen to see her father just yet. She hopes he'll be asleep and she won't have to talk to him.

But he must've been looking out the window, for the door opens and he comes out to meet her before she even reaches their twig gate.

'You're just in time. I've trapped us a hare. The stew is almost ready.'

The recent droughts ruined their crops and they have long since slaughtered all their chickens.

'I'm not hungry.'

'That's something new. Are you alright?'

The fact that her father avoided talking about her mother over the years only increased Mira's guilt about her death – it is for this reason that she has strived to become a great potter, to please him, to somehow justify her place in the world. And yet now it seems that the real reason they didn't talk about her mother was to spare her father's feelings. In his selfishness, he has never once thought how she might feel about all this.

'Rozalia told me about my mother. I know what—'

'Don't listen to her.' He looks about to make sure no neighbour has heard them and bundles her swiftly into the hut.

'You don't like her because her powers are stronger than your prayers.'

'What are you saying, child?'

'Why didn't you pray for me like you prayed for my mother? When I fell through the ice, you didn't call upon God to save me. Instead you pleaded with Rozalia to chase the chills out of my bones and keep me alive. If only—'

'Mira!' Her father raises his hand in the air as if to strike her, which he has never done before. He catches himself and steps back, a moment of silence spreading between them.

'If I could change anything, I would,' he whispers, burying his face into his hands.

Mira stares at the dry blood in the creases of his old fingers. Barely visible but indisputably there. She knows it's from the hare he'd skinned earlier, but her mind takes her elsewhere. Her mother didn't have to die.

HEATHEN

The morning after the ball, Elina sneaks to the kitchen to collect a fistful of smouldering ash. The world outside is cloaked in a new layer of snow, the ground smooth and impeccably white, hiding all the marks of the skirmish with her uncle from the night before. Her shameful secret is safe for now, but her uncle has made it clear it won't always be so, if she disobeys him.

She rides to the woods, the only place where she feels safe, with her bow on one shoulder and a bundle of bloodied linen under her arm – her smeared gown and the cloths she had used to clean herself with.

Fulger walks slowly, as though aware of her discomfort, faithfully taking her to the bend of the river, next to her favourite glade.

'You are a smart horse,' she says, and Fulger snorts like he agrees with her.

As soon as they reach the meander, Elina drops the linen and slowly slides down the side of the horse, her back against him, her face twisting with pain. When the cramps shooting through her spine ease off a little, she gathers an armful of twigs and shoves the snow with her feet to clear a patch of ground. But the wood is damp, threatening to put out the smouldering ash she has brought with her. Who would have thought lighting a fire could be so difficult? The servants make it look so easy. All they do is blow on the wood a few times and it magically bursts into flames, like they have fire on their breath.

When Elina loses all hope of coaxing the smallest of sparks, she tosses the smeared linen straight into the unyielding ash, cursing her uncle. Her mind drags her back through what happened the previous night. Over and over and over again. She pulls at her hair, but there's no stopping the images and words swarming in her brain. The heat of shame rises from her groin to her belly, chest, throat and, finally, singes the back of her eyes. She slips off her mantle and kneels in the snow, grabbing handfuls of fresh powder, which she rubs into her face and neck, even shoving it down her dress. But the snow melts and trickles on her skin like warm milk. Only one thing will quell the flame of disgrace.

The icy river.

She pulls off her boots and removes her layers of clothes, walking towards it with her arms open wide, embracing the crisp air. Her breath is severed the moment she steps into the water, but she welcomes its chill and dips her head under the surface, keeping it there until the river pushes her back up. The corner of her eye catches a splash of colour. The fire she so struggled to light is now roaring on the shore, destroying the evidence of her disgrace. Elina stumbles out of the river, but instead of drying herself by the flames, she wraps herself in her mantle and sits, leaning against a tree not too close to the fire. Getting comfortable will bring back her misery. There isn't a better painkiller than a sharp frost.

Despite the cold burrowing deeper into her bones, and the bark digging into her back, the previous night's sleeplessness finally starts catching up with her.

She dreams of someone calling her name. A woman's voice. It's her mother, standing in a field shimmering with butterflies, her arms wide open. But the faster Elina runs, the further away her mother drifts. The voice, however, sounds closer, louder. Someone is shaking her awake now. How frustrating.

She tries to open her eyes, but the dream is too sweet, and it pulls her right back into the field with butterflies. She's about to reach her mother's open arms when someone starts pinching her cheeks.

'Wake up, miss. Wake up, I say. D'you hear me?'

Elina cracks her eyes open to see a frowning face, a pair of green eyes.

'Hold on to my neck, miss. Here, let's put your boots on. And your mantle… I'll take you somewhere warm.'

No, Elina doesn't want to go home. Not today… not ever… but her lips won't obey and all she can hear herself whispering is: 'No… no…'

'It's alright. It's me, Mira, the potter's daughter, remember me?'

Why is she dragging her up? She doesn't want to—

The field of butterflies, she's now flying over it, snug in her mother's arms, only the breeze tingling her face. She nestles further into this warm embrace.

'Don't fall asleep, miss. We're almost there.'

She doesn't want to go anywhere. Here, with her mother, is where she wants to be…

Elina jolts awake with her mouth burning. Rozalia is forcing a drink down her throat, which leaves a trail of warmth all the way to her belly. There's a mountain of sheepskins piled over her, and her feet are in a bowl of water, which – like the snow earlier – freezes and scorches her flesh all at once.

Mira sits on the floor watching her. How did she manage to bring her here, especially with her injured hand? Probably on her sledge, but even so – she must be strong despite her frame.

'Where did you find her?' Rozalia asks.

'By the river,' Mira says.

'Was she alone?'

'Yes.'

'What happened?'

Mira hesitates, which worries Elina. How much has she seen? Had she spotted the bloodied linen before it burned? If Elina's knowledge of servants is anything to go by, peasants aren't as simple as they look, and usually know a lot more than they let on.

She locks eyes with Mira, willing her to keep her mouth shut, for even if she herself hasn't worked it out, if she mentions the burned linen to Rozalia, the old woman will certainly guess her shame.

'She doesn't know how to light a fire,' says Mira. 'And almost died because of it. Or maybe she just fancies herself the Snow Maiden.'

Elina exhales her relief quietly. *She must be alright, she's funny*, she thinks to herself. But Rozalia, the wily old fox, isn't fooled. 'Who takes a dip in the river in the middle of winter?' she asks, looking at them in turn.

'I didn't… I… I…' Elina fumbles for words. 'I dozed off while riding and fell off my horse.'

'Of course you did.' Rozalia doesn't bother to hide the mockery in her voice.

Whatever it was she was given to drink, it has loosened Elina's tongue.

'We received some good news from the Court. I've been granted a change in my status – I'm now a "son", on paper anyway. Best kind of news for a boyar family with no male heirs. Father invited guests to celebrate, and I didn't close an eye all night. This morning I went for a ride and that's when sleep caught up with me.'

Rozalia's look softens and Elina knows she believes at least some of it. But then some of it *is* true.

'You must be very pleased,' Rozalia says.

'It's not set in stone. The voivode could change his mind if we don't build the church. And given that two masons have tried and failed, who's to say a third one will succeed?'

Rozalia's face clouds over. 'Is that the price for securing your inheritance?'

'The voivode calls it a favour.'

Rozalia turns her back, busying herself with stirring something in a pot. Elina wonders if that's because she's embarrassed at the memory of her own encounter with the voivode.

During a hunting party a few years back, the voivode, in response to her father's initial request about her change of status, had demanded a church to be built where his arrow fell. Everyone had scattered, combing the woods with their eyes, hoping to be the ones to find the arrow. Elina too had wandered off, more concerned about her red ribbon – a present from her mother and which the ruler had asked to tie his arrow with, so as not to lose it in the sea of greenery. When she'd caught glimpse of the bright flame of her ribbon fluttering at the top of the hill, she'd spurred her horse and arrived just in time to see Rozalia, who was their beater at the time, trying to make off with the voivode's arrow. What was it Rozalia had told her then? 'It's not too late to avoid misfortune. Don't breathe a word about this. Pretend you never saw me.' But Elina was no fool. She knew servants stole from their lords all the time. She had demanded that Rozalia hand her the arrow. 'You're too young to understand the wrong that's being done,' Rozalia had begged. 'One day you will, but it may be too late by then. Please trust me…' But Elina hadn't.

Is that what Rozalia is thinking now? Is that why she won't tell Elina the secret about her mother which she has promised to reveal one day? Of course, she has never forgiven Elina for not letting her get away with stealing the voivode's arrow. Though who knows why she would want it; it wasn't made of gold.

'The broth will be ready soon,' Rozalia says and lights a candle.

Even though it's still daytime, the hut – half buried in the ground – is dim and dingy. The smell of melting tallow reminds Elina of her uncle's fat, sweaty flesh, and she retches.

'Don't you have any beeswax?' she asks.

'This isn't a manor house,' Rozalia says. 'And you didn't mind the tallow candles last time. What's changed?'

Elina is caught off guard. 'I didn't want to say anything last time. Never mind, it will pass.'

'Are you going to tell me what's the matter?' Rozalia's eyes are heavy on her. She is a dog with a bone. But two can play at this game.

'Is it true my mother wasn't well in her head?' Elina searches Rozalia's face for clues of what the old woman won't tell her.

'Where's that come from?'

'Someone told me I have her madness lurking in my eyes.'

'Whoever said that didn't know your mother at all—'

'Is that why she had those awful headaches? Tell me, was she wrong in the head?'

'This isn't the best time to talk about this,' Rozalia says and looks at Mira, who has remained so still as if she has fallen asleep sitting up. She immediately gets the hint and rises to her feet, ready to leave.

'I trust her,' Elina says, thinking to herself that Mira is her accomplice now, given that she hasn't told Rozalia everything she knows about that morning. She has proved much worthier than some boyar women.

'Please tell me the truth.' Elina turns to Rozalia, who is busy stirring in the pot. 'If there was something wrong with my mother, I'd like to know—'

'There was nothing wrong with her at all. Your mother was a gifted woman, and she was smart about it.' Rozalia tastes the food. 'Almost ready.'

Elina thinks of the strange pieces of advice her mother used to give her when her father was out of earshot: 'Do not follow blindly'; 'Question things'; 'Be curious about the world'; 'Be true to yourself'.

'Why won't you just tell me?' Elina's voice is almost a whisper. 'What's it going to take?'

'Trust. Right now neither of us thinks much of the other. I need to know you can handle it. For that—'

'I need time – yes, you told me that already. But what if we don't have much time? You are old, what if—'

Rozalia laughs. 'Your mother might've taught you many things, but patience wasn't one of them. The very thing that made her legacy possible.'

'Women don't leave legacies, only men—'

'Some women do. Your mother's greatness will be praised for centuries to come, though nobody will ever know her name. Right, I need to fetch more logs. The fire is dwindling,' Rozalia says and is out the hut in a blink.

Though Elina has regained some feeling back in her hands and feet, the pins and needles aren't totally gone. She drops the sheepskins they've piled on top of her clothes and mantle.

'How did you find me?' she asks Mira.

'I was gathering firewood and saw the smoke…'

'Thank you for not telling the old crone everything. And calling me a Snow Maiden—'

'I'm sorry, I didn't want to insult—'

'You didn't,' Elina says, running her fingers through her almost dry hair. 'I see you've got a neat plait. Can you do mine? I can't go home dishevelled like this.' Seeing Mira's hesitation, Elina asks, 'How's your hand? Does it hurt?'

'Oh no, it's not that… I can plait your hair,' Mira says, but she still doesn't move.

'Today would be nice.'

Mira approaches like Elina is a wild beast who could bite at any moment. She kneels behind her, gathering her hair and untangling it slowly. She's got a gentle touch. It reminds Elina of her mother when she used to plait her hair. They used to chat and laugh and play. That is, when her mother didn't lock herself in her room. How Elina hated Rozalia, who was the only person her mother wanted to see when she was ill, whilst Elina's pleading was ignored as she scratched in vain at the door. Many a night she went to sleep crying and craving to be with her mother, to look after her and make her feel better, to caress her fevered skin and wipe her sweat away. Perhaps if Rozalia hadn't been her mother's maid – and her friend, as it turns out – she would have got to do all those things.

Why is Mira taking so long with plaiting her hair? It's probably because of her injured hand. But it feels good, and Elina closes her eyes and wishes this would never stop.

'You have such beautiful hair, miss,' Mira says. 'So long and soft and shining.'

Elina is suddenly aware of Mira's breath on the nape of her neck. Has she just leaned in and smelled her hair? The warmth, the closeness of another body, makes Elina dizzy with longing. Longing to be held, to be told all will be well. She doesn't even know why, but tears tickle the corners of her eyes briefly before rolling down her cheeks.

'I'm sorry, miss. Am I pulling at your hair?'

'Elina. My name is Elina. And no, you didn't do anything wrong. I just… I don't know… What? Why are you looking at me like that?'

'I've heard rich people don't cry.'

This makes Elina smile, and she wipes her face with the back of her hand. 'I see you're mocking me.'

'They say you hardly have any reason to.'

'Is that what you think?'

Mira hesitates.

'It's alright. You can be honest with me,' Elina says.

'That's another thing they say – never trust a rich person.' Mira also smiles. Hers is open, effortless, unlike the strained grins Elina is used to amongst the people of her own ilk.

'And who's teaching you all this great wisdom?'

Mira shrugs. 'Life.'

'Alright, you win. But really, honestly, I'm not that bad. As you said the other day, you know what it's like to lose your mother. And Rozalia isn't helping by teasing me with secrets about my mama's life.' A fresh wave of anger surges in her chest and Elina clamps her jaw. She can't keep crying in front of a peasant. It shows weakness and fear and…

She jumps to her feet, turns around and hugs Mira, burying her face deep into this stranger's neck. She blames it on whatever it was that Rozalia gave her to drink earlier. Or maybe it's because she's recognised a kindred spirit. After all, this young peasant woman is the only one who understands – no – who *feels* what Elina is going through.

Afraid that Mira, wide-eyed and stiff, may pull away, Elina holds on to her tighter. 'Don't let go. Please don't let go.'

The herby scent of Mira's skin and her sweet breath are soothing. Why did she think Mira smelled bad the first time they met?

'I see my medicine has made you all soppy,' Rozalia says, dropping an armful of logs by the hearth. 'A little food will sort you out.' She tastes the simmering broth. 'It's ready.'

The unmistakable aroma of summer savory, Elina's favourite herb the year round, fresh or dry. Just as they are about to tuck into their food, Rozalia closes her eyes and clasps her hands in prayer:

Blessed be the Earth for growing this food,
Blessed be the Rain for quenching its thirst,
Blessed be the Wind for giving it breath,
Blessed be the Sun for nourishing it,
Blessed be the Moon for her Love and Light,
Blessed be!

Rozalia opens her eyes and starts eating in silence. Elina stares at her, unmoving. What she's just witnessed – heresy – is a crime punishable by burning at the stake, and yet this woman behaves like she has done nothing wrong.

'I cannot share your meal,' Elina says. Mira also stops chewing and looks up.

'It's not a crime to say a simple gratitude for the food that's given up its life so we can eat,' Rozalia says.

'It didn't give up its life. You killed it.'

'Anything we eat, plant or meat, has to die for our sustenance. Isn't it disrespectful not to thank your food for its sacrifice?'

'That's why we say grace to our Lord Jesus Christ.'

'He isn't the one we're eating right now, is he? It's never him. It's what comes from the Earth and the Water, the Air and the Sun. Thank the source, not your Lord. He's just one of its many manifestations.'

'Did Mother know about your…'

'Creed?'

'I was going to say blasphemy. Heresy.'

'There was nothing your mother enjoyed more than questioning things—'

'It all makes sense now,' Elina says, 'you're a heathen. That's why you wanted to steal the voivode's arrow. To stop our ruler from choosing the spot for a new church.'

Not getting a reaction from Rozalia, who sips quietly at her broth, Elina looks at Mira, raising an eyebrow as if to say – *Beware, she's not to be trusted.*

But Mira's response takes her by surprise. 'She's kinder than many villagers who go to church—'

Elina doesn't wait to hear the rest of Mira's words. She jumps to her feet and storms out of the hut.

How could her mother have been friends with a heathen like Rozalia?

Unless Rozalia is lying about their friendship.

WHAT IS A MAN WHEN HE'S BLIND TO ANOTHER?

Elina has never awaited a Sunday so eagerly. She has spent the entire week praying, asking the Lord to forgive her for spending time with that sinful, godless woman, listening to her take His name in vain. She should have challenged Rozalia more. She should have tried harder to defend her god and her religion.

After hours of arguing with herself and changing her mind repeatedly, Elina decides to confess to the priest about Rozalia's deathly sin. She's a woman who not only practises heresy, but preaches it with such conviction as if hers, and not Christianity, is the one and true faith. Elina will answer the call of her creed. She'll do her duty in weeding out the evil that's flourishing so close to home. Rozalia has been teasing her with supposed secrets about her mother to keep Elina from speaking against her. But she won't be fooled any more.

Elina wakes up early and gets ready hours before they need to leave for church, keen to have her confession heard as soon as possible.

Her father instructs Neculai to bundle up half a wild boar and seven hares from their hunt the previous day.

'Don't forget the jug with the priest's favourite red wine. And catch up with us before we get there. Neither I nor the Holy Father enjoy waiting.'

'Yes, sir. On my way already,' Neculai says, unbolting the gate for them.

The icy forest glitters in a sleep so deep that it's a wonder it comes back to life each spring. Despite the bright sunshine, the air has a sharp bite. Elina spreads the train of her squirrel coat over Fulger's back to lessen the sting of the frost and clasps her hands back in her fur muffs. She doesn't need to hold the reins, now looped around her wrists – Fulger knows the way.

'You're quiet today,' her father says. 'Not running a fever, are you?'

'Don't you remember the priest's counsel? To refrain from eating before confession and maintain silence prior to receiving our Lord's grace.'

The truth is that Elina's mind could not be more cluttered. Rozalia's heresy, her uncle's shameful act, Mira's gentle touch – thoughts swirl and toss in her head, not only making her dizzy but unsettling her belly too. She worries that if she talks too much, she may be sick.

'I'm so proud of you,' her father says. 'A beautiful young woman worthy of the richest prince. Or the voivode's youngest son. I've heard he's a fine man. Can't promise he doesn't eat garlic though.'

Her belly twists like it wants to turn itself inside out. 'Not marrying my cousin any more? Does Uncle Bogdan know about it?'

'My greatest wish is for you to be happy. If your cousin Mihnea doesn't suit you, I'm not going to force you to marry him. And anyway, given your judicial status now, you can definitely marry better than that.'

She remembers her uncle's words – *I don't even want to do this, but I have to. It's the only way to make sure you marry m'boy, for no one else will want you after this.*

Her throat goes dry, and she scoops the snow off a tree branch, shoving it in her mouth by the fistful. Neculai catches up with them and her father changes subject.

'The Advent starts tomorrow, and the priest has invited us to join him for lunch today after the service.'

'Lovely,' Elina says under her breath.

When they turn the corner, she notices a stooped figure lingering outside the church gate, a long stick in one hand testing the ground, the other outstretched, begging for food.

'What is a man when he's blind to another? What is a man when he's blind to another?' His sing-song words rise and fall as though kindness was a coy bird he was coaxing out of strangers' hearts, but people hurry past like he's not there.

The gate of the church squeaks opens, and the priest welcomes them with a wide smile. He then turns towards the sightless man, who is instantly obscured by the priest's belly. 'The drought has been bad for all of us this year,' he says and hands the beggar a small *posmag*.

'Thank you, Holy Father, God bless.' The man bows his head in gratitude.

Elina looks over her shoulder at the toothless man struggling with the piece of dry bread as though he were an old dog with a tough bone. She slips – fooled by the layer of snow concealing the ice underneath – and grabs for the brick fence to her side, its sturdiness reassuring whilst she finds her feet.

During the morning liturgy, Elina and her father stand in their usual spot at the front of the church, well away from the dung-smelling villagers who huddle at the back, squeezed into a space half the size. And, as always, the same pair of huge green eyes studies her from behind. Elina looks over her shoulder, but each time Mira drops her gaze or averts it before their eyes meet.

Her father squeezes Elina's hand reassuringly. 'Never far enough away from them,' he whispers in her ear. 'The new church we're going to build will be much bigger. We won't be so close to them then.'

Elina watches the priest like she's drinking his sermon, while her mind ponders on the mossy green of Mira's eyes. They remind Elina of valley wells – cool and quiet and unfathomable. Elina is intrigued by this peasant's loyalty. In the boyars' world, such gestures are few and far between, and usually cost a dear coin.

The least she could do is thank Mira for her discretion, her thoughtfulness—

There's a tug at her sleeve. 'The service has ended,' her father says. 'Make the sign of the cross. We're being watched.'

When they are called for confession, Elina's earlier resolve to confess about Rozalia's crime has waned somehow and she asks her father to go first, hoping that by the time it's her turn, she will have figured out what it is that's bothering her.

However, her father comes out much sooner than expected. His confessions are always shorter than hers and she wonders why the priest doesn't ask him as many questions as he asks her.

Elina starts her confession by saying she's been eavesdropping again – on their servants, on her father and uncle as they discussed her inevitable marriage to her cousin. The priest assures her that there's nothing wrong with keeping an eye on the servants, but that she should trust her father for having her best interests at heart. To her own surprise, Elina says nothing of Rozalia's heresy, or of her uncle's disgraceful behaviour, or of the anger sitting heavy in her heart at the priest's lie to the blind man. Every Sunday they bring him wild game and wine. She knows the priest has enough food all year round, drought or no drought. And she's seen him feed to his dogs what his family don't eat.

The clergyman pries her with further questions, but she assures him she has nothing else to confess to.

They join the priest's wife and two daughters for lunch and as the six of them take their seats at the table, Elina looks around, searching for the army of people this mound of food surely has been cooked for. The priest blesses the food with a short prayer, and they tuck in.

Elina reaches for a *cotlet*. 'I'll take this to the blind man—'

The priest shakes his head. 'Feed one and they'll all come flocking. Don't worry, miss, he'll live. Unfortunately.' He bursts into a belly-shaking laughter, with his wife and daughters joining in. Her father looks at her as if to say, *Don't embarrass me*.

Elina sips at her water – nothing else is easy to swallow. She's glad she hasn't told the priest about Rozalia's sin. Not because she has forgiven the old woman, but because things which were straightforward once aren't so simple any more.

What is a man when he's blind to another? The blind man's sing-song words reach them through the swinging door as servants bring in more food.

What is a man—

THE CALL

Despite Rozalia's herbal potions and urgent whispers, the strength in Mira's right hand isn't what it used to be. Her chores of cooking and tidying up are taking longer than usual. She often has to stop in the middle of something because her hand goes hot or cold for no reason. One moment ice shards needle her flesh, and the next she can swear hosts of fire ants are marching down from her shoulder to her fingertips. The pain she can manage, it's her father's furrowed brow that she can't stand.

He comes from a very long line of potters and, ever since Mira can remember, she has played with clay. He's always told her how proud he was that she'd carry on their ancestors' craft. Compared to his skills – the clay in her father's hands isn't just a ball of lifeless mud but some dormant creature coming alive with the slightest of his touch – her work after her injury is sloppy and clumsy and just not up to the mark.

As unthinkable as it may be, it's just as real – she won't be able to make pots any more. Though her father won't say it out loud, she can see his disappointment in his unfinished meals, can hear it in his midnight sighs.

At least if she could still paint the vessels like she used to, then not all of her skills would be wasted. Mira decides to try her hand on a small pot. She fetches the cow's horn and checks it for cracks before filling it with dye. The colour flows smoothly through the feather tip as she tickles the pot. For the finest work – the traditional spirals and waves – she uses a special brush made out of strands of boar hair.

When she's done, Mira turns the pot on all sides to appraise it. There's no denying it – the patterns are skewed, making it look like it's the work of someone who has gorged on barley beer. She smudges the paint with her maimed hand, making a mess of the whole thing, and takes the shameful dish to the garden where she can smash it before her father sees it.

Suru runs in circles around her feet, his high-pitched barks calling for play. Mira ignores the dog, and perches the pot on a boulder by the twig fence. She grabs the hammer but cannot bring herself to lift it. Suru's wagging tail whips her across her legs and she squats to scratch him under the chin.

She rescued him as a puppy when the village men culled a pack of strays last spring to control their number. There was this furry ball shaking and whining next to his dead mother and Mira brought him home. Her father didn't want him at first – 'Might be diseased,' he'd said – but she begged him until he relented. Suru won his heart several months later when he dug out the mole that had been destroying whatever little crops had survived the drought. Suru squeezed the creature between his jaws and dropped it dead at her father's feet, yelping in triumph.

'Keep quiet,' she tells Suru now, and picks up the hammer again. The dog bolts away suddenly and Mira laughs. 'I wasn't going to use the hammer on you, silly—'

The rest of her words are cut short as she sees her father standing behind and Suru running circles around him now.

'Let's not pretend, Mira. The sooner you face—'

'My left hand is getting stronger every day – it will help to redress—'

'I'm getting old. The tithes to the church and the voivode … We can't afford them much longer. We're facing falling into serfdom like so many of our people.'

Mira heads back into the hut, hoping to cut her father off before he launches into his same old rant, of how this was once a proud village of free peasants, of how they had been driven into servitude to the Turks, of the burgeoning taxes and the loss of land and freedom – she has heard it all before, time and time again. But it doesn't work.

'You know as well as I do,' he went on, following her inside, 'that serfs aren't much better off than slaves. Yes, they have various duties they're obliged to pay the boyar, but they are also bound to his estate, they need his permission to marry and – worst of all – their children too are born into subjugation.'

Mira breathes in the smoke from the *tizic* burning in the hearth, drawing it deep inside her, hoping it will dull her fury. 'Maybe with time—'

'It'll never be the same.' He shakes his head like he doesn't believe her. Mira wonders if her father means her hand or their circumstances. Perhaps both. 'A potter's work is half science. Nine fingers will never do the work of ten.' His voice is stern yet kind, and she knows this is just as hard for her father as it is for her. 'I'll keep going for as long as I can, but sooner or later, we'll have no choice but sell our home and land to the boyar. Unless…' There's a glint of hope in her father's eyes.

'What?'

'Our only hope is that you marry well, but given your condition…' The disheartened wave of her father's hand tells Mira what he's truly thinking.

'I don't have to marry—'

'The nunnery isn't for you, isn't for the likes of us. The church calls for a decent dowry, so—'

'It's not the church I was thinking of.'

'There's no other choice but to pray for a good marriage.'

'I can live like her. Like Rozalia.'

Her father winces like her words have pincers. 'She has healed your injury. Now you should stop seeing her. People will start talking—'

'That woman saved my life, Father. And she'd have saved my mother's too if you didn't get in her way—'

A loud knock on the door startles them both. Nobody has ever knocked on their door before. Neighbours or merchants wishing to buy their pots call her father's name – Pavel! Pavel! – well before they reach their hut.

Her father opens the door slowly, peeking through the tiny crack, and immediately wrenches his hand away like the handle has burned him.

Elina, the boyar's daughter herself, is standing on their doorstep.

Even in the low glow of the *opaiț*, Mira can see her father's face has drained of colour, his hand hovering in the air as if he's about to cross himself. She knows what he's thinking – the boyar's daughter doesn't usually call on the village peasants, and the fact that she's now standing in their doorway can only mean trouble.

Why didn't Suru bark to alert them to the unexpected guest? Useless dog.

'May I come in?' Elina asks, but doesn't wait for them to find their tongues. She steps inside and closes the door behind her. 'I came to thank you for my vessel.' She looks at Pavel. 'The one your daughter made for me. It's beautiful.'

'You paid us for it,' Pavel says. Mira notices her father's consternation is gradually replaced by suspicion as he scowls sideways at Elina.

'It's not the same as showing my appreciation.' Elina smiles. 'Here, I brought you this.' She hands Mira a small pot with honey.

'Thank you, miss.'

'Call me Elina, like I've asked you before—'

'Before?' Pavel steps protectively in front of Mira.

'When your daughter brought me the vessel,' Elina lies.

Mira is startled by how quickly Elina thinks on her feet, how convincingly she lies. She must have heard enough of her row with her father to refrain from mentioning Rozalia's place.

'It's awfully cold outside.' Elina rubs her hands together. 'Thought the winter was on its last legs but it's a stubborn one this year.'

'Travelling in this weather won't help your cold,' Pavel says. 'We'd offer you hot milk for your throat, if we had any.'

'Father…' Mira is appalled at her father's blunder.

Elina laughs. 'That's just my voice, I'm afraid. Croaky from birth.' She rubs her hands again, over the hearth this time, and thanks them for their hospitality.

Mira sees their guest out. With the snow melted and the sky clouded, the nights are confusingly dark. Perhaps sensing his mistress is coming, Elina's horse gives a little neigh and Mira can spot the patch of deeper black on black by the gate.

Elina trips into one of the many potholes in the courtyard and Mira grabs her arm. 'Hold my hand,' she tells Elina. 'I don't want you breaking your legs here. Your father will skin me alive.'

But right away Mira realises this is a terrible mistake. Elina's hand is smooth and soft as a piglet's skin. What will she make of Mira's palm – coarse and callused as a beggar's sole? But it's too late to pull it away.

'The real reason I came here tonight was to thank you for saving my life,' Elina says. 'The other week…'

Perhaps encouraged by the surrounding darkness, Mira says what's on her tongue. 'You didn't seem very happy that I found you.'

'It hurts just as much as the day my mother died. Time is no healer of grief, despite what they tell you.'

They've reached the gate but Elina is not letting go of Mira's hand. Something about this makes Mira's belly stir in a strange but pleasant way.

Elina hugs Mira like she did last time at Rozalia's, holding on to Mira's neck as though it were a log to save her from drowning. At a loss, Mira strokes Elina's back, saying the first thing that comes to mind. 'There's no shame in grieving. One day this ache is bound to—'

Her words are cut short as Elina's mouth brushes against hers. Was that a kiss? Or has Elina lost her bearings in the darkness and touched her by mistake? But something about the gesture is too deliberate and unapologetic to be a mistake.

Mira's face burns hot, not at the sinful act, surprisingly, but at the thought that her breath must stink of onion soup, while Elina's is sweet with honey and fragrant spices, which Mira has never smelled before.

Without a word, Elina jumps into the saddle and becomes one with the night. Mira listens to the galloping hooves fading away, the thuds without matching the pounding in her head.

It was just a friendly kiss intended for her cheek surely, but which, in this darkness, landed on her lips unintentionally, Mira tells herself. Still, her flesh tingles with a pleasant warmth despite the chilly night.

'What took you so long?' her father asks when she comes in.

Mira busies herself, tidying up the dyes, the cow horn and the brushes she had used earlier, whilst making sure to hide her face from her father, lest he spots something he shouldn't.

'I tell you somethin'—' he continues. 'People like her don't help people like us for nothing. Trust me, she's got a reason. Stay away from her—'

'She's just lonely and upset.'

'Don't be a fool. Where have you heard a wolf befriending sheep?'

The dry cow dung flares and hisses in the stove as if to agree with her father. Mira says goodnight and lies down to avoid any further talk, but the memory of the kiss is still burning her lips and won't let her sleep.

Why did Elina do that? Was it because the rich can do what they please without fear of consequences? Or did she do it because she knew Mira would like it? If it's the latter, then Mira is in trouble. Elina could be teasing her, testing her virtues, only to expose her later as a sinner. And no matter how much Mira would deny everything, who would ever believe a peasant over the landowner's daughter?

She must pretend this never happened. And she must stop thinking about Elina. Her father is right, the rich are a different breed and she had better remember that. It's not only foolish, but insane and dangerous to imagine anything else.

When her father's snores grow loud and steady, Mira gives up on her rest and sits up in the darkness, the embers in the hearth barely flickering.

Too many thoughts chasing each other in her head. Only one of them she can do something about. Mira tiptoes out of the hut with the silence of a ghost.

DISCIPLE

Despite the time of night, there's a soft glow in Rozalia's window. Mira is glad to see the old woman is still awake, but when she reaches the door, she can hear soft singing inside. She didn't think Rozalia had any friends, not in their village anyway. Mira turns on her heels when Rozalia calls out. 'Now that you're here, go fetch an armful of straw from the garden.'

Is Rozalia talking to her? How did she know—

'I don't have all night. Hurry up.' There's an edge to Rozalia's voice and Mira dashes to the garden for the straw.

When she walks into the hut, she sees Vera – the broom-maker's wife, who's always the first to badmouth Rozalia – now lying on the old woman's floor, all colour drained from her into the bloodied straw underneath.

'Gored by a bull in her thigh.' Rozalia answers Mira's silent question. 'Help me replace the layer of straw so I can gauge her bleeding.'

It takes some pushing and pulling as they turn the woman on her side to clean the mess, yet Vera doesn't show any sign of life.

'She looks—'

'She'll be fine,' Rozalia says. 'They brought her to me in time.'

The old woman mixes a drink, which she forces between

Vera's lips. The medicine smells and looks like the water where a toad has bathed, and Mira turns her head away.

Rozalia breaks into the same soft singing Mira heard earlier. A kind of chanting, or is it a foreign language? When she's done, Rozalia holds Vera's wrist with such attention as if it tells her secrets of the body.

'What's keeping *you* awake at this time?' Rozalia asks suddenly, startling Mira.

She had her request on the tip of her tongue when she arrived, but now her courage is gone. She watches the colour returning to Vera's drawn and waxy face, her limbs lifeless only a moment ago now twitching… Dark magic or not, anyone who can coax life back from the brink of death like that is nothing short of a miracle worker.

Mistaking Mira's hesitation, Rozalia says: 'Don't worry about Vera. If she can hear anything, she won't remember it. So what is it?'

'I'd like to learn about herbs and healing. Will you teach me?'

'Why would you want that?'

Mira stares at the gap between her right thumb and middle finger. 'I'll never be a potter again.'

'Your desire for my teachings should come from within, not prompted by circumstances.'

'That's not all,' Mira adds quickly. 'I want to be able to help women like you wanted to help my mother. You would've saved her life if my father… She'd be alive today, wouldn't she?'

Rozalia watches her for a long moment. Mira returns the stare, unflinching.

'Pottery was my father's idea, his desire for what I should do. Learning to work with herbs is mine.'

'It's not an easy path. You know what people think of me—'

'I also know whose help they seek when they're in pain.' Mira looks at Vera to prove her point.

'Alright. I'll give you what you're after, but I want something in return.'

Mira shuffles on her feet. 'Not sure I have anything I can trade… You know our means.'

'I want a disciple.'

'To teach the secrets of herbs?' Mira checks she has heard right. 'That's what I'm—'

'That's not all. I'm a guardian of the ancient wisdom, and I need someone to pass it on to.'

Mira swallows hard. 'What's that? What do I have to do?'

'It requires an oath of commitment and devotion to keep these teachings alive and pass them on to the right person when the time comes, so that the sacred wisdom isn't lost with your own death.'

'These teachings, what exactly are they?'

'Ancient traditions of attaining higher consciousness. Transcending human limitations—'

'Some people might say it's witchcraft, black magic.'

'That's what people call things they fear or don't understand. None of this will make any sense right now, but trust is everything. Initiating you into these secret teachings will give you tremendous powers, which go far beyond anything you can imagine right now.'

'I was only looking to learn about plants.'

'Plants are part of the whole – they cannot be taught separately. Knowing only fragments is dangerous. You're either in, or you're not.'

Mira takes a moment to think about it before she nods. 'I'm in.'

SHELL

It is one of those sunny, dazzling days that might fool you into thinking winter is over. But the chill in the air and the patches of frozen snow in the garden are proof that the old season still holds the upper hand. Elina is eager to see the back of this long winter which, despite its brightness and purity, has left a permanent mark of shame on her soul.

Behind the window of the day room, where the cold doesn't reach her, she basks in the fuzzy warmth of the low sun. She cracks walnuts with a hammer, dreamily picking at their sweet kernels. Her body is soft with thoughts of Mira's lips the other night: full, moist, willing. She closes her eyes, following the thrill running through her body.

She can hear the gates opening – the heavy bolts being drawn, the creaking of wood, her father's coach rolling in – he must be back from his meeting with the priest. They've received word from mason Barbu about his impending arrival with his men, and her father went to make arrangements for their lodgings.

He is back sooner than expected, and this sends a flash of annoyance rushing through her. She was enjoying the quiet room, being alone with her thoughts of Mira. Now her father will ruin it. She quickly goes to kneel in the eastern corner of the room, under the icon of the Virgin Mary, where she pretends to pray, hoping he'll leave her in peace a little longer.

When the door opens and his heavy boots step in, she keeps her body still, holding her breath, waiting for him to walk straight out. But he doesn't, and she jerks involuntarily as anger spills hot in her chest. She doesn't hear the sigh her father usually makes as he sits down. He must be standing, and this gives her hope he may still turn around and leave when he realises she's intent on her prayers.

She focuses on her breath, preparing for a battle of wills, when she's suddenly aware of her skin prickling at the back of her head. A cold shiver shoots between her shoulders and she springs to her feet, turning to see what her body already knows.

'Ho!' Bogdan says it the way he'd call out to a spooked horse.

'We weren't expecting you.' Elina's breath comes short and quick.

'Thought it would be a nice surprise.'

'Father will be delighted to hear that.' She somehow manages a strong voice despite the terror coursing through her. 'I'll go and let him know.' She makes for the door, but he steps sideways in her way.

'He's not home, I've been informed. Your gateman is a chatty fellow.'

Elina makes a dash for the hammer lying on the table where she was cracking nuts, but her uncle is closer and grabs it, holding it out of her reach. At a loss, her hand closes over a jagged walnut shell.

'You can try to fight me—' he says, dropping the hammer on the floor and kicking it a long way behind him, '—but this will only prolong our time together. If that's what you want, I won't complain. Or you do as I say, and this will all be over in a blink.'

'Get away from me or I'll scream for help.'

'Go ahead. But then you can forget about a decent marriage or your inheritance. At best your father will send you to a nunnery, or if the voivode catches wind of your promiscuity, he'll certainly find an excuse to slaughter your father, seize your coveted estate and add you to his harem of concubines.'

Elina's breath flutters in her throat as the truth of her uncle's words sinks in. She has heard of the voivode's greed and his killing of boyars whose properties or women he desires.

She squeezes the rough shell in her fist until it breaks her skin.

'I know you're smart enough to know what's best for your family and your reputation,' Bogdan says, approaching her. 'I'll keep them both safe in exchange for a sweet kiss.' He lifts his *anteriu* over the budge of his solid belly, revealing a birthmark under his navel: two red blotches coming together in the shape of a large bug.

SECOND CHANCES

When Elina refuses to go to church for the third Sunday in a row, her father isn't pleased.

'The priest is asking after you. I told him you weren't well, but this is getting embarrassing.'

'I'll go to church when I feel better.'

'Just what's wrong with you, may I ask? Whatever it is, it doesn't stop you from going out hunting.'

'Fresh air beats frankincense—'

'Look, my dear, I don't want to have this conversation every Sunday.'

Elina knows she'll have to go to church again at some point – her father won't have it any other way – but she hopes it won't have to be so often. She can't ignore the tug of war in her heart. Her faith has been shaken since the incident with the blind man and she questions everything the priest says.

Besides, she'd rather not go to confession at all than have to lie and say she has nothing to confess. With the snow melting away and the weather getting warmer, her uncle has taken to visiting them more often, and only the two of them know his true reasons. She does her best to keep out of his sight, but his cunning and brutality are tireless in feeding his vice.

Elina spends as little time at home as possible, riding in the woods, or hunting, all the while thinking about the potter's daughter. If Mira were here, then the manor would be a more bearable place. Maybe she could bring Mira to live here.

An idea strikes her.

On the way to the village, Elina stops to hunt some small game. Mira and her father must be short of food if they are setting hare traps in their yard.

The woods, though still bare, are noisy with trilling and cooing and chirping and squeaking. Do the birds know spring is on its way, or are they calling for it? Two garrulous grouse are squabbling in a tree and Elina sets an arrow in her bow, taking careful aim with one eye closed.

One of the birds drops to the ground.

Holding the reins in one hand and the limp grouse in the other, Elina prods Fulger into a sprint. Just before she reaches the village, she spots a fire smoking in Rozalia's yard and would have ridden past it if it wasn't for the thin figure burning armfuls of straw. Despite the large shawl and drab clothes, Elina recognises Mira. She dismounts Fulger with one quick jump and walks straight into the courtyard.

'A spring clean already?' she calls from the gate. 'The weather could still turn.'

Rozalia gives her a sideways look, visibly amused at Elina's comment. After all, nobody knows the weather as well as this old woman.

'Courtesy of a sick visitor last night who bled all over my hut,' she says. 'You're just in time with the game.' Rozalia reaches for the grouse, which she plonks into a pot of steaming water.

'Feathers and all?' Elina asks.

'It's called scalding, the easier to pluck the feathers.'

Why does her father say that the peasants are ignorant people? They may not know their letters, and they may be in the dark about the law and country affairs, and many other things which the rich are privy to due to their social standing – but the peasants are certainly not stupid. They are wise about life and survival in a way that boyars could never be. Put simply, Elina is convinced that the villagers would have no trouble sustaining themselves in the absence of landowners, who only burden their lives with hard work and tithes – why, they'd truly thrive. But how long would she and her father survive without their servants at the manor?

'I'll go get the fire going to cook us this fat grouse,' Rozalia says.

Mira jumps to her feet. 'I'll take care of it,' she says. 'You've done enough today. You could do with a little rest.' There's a quiet yet clear pleading in her voice – Mira is obviously wary of being left alone with Elina.

Rozalia, however, waves her off. 'I'm not as old as you think I am.' And turning to Elina, says: 'Give her a hand with the plucking. You'll learn something useful.'

With Rozalia gone, Mira avoids looking at Elina. She goes about her work in silence – fishing the grouse out of the hot water with a wooden spoon, placing it on a log and starting to pluck at the feathers. When Elina squats next to her and tries to copy her movements, Mira is quick to find fault.

'We start with the tail and the wings.' She turns the bird so that Elina can reach the other wing. But even so, their hands touch as they go about the plucking. Each time Mira pulls her hand away like she has touched a rosehip bush.

'A few feathers at a time, please,' Mira says, without looking up. 'You're ripping the fowl's skin with your pulling.'

Elina is really trying, yet her work isn't showing her efforts. 'I know what you're thinking,' she tells Mira. 'But I want you to know that you can trust me, I promise.'

'If it's about the other night, I totally understand. Grief isn't easy to—'

'You know very well what I'm referring to.' Elina studies Mira's face for clues of what she won't say.

Mira stares back. 'Look, I'm just a peasant girl and you're… you're… The truth is that an onion can only ever sprout an onion.'

'What's that supposed to mean? That I smell?' Elina grabs a fistful of wet feathers and throws it playfully at Mira, whose reaction is a brief laugh – and that is so lovely – but she quickly composes herself.

'You belong to a different world, always will.' Mira flushes and her fingers resume the plucking.

'I know you can't make pots any more because of your injury – yes, I couldn't help eavesdropping the other day before I knocked on your door – but I have an idea. I'll ask my father to take you on as my maid. This way you can still provide for you and your father, *and* we can be close friends—'

'Given the pleasant weather, why don't we cook dinner outdoors?' Rozalia calls to them, approaching with a large bowl and a knife. 'What's up with you?' The old woman has noticed Mira's flushed face and jittery fingers.

'It's my incompetent plucking,' Elina says. 'Apparently, I'm breaking the grouse's skin.'

'We've got food, and for that we should be grateful,' Rozalia says, but the way she's watching them proves she doesn't believe Elina. 'I'm going to say this once and you better remember it, both of you: in my house, there's no social standing. You leave your status at the gate.' She glares at Elina. 'Here we're all equal, respectful of one another. I won't allow any airs and graces.'

Neither of them says anything to contradict Rozalia. And though part of Elina knows it's better the old woman thinks she's been unkind than suspect the truth, another part of her wishes Mira would come to her defence. But Mira is now gutting the bird, all her care and attention focused on the dead fowl.

Elina picks a log to help Rozalia with stirring the fire. 'We were also talking about becoming friends,' Elina says.

There's a gasp as Mira drops the knife, and it's not clear if she's hurt herself or not, her hands already glistening with the grouse's blood. She swiftly picks it up, runs it through the flames for cleansing and resumes her work, as if letting a sharp blade slip through your fingers and allowing it to drop by your big toe were part of the gutting ritual.

'Are you alright?' Elina asks, genuinely concerned, but also pleased to notice Mira isn't as composed as she'd have them believe.

'Nothing that won't heal,' Mira says, looking away, and though Elina can't be certain, she thinks she can sense a barb in these deliberately ambiguous words.

'Friends, huh?' Rozalia asks.

'Why are you scowling at me? You and Mama were friends notwithstanding your class differences, weren't you?'

Rozalia starts skewing the pieces Mira has chopped. 'Young meat – it won't take long to roast. Will you share our meal today, or does my heresy still offend you?'

Words are eluding Elina, like they are fish she's trying to catch with bare hands. She has been questioning her faith, and despite all her reticence and doubt, there's no simple answer.

And she is grateful Rozalia doesn't wait for one, as she instructs Mira to fetch three *străchini* from the hut.

While turning the meat over the fire, Rozalia tells strange stories about Old Gods – deities who breathed the world into existence way before the man-shaped god came along. Between the Sun God who blesses their crops and the Moon Goddess who holds all life in Her enthralling powers, Rozalia talks about a whole cohort of spirits who protect nature – the Spirit of the Land, that of the Water, of the Fire, the Forest Deity…

'Sounds like there's a whole invisible world out there,' Elina says, eager to let the old woman know that accepting her food – the roasted wing Rozalia places in her *strachin*ă – doesn't mean that she swallows her tales too.

'We see what we deserve to see. Only when you approach nature with the attention and respect it's worthy of will it lay bare its secrets.'

'And its spirits? You know, I spend a lot of time in the woods, and I've never caught a glimpse of any of these creatures you talk about,' Elina says. She turns to Mira, hoping for a furtive smile or a wink of support, but Mira lowers her eyes, busying herself with the bones in her plate, picking them clean.

'They certainly see you,' Rozalia says, looking at her from across the fire.

Elina's laughter burbles up from deep in her belly. 'And you know that because they tell you?'

'Because I make offerings to them to look after you.'

The laughter dies in Elina's throat. The woods are an escape for her, the place where she feels most at home, free and happy like nowhere else. Could this be partly thanks to Rozalia's placating of these unseen spirits? And if that truly counts for the safety and joy she feels wrapped around her deep among the trees, is there also a spirit who protects young women from their uncles' abuses, whom Rozalia could supplicate on her behalf?

But Elina doesn't ask. She gulps it down with a sip of water and finally bites into the juicy meat, fragrant with wild garlic and parsley. The bad taste in her mouth, however, ruins the food, and she pushes the plate away.

The gathering darkness shields half of Rozalia's face, the other half glowing from the flames. Her voice, as she carries on telling her stories, is lilting and Elina finds herself hanging on Rozalia's every word, as though under a spell.

For all her reservations about this old woman, being in her presence right now eases off the sharp claw that's been gripping Elina's chest for weeks.

The more she tries not to think about going home, the more fear courses through her.

What if her uncle has dropped by unannounced again?

MEDICINE

To prepare Mira for her initiation, Rozalia has instructed her to fast regularly. This is not only unpleasant but inconvenient too, because she's used to eating when there is food and starving when there isn't any. Now she has to fast on certain days – something to do with the phases of the moon – regardless of whether she's eaten anything the previous day or not. However, Rozalia is right about one thing – when done by choice, hunger isn't painful.

The next thing Rozalia teaches her is overcoming the fear of darkness. One night during a fierce storm, she takes Mira to the back of her garden, then into the forest. The trees creak and groan all around, some of them snapping off in their path. Mira begs to go back, but Rozalia marches on, saying, 'At the heart of any storm, whether it's around or inside you, there's a place of quiet like no other. When you find that place, you gain such strength that nobody could ever take that away from you. Now watch your breath, Mira! Closely. Carefully.'

The howl of the storm makes her body shake so hard that Mira thinks her joints will come undone. Rozalia doesn't hold her hand or speak much, and Mira wonders if this is done on purpose. It makes her think of fledglings on their first flight. They either take off and survive, or plunge to the ground, spilling into a mess of guts and bloodied feathers.

Just when she thinks her chest and lungs are too small to cope with the ball of fire rolling up inside her, she can hear Rozalia say, 'Let it out', and Mira finds herself bent forward with hands planted on her knees, roaring like a demon. Her scream entwines with that of the tempest, looping around the twisting, swooshing trees.

When her chest is empty of breath, she is certain something has ripped inside of her. Because whatever it was that shook her body so wildly has now gone from her bones, leaving her light and still, as though she has reached that heart of the storm Rozalia was talking about.

'A good scream is a powerful medicine,' Rozalia says and hugs Mira for the first time that night. 'Those unversed in the laws of the body and life see it as a fit of madness or being possessed by the devil. But now you've learned the truth and what it's worth.'

'I've learned its power, but its workings are a mystery to me.'

Rozalia holds her hand, leading her out of the woods. 'A good scream, when done properly, cracks an opening into your binding and alters it slightly, just like a torrent of rain alters the grooves on a well-trodden road.'

As part of her training, Mira also has to kneel, learning to be still for many hours a day. When she makes the mistake of complaining to Rozalia that her knees are starting to swell, Rozalia's reply is as clear as most of her advice: 'Before we can do any work with the soul, we need to deal with the flesh, or it won't let us get anywhere.'

'How long is this preparation going to take?' Mira asks.

'As long as it takes for your body to stop hurting.'

Alongside the mysterious practices, the wise woman teaches Mira all there is to know about herbs and their uses, and *this* is what makes it all bearable. One day Mira will be a healer, skilled and knowledgeable enough to save the lives of women who would otherwise have her mother's fate. This is enough to alleviate the worst pangs of hunger and ease the pain in her joints from prolonged kneeling.

It's the month of the opening buds and Rozalia says it's the best time to stock up on wild garlic. She hands Mira a basket while she carries a peculiar pouch made of three badger snouts sewn together.

'What's that for?' Mira asks.

'My medicine bag, to collect herbs.'

Instead of setting off for the woods through the back end of her garden, Rozalia leads the way alongside the lake.

Since her near-drowning a few moons back, Mira avoids the lake whenever possible, and when there's no choice, she scurries past it, cupping her hand to the side of her head to block it out. It's a silly fear, but she can't shake it off. Her flesh prickles and she sweats every time she comes anywhere near it.

Mira almost cries out with joy when she sees Elina riding out of the forest but swallows her excitement at once, lest Rozalia notices it.

'Good day to you both,' Elina calls to them as she alights. 'Where are you off to, looking so purposeful?'

'The usual, foraging for food and medicine,' Rozalia says.

Mira jumps at the opportunity to ask her burning question. 'Shouldn't we be in the thick of the woods for that?'

'There are plenty of herbs you could be learning about on the way there,' Rozalia says, a little too impatient.

'Can I join you?' Elina asks.

'Someone may see you. Your father won't like it if he gets wind of it.'

'I'll blame it on you. I'll say you've bewitched me.' Elina sends her horse off grazing with a pat on his neck and, with her *cobză* on one shoulder and her bow on the other, she falls into step beside Mira.

Rozalia, as if to reinforce her earlier point, shows them

various plants and leaves, describing their uses. Mira keeps her eyes on the ground to avoid seeing the lake, half listening to Rozalia, half wondering about Elina, who has taken to visiting Rozalia frequently. Of course, Elina is after answers about her mother, which the old woman is withholding, but Mira can't help feeling there's something else that brings Elina here. Like she's running away from something, or perhaps – someone? Otherwise, why is there so much sadness – often fright – in Elina's eyes when she has to go home?

Maybe she's just imagining it all. Because as the boyar's daughter, nobody in their right mind would dare upset Elina, let alone harm her in any way, unless they wanted to be carrion for crows.

Rozalia's enthusiastic patter is interrupted by Elina. 'You make it sound like the entire forest is packed with medicine.'

'All herbs are useful. It's only that people are ignorant of their benefits.'

'You have an answer to everything.'

'Wouldn't that be wonderful?' Rozalia says and immediately finds another plant to talk about.

The old woman is unusually chatty today, Mira thinks. Either she's truly excited about sharing her vast knowledge with them or she's—

Mira suddenly realises that, instead of entering the woods, they are following the curve of the lake, approaching the spot where she fell through the ice. Panic gathers in her belly, and she squats, pretending to tie her *opinci* so she can catch her breath and think of a way out.

'I'm sorry, but I have to go,' she says, still fiddling with the string of her *opinci*. 'Just remembered, my father has asked me to foot-wedge a batch of clay for him—'

'We're almost there,' Rozalia says.

'Where?' Elina asks.

'To the place where Mira is going for a quick dip.' Rozalia resumes her walking.

'Isn't it a bit early for that? It's not even proper spring yet.'

'Medicine isn't always pleasant,' Rozalia says over her shoulder.

'What's going on?' Elina asks in a whisper.

'She tricked me, bringing me here—'

Elina elbows her. 'I've been for a swim in the middle of winter, remember? It can't be any worse than that.'

'It's not the cold water…' Mira says, prickly shivers running rampant over her body.

'We haven't got all day,' Rozalia calls to them from up the path.

'We can do it together,' Elina says in a sing-song voice. 'I'll come in with you, if you want.'

The thought of having to step into the lake brings bile to her throat, but not doing so and embarrassing herself in front of Elina feels just as sickening, and Mira scuffles forward, doing all she can to put one foot in front of the other.

By the time they reach Rozalia, the old woman has already gathered a handful of twigs. 'I'll make a big fire so you can dry after.' She rummages in her grisly pouch, taking out a flint rock and a fistful of *iască*, a specially dried mushroom that catches sparks easily.

Mira stands with her back to the lake, taking deep breaths to settle her stomach.

'You trusted me the last time. You did what you were told…' Rozalia says while kindling a flame with her breath.

'I had no choice then. It was facing you, or death by drowning.'

'If you don't take that dip, this lake will haunt you for the rest of your days.' Rozalia's voice is soft and encouraging.

Mira has nothing to say to this, but her right eye twitches with anger. Elina has propped her bow and *cobză* against a pine tree and is now undressing. 'Hurry up,' she says. 'The sooner we do it, the sooner it'll be over.'

Mira has bathed in the lake with village women before the accident and it's not the bare flesh that's holding her attention. She realises that, without her rich layers, Elina doesn't look any different to her. Taller, yes, but just as thin. Mira eats when there is food. What's Elina's trouble? Word is, they don't lack anything at the manor house.

'Don't keep me waiting. It's a little chilly,' Elina says, hugging herself.

Mira's whole body is squirming in protest at having to go in the water, but what will Elina think of her if she doesn't do it? A quick dip. A very quick dip. In and out. How bad can it be?

Mira doesn't have as many layers and sheds her clothes in one breath, before she can change her mind. Elina hooks her arm through Mira's as they walk towards the water. 'To keep us warm,' she says, and perhaps noticing Mira's trembling limbs, she adds: 'I'll keep hold of you at all times. I won't let go. It'll be alright.' Her whisper is so close that Mira's cheeks flush hot.

'You smell nice,' Mira says, immediately anxious about her own body odour, which she knows won't be as pleasant.

'Orris root powder. A trick Rozalia taught my mother. Look, we're here already.' Elina dips her toes in the water. 'Nippy' – she shivers as she steps in, pulling Mira after her – 'but we'll live.'

Mira looks over her shoulder. They are obscured from Rozalia's sight by a fringe of reeds. She could just wet her hair and body, and Rozalia would be none the wiser.

'It's not her you'd be fooling,' Elina says, guessing Mira's thoughts. 'Come, it'll be over before you know it.'

Arm in arm, they wade through the numbing water until it reaches their shoulders.

'How 'bout qui' paddle? 'T'will warm us up.' Elina's words are clipped with stutters and sharp intakes of breath.

Mira's toes grip the hard-pressed silt of the lake bed.

'You got to take a dip t'wet y'hair,' Elina says, shivering, and takes Mira's hands into hers. 'We'll do it t'gether on three. Ready? One… two… three…'

With a deep breath, they go under at the same time. Mira

doesn't want to be submerged any more than necessary and comes up for air at once. Elina takes her time to resurface, making Mira uneasy with each passing moment. She stares into the water, but having disturbed the mud at the bottom of the lake with their feet, she can't see much. Just small grey waves bobbing up and down, glinting in the setting sun like the scales of a giant fish.

Someone grabs her shoulder from behind, and though she knows it can only be Elina, her body reacts before her mind can catch up, and she gives out a panicked yelp, turning around so sharply that her feet slip on the silt and – flailing – she ends up swallowed by the lake once more.

When Mira comes up again, coughing and spitting water, Elina teases her. 'Enjoying it too much, are you?'

Mira can think of a few words she'd like to say to Elina, but she manages to hold her tongue and heads for the shore.

Elina bars her way. 'Why such hurry to get out? You look at home in the lake.'

Sensing a trap, Mira halts, looking suspiciously at Elina.

'What with your big green eyes, you look like a frog paddling about.'

Instinctively, Mira hits the water with her palm, splashing Elina, but she immediately catches herself: Elina isn't just another village woman she can play with like that.

To her surprise, Elina laughs and splashes her right back. 'You mocked me when you called me a Snow Maiden, implying I was stupid enough to think I could beat the frost. You can dish it out, but you can't take it, eh, Froglet?'

'Snow Maiden.'

They are both laughing now, engaged in a water fight. Elina leaps forward and wraps one arm around Mira's waist, the other playing with Mira's hair, sweeping it off her face, tucking it behind her ears. They are so close their breasts are touching. A hot shiver uncoils somewhere between Mira's belly and her lower back – sinful, shameful, yet too pleasant to deny. Elina's wide eyes are asking an unspoken question and perhaps Mira's tingling skin covered in goosebumps is all the answer she needs. With a quick look over her shoulder, Elina locks them into a tight hug, their lips brushing into a lingering kiss.

What if her father is wrong? Mira thinks. What if Elina doesn't have any dubious motives for befriending her and genuinely feels the same way Mira does? This, of course, doesn't change the fact that what they are doing is dangerous and they could never be together as they want to. Yet despite all this, it feels… right somehow.

Suddenly, Elina breaks away. 'Catch me,' she says, chuckling and wading towards the shore.

All that earlier fear has been washed out of Mira's body. She wishes they could stay in the water a little longer. Just the two of them and their kiss. But Elina isn't coming back, and Mira follows reluctantly, splashing more water on her face, lest Rozalia notices the guilty flame that's burning her lips and cheeks. Mira stops on the other side of the fire from the old woman.

'I see you've survived,' Rozalia says.

'All that water I swallowed kept me afloat,' Mira says, wringing and twisting her hair, and avoiding looking at her.

The dusk is creeping in, and with it, a light breeze ruffles the lake. Somewhere an owl is hooting. Elina must dislike them, judging by her frown as she looks about the trees searching for it. Unable to locate the bird, Elina picks up her *cobză*, intent on drowning out its offending call. The thrum is tender, unhurried, as though she chooses it with great care from a pool of many sounds, singing a song of deep yearning.

Mira recognises the longing which refuses to be named. A flicker, a flutter she's sensed forever trapped in the chambers of her heart. She licks her lips, tasting honey every time she thinks of their kiss.

In singing, Elina's already coarse voice grows deeper as her music ripples through the air, its unseen thread tying them all together – the lake, the breeze, the hooting owl and the ancient trees.

Elina's skirt lifts as she perches her foot on a rock the better to hold the *cobză*. Mira can't help stealing glances at Elina's bare legs. Too shy to look at her naked body earlier, now that Elina has closed her eyes, absorbed in her singing – and with Rozalia busy tending to the fire – Mira watches Elina closely, as if she were a fairy trapped in their world.

The flickering flames throw playful shadows all over Elina, save for a few dark marks on her legs which don't shift like the rest.

Mira leans in for a better look.

There is a cluster of bruises – bold and ugly – scattered down the inside of Elina's thighs. How did she get them? From riding, perhaps? Not that Mira knows anything about riding, but these look like pinching bruises from thick fingers.

Could she be right, after all, about Elina fearing someone? It's hardly possible, given Elina's status and her temperament, but how else to make sense of these injuries?

Unable to say anything, Mira kneels behind Elina and starts plaiting her hair, making her touch as gentle as possible, as though her tenderness could soothe the pain of whatever it was that caused those angry marks.

Mira whispers a wish, knotting it tightly into Elina's plait and hoping it snakes its way into her head and heart until it comes to pass.

MASON BARBU

Something makes Mira look over her shoulder and it's not because of any noise. She has noticed this before; she can sense someone's presence before she can hear them. A kind of odd stillness in the air that sends her skin crawling.

Rozalia must've sensed it too, for the two of them look towards the woods at the same time. Seeing nobody there, Mira turns back, thinking she must have imagined it, but Rozalia remains still and unblinking, as though by the power of her stare alone she could conjure someone up.

And she succeeds.

A shadow peels off a tree, striding towards them. A tall, dark-bearded man, his shoulders wide as a breeding bull's.

Elina stops playing the *cobză* and steps forward, standing poised and pompous, as befits the mistress of these lands.

'They told me many beautiful women lived here,' the stranger says by way of greeting. 'They haven't lied.'

'Who do we have the honour of welcoming to our village?' Elina asks, the excessive friendliness in her voice tying a knot in Mira's stomach.

'Master mason Barbu. I've been summoned—'

'Good evening, mason Barbu. I'm Elina, the daughter of Boyar Constantin. My father will be pleased to know you've arrived. You're our last hope for building the church. A few architects have tried their skills but alas…'

The mason bows to Elina. 'So I've heard. I promise to do my best.'

'On your own?' Elina tilts her head in surprise.

'Thirteen men. Two are with me.' He nods towards the lurking shadows in the woods. 'The rest will arrive in the coming days. All skilled masons like myself. And, of course, we'll get a helping hand from your local men, the devout Christians they are. It happens everywhere we work, up and down the country,' he says and looks over Elina's shoulder.

'This is Mira, the potter's daughter,' Elina says. 'And this is Rozalia – the best healer around here.'

As the man steps forward, a shiver shoots up Mira's spine. The stranger's face, now tinged with the glow of the fire, bares a hardness at odds with his chat and cheer. It's as if the chill of the stones he works with has crept into his gaze. Mira shudders and drops her head, busying herself with feeding twigs to the fire.

The air grows heavy with a fraught silence as the mason locks eyes with Rozalia, an exchange of silent words crossing between them.

'A wise woman, I see…' he says, drawing out his words. 'We'll get along just fine. A wise woman knows where her place is, where her limitations lie.'

'Wisdom is also the absence of fear,' Rozalia says, her voice flat.

Another silent spell follows, and the mason does something unexpected and unheard of. He bows to Rozalia, and she returns the gesture. No man of his status would ever bow to a peasant.

When Barbu takes his leave and returns to the woods, Rozalia stares into thin air long after the mason has become one with the night.

Elina is the first to find her tongue. 'How do you know him?' she asks.

'I don't.'

'You bowed to him—'

'Neither of us bowed to each other. But to the Oneness we recognised in one another. I believe he too may be a follower of the ancient wisdom.'

'He doesn't strike me as a medicine man,' Elina says.

'No, I don't think he is. There's a darkness about him I don't trust.'

'The important thing is – will he succeed in building the church?'

Rozalia is quiet for a moment. 'He might,' she says finally. 'But if he does, there'll be a dear price to pay, and I don't mean just your father's coins.'

'What else could it be?' Elina asks.

'You don't want him to accomplish the job. That's all I can say.'

'Why do you have to be so obscure all the time?'

'Because you wouldn't believe me if I told you. You'll just have to trust me.'

'That's what you said when you wanted to steal the voivode's arrow back then. You're asking for the same thing now – trust you – but on what grounds?'

'Nothing I say will make sense to you at present.'

'You know how much the building of this church means to me—'

'For selfish reasons. You're thinking of your inheritance.'

'Of course I am. You said my mama was a smart woman. But a woman can only afford to be smart if she's either lucky to marry well, or if she's financially independent. And that's what I'm aiming for, because I don't wish to rely on luck.'

'Fair enough. But you don't know the forces you're reckoning with here.'

So I was right – Mira thinks of the hunch she had about the mason.

'You keep saying that. Please, enlighten me,' Elina says, looking at Mira, perhaps seeking her support.

'Rozalia has done nothing but help us so far,' Mira says, barely audible. She doesn't like being caught in the middle. 'Your mother trusted her. Perhaps we should too.'

'Yes, my mama trusted her. And where is she now?'

'Through no fault of Rozalia's, as I've understood.' Mira is surprised by the sharpness of her own words. She can only rely on the conversations she's heard between Elina and Rozalia, but she has no way of knowing what really happened to Elina's mother. The glint of disappointment in Elina's eyes is confirmation that Mira has said the wrong thing. But the words have been spoken and she cannot take them back. She's glad for Rozalia's intervention.

'There's something we must do,' the old woman says. 'A little warding ritual to protect the two of you.'

'Has Satan himself just walked into our village?' Elina asks.

'You can mock me all you want, as long as you come visit me on the next new moon. On an empty belly.'

'But protect us from what?'

'I promised your mother I'd look after you. You don't have to believe anything I tell you. Just turn up. Do it for your mother.'

WARDING RITUAL

Mira burns a sprig of sage in preparation for the ceremony, guiding the acrid smoke around the corners of the ceiling, where Rozalia says bad spirits like to roost.

'What if Elina doesn't come?' Mira asks.

Rozalia hums something under her breath as she forms a wide circle on the floor with an array of rocks of different sizes. Inside it she places two little stones the colour of the harvest moon when it hangs low in the sky. One is shaped as a crescent, the other as a teardrop.

'Amber,' she says. 'It will protect you.'

'Am I in danger?'

'It's good to be prepared.'

'For what?'

Rozalia ignores the question and swings a flame about Mira's head and shoulders. 'To cleanse your spirit,' she says. When she's done, Rozalia kneels inside the circle of rocks and asks Mira to join her.

'What about Elina?'

'Repeat after me,' Rozalia says and hums something unintelligible.

'But it doesn't make any sense,' Mira protests.

'It doesn't have to. It's a chant, not a love song. Don't expect any clear words – they belittle the purity of sound, therefore diminishing its power. You just follow my rhythm and stay with it.'

Mira learns the strange tune and carries on repeating it until Rozalia brings the pitch down and finally stops chanting altogether. She picks the two gems and holds them in her balled fists, whispering something into them, then hands Mira the one shaped as a crescent.

The door squeaks open, with Elina peering in, as though she's still not sure about coming here tonight.

'Am I too late?' she asks, dropping a heavy bundle on the ground.

What tasty food has she brought this time? Mira wonders.

Rozalia holds out the teardrop amber, still warm with her breath. 'This one is for you. A talisman to ward off evil. Keep it on you at all times.'

Elina rolls it between her fingers. 'Bewitched, is it?'

'Fasten them securely around your necks.' Rozalia tosses them a spool of thread and then she squats to clear the rocks away, moving them into a corner of the hut where she hides them under a hare skin.

Elina offers to help Mira with tying her string, which sends shivers down Mira's back at the first touch. Elina's breath is hot and shaky. Either she's struggling to make a knot or she's taking her time on purpose. Choosing a moment when Rozalia has her back to them, Elina kisses Mira on the side of her neck. Convinced her hair is standing on end, Mira immediately pats her head, lest she looks like a frightened cat.

'Will you help with mine now?' There's a playful glint in Elina's eyes, inviting Mira to return the kiss.

Though she's grown more confident about their friendship, Mira can't discard the peasants' stories she's heard all her life about the fickle whims of the rich and their cruelty. If word got out about their unconventional bond, it wouldn't be Elina who'd be punished. People of her class don't have to worry about consequences. And yet, Mira chooses to push back these thoughts, as if the strength of her will is a fair match against the way of the world.

She leans in for a furtive kiss, and that's when she notices the mark. To make sure of it, Mira pulls at the collar of Elina's dress on the pretext of adjusting it, and sure enough – there's a purple bruise blooming down Elina's shoulder. Mira kisses the blemished skin, planting a silent wish of healing. She's almost caught out by Rozalia, who turns towards them suddenly, her voice as relaxed as it is urging.

'It's not essential, but if you can remember your talisman when you go to sleep and upon waking up – thank it for protecting you – this way its power will increase. And don't lose it!'

Mira immediately checks she's made a tight knot on Elina's string, hoping the blessed gem will safeguard her friend against any further harm from now on.

'Are we immortal now? Invulnerable?' Elina's mocking smile spreads wide on her face.

'Like gratitude, belief is another ingredient that makes our day sweeter. None of your father's rivers of honey will take away grief, or pain, or longing. But you already know that, don't you?'

'Plain-speaking as ever.' Elina holds her smile, but her foot is tapping fast.

'I have partridge stew,' Rozalia says and starts pottering about the hearth, dishing out the food.

Elina unties the bundle she brought with her earlier to reveal a small crock with fruit jelly. She never comes empty-handed, always bearing gifts they can eat – meats, honey, nuts and spices from faraway lands. More than the food, Mira enjoys Elina's fierceness. Not that she can ever dream of behaving like that, but it's heartening to watch someone who can, even if Elina's warrior spirit isn't enough to protect her from whoever gives her those ugly bruises.

Gathered around Rozalia's hearth and listening to her stories about the Old Gods – with Elina challenging most of it – Mira wouldn't want to be anywhere else. These two women, who often argue with each other, are the closest thing Mira has ever had to a proper family.

When she readies to leave, Elina also stands up. 'Time for me to go too,' she says, and there's that sadness clouding over her eyes again.

They walk along the lake shore, keeping to under the trees to avoid the moonglow. The villagers are usually indoors as soon as the sun sets, but it's best to be careful. The spring night, still chilly, is thick with life: flapping of wings, the rustling and snuffling of hunting for food or a mate.

Elina takes Mira's hand, the touch sending a hot tingling across her breastbone. She speaks, for an excuse to breathe in more air.

'Funny thing that you prefer Rozalia's burrow to the grand house you live in.'

'When was the last time you spent a full day at home yourself?'

'If I lived in a manor—'

'Speaking of which…' Elina lets out an angry huff. 'I've asked my father about making you my maid, but he says I already have Ana. He doesn't want to let her go because she's been with us for years *and* because she has four mouths to feed.'

Mira is lost for words for two reasons. First, because she didn't believe Elina would really ask her father about it; and second, that Boyar Constantin cares about his servants.

'Say something.' Elina leans in closer to her.

'It's great to hear your father isn't the beast people believe him to be.'

'That doesn't help *us*.'

Mira, who is used to following advice, not giving it, whistles a little air through a pursed mouth. 'Maybe if we wait a little…' She tries to find the right words.

'Yes, we'll wait until Barbu builds this church. Once that's done and the voivode is pleased with it, my official "male" status will put me on an equal footing with my father. I won't need his permission to make you my maid then.' Elina pulls Mira into her arms. Their lips find each other in the darkness and Mira relishes how right this feels, despite the warning pounding in her chest, demanding to be heeded.

Later that night, Mira has a dream that wakes her up in a cold sweat.

She's trapped in a strange kind of place. Familiar in that it feels heavy and smothering like when she was stuck under ice, yet different. This is an unyielding wall surrounding her from all sides, with no doors nor windows, or else she can't find them. The confined space is dark and silent as though she has fallen into an empty grave. She searches for a way out by clawing at the walls until her hands are stubs of jagged bones. But the stone, instead of giving way, squeezes in on her with the strength of a sly serpent until she fails to draw another breath.

Mira bolts up, gasping for air. Not even when her father's peaceful snores reach her jumbled mind does she feel a respite in her terror.

She wipes the sweat off her face, has a sip of water and tries to go back to sleep, only to wake up again by the same dread that she's trapped deep underground.

The dawn finds her with a twitching eye and throat clogged with fear – thick and slimy like cold grease. Has this anything to do with the warding ritual from the previous night? Has Rozalia given her a cursed gem to wear around her neck? That woman is a witch after all.

Or could this dream be a warning? Does Rozalia have a cellar? She must do. Almost everyone in the village does. Why has she never talked about it, or shown it to Mira?

Don't be stupid, she tells herself. She won't let her father's fears play on her mind. She has to stick with what she knows, not what other people tell her to believe. That's what Rozalia's teachings are all about – learning to find your own truth.

But what if the old woman isn't all she seems to be?

CELLAR

Tired and troubled by the ghastly dream, Mira crouches on the doorstep, hoping the dampness of the dew outside and the gentle breeze will clear her head. The day is breaking with a thin grey light spilling over a bruised and battered sky. What demons did the heavens have to battle overnight?

With birdsong for company, Mira watches the small, dark clouds merge and fray and merge again, turning from scars and blemishes into pots of gold as the sun peeks over the eastern hill. The breath of the new morning warms her face and bones, lifting the cold terror that's been pooling in her heart. She must confront Rozalia about it. How is it possible that Mira – who is usually too tired to have any dreams at all, and when she does, they are fleeting, silly and forgetful – is all of a sudden haunted by a nightmare more real than life? It's uncanny that this should happen following the strange ritual they performed last night. The old woman must be hiding something.

When she can hear her father stirring, groaning as he stretches his old bones, she picks up the bucket to go fetch water from the well. Something in their garden catches her eye – a hare hanging in their trap. Her stomach growls as she thinks of the tasty meals she's going to cook for the next few days. But then she realises there's something wrong about it, about the way the hare hangs in the noose. Unnatural somehow.

She goes to check on it and is surprised to find a dark stain on its fur. None of the hares she traps ever bleed. This one has a tiny injury in the neck. Like it's been speared. Someone has hunted this hare and placed it here to make it look like it's trapped itself.

Mira smiles. There's only one person who could have gone through all this trouble – who would've had the means to. Warm joy sloshes through her middle as she thinks of Elina.

For the rest of the day, Mira's head is full of Elina, whose face she can see everywhere – in the well when she goes to fetch water, in the hotpot she cooks with the gifted hare, in the clay she foot-wedges for her father.

But as the shadows draw out and daylight dips, Mira gets restless, dreading the night ahead. She has to see Rozalia and ask her about the dream. She needs answers from the old woman.

Mira finds Rozalia sorting through a basket of shallots, peeling the dry layers, chopping out the rot.

'I wasn't expecting you this evening. Everything alright?'

Mira goes to squat next to Rozalia and give her a hand with the bulbs. 'Do you have anything to help with sleep?'

'What's eating at you?'

Mira keeps her eyes on the onions, turning them in her hands to make sure that even if they're damaged, their roots are intact. She's learned that scraps of shallots will grow into a healthy crop as long as their root tips are sound.

'Do you have a cellar?' Mira fixes Rozalia with a stare, wondering if the old woman will tell the truth.

'I can play your game by answering every question with another question.' Rozalia drops her work and returns Mira's stare. 'But if you want answers, you have to start talking to me. What's going on?'

Mira recounts her nightmare, the vivid horror of the

grave-like space she was trapped in. The skin-prickling fear she couldn't shake off the entire day. Is this connected to the warding ritual from the previous evening? Could something have gone wrong with it?

Rozalia, who is usually so serene, is now frowning. 'And you think this awful place is my cellar where I'm going to trap you, is that right?'

'You said if I talked, you'd stop asking questions. I'd like some answers. Please.'

A moment of silence grows into a spell and neither of them breaks it. Mira is waiting to see what Rozalia has to say for herself, but the old woman is quiet, her eyes focused in mid-air like she's trying to untangle something only she can see.

'Time has come for your initiation,' Rozalia says finally. 'But for it to work, you must trust me, because it won't be an easy path. Many of your questions will go unanswered, my instructions will seem pointless and frustrating, yet you'll have to follow them precisely, with no room for error or digression. If you have any doubts about me or my motives, then you're wasting my time. And in your case, you're playing with your life.'

'So you know this place?'

'It's not my cellar.'

'Where is it then?'

'You'll find out soon enough. Come, we have work to do, but first – do I have your trust? Whole and unconditional?'

Mira thinks of everything Rozalia has done for her. Sure, the old woman has been after a disciple all along, but she's also teaching Mira what she's asked for – the way of herbs and healing. And it's hard to believe that someone who saved her life would want to harm her now.

Mira gives a decisive nod. 'I trust you.'

Rozalia drops the shallots and takes Mira's hand. 'Now listen carefully to my instructions and do exactly as I tell you.'

INITIATION

A feisty wind picks up around midnight, bringing the world alive with whispering shadows. Even so, Mira's feet take her to Rozalia's hut without once tripping or tumbling into the gullies of the road.

She has followed Rozalia's instructions exactly as she's been told: singing a particular chant every night after her father falls asleep, kneeling for hours, and fasting for three whole days before the new moon tonight.

'I started to think you changed your mind,' Rozalia says when Mira walks in.

'Father took forever to fall asleep. Tossed and turned and sighed like he could tell I was up to something.'

'Have you heeded my advice?' Rozalia asks.

'I've noticed that when done by choice, fasting isn't difficult. But I can't imagine doing it for weeks, like you do sometimes.'

'We don't know our true power until we're tried by life.' Rozalia points to a bowl on the floor. 'Wash your face in there and trickle some of the water on the crown of your head.'

The water is unexpectedly cold and fragrant with hints of cedar wood and acacia blossom.

'Now you're refreshed and receptive for what's to come. There's no going back after this. If you have any doubts, now is the time to—'

‘I’m ready,’ Mira says and steps into the circle of rocks marked on the floor, similar to the one they had had at the warding ritual.

‘As you already know about chants, they have neither words nor meaning. But when used for a certain purpose, they work like a key for the right lock. And you have to keep up with me for as long as I go. Don’t stop, or it won’t work.’

‘Alright.’

‘And keep completely still and focused. Your body will itch, hurt, most probably go numb too, but you must ignore it all and stay with the chant. Nothing bad will happen to you. You have my word.’

They kneel inside the circle of rocks and Rozalia establishes a rhythm with a certain sound, which the two of them sing until a warm glow unfurls in Mira’s belly, spilling into her lower back and out to her limbs.

Her mind, however, is slow to settle. Her skittish thoughts keep flitting to Elina, to their touches and embraces and kisses. She can smell Elina’s iris-root scent as if she were right here in her arms. Mira’s daydreaming is soured with drops of shame. What would her father and Rozalia think if they knew of her strange and sinful feelings for Elina? What would people do to them if they found out? As the boyar’s daughter and the mistress of these lands, Elina surely wouldn’t be punished. It’s a comforting thought and Mira’s breath seeps in deeper like the gush of a river when a boulder is pushed out of its way.

Staying with Rozalia’s chanting is an increasing effort. It’s not easy to sing on an empty belly. Mira has done her best to follow the rhythm, but her strength is dwindling. The weaker Mira’s voice gets, the more Rozalia raises hers to make up for it. Sensing the old woman’s effort, Mira scrapes for any last bits of her strength to keep going.

A kind of low rumbling spreads under her skin. How long have they been chanting? Her legs, folded under her, burn with pins and needles, and her back has curled forwards, ready to tumble over at any moment.

When Rozalia places her hand on Mira's head, a light brighter than the midday sun flares up behind her eyelids. All the pain in her back and neck and shoulders melts away and she has the strange sensation that her body has cracked open, shedding her skin as though she were a butterfly finding her wings. Is she fainting?

Yet, she remains fully aware throughout what follows…

…If someone had told her this was possible, Mira would've dismissed it as the wild ramblings of an unhinged mind. Now that she's experienced it herself – this boundless state, this floating, this conscious dreaming – she can never go back to who she was before this evening. She has crossed the threshold of this world and had a glimpse of what's on the other side…

'Could I do this on my own?' she asks Rozalia. 'Or is this something only you can—'

'You could. But to succeed on your own, your effort and focus will have to be a lot more fierce. But it's not impossible. It all depends on how much you want it. Like with most things.'

'Why the top of the head?'

'It's the secret door to the world beyond the reach of our senses. Yours is open now. Be responsible with it.'

Rozalia leans in to seal Mira's initiation with a few secret whispers. When she's done, she snuffs out the candle and tells Mira to follow her out.

They stop in the doorway where Rozalia listens for a few moments, then she leads the way to the far end of the garden where her twig fence marks the end of her property and the beginning of the woods.

Mira notices two boulders close to each other and a few logs scattered near them. Rozalia kicks the largest rock and feels under it as though it were a hen and she is groping for eggs. The rock lifts at one end, which Rozalia props up with a log and then she suddenly disappears like she's been swallowed by the earth. A trapdoor? When Mira walks around, she sees a hole and Rozalia getting smaller as she descends into it.

Rozalia's cellar.

Mira's heart flaps like a trapped turtle dove. Is this the place from her nightmare?

'You coming?' Rozalia calls from deep underground, where she can be heard striking the flint rock. Shortly, a weak light beacons at the bottom of the stairs.

As Mira wobbles down the uneven steps, her skin shrinks and prickles, but the moment she catches the scent of herbs and medicine, she swallows down her fear. This is not the sharp tang she remembers from her nightmare. Besides, there's a warmth here that's certainly missing in the place that's haunting her nights, where the cold and darkness are bone-crushing.

Rozalia hasn't lied. This isn't the prison that's tormenting Mira in her sleep.

Final proof comes when she steps into the room at the bottom of the stairs. It looks like someone lives here. A small table and a wood log for a stool, a bed of sprigs and rushes in one corner and a trunk the size of a coffin in the other. Drawn by its wax polish, Mira steps towards the trunk, but Rozalia calls her attention to the shelves hanging around the walls, burdened with herbs and potions. 'You know most of them,' Rozalia says. 'A few more to learn and you'll soon do this work better than me.'

Mira spots a pile of men's clothing on the floor. Why is Rozalia keeping the garments of her dead husband?

'They come in handy sometimes.' Rozalia answers Mira's unspoken question. 'When I don't want to be noticed.'

'What do you mean? You dress as a man? Why—'

'You'll live and learn. Women aren't welcome in many places.'

Mira has many questions, but Rozalia doesn't give her time to ask any of them. She goes through what potions are stored in which pots and what they are good for. She trains

Mira to remember them by their scent, or stench in some cases, or even taste. 'Eyes are not to be trusted,' Rozalia says.

By the time they are through with them all, Mira's head is spinning, and her legs are so light she's certain her heels have sprouted wings. She starts laughing for no reason.

'We're done for today,' Rozalia says and starts walking up the stairs, which lead up to the soft light of dawn.

The chill of the early morning clears Mira's head a little, leaving her to marvel at how much has happened in one night. If only her father knew, she thinks, and breaks into another fit of laughter.

Back inside the hut, Rozalia gives Mira plenty of water to drink, and only allows her to go home when her jollity subsides.

On the doorstep, the old woman plants her hands on Mira's shoulders, looking her square in the eyes. 'The secret of my cellar stays with you and me. No one else. Not even your new best friend.'

Mira nods soberly, her heart squeezing with longing at the mention of the woman she loves.

HARVEST FAIR

Yet another dry summer and the cracks in the parched ground are so wide that the cattle break their legs. Another hungry winter is awaiting them.

Mira is grateful for the hare she finds in her trap every week – a secret gift from Elina, whose game Mira plays by pretending she doesn't know about it. Each time she only cooks half of the hare, the other half she smokes and stores in their cellar for the lean months ahead.

As Rozalia's apprentice, Mira doesn't only learn of herbs and healing but is also initiated into sacred ceremonies where, by making offerings of food and fire, they can appease the Old Gods and plead with them to end the droughts.

Rozalia says the rain has got lost in the mighty skies. They tie snails with strands of wilting grass and sprinkle them with water, calling upon the winds to bring clouds their way, until Rozalia – her neck stretched and nostrils sniffing the air – can catch the scent of rain. But each time the showers are quick and short, barely quenching the thirst of the gaping earth, and they have to start their pleadings anew.

The dry weather has brought hordes of mice above ground and today Rozalia shows Mira how to rub tansy leaves in all corners of the hut to keep the pests away. However, judging by the restless glint in Rozalia's eyes, something worse than mice is on her mind. But Mira won't prod. She's learned that the old woman will only speak when she's ready.

'Such a strong smell.' Mira wrinkles her nose at the tansy. 'No wonder the mice hate it.'

'You better get used to it. Do you remember what else it's good for?'

Mira nods. She's been taught the power of a tansy bath and mugwort drinks mixed with hemp seeds. It's what Rozalia uses to rid young women of 'unwanted burdens'.

'The harvest fair is in a couple of weeks and some unlucky women will need our help soon after that,' Rozalia says. 'The tithe collectors usually grab more than grains when they swoop on our village. Make sure you stay well away from those men.'

They finish smearing the walls with tansy and Rozalia still says nothing about what's bothering her. Mira helps tidy up and is about to leave when Rozalia's words root her to the spot: 'He's an adept of the secret teachings.'

'What? Who?'

'Master mason Barbu,' Rozalia says. 'I saw him by the crossroads yesterday at the crack of dawn, digging clumps of earth and spraying them with milk.'

'He sounds like us. We too beseech the Old Gods—'

'We do it for a greater good, but he… He's pursuing his own interests, seeking to please his pride. The fool.'

Mira's heart is torn. On the one hand, she hopes Barbu succeeds in building the church, enabling Elina to keep her status as a man in the eyes of the law and subsequently come into her father's inheritance. She would gain the independence she needs to make Mira her maid, and thus avoid raising suspicions of their close friendship. On the other, if the new church is built, the false faith of the crucified man will grow deeper roots in their village. This will not only put Mira and Rozalia in danger for their practices, but it will threaten the very survival of their ancient wisdom, which the two of them are to protect with their lives and pass on to future generations.

It would have been an easy choice before her initiation. But now that Mira has been entrusted with this non-material treasure, it's not so simple any more.

'My strength isn't enough to stop him,' Rozalia says. 'I need your help.'

She is asking for the very thing Mira fears most, to choose whom to betray – the woman she loves more than anything in the world, or the ancient teachings she's now a guardian of.

'When?' Mira asks, the word trembling on her tongue.

'On the night of the harvest fair. The largest full moon this year. Show your face at the fair, then come meet me on the hill of the Three Springs, where they're building the church. And don't forget – stay well away from those tithe collectors,' Rozalia says and blesses Mira with a few whispers.

Though the harvest is scarce, villagers still gather to celebrate. Boyar Constantin provides food, wine and music for the fair each year and this is one day when nobody goes hungry.

When the boyar's suite arrives, accompanied by lively fiddles, people whistle and cheer to welcome them. Mira's eyes are fastened on Elina, who looks like a goddess. Her hair – black as a moonless night – is gathered into intricate plaits and adorned with a wreath of red dahlias. Her gold bangles clink and jingle as she walks, and when she passes Mira, their hands brush surreptitiously, leaving Mira's skin burning where they touched.

Who is the man next to Elina's father? They look alike. Perhaps the boyar's brother? The three of them sit on the raised stand, specifically built for Constantin and his family to watch the celebrations.

Makeshift tables are laden with roast boar and grouse and a barrel of wine is gurgling to keep the villagers sweet and loyal to the boyar; small boys leap through the flames of the bonfire in a contest of bravery, as well as to ward off illness and bad luck; a cluster of young men, wearing only their slacks, engage in foot racing or wrestle in *trântă*.

The priest condemns the harvest celebrations and would have banned them a long time ago if it wasn't for Constantin, who not only attends them each year but also provides gifts – sheep or goats – for all those who win at games and races.

The music gets people dancing, either in a circle with their arms on each other's shoulders, or pairing up and spinning around the bonfire, ankles flicking everywhere. At the far edge of the village square, Mira spots a pack of stray dogs, whose shiny eyes make it look like a strip of starry sky has fallen to the ground.

Five horsemen approach in a cloud of dust, sending the dogs scampering away. Mira watches them dismount and tether their frothing beasts to trees and fence posts.

The tithe collectors have arrived. Those who haven't paid their dues will try and hide, but with so much wine flowing, villagers turn against each other, alerting the collectors to buried grains and crops. Though they've scraped just about enough to pay the tithes this year, Mira wonders how they will be able to manage next year.

Her father is talking to somebody and, when she turns around, Mira steps back in surprise. It's the master mason.

After meeting Barbu for the first time at the lake, Mira has seen him often about the village – he and his men have been accommodated on the priest's property – but each time she spotted him, she turned back or changed ways, unlike many other local women who seemed to enjoy greeting the mason and exchanging pleasantries with him.

A jab in her ribs from her father helps Mira find her words. 'Good evening, master mason,' she says and bows her head.

'I brought you some food before it all disappears.' He holds out a tray with freshly baked pies and chunks of roast boar.

'Thank you, but I'm not hungry,' she lies.

Her father, however, steps forward and takes the food. 'That's very kind of you, master mason. God bless you.'

'How about a dance then?' Barbu proffers his hand. 'It will surely help you work up an appetite.'

There's another jab in her ribs from her father, and Mira takes Barbu's hand.

He is a good dancer, twirling Mira with such ease and skill as if he's spent his life attending fairs and not dangling off scaffolds. His callused hands have a gentle touch, yet his arms and shoulders are solid, as though it's not flesh but chiselled stone that's laid out under his skin.

Mira looks over her shoulder to find Elina, but she's all blurred out in the dust rising from people's feet. This is a never-ending song and, though dizzy and annoyed, Mira cannot abandon her partner in mid-dance. Such embarrassment would feed the village gossip for months to come.

When the music finally stops, she gives Barbu a quick bow and returns to her father's side.

'Handsome man, isn't he?' her father says, but Mira ignores the hint. She searches for Elina, who is nowhere to be seen.

'I'll go for a little wander, see what else is happening at the fair,' Mira says and slips away.

The moon is low in the sky, pinning the dark mantle of the night with the shine of a new coin. Giving a wide berth to the tithe collectors, Mira keeps to the edge of the gathering for a better view, while she can stay out of sight.

Where is Elina? She's not next to her father on their viewing platform, and neither is she dancing. Has she gone home already? But the boyar's coach is still here. Unless she got upset because Mira danced with Barbu, and decided to return home early, on foot – in which case, she should be able to catch up with her if she hurries.

Her mind made up, Mira walks casually to the birch grove beyond the village square, and as soon as she steps into the shadows of the trees, she breaks into a sprint down the path Elina would have taken towards the manor.

The clamour of the fair fades behind her and now there's only the wind whistling in her ears.

Then a curtailed scream.

Mira halts. A bird of prey? She listens again to the darkness around her. Just the breeze tousling the leaves and a hooting owl. There's something else.

A frantic jingle comes from somewhere to the left. Is that Elina's bangles?

Sharp boughs whip at her face and briars grab at her ankles as Mira dashes through the thicket to where she can hear grunts and muffled voices. Two people are scuffling on the ground.

The tithe collectors, she thinks, and a chill shoots down her back as she recognises the dress, its beads and goldwork twinkling in the moonlight.

'Get off her,' Mira shouts and grabs a stick. 'Can't you see she's the boyar's daughter? You'll have a rope around your neck before the night is over—'

A tall, broad figure scrambles to his feet. He's not one of the tithe collectors. Mira narrows her eyes – isn't he the other boyar who accompanied Elina and her father at the fair this evening?

She's confused, and for a moment, Mira thinks she may be the one in trouble for being nosy. But the man waddles away, disappearing through the trees, and she dashes to Elina's side.

'Are you alright? What happened?'

Mira doesn't need to hear the answer; she can see it. Elina's face is smudged with tears and dirt, her dress is torn at the neck and chest, revealing her amber charm, glowing wet and warm between her bare breasts.

'Who is he?' Mira's question is a sharp whisper.

'My uncle,' Elina says, hiding her face in the crook of Mira's neck.

'It's alright, he's gone now. It's alright.' Mira cradles Elina in her arms.

'You don't understand. He'll be back.'

'I know. I've seen the bruises on your body. The burned linen at the lake, you wishing to fall asleep in the snow – it all makes sense now.'

Elina shrinks, like she's seeking to burrow herself into the ground. 'I'm so angry, and scared, and…'

Mira squeezes Elina tighter into her hug. 'I'll look after you, I promise. I'll do anything to… Come, we have to take care of something.'

The two of them lock fingers, their grip firm and unreserved. Elina follows without asking any questions, but when she recognises where they are headed, she pulls away.

'I'm not telling Rozalia about it.'

'We're not.'

'You're taking me to her—'

'She's not at home. She better not be.'

Mira hopes Rozalia has gone to the hill of the Three Springs by now to get things ready for their midnight worship. Her instruction had been clear: *The secret of my cellar stays with you and me. No one else. Not even your new best friend.* However, Rozalia could not have predicted this awful situation. Mira has no choice. She can't leave Elina alone in the woods after what's happened to her while she goes to fetch the herbs. She has to take Elina with her.

The reluctance in Elina's eyes turns to curiosity as they circle round Rozalia's hut and make their way to the bottom of her garden.

'Where are we going?'

Mira places a finger on her lips, asking Elina to be quiet as she listens carefully into the night. Though Rozalia's hut has sunk into darkness, she's learned that eyes aren't always to be trusted. The ears and the nose should be equally engaged.

Pleased with her assessment, she pushes aside the largest of the two boulders and slips into the hidden passage.

'Don't let go of my hand,' she whispers to Elina. 'The steps aren't even.'

Mira fumbles for the flint stone and the *iască* which Rozalia keeps in the same spot at the bottom of the stairs. She strikes the rock until a spark hits the *iască*, and with gentle blowing Mira teases out a flame.

Elina whistles in surprise. 'So many pots and jars. Looks like she's sampled the whole woods. I see the rumours about her are true. She's a—'

'A wise woman,' Mira says before Elina can utter something she won't be able to take back. 'But you already know that. You've heard her talk about plants and—'

'I thought she was making it all up. Like she did with that warding-off ritual when she gave us our charms. Blessed to protect us, isn't that what she said? Well, mine hasn't done a very good job of it tonight, has it?' Elina pulls at the amber around her neck, but the thread is strong.

'I tied one of my best knots,' Mira says. 'Please keep it on.'

'What's in there? A dead body?' Elina points at the trunk at the other end of the cellar.

'We must hurry.'

'A secret lair, who would've thought?'

'You can't tell anyone about it. I've broken my oath to Rozalia by bringing you here.'

'Why did you bring me here?'

'I'm worried about…' Mira picks up a small bundle from one of the shelves. 'Here's some chamomile and comfrey for your bruises. And this is mugwort. Make a strong brew and drink it for three days. To kill his seed.'

'You think—'

Mira can't tell Elina what she's really thinking. That it's not a pregnancy she fears for Elina – a disgraced and disowned Elina would be more attainable, after all. It's the danger of losing Elina, should she have a difficult labour like Mira's mother did.

'And if it doesn't work?' Elina asks.

'Then you *must* see Rozalia at once. Her tansy bath will sort you out, if nothing else does.'

'Can I have some of that too?'

'It's a dangerous plant. Let's hope you won't need it.'

Elina looks about the cellar. 'What does it look like, this *dangerous* plant? I'm curious.'

Mira points to the clumps of dry stalks adorned with yellow flowers in the far corner. Elina walks towards them and after a quick sniff, she turns her head away. 'They stink!'

'Tell me about it. We rub our walls with it to keep the mice at bay—'

'And how does it prevent, you know…'

'Makes you bleed. Come, let's go now.'

Elina doesn't move. She stares at the bundle of mugwort in her hands.

'He did this to me so that I can't marry anyone else but his son. But living under the same roof as my uncle means I'll never get away from him. I'd rather die than be his daughter-in-law.' Elina's eyes glisten, shooting fury and a spark of madness.

'There must be another way.'

'Yes, there is. Being shut away in a nunnery somewhere.'

Mira blinks rapidly, trying to swallow the thickness building in her throat. With Elina in a convent, they would never see each other again. The look on Elina's face says: *My thoughts exactly!*

'Hence there's only one option for us, my Froglet. That I remain an unmarried woman by choice and make you my maid. But for that to happen, I need to be my own master. The sooner the church is built, the sooner I'll acquire the "male" status permanently and unequivocally. Then I can bring you to the manor.'

'What if…' Mira takes a deep breath. 'What if the church can't be built?'

'Barbu would've left by now if he didn't think he could do it. But he's still here. He's still trying… Or do you know something I don't?'

'Rozalia says she can see darkness in his soul.'

'Fancy a chip laughing at a broken pot. Has it occurred to you that she may be pointing at Barbu to save her own skin?'

It's true that many things Rozalia does and says don't make sense, but it's also true that she has saved their lives. Has Elina forgotten about that?

'Hold on!' Elina whispers, a frown pinching her brows. 'You seem to have learned a lot about herbs… giving me these tonight…' She shakes the mugwort in Mira's face. 'Are you becoming like her? Are you Rozalia's disciple?'

'She tells me things and I remember them.'

'You don't question anything. You follow blindly—'

'Prying and probing is more fruitful after attaining a little knowledge first.'

'You're starting to sound like her too. Tell me something. Are you and Rozalia interfering with Barbu's work?'

'Don't put all your hopes in this church. I hear our ruler is a capricious man. He could change his mind about your status—'

'Do you have a better plan?' Elina's anger makes her hoarse voice harsher.

No, Mira doesn't have a better plan. And what if Elina is right? What if this is her only chance of gaining her independence – of them being together – and Mira is spoiling it for them? Her mind is a jumble, and she no longer knows what to do.

'I was wrong about you.' Elina steps away from Mira. 'I thought you were on my side. I thought we were… You've betrayed me.' Elina breaks down into sobs which shake her shoulders and bring on an uncontrollable cough. She mouths: 'Water!'

Mira scrambles up the stairs and out of the cellar, running across the garden towards Rozalia's hut, almost stumbling over the water bucket by the door. She scoops a jugful and rushes back, spilling half of it in her haste.

'I'm coming, I'm coming,' she says, clambering down the steps. She can't hear Elina coughing or crying any longer, and Mira dares hope the worst is behind them.

But when she gets to the bottom of the stairs, she halts there, blinking in disbelief: Elina has vanished.

She must truly be upset if she's run home without waiting for the water, thinks Mira. She considers whether to go after her, tell her she's sorry, that she's on her side, always will be no matter what.

But a deep breath makes her change her mind. It may be best to let Elina rest after everything that's happened tonight. They will talk again soon. Everything will be alright, as long as they don't fall out with each other.

Despite what Mira wants to believe, an alarming thought is thrashing around in her head. Will Elina ever forgive her this betrayal?

CONFESSION

By the time Mira arrives at the hill of the Three Springs, Rozalia has already laid out a makeshift shrine: a circle of rocks, inside which there's a bunch of sage, a long hawthorn spike and a small pot with smouldering ash. Rozalia is so still that is seems like she is just one more boulder amongst the many that have already been gathered here in preparation for the building works.

Mira walks to the stream purling on the side of the hill, its moonlit flow shimmering with a thousand scales as she wades in to her knees. She splashes water on her face and the top of her head, the spot which Rozalia says is the gate between the seen and the unseen world. The fresh water cools her blood and the beat of her heart.

'What took you so long?' Rozalia asks, half her face caressed by the glow of the Goddess Moon and the other shaded by the wing of night.

Mira can't bring herself to tell Rozalia that she has broken her trust. Of course Elina won't tell anyone about the secret cellar, but that's not the point.

'I danced with the mason,' Mira says, kneeling inside the circle of rocks next to Rozalia. 'If his hands are as good as his feet, we don't have much chance of stopping him from building this church.'

'We'll see about that,' Rozalia says and lights a bunch of sage. Her lips are busy with a string of mumbles as she sways the billow of the acrid smoke from side to side and claps her hands once or twice, the better to cleanse the space.

They beseech the Old Gods to stop the mason and his mission. They call upon the Spirit of the Land to shake the ground and knock down any walls that go up. They urge the Mother of the Forest to unleash her fury on the men whose axes kill her children by the dozen, felling trees with neither a prayer nor remorse in their hearts.

Mira's attention isn't as sharp as the process requires. Her mind is entangled with thoughts of Elina and the hurt she's suffered at her uncle's hands. Now she understands this is why she visits Rozalia so often, despite their constant quibbles. How wrong Mira has been all this time. She has admired and envied Elina in equal measure – her status, her home, her rich life. But things aren't what they seem. While Elina's belly is never empty and she wears dazzling dresses and jewellery, she's no less a prisoner of her world than Mira is of hers. And if she's been so blind to Elina's hurt, what else could she be wrong about?

Perhaps sensing Mira's poor focus, Rozalia gets them chanting a special sound, which she says helps to unburden the mind. It's hardly louder than a whisper, but its power is such that Mira feels a hum rising in her belly, rolling into her chest and head and out towards the sky to meet the grace of their goddess as they plead with her to muddle the mason's mind and send him fleeing from their village.

Rozalia picks up a small stone from the circle of rocks and hands it to Mira. 'Hold it tight as you make your pleading. Rocks have a memory far greater than you can imagine. It will preserve the urge on your breath for a long time.'

Judging by the shift of the stars above them, hours have passed by the time they finish their devotion. Mira's mind and body are so still she can hear the dew falling.

Before they stand up, Rozalia passes her the hawthorn spike. 'We need a drop of your maiden blood to complete the worship, an offering to the Old Gods. Prick the side of your finger. It's less painful.'

Rozalia guides Mira's hand so that her blood drips onto the stone she's been holding in her fist throughout the ceremony.

'We need to bury it before the blood dries out,' Rozalia says, pointing to a small dip next to where the foundation of the church has been marked up.

Mira places the smeared stone with great care, and a little guilt, as though she were burying a piece of herself.

She remembers Elina's reproach: *You don't question anything. You follow blindly*. The words, though true, are like pebbles which have sunk in the well of her belly.

Mira shoves a heap of soil over her offering, fearing that, with it, she has also buried Elina's chance at independence.

RECKONING

Mira and Rozalia are squatting by the hearth, grinding burdock root, when they hear a soft scraping on the door.

'Rozalia!' An urgent whisper.

Mira leaps as though the burning wood threw off a spark at her bare feet.

'Who's there?' Rozalia asks.

Another whisper on the other side and Rozalia lifts the latch. Andrei, the shepherd's son, staggers in.

'Father is dying,' he says, his words muffled by his beard, which shines wet, like the rest of his face. He must have run all the way here.

'I've heard the priest has been visiting him lately,' Rozalia says.

'He's asking for you.'

Rozalia hesitates and the look in her eyes is not because she doesn't want to go – she sometimes refuses to help people, saying their illness is a lesson they must learn – but because the shepherd, a lifelong churchgoer, has only accepted Rozalia's wisdom recently. She helped him wake up from a dead faint after an oak tree fell on his head. Following his recovery, the shepherd has often brought her milk and cheese in secret – always at night, to avoid being seen at the witch's house.

Rozalia turns to Mira. 'You've got the burdock powder

you came for, but spare a thought for the shepherd's daughter. She's about your age – Smaranda – isn't she? I'm sure she'll appreciate some company.'

Mira hears the instruction in Rozalia's casual suggestion. Over the past few weeks, Rozalia has taught her their version of the last rites, and it sounds like today she's going to witness this practice being carried out in real life.

'Certainly,' Mira says. 'I'd be glad to help, if that's alright?' She looks at Andrei. It's polite to seek his permission.

'That's very kind of you,' he says, too preoccupied to notice Mira's relief.

'You two go ahead,' Rozalia tells them as she mixes powders from three different bundles. 'I'll be right behind you.'

Mira knows this is an arrangement so that the two of them aren't seen together. The very preservation of the ancient wisdom depends on their caution. Their ties of teacher-disciple have to remain a well-guarded secret.

Andrei doesn't say a word on the way back and his stride is so wide that Mira hops to keep up with him. When they reach the shepherd's house, Andrei grunts something which Mira understands as *wait*. He goes to restrain their dog before waving her in.

The stench of the hut makes Mira want to dash back out again, which is odd, because she's used to all sorts of unpleasant smells – of the cow dung they burn to keep warm in winter, of villagers' rotting teeth, of bedpans. But this is different. It's the smell of this man's illness, the smell of his own death. She takes a deep breath like Rozalia taught her to do whenever a strong odour or taste clutches at her throat.

The shepherd lies on a blanket of straw in the far corner of the room, his lungs struggling for air. Smaranda is wiping the sweat off her father's face with a rag. Lisaveta, the shepherd's wife, is cleaning a fleece of burrs and beetles in the opposite corner, mumbling to herself. At first, Mira thinks the woman is praying, but then she catches a few cursing words and realises the shepherd's wife is upset with her dying husband.

When Rozalia glides into the hut, quiet as a shadow, Lisaveta jumps up, utterly spooked, and flaps her arms about, shooing Rozalia back out and wailing that the witch will curse her home.

Andrei tries to appease his mother, but she waddles out, saying she won't be under the same roof as a heathen.

The shepherd's face twists with pain as he greets Rozalia. 'The herbs you sent me helped my pain more than the priest's prayers.'

She kneels and takes the dying man's hand, checking for the throb in his wrist. He tries to smile. 'Last time I was ill, you stopped my soul from crossing over to the other side, guiding it back into my body, saying it wasn't my time.'

'There's nothing I can do this—'

'It's not more days I'm askin' for... just peace for my soul... and something for the pain.'

Rozalia scoops a fistful of powder from her badger-snout pouch and stirs it in the cup of water by his side. Supporting the shepherd's head with one hand, she holds the thick potion to his mouth with the other.

The frowning on his face softens after a few sips and by the time he drinks half of it, a languid smile quivers on his cracked lips.

Rozalia starts whispering the first chant – a pleading with Mother Earth to welcome the returning son back to her womb. This is followed with incantations – senseless, unintelligible singing where the pitch of sound is all that matters and not the meaning of words. Rozalia's gaze changes as she enters the dream state where she can gain the space and tools necessary for this task. No interference or intrusion is allowed. A fruitful result is entirely dependent on the ability to maintain a fierce focus.

That's why Mira isn't surprised at Rozalia's commitment even when the dog starts barking outside, warning them of a visitor. How did Rozalia manage to slip by the dog unnoticed earlier? Smaranda takes a quick look through the window and spins around at once, her face turning white.

'It's the priest,' she says and runs towards Rozalia, but

Mira jumps in her way and grabs her elbow before she can touch Rozalia.

'She's not to be interrupted,' Mira says, and looking over her shoulder at Andrei – who has also sprung to his feet – she instructs him: 'Make sure she's allowed to finish her work. For your father's sake.'

Mira guides Smaranda behind the hearth, where the two of them squat low on the other side of the wall. 'It's better we stay out of the way,' she whispers to the shepherd's daughter, whose eyes are wide with terror.

'May our Lord Jesus Christ bless this home.' The priest's impassioned voice, accustomed to the high ceiling of the church, booms in the shepherd's tiny hut.

Mira peeks behind the wall. The priest, his face red with effort – from haste? Anger? – stands in the middle of the room, with Lisaveta at his heels.

Andrei mumbles a reply, but Rozalia keeps up with her chants like she hasn't heard the priest. Mira can only imagine how difficult it must be for Rozalia to carry on with her work in the presence of the man she dislikes most. She'd told Mira once that she didn't fear the priest, but that she was well aware of his influence and power.

'In the name of the Lord and all that's holy,' the priest says, stepping towards Rozalia, but Andrei bars his way.

'It is my father's bidding,' he says. 'Please allow a dying man his last wish.'

'It's the light of our Lord that your father needs, not the devil.' The priest crosses himself, but Andrei doesn't budge, towering head and shoulders over the clergyman.

The two men look so tense against each other that Mira fears the priest will storm out and call for the boyar and his men to drag Rozalia out of the hut. Instead the priest drops to his knees. 'The illness has weakened your father's mind and heart. It's my duty, as our Lord's messenger, to guard your father's soul. I won't abandon him when he's in most need of the love of our

Lord.' The priest closes his eyes and starts praying out loud, his thundering voice prevailing over Rozalia's chants.

To prevent the dying man from getting confused in the ensuing clamour, Rozalia places his limp hand against her belly and holds it there. By feeling the rhythm of her breath, the shepherd will find it easier to stay with her chant.

Watching from behind the hearth, Mira can see it's working. The shepherd's lips start moving in time with those of Rozalia, his breath matching hers in the certain beat she has set to guide his soul out of his broken body.

'It is done,' Rozalia whispers to the shepherd. 'You can go in peace now. When you're ready, close your eyes and follow the light, and most importantly – do not be fearful. I've blessed your passage. You're safe.'

The shepherd doesn't need to speak his gratitude; it spills into his eyes, before he shuts them for the last time.

The priest is up on his feet the moment Rozalia leaves the shepherd's side. 'I won't let this be forgotten,' he says. 'Such blatant disdain for our Lord. Worshipping Satan in the house of good Christians.'

'I've only helped alleviate this old man's pain,' Rozalia says. 'Help thy neighbour. Isn't that what the Lord teaches?'

'The shepherd needs a priest, not a… You're an impostor, meddling where you have no authority—'

'It's merely knowledge. Knowing the works of life is all there is. And for that I don't need to be a priest.'

'Playing God,' the priest snorts. 'I've just witnessed your heresy, all those jumbled words and spells—'

'The virtue of sound lies in its pitch. You want to give it meaning so the mind can grasp it, but my work is not with the brain.'

'Of course not. You haven't got one. Just listen to yourself talk, nonsense all of it. Black magic right under my nose—'

'Everything is magic when you don't understand it.'

'No, no, no.' The priest shakes his head. 'You can't inflict your madness on others. I won't allow it. Only one place for the likes of you. The stake and the eternal flames of hell.'

A prolonged silence settles between them, their eyes locked into a stare. When Rozalia speaks again, her voice has an edge Mira hasn't heard before.

'What is not understood will always be feared,' she says and is out of the hut before the priest can reply.

Mira waits behind the hearth for the priest to leave too before she can make a move, which isn't long. After a few prayers over the dead man's body, the priest walks out without saying goodbye to the grieving family.

It's late into the night, but Mira doesn't want to go straight home. Though there isn't much she can say or do to take away from the priest's threats, she hopes a little support won't go amiss, even for a fearless woman such as Rozalia.

Despite the ungodly hour, she finds the old woman brewing tea with the burdock root they ground earlier.

'You needn't have come back here. Our work is done for today,' Rozalia says, handing Mira a cupful of the brew.

She swirls it in her mouth. 'Not bad. Smells nice too.'

'I may have to go into hiding for a while,' Rozalia says.

'Why did you confront him?'

'I've tried avoiding him over the years. This time he caught me in the middle of my work. You know I couldn't stop what I was doing.'

'Where are you going to hide?'

'Not far. My cellar is the only place where I'm safe. No one knows about it but you and me.'

Mira's chest tightens. She can't confess her betrayal to Rozalia, even though she did it out of care for Elina. Rozalia has enough to worry about right now than to add to her troubles. Besides, Mira is certain Elina won't tell anyone about the cellar. Their secret is safe.

'Hopefully, I won't have to be in hiding for long.'

'Do you think the priest will ever forget?'

Rozalia looks away. 'The pompous fool will never forgive me. I might have to move to another village, or even better – a town. It's easy to hide in a town. Nobody knows anyone there. The town of Galbena may be a good choice – it's not too far away, only a couple of villages down south, but far enough to keep me out of harm's way… Of course, there's also the chance I may get caught.' Rozalia falls quiet, sipping at her tea.

'No, you won't.'

'If they take me to the stake, you have to do something for me.' Rozalia stirs the embers in the dwindling fire and shoves in another log. The wood groans and hisses and throws sparks in the air. She sits on the sheepskin, facing Mira.

'Listen carefully…' Rozalia drops her voice to a whisper as she goes on to describe what sounds like a nightmare. One that Rozalia says may happen in real life. The precise details she goes over – how Mira should prepare a certain type of bread, the process of dampening soft firewood like cedar and pine spruce and preserving Rozalia's hair – makes Mira think the old woman has been long preparing for such eventuality.

'I hope there'll never be any need for that,' Mira says, but Rozalia leans in and squeezes her shoulder.

'I want you to repeat everything I've said.' Her voice has never sounded more urgent. 'I need to know you'll remember it all if it comes to it.'

Mira recites the instructions and, when she's finished, Rozalia nods and reminds her of one last detail. 'The trick is not to dampen the wood too much that it doesn't burn. Just enough to make it smoke before it catches fire. There has to be lots of smoke.'

It's Mira's turn to nod now, though she does it only to please the old woman. It's hard to imagine that such an awful fate may await Rozalia. She's just being overly cautious, that's all, and sipping the last of the brew, Mira stands up. Rozalia is also on her feet at once.

'No need to see me out…' Mira says.

'I'm not. I'm going to my cellar. There's lots to do before they come for me,' Rozalia says and is out the door like a gust of wind has plucked her away.

THE SKETCH

Elina steeps the mugwort in secret, hidden in her room. But has Mira given her the right herbs? They taste like poison – so bitter and revolting that her stomach contracts towards her spine, refusing to accept it. Honey does little to improve it. Pinching her nose, she downs the drink in one go and follows it with more honey.

Will the mugwort do the job? If not, she'll have to use the tansy she stole from Rozalia's cellar. Did Mira notice some of it was missing when she returned with the water? Even if she did, she wouldn't tell Rozalia about it, because then she'd have to explain why Elina was there in the first place.

Elina is startled by loud voices coming from the courtyard. Barbu must have arrived. Her father has summoned him to demand an explanation as to why he too is failing to erect the church.

By the time Elina reaches the hallway, her father is already greeting their guest. She does a quick bow. 'I hope you have good news for us, master mason.'

'I hope so,' Barbu says, and reaches for his saddlebag which he has tucked in the corner by the door. He takes out one of the two tight scrolls Elina notices peeking out of the bag.

Once they are in the room where her father proudly displays

his hunting trophies, with the door shut behind them, Barbu is lost for words as he glances from the boyar to Elina and back.

'It's alright,' her father says. 'Feel free to talk in her presence. She's my heir now. The building of this church concerns her more than anyone.'

Barbu nods and unrolls the parchment. Her father lets out a low whistle. 'Breathtaking. The voivode will be well pleased with such splendour.'

Elina moves her hand over the drawing, expecting to touch the coolness of stone, so exquisite are the details and the play of light.

'Do you like it?' Barbu asks.

'It's one thing to draw it, but can you achieve this in real life?' she asks, holding his gaze.

'I'm working on it, miss.'

'You've arrived in spring and it's almost winter now. Can't say you're doing a much better job than the previous masons.'

'Unlike them, I'm still here. I'm still trying.'

Her father clears his throat. 'By the way, master Barbu, the other masons slaughtered many roosters and wild boars whose blood they used to try and break the curse of that piece of land. What I'm saying is, don't be shy – if you too need roosters or anything else, just ask. I want this church built, whatever it takes.'

'Sounds like the others were bumblers, not proper masons,' he says, and Elina detects a sly smile on his fat lips. 'Rest assured, you've got the right man for this job. I just need a little more time, that's all. Trust me, I've done this three times before. I know what it takes—'

Loud clamour in the courtyard makes them turn towards the window. Dogs are barking and someone is shouting. None of their servants ever raises their voice; it must be an unexpected visitor.

Elina sticks her head out. 'It's the priest. Our dogs are upon him,' she says, and they all rush out. By the time they reach the front door, Neculai is already showing the priest in.

'Are you alright, Holy Father?' The boyar offers the priest his hand for support.

'Your beasts were that close from sinking their teeth into me.' The priest's forefinger and thumb are almost touching.

'Elina, dearest, go fetch us some water, will you.' Her father tells her to hurry, but the priest stops her.

'I'd prefer something stronger,' he says. 'Something that will ease my palpitations.'

The boyar sends Neculai running to the cellar and, together with Barbu, they help the priest into the room.

'In fact, a little water may come in handy after all,' the priest says, taking in his smeared robe where he'd fallen on his side. 'The fog has turned your courtyard into a right mire.'

'I'll call the maid,' Elina says, already gliding out of the room, past Neculai as he enters carrying a pitcher of wine and a tray of smoked meats as *zacuscă*.

Ana is wiping the mud the priest has brought into the house. After instructing her to fetch what's necessary, Elina is about to return to the guest room when something catches her attention. The second scroll, which Barbu didn't show them, is peeking out of the saddlebag. She tiptoes towards it and, without any hesitation, plucks it out with one swift move.

Unlike the drawing Barbu shared with them, this one isn't pretty at all. More like a framework for the real thing. A mesh of lines shoots out in all directions with meaningless numbers scribbled all over them. *A total mess*, Elina thinks, yet something about it is orderly, with a purpose known only to the one who made it.

However, it's not the incomprehensible structure that unsettles Elina but the faint sketch on the side of it. The image is barely visible, as if Barbu has tried to capture a fairy, or an angel. Contrary to the bold and precise lines everywhere else on the parchment, the image looks impermanent somehow, reminding Elina of the daintiness of snowflakes.

Even so, she recognises the mason's muse.

It's Mira.

He must be hopelessly in love with her if she's on his mind even when he's working. Does Mira know about it? Did Barbu say anything to her when they danced together at the harvest fair? Surely Mira would have told her if he had. But then Mira isn't being totally honest about her work with Rozalia. She could be hiding other things too.

Though still upset with Mira from the night of the fair, Elina can't deny the jealousy that prickles her heart.

Hurried steps squelch in the courtyard – Ana must be returning from the kitchen. Elina places the scroll back inside the saddlebag and turns just as the door opens.

'I'll take these,' she says and carries the bowl of water and the cloth to the guest room.

As a woman, she's not allowed to touch the priest's holy robe and so her father offers his assistance, but Barbu is quicker to step forth and take the load off her hands.

'I'm very sorry to hear about all this,' her father says as he tops up the priest's glass. 'She's a rude old woman, but – heresy and blasphemy? Well, that's unforgivable.'

Elina's heart speeds up. She knows who they're talking about.

'A rotten apple,' the priest says. 'We must protect our community from her evil.'

'What do you advise we do?' the boyar asks and takes a large gulp of wine.

'This conversation isn't for the ears of young ladies.' The priest frowns.

'Elina, dearest, why don't you go ask the cook to prepare an early lunch for us all? We'll be in the dining room shortly.'

'Certainly.' She bobs and walks out, stopping on the other side of the door, her ear close to the keyhole.

'That widow is a witch. Satan's servant. There's only one fate for the likes of her.' The fire in the priest's words is making him cough.

'She's a great healer though,' the boyar says. 'She often treats my horses for injuries after hunting parties.'

'She works with herbs, she doesn't come to church,' the priest scoffs. 'What more proof do you want that she's a heathen?'

There's a pause on the other side of the door and Elina fears the men may have sensed they're being listened to. She's about to flee when her father speaks again.

'We can't take her to the stake. Not yet anyway.'

'Why not?' Barbu asks. His words are measured, no doubt meant to sound curious, but they can't fool Elina's sharp ear. She catches reproach, contempt, even incitement under the guise of curiosity.

'The shade of vermilion in my illustrations – she is the one who cooks the dye for me.'

'I won't have any dye cooked by the devil in my church books.' The priest's voice is shrill with indignation. 'You'll have to find someone else to cook them for you.'

Another pause.

'Alright,' her father says. 'Give me a little time to get a servant to learn the trick from her, then she's all yours.'

'Make sure you find someone God-fearing and faithful, someone who wouldn't be led astray by that wicked woman.'

'I will, Holy Father.'

'You may want to keep an eye on your daughter,' Barbu says. 'I saw her chatting with Rozalia around a fire in the woods.'

How dare he? Elina steps back from the door, lest they hear her indignation.

'She was her mother's maid, for God's sake. And if my daughter wants to speak to her, to remember her mother, then she may do so.'

'You don't know what the old woman may be teaching your daughter. It's best to be cautious.'

'Thank you for your concern, master mason, but that's not why I summoned you here. I need a straight answer – when are you going to build that elusive church?'

'We're making progress,' Barbu says. 'You'll soon see it for yourself.'

'May the Lord hear you.' The priest sings an 'Amen'.

The sound of a chair scraping against the floor sends Elina scuttling off to the kitchen, to let the cook know about the early lunch. Her heart is thumping and it's not from the run.

She has to tip Rozalia off. Whatever she may think about the old woman, Elina is still hoping Rozalia will tell her what secrets she knows about her late mother.

But she cannot deliver the message today. Her sudden absence will be suspicious, especially after Barbu's warning. She'll do it first thing tomorrow morning, before her father wakes up.

GILDED GAOL

An unrelenting starling perched outside her window wakes Elina up. It's still very early – the sky is low and dull – and on a different day, Elina would shoo the bird away. Today, however, she sits up at once, grateful for this timely call. The sooner she goes to warn Rozalia about the priest's plot, the sooner she can return to the manor, and her father will be none the wiser.

Burning a candle will alert the servants that she's awake, and so Elina dresses in the murky light of dawn. She drops the hood of the cloak low over her eyes and is about to leave the bedroom when her stomach is suddenly in her throat and she's retching. Scrambling for the chamber pot next to the door, she leans over it, but only bitter bile drools out of her mouth. She did think last night's partridge stew was a little too herby for her liking – the cook loves her dill.

Outside, the world is swathed in a heavy mist, which will certainly provide the best cover she can hope for. A candle is already burning in the kitchen. Florica must be brewing some sort of fruit punch, judging by the sweet scent filling the courtyard. Their cook is famous for her tasty dishes. The woman knows seventeen ways of preparing crayfish and thirteen ways of cooking eggs. Like Rozalia, Florica too uses the kitchen as a workshop to experiment with ingredients.

However, unlike Rozalia, who seeks to ease people's suffering and pain, the cook is concerned with tickling their tongues and indulging their bellies.

Elina wonders about Rozalia, Florica, her own mother – all three of them have stayed true to their passion but have had to do it behind closed doors.

Is this what lies in store for her too? She hopes not.

Elina pinches her nose as she skulks by the kitchen and only stops for a deep breath when she's well past it. But Florica's *compot* has filled up the entire world with its sickly-sweet scent, making her retch again. She loves the cook's fruit punches. Why is she so disgusted by it this morning?

She holds her breath and scurries towards the stable. Fulger snorts as soon as she opens the door.

'Good morning to you too, my friend.' She kisses his nuzzle. 'Keen for a ride, are we? Keep quiet till we're out in the woods.'

She leads the horse towards the garden gate when a voice calls from behind.

'The boyar is asking for you.' It's Neculai. He must've heard her being sick and woken her father up.

Keeping hold of Fulger, Elina walks towards the front of the manor. Her father, wrapped up in a mantle and wearing his squirrel fur slippers, is standing on the porch, yawning.

'Are you too having a bad stomach?' she asks from afar by way of greeting. 'I must tell Florica to go easy on that dill.'

'Food has never given me any trouble.' He pats his bulging belly. 'Is that why you're up so early?'

'Can't sleep. Thought I might as well go for a ride, get some fresh air.'

'Not fresh enough for you here?'

Elina decides to ignore her father's teasing. 'I won't be long—'

'Lying down will help you more than exerting yourself. Neculai will take the horse back to the stable. You go and try to get some rest.'

Elina knows pushing any more will only make her father dig his heels deeper and she smiles and bows her head, certain it will please him, but in her mind, she's already planning how to go behind his back.

Despite her best efforts, her father is ahead of her. He must have asked the servants to keep an eye on her, for she feels watched. The maids, no doubt, keep him apprised of her upset stomach and poor appetite. Florica is doing her best with all sorts of wonder soups, as she calls them, but nothing seems to help.

When Elina discovers that her saddle has mysteriously disappeared, she storms into the day room where her father is playing cards with Neculai in front of the fire.

'Where is my saddle?' she asks, pinning her father with a fierce stare. She could certainly ride bareback, but that's not the point.

Boyar Constantin shifts his weight on the divan piled with cushions. 'You have your mother's nervous disposition,' he says. 'The older you get, the more like her you become.'

'I'd like to go out for a ride. I miss the woods.'

'Fine, let's go. I'll join you.' He makes to stand up, but he struggles to lift his weight.

'Why are you doing this? Don't you trust me—'

'It's not that.'

'What is it then?' Elina's hands are balled into fists at her sides.

The boyar dismisses Neculai with a flick of his wrist and waves at Elina to sit next to him. She remains standing.

'I'm worried about you. You don't seem yourself lately and I don't want to make the same mistake I made with your mother, God bless her soul. Couldn't live with myself if something happened to you—'

'Don't turn the manor into a gilded gaol then. What's the use of all this' – Elina looks around – 'if I can't be free?'

Her father scoffs. 'No one is really free, my dear. I'm at

the behest of the voivode and he is a vassal of the Ottoman sultan, and so it goes. Real freedom doesn't exist, and if it did, I'm not even sure we'd want it. You're yet to learn the whims of the world.'

'Until then, I want my saddle back.'

Her father watches her closely. 'What is it? What troubles you? You know I'll do anything for you. And I mean – *anything*. Has anyone upset you?'

The concern and love in her father's voice makes her wobble and she sinks next to him on the divan, unable to stop her sobs. She buries her face in his chest, afraid she may say things she will regret later.

'It's alright, my angel, it's alright. Crying will make you feel better and then you can tell me all. I'll have neither man nor beast upset my little ray of sunshine.'

The tears do wash away some of her distress, but Elina could never tell her father about the deep hurt and shame his own brother has caused her. Has the mugwort brew worked? Is she going to get her monthly bleeding soon?

'So? What is it?' her father prods when she wipes her face dry.

She decides to mention the other thing that sits heavy on her mind. 'It's about Rozalia. You and the priest are plotting against her. You know she isn't as bad as he makes her out to be.'

Her father lets out a laugh which shakes the many rings of flesh around his belly.

'Is this why you're upset?' he asks and laughs some more. 'Didn't you hear what I told the priest? About needing to find out her secret for cooking my colours? I'm buying her time, that's what I'm doing.'

'You did that on purpose?'

'Of course. I don't really like her, but who's going to treat my horses if she dies?'

'I need to go and warn her—'

'If she's had a confrontation with the priest, she'll know

he's after her, don't you worry about that. That woman is no fool.'

Her father is right. Surely Rozalia, who can smell the rain from days away and who can understand the whispers of the wind, surely she would sense the danger that's coming her way and prepare for it.

How?

Elina can't begin to imagine, but then Rozalia must be a resourceful woman to have survived so far.

'Is there anything else on your mind, my angel?' Her father is watching her closely.

Pray that the mugwort has worked, she wants to tell him.

'No,' she says, and to convince him of her lie, Elina does her best to smile.

TRAPPED HARE

Mira has taken up combing wool for those who own sheep in the village. It helps to put food on the table, especially since she hasn't caught anything in her snare recently. Elina's regular gifts of hares have stopped too. But her friend's refusal to forgive Mira – it's been a few weeks since she's seen her – is more painful than the hunger pangs.

With the harvest over and the cold weather setting in, the *clacă* starts – a weekly gathering where people come together to help each other with any work that needs doing, such as spinning wool or weaving clothes. The men join them to help with rolling the thread into skeins, but mostly to tell jokes and stories. This is also an opportunity for young people to get to know each other better, the evenings often ending with singing, dancing and furtive kisses.

Mira attends them once in a while to please her father, who hopes she'll find herself a suitor at these gatherings. There is a particularly keen young man – Simion, the skinner's son – who always offers to help Mira with teasing and pricking the wool as she works the drop spindle.

Each morning after a *clacă*, her father asks how it went. She knows what his real question is, and when she tells him she's not interested in anyone, he says she's fussy.

'You better find yourself someone soon,' her father says.

'I caught wind of peasants' uprisings all over the country. Sounds like our voivode has increased the tithes to cover the yearly tribute to the sultan. He's bleeding us dry. Our young men might also be tempted to take up forks and axes and go to battle.'

Mira would like to tell her father that such a situation would suit her just fine. With no men left in the village, he won't be nagging at her to find a husband.

'I'll go do some washing,' she says and fetches the wicker basket piled up with rags.

As soon as she turns the corner of the road, Mira heads in the opposite direction to the river. Rozalia has asked that she visits every day, so that she can pass on as much of her teachings as possible before the priest comes for her.

The tiredness from the many nights when she tosses and turns with worry for Elina dissipates at the thought that maybe today she will be at Rozalia's. Surely she won't hold a grudge forever.

Rozalia is cooking something tasty, if the smell is anything to go by. After sweeping the hut with a quick glance, Mira's heart sinks: Elina isn't here.

'You look more sapped and sleepless than me. And you don't have the church seeking to burn you at the stake.'

'I'm worried about you.'

'Don't be. I'm already spending the nights in my cellar. They won't come for me in daylight. Let's go – we've got lots to do,' Rozalia says and leads the way towards the secret place at the end of her garden.

By the time Rozalia is done with the teaching, Mira's head is swimming from all the herbs and potions she's had to smell and taste. The fact that she isn't laughing herself silly any more means she's growing accustomed to them.

The waning moon has long passed the ridge of the third hill. A flock of clouds glides towards the crescent, veiling it at first and then smothering it altogether, sinking the world into total darkness. Mira, who knows this road like the back of her hand, sprints all the way home without once putting a foot wrong. She reminds herself to check the trap before going to sleep. With some luck, they could be eating hare stew tomorrow. Even better if Elina brings it – it would be a sign of reconciliation.

A weak light flickers in their hut. How come her father is still awake? Is the cold weather troubling his bones, like it's doing with her damaged hand?

Suru meets her with excited yelps, which she hushes by patting the dog, telling him to be quiet. She sidles along the front wall and can hear her father talking to someone.

She knows this voice.

It's Barbu.

All air goes out of her lungs, and she leans against the wall. What's he doing here, visiting at this ungodly hour? What kind of news is this to be brought at night?

The *opaiț* in the hut spreads a soft glow out the window and Mira catches sight of the hare hanging in her trap. With the slight breeze swinging the choked animal from side to side, their guest would have seen it too.

She dashes to check the fur on its neck, but there are no stains on it. It's not a gift from Elina.

BETROTHAL

As Mira walks in, a pungent smell she doesn't recognise hits her in the face.

'There she is.' Her father stretches one arm towards her. He's holding a cup in his other hand, which he downs in one go, wincing.

'You've got a brave daughter' – Barbu smiles – 'to be wandering out on her own at night. Can be dangerous, what with all the stray dogs you've got roaming round here. Anyway, I better be going,' he says and picks up the flask next to him. 'There's a little left.' The mason shakes the flask and turns it upside down, pouring a cloudy liquid into Pavel's cup.

That's what she could smell when she walked in. Neither wine nor barley beer, it certainly is some sort of a tipple, judging by the jolly glint in her father's eyes.

Barbu corks the flask with a peg of wood and pulls his sheepskin hat on. 'Perhaps I'll come join you for a hare stew soon.' He winks at Mira and takes his leave, stooping to pass through their door.

Pavel follows him out and Mira can hear the two men talking in low voices in the courtyard before her father returns.

'Where have you been?' he asks as soon as he shuts the door, his voice not as sweet now.

But Mira has her own questions. 'Why was the mason

here? What did he want?' She draws closer to the oil lamp. Her damaged hand hurts less when she warms it up.

'You're a young woman and… you need to protect your reputation. You can't be seen out on your own at night.' Her father sighs and shakes his head.

'Why did he come here?' she asks again.

'Aren't you honoured to receive such a worthy guest? He's the master mason who's going to build a church in our village—'

'It couldn't have been your pots he was after – the priest feeds him.' Mira's hands have warmed up, yet she keeps them by the open flame.

'He's a nice man, Mira, and I'm getting old. The tithes have gone up and…' Her father fixes her with a heavy stare. 'You need a husband.'

'Is that why he was here?' She moves her hands on top of the flame where the burn is stronger.

'Barbu is the answer to all my prayers for you—'

'I'm not marrying him.'

'The matter is settled, Mira. He asked for your hand, and I said yes. You're betrothed – he's your lord now. The best marriage a woman of your standing will ever see.'

Mira hovers by the *opaiț*, refusing to let the words sink in. Her hands are stinging from the burn, but it's not painful enough and she dips them closer to the flame.

'What did he give you to drink?' she asks.

Her father's face lights up again. 'Like water, but better. With fire in it. It's from the monks.'

'What monks?'

'The ones Barbu built a monastery for somewhere up the country. He's learned the secret of their drink. He's a very smart man, I tell you.' He chuckles as if remembering a story Barbu may have told him. 'Three churches so far. The one he's going to build in our village will be his fourth. You should've seen the joy in his eyes when he spoke of his work. He's a creator like us…' He quickly corrects himself. 'Like me with my pots, but on a much grander scale. You'll do very well to be his wife.'

'But then I'll have to follow him all over the country, wherever his work is, won't I? I may never see you again,' she says, hoping this will make her father think twice about marrying her off to a stranger.

'Oh, you needn't worry 'bout that. He's promised me he'll never take you away from here.'

'But—'

'It's the best thing that can happen to you… and there might still be a chance I can pass on my potter's craft. You could have a little boy this time next year.'

So this is what it's all about. Her father is after a successor, not concerned with her happiness. Now that she can no longer make pots, he has given up on her and is dreaming of a grandson. She already hates the unborn child.

'Mira, you know I love you more than anything in this world… I only want what's best for you. And I'm tellin' you, the mason is a gift from heaven.'

Mira has a lot to say to her father, but none of her reasons will make him change his mind. She thinks of the string of births and nursings ahead of her and shudders.

How will Elina take this news?

Later, as Mira is crying about her fate on Rozalia's shoulder, the old woman doesn't seem surprised, as though the wind has brought the news ahead of her. She strokes Mira's head and, when her sobbing subsides, she takes her hand and looks her in the eye.

'That's our lot – to be a wife and a mother, or risk being shunned by our community.'

'I want to be like you.'

'I was married once too,' Rozalia says.

'What happened to your husband?'

'I'm a widow now. You too have to do what you have to do—'

'Didn't you say you could see darkness in Barbu's soul? That he's exploiting the secret teachings in favour of the false faith? How can I marry someone like him?'

'Come here.' Rozalia pulls her into a tight hug. Mira can smell the entire earth on this woman's skin. The scent of herbs and flowers and fruit and soil and rain. It's all there, as though she's the Spirit of the Land in the shape of a woman.

When Rozalia looks at her again, there's something about her that unsettles Mira. She senses a heightened state of waiting, a stealthy kind of stillness. She looks relaxed and yet alert, ready for action, but for what exactly, Mira cannot tell.

'There's time to stop him,' Rozalia says. 'Barbu and his men won't resume their works until spring, so plenty of time to change his mind.'

'Do you think that's possible?'

'There's a lot to be said about a woman's charm.'

'But I don't love him—'

'You don't have to love him.' Rozalia smiles, like she knows something Mira doesn't.

'I don't know. I'm worried...'

'Is there something else you're not telling me?' Rozalia studies Mira.

No matter how much Mira wants to confess her forbidden love for Elina, her mouth won't speak the words out loud. Not because she fears Rozalia will expose them, but because the old woman will only tell Mira what she already knows. That she should stop fooling herself with an impossible love.

'So what is it?' Rozalia insists.

Pressured for an answer, Mira talks about the other thing that keeps her awake at night, the dream where she finds herself trapped in a black pit, withering away. 'It's the same old nightmare I told you about. It leaves me in a cold sweat each night. You said you'd explain it to me one day—'

'I've done more. I've equipped you to overcome it.'

'How?'

'You have to stop fearing it first.'

‘You don’t know what terror is, if you think—’

‘I’ve shown you the way out of that place. You will know what to do when the time comes.’

The old woman is full of riddles this evening, but Mira has learned not to push it. Elina, no doubt, would laugh at her unquestioning trust.

Elina! Why can’t she stop thinking about her? There’s no hope for them, so why torment herself with silly dreams like that?

Unless…

But Elina would never agree to this. Yet, if Mira is prepared to give up on her comfortable future as the mason’s wife, so must Elina be willing to sacrifice hers. Are Elina’s feelings strong enough to take a chance with Mira’s idea?

She looks at Rozalia, this woman who lives by her own rules. She has survived. And if she has, there’s a possibility they might too.

At least they must try.

THE WILL OF SNOWFLAKES

Elina's efforts to swallow and keep down the bitter mugwort haven't paid off. Her monthly bleeding is late.

She imagines her belly growing. Her father will think she has finally started to eat properly, and he'll be happy. But then, of course, her belly will grow bigger and bigger and so will her shame. Her disgrace will be obvious for all to see.

She crawls under her bed where she's hidden the tansy, wrapped in layers of linen to stop its awful smell spreading about the house.

If this is what Rozalia uses to help women in her condition, it must be a powerful herb. And how difficult can it be to make a bath with it? She isn't as squeamish and helpless as Mira thinks she is.

She'll do it on Saturday. The servants will be suspicious if she has her bath earlier in the week. They may have already guessed something is amiss. With so much on her mind, Elina had forgotten about the monthly wash and boil, and when Ana asked about her cloths, Elina had to stain a few strips of linen with pig's blood and present them as her own.

Will the tansy work where the mugwort has failed? Only one way to find out.

Winter storms into the village on Saturday morning, blowing icy winds and sifting heavy snow from a gloomy sky.

Elina asks the maid to get the fire going in her room. Today is the day. There's a part of her still hoping that, by the time Ana gets the bath ready this evening, her monthly bleeding will start at the last moment, and she won't have to tempt the tansy.

Her father has dealt the cards, waiting for Neculai to finish chopping the firewood outside so they can start their game. Though he's taught her how to play, he rarely allows her to join in because, unlike Neculai, she doesn't let him win.

Nestled on her favourite tasselled cushion – a present from her mother – Elina plays the *cobză* softly by the window, her back to the men. She watches the snowflakes swarming outside, as if they are choosing where to settle. Who is she fooling? Of course it isn't up to them where they end up. It's the invisible wind that's tossing them about, teasing them with the promise of free will.

Will she be rid of her shameful burden this time tomorrow? How will she know if she's done it right?

To take her mind out of this dark place, Elina thinks of Mira, her Froglet with the striking green eyes. It's been hard not seeing her all this time. Why is Mira being so stubborn? Can't she see she's harming their chances of being together? If only she didn't listen to that batty old woman. Elina must speak to her, make her see reason.

But first things first. She'll get this blasted bath over and done with this evening, and tomorrow she will talk to Mira.

When dinner is served – roasted pheasant rubbed in garlic and drowned in red wine – Elina shoots to her feet, heaving and covering her mouth.

'Are you alright, my angel?' her father asks.

'My stomach is still a little tender for such a rich meal.

A hot bath and an early night tonight, and I'll be fine in the morning.' She bids him goodnight.

'Sweet dreams, my angel,' he says, his beard glistening with fowl grease.

The bathtub has already been brought to the room. It's disturbing seeing it empty like that; it reminds Elina of her mother's coffin. *Don't be silly*, she tells herself. It's the same bathtub she's always used – waxed oak wood caulked with dry leaves of cattails to stop it from leaking.

But her mind does its own thing, taking her back to the darkest day of her life – her mother's funeral, the memory of which is all a blur. Clipped images and scraps of talk swim around Elina's head. She remembers the priest burning so much frankincense around her mother's body it seemed he was trying to bury a demon, not a human being. Yet she relished the heavy incense, which together with Rozalia's mysterious brew made her light-headed, lifting the woe and sorrow from the pit of her heart. The next thing she knew, she was laughing as her mother's body was being carried out of the house. And after that, total blackness until the following day, when her father had taken her to the graveyard to show her the fresh mound of earth.

The maid walks in with two buckets of steaming water. 'Piping hot, miss, as you've asked.' Despite the cold snap outside, Ana is flushed and sweaty. Right behind her, Neculai is holding two more buckets.

'That'll do,' she tells the maid when she's half-filled the tub. 'You can clear it away in the morning. I don't wish to be disturbed once I fall asleep after my bath.'

As soon as the maid's steps fade away, Elina jams the door from the inside by feeding the broom through the handle, like her mother used to do. She reaches for the tansy under the bed. How much should she use? Uncertain, she throws it all in, soaking the herbs with the fire poker, watching the water turn into a cheerless yellow, then into a baleful brown.

When it has cooled down a little, she steps into the murky bath, almost making the sign of the cross, when she reminds herself she doesn't believe in Lord Jesus Christ any longer to seek his protection, or indeed, to expect it. Whatever happens, she hopes it's quick and painless.

And so, she lies in the bathtub and waits.

GODS' BIDDING

Their wedding is to take place at the beginning of spring. However, the winter has only just started, and Mira tries to find some consolation in that. She should have enough time to act on her plan.

Barbu has invited himself for hare stew the following evening, but Mira isn't in the mood to entertain guests. Her mind is on Elina. They really need to talk. If she's not at Rozalia's tonight, Mira will have to go up to the manor tomorrow. She'll take one of her father's best pots as a gift so they let her in.

Mira tells her father she's going to the *clacă*, but instead heads to Rozalia's.

She finds the old woman spinning wool by the stove, her eyes half closed. Not wishing to disturb her contemplation, Mira waits quietly at the door, taking deep breaths of the sweet pine smell that's filled the hut.

'Are you going to tell me what's bothering you?' Rozalia asks, startling Mira. 'You look like you've been chewed by a cow and spat back out again.'

Mira squats next to Rozalia, telling her about Barbu's haste with the wedding and how she hates him for it.

'And he's coming for supper tomorrow. I'm afraid I won't be able to hold my tongue.'

Rozalia takes Mira's hand. 'You don't realise the great duty the Old Gods have chosen you for. Only you can stop Barbu from building that cursed church. And one way is to marry him.'

'What's the other? I'll do whatever else it takes—'

'The other way is through means which our faith doesn't allow. Unless it's absolutely necessary.'

'Who decides? Because I feel it's absolutely necessary. I don't love this man, and I don't want to marry him—'

'You are yet to know your powers.'

A spell of silence settles between them, and to make it more bearable, Mira pokes the fire to liven it up.

'But this is not the only thing that's troubling you, is it?' Rozalia asks.

'What do you mean?' Mira turns suddenly, dropping the poker on her foot. Has the old woman found out about her and Elina?

'Perhaps it's something to do with the tansy that's gone missing from my cellar?'

'What missing tansy? I don't understand...' Mira's heart is pounding like it already knows something her mind is yet to catch up with.

'You tell me. You've either given it to someone without my permission, or you've betrayed my trust by bringing someone to my cellar. I need to know if my hiding place isn't safe any longer.'

Mira's mind races back to the night of the harvest fair – Elina's coughing fit, and her running away before Mira had returned with the water.

Mira cradles her head.

'Talk to me.' Rozalia's voice is calm yet demanding.

'Elina. She was distressed. I had to get her away from the fair. I gave her mugwort to avoid... But not the tansy. I swear I didn't give her the tansy.'

'But you must've told her about it. That was your mistake. The knowledge you've acquired from me comes with huge responsibility. You can't be reckless with it, or it would hurt people instead of helping them.'

'I'm sorry, I'm so sorry—'

'We don't have time for apologies.' Rozalia drops her spindle and jumps to her feet, going through a few pots and bundles, measuring and mixing herbs. 'Who is he?' she asks.

'Her uncle.'

Rozalia nods as though she's known this all along.

'Are you good at climbing walls?'

Mira gapes at Rozalia's strange question. 'I'm good at climbing trees. Why?'

'We're going to the manor. The mugwort hasn't worked, or we would've seen her by now. We have to get to her before she uses the tansy.'

'What if—'

'You better pray she hasn't.' The urgency in Rozalia's voice hits Mira in the pit of her belly. If Rozalia is worried about something, it must be serious.

'Elina could be avoiding coming here because of what we're doing to her,' Mira says, taken aback by her audacity to doubt her teacher.

'What are we doing to her?'

'You know very well that our efforts to stop the building of the church are also harming her future status, her independence—'

'Things aren't always what they seem. You of all people should—'

'What if she's right?'

'I wish she was,' Rozalia says. She stuffs the medicine into her badger-snout pouch and throws it over her shoulder. 'Let's go.'

TANSY BATH

The smell of soaked tansy is unbearable, but if she gets out of the tub now, it may ruin the result. To stop herself from being sick, she sits up and pinches her nose. Apart from the usual light-headedness when having a hot bath, there's nothing else happening. It could be a long wait. And if it doesn't work? Icy fingers grip the back of her neck.

A faint throb in her belly grows loud and urgent, like something trapped inside her is seeking to get out. Is this it? Has it worked? The water has certainly turned darker, but it's hard to tell if it's the tansy or her blood. She stands up in the tub and there it is – a thin red trickle weeping down her inner thigh. Her bleeding has finally been summoned, like an errant rascal, by the power of this magical plant.

She has done it. She is bleeding her shame away, saving herself and her family from a public disgrace. The last time she felt such lightness was years ago, when her mother was still alive, pushing her on the swing tied to the plum tree, that same plum tree that has witnessed her dishonour.

How much longer does she need to stay in the tub? Maybe a little longer to make sure… But her limbs grow heavy and wild tendrils start dancing in front of her eyes. She steps out of the water and ties herself with the strips of linen she has cut earlier. Her movements are slow as though she's just woken up from a deep sleep.

To her alarm, the layers of linen are soon soaked with blood, and she has to replace them. These too blossom red stains far quicker than she has expected. The room blurs. She lies down, hoping to ease the blood flow, but when the walls start spinning and the ceiling closes in on her, she sits up, struggling for breath.

She has to see Rozalia. At once. Before she bleeds herself dry.

With more linen strapped between her legs, she staggers out of the room. Her right foot is going limp with pins and needles as she waddles towards one of the sheds in the garden. She comes out with a small sledge. It will take less effort going down the hill on this than riding. Besides, leaving her horse behind will tell her father she hasn't gone far, if she doesn't make it back in time before her absence is discovered.

Elina unbolts the gate. All she needs is a gap so tiny a cat could squeeze through. And then she's out, the wind hissing in her ears as the sledge flies down the frozen snow.

WHITE NIGHT

Just as Rozalia is about to blow out the candle, she snaps her head up. 'Did you hear that?'

The crunch of snow under someone's feet. Followed by a brief silence and then a thud, like a sack of grain has been dropped in the courtyard.

Rozalia peers through the window. A frown, a sudden gasp and she darts to the door, flinging it open with such force that it swings on its hinges. Mira follows her out, watching Rozalia run towards someone who has collapsed in a heap by the gate, their clothes smeared in mud. Where did they find mud at this time of the year? The world is covered in snow—

'Stop staring and give me a hand here.' Rozalia's urgent voice tears through Mira's shroud of confusion, through the wall of denial which her mind is so feverishly building to repress what her eyes are seeing.

Her feet spring into action and she reaches the gate in one breath, helping Rozalia to bring Elina inside. Her nightdress under her cloak is stiff with blood – some frozen, some blossoming afresh. Her eyes are half open, only the whites showing, and her face – drawn and eerie – reminds Mira of the women Rozalia has tried to help in the past, but who have bled dry right before their eyes.

'Go get the horsetail powder and the shepherd's purse and the lady's mantle. Grab a bunch of yarrow too. Hurry!'

Sliding and slipping in the snow, Mira can swear Rozalia's cellar has moved further into the woods. The frosty air slashes at her eyeballs and stings her throat. Once in the cellar, she lights a candle briefly to grab what she needs and scrambles up the stairs, only to realise she's left the candle burning. Back down the stairs, blows it out, up the stairs again, through the length of the garden, trying to keep her footing…

When she's finally made it back into the hut, Mira stops in the doorway, her strength seeping out of her all at once. Elina is no longer there. In her place, a corpse is lying on the ground.

'What's got into you?' Rozalia glares at her. 'Snap out of it and start mixing the horsetail like I taught you. No room for errors tonight. Here, hold this steady.' Rozalia pushes a stick in Elina's mouth. 'She's got to drink this in one go.'

They work in silence, apart from Rozalia's urgent chants as she does a certain ritual to keep Elina's soul tied to her weakened body. Mira knows things are getting worse when Rozalia twists a ring of wire around Elina's limp ankle – the utmost measure to bar a soul from leaving the body. They remove the soaked mess from under Elina and replace it with dry straw, to gauge her loss of blood.

'There's nothing else we can do now but wait and trust that our efforts and the medicine will bring her back to us,' Rozalia says and slides to the floor, sweat trickling down the sides of her face. Mira wishes Rozalia would go out for some fresh air so she could hug and kiss Elina back to consciousness. All she can do is hold her friend's cold hand and try to push away the dark thoughts circling her mind.

She searches Elina's face for the faintest sign of life – a tinge of colour on her cheeks, a flicker under her eyelids, a stir, a moan, anything at all. If Rozalia hasn't given up, it means there's some breath left in her body. Why can't she spot it? Maybe she's not looking hard enough. But if she looks too hard, all she can see is a dead child, not the young woman she loves.

Mira turns away and looks out the window. The crisp light of the moon spreads a shivery sheen over the snow-cushioned trees, hunched under their glinting weight. Their fortitude annoys, no, angers her, and she wishes their trunks snapped to pieces.

Save for the fire in the hearth, nothing stirs in the hut or outside it. Winter must be the most powerful season of all, to freeze time in its tracks like this.

When a low murmur escapes from Elina's lips, Mira thinks it's her friend's last breath and almost clamps her hand on Elina's mouth when she suddenly hears Rozalia's relief. 'You took your time, Miss Stubborn. Welcome back!'

Though there's no other sign of life from Elina, Rozalia's shoulders have relaxed and the hammering in Mira's chest also subsides.

When she comes to, Elina's gaze is empty of all recognition as her eyes dart about the room.

'It's alright. Everything is alright,' Mira says, biting the inside of her cheek to stop the tears pooling into her eyes. 'You're safe now.'

'Is it done?' Elina whispers.

'It's so done we almost lost you too.' Rozalia smiles, but the chiding in her voice is obvious.

'You're in danger. The priest… he's after you.'

'Not the time to waste your breath—'

'But if something happens to you… I'll never learn about my mother's secret—'

'Nothing will happen to me.'

'It's so easy to slip away… I wouldn't have woken up if… it wasn't for your efforts. But can you guarantee my life tomorrow? Or yours, for that matter?'

Mira looks at Rozalia, waiting to see how she'll respond to Elina's challenge, but – for the first time ever – the old woman is lost for words.

She stands up. 'I'll be back in a moment.'

'I won't fall asleep or forget about it,' Elina says, but Rozalia is already out the door. She turns to Mira. 'Don't stare at me like that. You don't look any better yourself. Wait, I know, you're going to say how much you missed me—'

'No. I didn't miss *you*. Only the hares you used to place in my snares.'

Elina's weak smile looks more like a grimace. 'How did you—'

'Shh, there are other things we need to talk about before she's back. I've been betrothed to Barbu. He's asked for my hand.'

'He's in love with you. I saw his building plans – he's sketched you on one of them.'

'I don't love this man and never will. But the wedding is in spring.'

'So quick…'

'Even if he succeeds in building this church and you gain your independence, it will be too late for us. I'll be his wife by then, burdened with his children, following him up and down the country, wherever his work may take him.'

'What are we going to do?'

Mira looks over her shoulder. She drops her voice even lower, and she tells Elina about the plan she's been hatching. 'We'll run away. To a busy town where nobody knows us and pretend to be orphan sisters.'

'How are we going to survive? You've seen me – I can't even make a fire.'

'You're good with your bow and arrow. All those hares you left in my snare – clean shots, each one of them. We won't starve. We'll cope, you'll see.'

'I don't know—'

'It's the only way if we want to be together.'

Elina blinks slowly, like she's about to fall into a deep sleep.

'Look,' Mira says. 'I'm giving up on a safe future as the mason's wife. Marrying him, I'll have a status and enough food on the table for the rest of my life. But I'm choosing you. Us. It may be a foolish choice – certainly dangerous – but I'm standing by it. Are you ready to do the same?'

The crunch of snow outside – Rozalia is coming back. Mira bends over Elina with urgent whispers.

'You'll be fine in a few days. Drink lots of beetroot juice to help with your blood loss, and on the night of the next new moon, come to Rozalia's cellar. Don't bring much stuff, only what you can carry… I'll be waiting for you…'

The door opens and Rozalia walks in with a bunch of scrolls in her arms.

'Are they my father's drawings?' Elina asks. 'Why have you got them?'

'They are not your father's.'

'Whose are they?'

'Your mother's.'

'I don't understand. Did she also paint? I never knew—'

'Your father doesn't paint. Never has. It's all your mother's work – the church books and the scrolls – everything. Your father pretended for your mother's sake. She asked him to. Begged him even. She told me it wasn't easy, because your father refused to lie to the priest. But she insisted. Your mother knew what she wanted and how to go about getting it.'

'This can't be true—'

'Your father loved your mother dearly. And like her, he did what he felt was right in his heart, rather than yield to social conventions. These will always change, whilst the truth in our hearts is unwavering. When we trust our instincts, everything else falls into place. Is it easy? No. Possible? You bet. Worth the danger it may pose? Absolutely.'

Mira, who is still holding Elina's hand, squeezes it to pass on a silent message – *See? It's in your blood to break rules. Both your mother and father did it. You can do it too.*

'So this is my mother's secret you've kept all this time…'

'She didn't suffer from headaches. She locked herself in her room so she could draw in secret. If word had reached the priest that the church books were painted by a woman, well, imagine the scandal, the danger to your family.'

'And what about all those bundles of medicine you used to bring her?'

'It wasn't medicine, but dyes I cooked for her.'

Elina shakes her head, her eyes glistening.

'Your mother would have told you herself, if only she'd lived a little longer.'

'Let me see them,' Elina says.

Rozalia unfurls the scrolls one by one: a skylark in flight – its beak wide open – singing a silent song; a *cobză* propped against a giant disembodied heart; scenes from the Bible; a young Elina in a swing, riding in the woods, playing with puppies.

Mira gasps. 'Such bright colours. As if they've been painted earlier today.'

'Wait.' Elina frowns at Rozalia. 'If my father doesn't paint – that's why he was so flustered when the priest asked him about illustrating the new manuscript – if he doesn't paint, he doesn't need your dyes. And if the priest finds out the truth, or if my father changes his mind, then you're—'

'Your father may not like me very much, but he loves his horses more than he hates me. Who's going to treat them after his hunting parties if I die?'

'That's what he said, but he's unpredictable, as I've just found out.'

'Whatever they say about your father, he's a decent man,' Rozalia says with such conviction that she either truly believes it, or she's very good at lying. After all this time Mira has known Rozalia, she still can't tell which one it is.

'I see you haven't finished your medicine.' Rozalia holds the cup to Elina's lips but looks at Mira, who was supposed to ensure she drank it all. But in her rush to talk about their running away, she totally forgot about it.

'Why do your herbs have to taste so awful?' Elina scrunches up her face in disgust.

'If medicine was pleasant, people wouldn't learn their lessons.'

'What's that on the floor? Another scroll?' Elina leans to the side.

Rozalia picks it up and opens it. It reveals a pair of dark eyes, their stare so intense that it looks like an actual person is watching them through two holes in the parchment.

'I've seen these eyes before… Who is it?' Elina asks.

Rozalia shrugs and goes to potter by the hearth, but her gesture is too rushed and half-hearted to be telling the truth.

'I know them, I know these eyes…' Elina's words slur. She rolls her head, fighting to stay awake and remember something important to her. But no one's will, however strong, stands a chance against Rozalia's potions.

Mira cups Elina's face with both hands, and – making sure Rozalia isn't listening – she whispers: 'I'll wait for you on the evening of the new moon.'

But Elina's awareness has sunk from her eyes before they close. Will she remember their talk? Mira wonders.

'You can go home now.' Rozalia's voice is heavy with fatigue. 'The dawn will be spilling over the hills soon, and you need to get some rest before you play host this evening.'

It takes Mira a moment to remember that Rozalia is talking about Barbu. She has forgotten all about his visit.

'I'll be back as soon as I get rid of him.'

'Mira, we don't always recognise what our gods require of us. Don't forget, we've all got our purpose.'

'If only I knew what mine was.'

'Your heart will guide you.'

Mira struggles to suppress her irritation at Rozalia, who is so tight on words you'd think she had to pay for them. But an alert and heedful glint in these ancient eyes reminds Mira of this woman's wisdom.

'I'm sorry.'

'No need for any apologies. I'm very proud of you. I couldn't have chosen a better person to pass on my teachings to. Be bold and be safe. I'll watch over you. Always.'

'You speak like we won't see each other again.'

'One of our bedrock principles – to live each day as if it's our last. Remember?'

'I'll be back as soon as I get rid of Barbu,' Mira says, and with one last peek at a sleeping Elina, she heads out into the thinning night. The thought of their life together in the weeks and years to come makes her heart sing, lifting her weariness and quickening her step.

In the murky light of the early dawn, she spots a red yarn snaking away in the snow. Mira praises the Old Gods for giving Elina enough strength to reach Rozalia's hut in time last night. Judging by the winding blood trail, she was barely steady on her feet.

Mira follows the yarn all the way to the edge of the woods, shuffling her feet to wipe all trace, hoping that nobody else has seen it.

THE GUEST

Mira has hardly spoken a word to her father the whole day, her head drooping with lack of sleep and worry for Elina.

'You're aloof, have been for days,' he says. 'What's eating at your heart?'

'What good is it to talk? You're not hearing me.'

'Becoming Barbu's wife is the most fortunate fate you could ever wish for. You'll thank me for it one day.'

Mira doesn't answer. She goes about her chores, stewing the hare and stirring the porridge as they wait for their guest to turn up. The dusk is darker than usual. With so much *tizic* smoke coming out of chimneys, all she can see is one large smudge of soot straddling the sky. It will bring night sooner. She can't wait to get through the supper so she can go back to Rozalia's. Elina should be better by now.

When Suru starts barking outside, Mira dishes the stew and the grain porridge out on two trays. The food is supposed to be steaming when the guest comes in.

'Good evening, honourable host.' Barbu bows at the door, rubbing and blowing into his hands. 'A mean frost out there.'

'Welcome, honourable guest.' Pavel also bows. 'How I wish this winter was all over.'

'Oh no, not so fast,' Barbu laughs. 'It's the only season when I can get some rest.'

'You won't like it so much when you're my age. Old bones don't take kindly to cold.'

Mira waits on Barbu to place his sheepskin and hat into her arms. She can tell from the weight and the exquisite pattern of the stitches that he must have paid a dear coin for them, especially the shiny black hat made from what looks like the curly skins of four lambs sewn lengthways. She places his garments on a pile of fresh straw and goes to sit in the corner of the hut, teasing wool. Today is the first time she's grateful that she will eat after the men. It means she can disappear into a dark corner, where neither the flicker of the *opaiț* nor Barbu's piercing eyes can reach her.

When her father starts saying grace, Mira turns to check Barbu's manner of praying and finds he's watching her.

'Tuck in, master mason,' Pavel says, 'before the food gets cold.'

'Not before we take a sip of the health-giving brew I've learned to make from the monks.' Barbu pulls out a flask from somewhere in his shirt. 'Here's to the host of this house and to the beautiful woman who has cooked this feast.'

Mira pretends she's too busy to acknowledge his toast.

'Mira.' Her father's voice is impatient.

'Thank you, my lord,' she says without taking her eyes off the wool in her lap.

Barbu pours a drink for Pavel and, judging by the gurgle of the drink, he's pouring a lot more for his host than he poured himself a moment ago.

Slurps, sips and lip-smacking are followed by grunts of compliments for the food.

'How do you find living in our village?' Pavel asks.

'I love your community. And I love the *clacă* here. I attended yesterday for the first time, and I can tell you, I've been to many of these gatherings in other villages, but none so lively as yours.'

'My daughter enjoys them so much she never misses one,' Pavel says and looks at Mira. 'I hope you helped the mason feel welcome yesterday.'

Mira's heart turns into a pounding fist, and she shrinks further into the corner of the hut so that they don't see the panic on her face.

'Your daughter has been wonderful,' Barbu says through a mouthful of porridge. 'She's taught me the local songs and customs. I already look forward to the next one.'

Mira is stunned by his brazen lie. The fact that both she and Barbu know the truth makes her father look like a fool. Though she's angry with Barbu, she can't find her tongue to speak up and force him to admit to his lying, for then she will also be in trouble.

The ease with which he lies. And she can't tell if what she feels is gratitude for having saved her skin, anger that he's disrespecting her father in their own home, or alarm that her husband-to-be can lie so effortlessly that she'll never know when he's telling the truth.

He must be thinking the same about me, Mira thinks. *Good. Hopefully this will make him change his mind about wanting to marry me. Surely no man wants a wife who lies about her whereabouts at night.*

Mira has finished teasing the entire sheepskin and Barbu is still here. Should she go and clear away the empty trays, a little hint that dinner is over? But they may notice her trembling hands – she's still riled by his lying.

She wonders how Elina is doing. How she longs to be by her side again, hold her hand and talk about their running away, their life together…

There's a sudden silence in the hut and Mira realises she's been asked something. Barbu and her father are both looking at her, the first with a smile on his face, the other with a frown.

'I'm sorry, I don't feel very well. I'll go outside for some fresh air.' She pulls the shawl tighter under her chin and gets up from the floor.

'But our guest, your betrothed—'

'I was about to leave anyway.' Barbu also stands up, taking his empty flask with him. 'Thank you for your hospitality

– the juiciest hare I've ever had.' He shakes Pavel's hand. 'May good health be with you.'

Mira has no wish to be alone with Barbu. He'll probably expect her to thank him for covering up her lie, but she has no intention of doing so. She'll accompany him to the corner of the road, where she'll wish him goodnight and turn around, pretending to go home.

About two dozen steps.

They walk in silence, only the snow crunching under their feet. A dogged chill gnaws its way through Mira's sheepskin and prickles her skin. The air is so cold and dry that her nostrils stick together on the inside, and she pulls the shawl over half her face, keeping her eyes to the ground.

Less than a dozen steps left now to the corner of the road.

'What's that?' Barbu asks, stopping dead in his tracks. Mira lifts her head to see long tongues of fire lashing up at the sky. Just above where Rozalia's hut ought to be.

Does this mean Elina's bleeding has stopped and so Rozalia is burning the straw?

But something is not right. The flames are too thick and angry for that to be the source.

The crushing pain in her chest comes from nowhere, and while her mind is crippled with foreboding, her feet are kicking into a frantic sprint, tearing down the valley towards the raging fire.

A HEAP OF RUBBLE

Young and old have gathered by Rozalia's hut, their gaping faces awash with gold from the hungry flames. The thatched roof is long gone, the fire now chomping away at the walls of twigs and clay. The bleats of Rozalia's goat mix with the barks of men and dogs.

Mira spots Elina sat in the sleigh next to her father and the priest. Someone must've seen her come to Rozalia the night before and told the boyar about it. But when Mira sees the three hounds the size of calves circling the sleigh, she knows the beasts had no trouble sniffing the blood trail, no matter how well she'd kicked the snow to hide it.

She sneaks towards the garden and hides in the cellar, wedging the trapdoor open just enough to see. Two servants tie Rozalia behind the sleigh as everyone watches on. Including Barbu, who's just caught up and joined the crowd.

'You're a serf of Satan seeking to bathe in the blood of a virgin.' Boyar Constantin wags his finger at Rozalia as he hollers above the clamour. 'Look at my child! There isn't a drop of blood left in her—'

'Father, that's not true—' Elina stands up, but the priest

pulls her back down, making the sign of the cross above her head repeatedly.

The dazzle of the fire shines on the boyar's face, distorting it into a hideous grimace as he yells at Rozalia: 'The stake is the only place for an evil witch like you.'

'Amen.' The priest raises his arms towards the night sky glowing crimson.

Rozalia says nothing. She just stands there, tethered to the sleigh, her bare feet sunk into snow up to her ankles. Mira is angry that this feisty, wise woman doesn't put up a fight or try to break free, but then she knows that even with her exceptional speed, Rozalia couldn't outrun the hounds.

Elina is still protesting and crying, and Mira worries for her. She hasn't got the strength to be fighting like this. Her father, however, is deaf to her pleadings and waves at the *vizitiu* to set off. The two horses start trotting and Rozalia runs to keep up with the sleigh, but as the beasts speed up, she loses her footing and her body slides across the frozen snow with the lightness of a dry log.

Elina's shriek rips through the night, its echo hopelessly trapped in the icy trees. She lunges out of the sleigh, but her father and the priest hold her back.

And then all goes eerily quiet. The boyar's retinue melts into the night with the last of the serfs dragging Rozalia's goat behind him, and the villagers return to their hovels. Mira could almost think it was all just a bad dream if only she didn't have a nose to smell the burn, or eyes to see the smoke coiling up from a heap of rubble, all that's left of Rozalia's home.

A thunder gathers in Mira's belly, its rumbling familiar from the night Rozalia took her to the woods in the middle of a storm. She shoves the trapdoor open, clambers out of the cellar and runs for the trees beyond. The squall churning in her belly grows bigger and heavier, and when she's certain it's about to smother the beat of her heart, her body thrusts forward and her jaws open wide to release a wail that shatters icicles hanging from the branches.

She spends the rest of the night in Rozalia's cellar, thinking of bears and how they hole up during winter, the warmth trapped underground shielding them from the bitter frosts haunting the world above.

The next morning when she comes out, she spots a dark trail in the snow, but this one isn't meandering like the one she wiped with her feet the previous day. This is arrow-straight – as the sleigh dragged Rozalia behind, her flesh was slashed by the blade of the icy road.

Mira seeks out the men's footprints and sprinkles them with warm ash from under the ruins of Rozalia's home, before pinning each one of the prints with sharp sticks to send pain and death to their owners. Rozalia once told her a tiny bit of each of us is left whenever we touch something: the ground, a thing or another person. We don't see it, but it's there.

The hounds knew this truth when they picked up Elina's scent all the way to Rozalia's hut.

BIRTHMARK

Elina has been crying and pleading with her father for the two days since she was found at Rozalia's hut.

'Stop saying the witch is innocent—'

'She's not a witch.'

'She cast a spell on you, and you don't even know it. You don't know what you're saying. All that blood on your gown. I should have listened to what other people said about her, but she tricked us all – me, you, your mother.'

'Father—'

'She'll pay for it dearly. I'll see to it.'

The shameful truth singes Elina's tongue, yet it won't come out. Will her father even believe her? How can she prove her uncle's wrongdoing?

'I'm going to go for a walk in the garden.'

'You need to rest—'

'I need fresh air.'

She knows her father and the servants are watching her every move. But she has to go to the village this evening and find out where they've taken Rozalia. She can't let the old woman be punished for something she didn't do. And if being the boyar's daughter won't help to set Rozalia free, a few silver coins certainly will. That's the one truth Elina has learned from her father – money is the key to any lock.

Despite the cold prickling her nose and cheeks, her guilt is burning a hole in her chest. She doesn't stray too far out; she needs all her strength for the trip to the village. The willow bark and yarrow root Rozalia had slipped her moments before her father had burst into the hut and turned all their lives upside down has helped thicken her blood over the last couple of days and prevented further bleeding.

Elina returns to the courtyard and is sweeping the snow off her boots when she catches a familiar sound. One that sends an ice shard through her heart.

She can tell which boyar family is coming to visit just by the ring of their sleigh bell. Her ear has never failed her. Not her, who can play a tune on her *cobză* after only hearing it once.

This jingle belongs to her uncle's sleigh.

Pretending to go to the stable, Elina ducks into the garden shed where she grabs a coil of rope and hides it under her cape. She instructs the maid to tell her father that she's not feeling well and has gone to bed early. The moment she can hear her uncle's sleigh entering the courtyard, Elina shuts the door to her room, feeding the broom through the handle.

By the time the two men have finished their prolonged supper, and the house has finally succumbed to silence, Elina thinks it must be close to midnight. She waits a little longer so the two men can fall into a deeper sleep before she ties one end of the rope to the bed, thrusting the other out the window. She doesn't want to unbolt the door for fear her uncle may be lurking on the other side. She wraps herself in Ana's tattered cloak, grabs the rope and squeezes out through the small opening.

But this isn't as easy as she thought.

Her once strong arms can barely hold her weight as she starts climbing down. How is it possible to be so heavy after she's lost half her blood? Though the room is on the first floor, the window is high up and before she's even halfway down, her hands slip. The rope burns her palms and before she knows it, she's flailing her arms and tumbling to the ground.

Despite the pile of snow under the window cushioning her fall, the impact knocks the breath out of her. She lies there, jaws clenched, trying to ascertain the damage. The throbbing in her lower back makes her wheeze, but she's able to roll and sit up, reassuring herself there are no broken bones.

She stands up and staggers towards the stable, when a voice makes her reel back against the wall.

'So much for the reputation of a good boyar's daughter.'

She can't see him until a shadow breaks off the tree in front of her and grabs her arm.

'I'll let you go where you're about to go, but only after we're done,' her uncle growls in a low voice. 'We've got to make up for what we didn't finish last time.'

What's he doing out here? He must have been looking for a way to break into her room.

Elina tries to snatch her arm back, but her uncle twists it, bringing her to her knees. Her cries are muffled by his lardy paw as he fiddles with his fur-lined mantle, struggling to unbutton it with just one hand. Before he has time to lift his *anteriu*, someone is running towards them with an oil lamp and her uncle lets go, swearing under his breath.

'What's going on?' Neculai calls out. 'Is miss alright?'

'I caught her jumping out the window,' her uncle says. 'She tells us she's not well and then she tries to sneak out in the middle of the night. A secret lover perhaps?'

'I'll go wake master up,' Neculai says, but Elina won't be left alone with her uncle. She starts calling for her father at the top of her voice.

Dressed only in his nightshirt and slippers, her father lollops towards them.

'What in God's name are you doing, child?' He is angry and out of breath.

'Rozalia is no witch. You must tell me where she is, or I'll go find her myself.'

'You're out of your mind—'

'She's a wise woman who—'

Elina's words are cut short by a slap to her face. Her father has never raised his hand to punish her for anything. Not even when she plaited his beard once, while he was asleep, and then cut it to show him her beautiful work.

Her eyes refuse to focus, but she won't let them see her cry.

'It's alright, brother.' Her uncle steps between Elina and her father. 'The girl just misses her mother, hence befriending that witch. It will pass. Let her come live with my family for a little while. My wife will help to fill that anguish in her heart—'

'No!' Elina steps back.

'You lied to me,' her father says. 'You said you weren't well but—'

'I wasn't. I'm not.'

'You're well enough to jump out the window.'

'Look, brother, why don't I take her off your hands for a few months? My wife will look after her. And I'm certain my son would like to get better acquainted with his bride-to-be.'

'It might be for the best.' Her father nods.

'No, Father. Please don't.'

'I didn't ask for your permission.'

'If you make me go, I'll kill myself.'

Her uncle laughs. 'She's quite something, isn't she?'

Elina turns to face him. 'It's all your fault – all this has happened because of you. You forced yourself on me time and again. Rozalia was only trying to fix the consequence of that.' The words leap out of her mouth as if they have been hiding at the back of her throat, awaiting this opportunity.

'Oh, I see. Because threatening to kill yourself didn't work, now you're dragging me… You're sick in your head—'

'Quiet,' her father barks. He waves the servants away and grabs Elina's shoulder. 'What are you saying?' His voice is angry, but something in his tone reassures her that there isn't another slap coming her way. Not that she cares any longer.

'She's gone mad,' her uncle shouts. 'Just like her mother. You know what? Forget about my offer. I don't think I can take responsibility to look after her in this state of mind.'

'Hold up the oil lamp,' Elina tells her father and does something she never thought she'd have to do. She lifts her skirt and shows him her thighs, both of them marked with a string of bruises, some dark and old, a few freshly blossomed.

'She's a liar, a devious devil. What with her sneaking out in the middle of the night like that – anyone could have given her these—'

'*Uncle*' – she spits out the word – 'Bogdan has a red birthmark under his navel that looks like a big, disgusting bug.'

'Now this is… hold on…' Her uncle's words hang in the air. He makes to grab Elina, but her father charges at him, taking him to the ground. They grapple and roll over each other, throwing punches and swearing. Elina calls for Neculai, who appears immediately like he's been waiting for this to happen. He is followed by Bogdan's servant, who is holding a whip in his hand. The two of them pull the brothers apart.

'My daughter isn't just another thing I own which you can help yourself to. You've been stealing from me one way or another since we were just boys. But laying your hands on my daughter like she's some gypsy harlot… It's unforgivable. They'll cut your nose off for this.'

'If we go to court. But don't forget the public shame this will bring on your family. Why don't we settle it between us?'

Her father's mouth opens and closes, opens and closes. 'Fine, I'll wrestle you.'

'It's best if we do it with our bows and arrows. In the woods. Then we can pretend whoever gets injured has had a hunting accident.'

'No, Father, don't do it,' Elina pleads. Everyone knows which brother is the better archer.

Her father looks at her. 'And you… I'm afraid there's no option but to send you to the convent until you atone for your sin.' Though she's certain these harsh words are for the benefit of her uncle, Elina can't ignore their hurt.

To his brother, he says: 'Tomorrow at the crack of dawn. In the glade of the First Spring.'

MARKSMANSHIP

Her father's intention remains firm, leaving no room for change of mind or heart. How long will he send her to the convent for? Mira may well be married off to Barbu by the time she's let out again.

Elina's head spins, her sleep as wrecked as her honour. She gathers the blanket around her like a mantle and paces the room. Snow flurries dance out the window, their light and carefree whirl a mocking insult. Or perhaps a provocation?

There's no question about it. They can't wait until the next new moon to run away, as Mira suggested. They will have to do it imminently, or they may never see each other again.

But first they have to find out where Rozalia is locked and get her out. Sneaking away from the manor tonight is not an option. Judging by the creaking of the floors, the coughing, the opening and closing of the doors, she isn't the only one unable to sleep. Her father and uncle are equally restless, no doubt wondering which one of them will die tomorrow.

She can't let her uncle kill her father despite how much she hates him right now.

The house settles into a quiet spell just before dawn, and so does her mind, revealing a way which will set her free, and also fulfil her desire for vengeance against her uncle. She knows what she has to do.

Elina takes the oil lamp, which she has kept on a low flame, and tiptoes out of her bedroom, down the stairs, towards the armoury at the back of the house where her father keeps his hunting tools. She dips her fingers into the melted tallow and dabs at the hinges of the door to stop it from squeaking. Once inside, she heads straight to her father's quiver and replaces all his arrows with lighter ones which, due to their weight, will veer to the right of the target.

Cloaked in fur mantles and a heavy brooding, the two men leave the manor at first light, accompanied by their servants.

Elina is ready to follow suit. She has drunk the last of the willow bark and yarrow root from the batch Rozalia gave her. It's not much, but hopefully enough to prevent any possible bleeding from today's riding. She picks up the bundle she has prepared with a fistful of coins, as well as hers and her mother's jewellery, and on the way out of the house, she stops by her mother's room.

'I miss you so much,' she whispers.

She slings her mother's *cobză* over the other shoulder to where her quiver is and heads for the garden gate. The servants are awake, but caught up in their gossip about the boyars' skirmish from last night, they won't notice her disappearance.

Down the road from the manor, Elina turns for a last look at her home.

'Goodbye, my gilded gaol,' she says and prods Fulger into a gallop, aiming to arrive at the First Spring ahead of the men. But not before a quick diversion to the lake, where she buries her bundle of coins and jewellery next to the biggest rock on the shore, kicking the snow with her feet and digging the earth with the edge of her bow. They are safer in the ground than on her, until she and Mira have set Rozalia free and are ready to run away themselves.

The frosty air hurts her nose and Elina pulls her shawl right up to her eyes. She's looped the reins around her wrists and kneads her hands deep into her fur muffs to keep them warm. Frozen fingers won't do for the feat she's hoping to pull off.

When she arrives at the First Spring, the servants are marking the spots at the opposite ends of the ice-laden glade. The brothers are facing each other like two *zmei*, steam coming out of their nostrils.

Elina keeps out of sight as she tries to establish the best angle to hit her target. When she finds it, she remains astride and draws her bow. Fulger must have sensed her urgent stillness, for he too grows stiff.

There's a certain kind of hush in the snowy woods that is both desolate and equally charged. Teeming with unseen life sheathed in all this snow and ice. Elina can almost hear its subtle throb as she pulls back the string of her bow and holds her breath.

The two brothers also draw their bows and, as Neculai counts to three, Elina closes one eye and releases her arrow in time with the count. Her uncle's parted legs offer her an easy aim.

Her father's arrow whooshes past her uncle's left shoulder, getting stuck in the trunk of an oak tree on the other side of the glade. Her uncle's shaft lands on her father's right arm.

Yet both men cry out in pain at the same time.

Her father cradles his arm, his face distorted with confusion as he watches his brother lying on the ground with an arrow embedded in his crotch.

He'll live, Elina wants to say. But his seed won't, and that's what matters.

'There! She's right there!' Her uncle's servant is pointing at her.

A slight prod with her boot and Fulger springs to life, racing down the hill, towards the safe space of Rozalia's cellar. Riding bareback, she's a match to any male rider, and now she's also got a few moments' advantage over her pursuers, but just as she prepares to dismount at the edge of the woods, she looks over her shoulder to see her uncle's servant whipping his horse and hurtling towards her with the speed of a winged demon.

THE SECRET OF SOFT WOOD

The village elders have found Rozalia guilty of witchcraft, accusing her of performing black magic with Elina's blood. She is to be burned at the stake the following Sunday.

Mira goes about her chores like a shadow, her hands and feet doing what they do daily – fetching water from the well, cooking, changing the straw for their bedding, teasing or spinning wool – while her mind and heart do their own thing.

She returns to Rozalia's cellar every night the moment her father starts snoring, each time hoping to find Elina there. She needs her help in order to set Rozalia free. Doors forever locked to a peasant open freely to those of Elina's ilk. But the twigs Mira places on the cellar's trapdoor to tell her if someone has lifted it in her absence remain undisturbed each time.

She realises with dread that she may have to do what Rozalia made her promise she would do if it came to it. She remembers the instructions perfectly and, with a heavy heart, commences the preparations.

The night before Rozalia's punishment, Mira takes a bundle of food to the elders' cellar where the old woman is being guarded by Simion, the skinner's son. He is reluctant to take the food, but when Mira shows him it's only a loaf of mouldy bread, he snorts: 'Thought you were kinder 'an that. Not much charity in yer heart to give some'un such rot.'

'You'd be scoffing it yourself if it was any better.' Mira smiles and sighs with relief.

A village elder might have guessed the power of mould in rye bread but not Simion, and Mira praises the Old Gods for their grace.

She snuffed the oil lamp hours ago and has been kneeling in darkness all this time, whispering incantations like Rozalia taught her. The blizzard has been raging throughout the night and shows no sign of abating, but it won't stop Mira from carrying out her promise.

At the rooster's first crow, she unrolls the bundle of male clothing Rozalia gave her and which she has hidden under layers of straw. She gathers her skirt around her waist, pulls the *ițari* on, tucks her hair under the oversized hat and slips into the boots, which fit her with her own *opinci* strapped to her feet. She needs to wear her own clothing too, in case things go wrong and she has to shed her disguise quickly.

Her father's snores assure her of his deep slumber. Mira checks the wax cork on the water jug and, happy with its tight seal, she hides it in the sleeve of her sheepskin. Stuffing her mittens with the hot beets kept by the hearth throughout the night, she sneaks out of the hut.

Outside, there is a whirlwind of white that has blotted out the world, and she's glad for it. It covers her tracks and more importantly – it may save Rozalia.

She fetches the armfuls of pine twigs – softwood, Rozalia said – which she's kept out of sight behind the latrine and which she's doused with water for the past three days. She tops them with a few dry ones and straps the bundle on her sledge, the easier to carry it to the village square. She waxed the runners last night and the sledge moves with the slightest of tugs, following her with the eagerness of a summoned dog.

The blizzard tries to push her back, but she leans into its fury, glad for the weight of the sledge and the male clothes, which stop her from being plucked off the ground. The hat keeps slipping over her eyes and Mira wishes she'd layered it with a tuft of wool, but it's too late now. It may be for the best anyway – the less of her face showing, the better.

Soon she doesn't know where she is any longer, thinking she's trapped in a giant snowball, walking in circles. It angers her that a blizzard can wipe her senses like that. She's walked these roads for fifteen years; she can do it with her eyes closed. But it's different in a snowstorm and her feet act like spooked horses refusing to move. Yet it's not the storm wedging fear in her heart. She's listened to its whistles and whooshes each winter, knowing its eerie song is but a lullaby the Old Gods are singing.

She grasps tighter at the beets in her mittens to fend off the cold as she brushes the snow off the fence she's holding on to. Thanks to the rye stalks woven through the boughs, she recognises the broom-maker's house, meaning she's only around the corner from the village square.

Mira shuffles onwards until she spots blurred figures in sheepskins bustling about. Some of them are fixing the stake, others are binding a makeshift roof over the piles of straw and firewood to be kept dry from the blizzard.

She stops, not so much to catch her breath, as from the sudden dread uncoiling in her belly. They'll bring Rozalia here when the church bell rings after the morning service.

Despite the thump in her chest, Mira pulls at the sledge and heads towards the elders. She greets the first one and points at her load. 'More firewood to burn the witch. It's dry and ready to go,' she says in the harshest voice she can muster.

The elder takes a quick look and grunts approval. 'Over there, young man.' He waves her towards the clapboard. 'Drop it with the rest. Make sure it's out of the snow.'

Such relief to be called a young man that she almost drops the jug of water clasped under her arm.

Once she's under the makeshift roof and out of the elders' sight, Mira takes the jug out of her sleeve and sprinkles the water over the straw and woodchips to be used for the kindling of the fire. Rozalia had said, 'Not too much that the wood doesn't burn, but enough to make it smoke beforehand. Lots of smoke.'

When the jug is empty, Mira piles her own wet load on top of the wood already there and hopes they will be the first the elders reach for when the time comes.

She walks away as quickly as trudging through snow in oversized boots allows, hiding her sledge in a ravine by the side of the road and aiming for the closest haystack. The blizzard comes to her aid as she burrows her way deeper into the pile of fodder, snatching the straw from her hands and flinging it towards the sky. When she's in, she frays the hay around the edge so that she can see the village square but not be seen herself. The beets are barely warm now and she rubs her hands as fast as she can to stop them from going numb. The furring of the straw around her keeps her warm and she feels like a large sheep with a thick layer of wool. She hums the chants Rozalia has asked for – a kind of last rites – though she's still hoping for a miracle.

The rolling murmur lulls her into a haze where there's no anger, no sadness – a place the blizzard will never reach, still and silent as the womb of the heart.

Shrill and unrelenting, the chime of the church bell startles Mira, hurling her awareness back to her surroundings. The earlier heavy snow has turned into a fine powder, as though some wicked baker is sifting flour from above. People spill into the village square almost immediately – they must've been waiting behind doors, eager to witness the gore.

Rozalia isn't dragged to the stake as Mira has feared. Two villagers are helping her walk, her arms around their shoulders as if they are old friends. Barefoot and dressed only in a long shirt, torn and smeared with dark stains, she looks weak, and Mira knows it's not with fear. Her head keeps dropping to her chest, but she lifts it up each time. Not even the whiteness of the swirling flakes can hide the blues and purples on Rozalia's face. Her usually neat plait is now unravelled, blowing about her head like a knot of restless snakes.

A wave of heat rises in Mira's belly, and she wants to unleash the howl that's growing too big for her chest. She reaches out of the haystack for a fistful of snow, which she rubs on to her face, and then another to stuff her mouth with. The relief doesn't last long before she grows short of breath again.

Rozalia's sudden bursts of laughter, erratic and out of place, bring a drop of joy to Mira's weeping heart. Simion has stayed true to his word and given Rozalia the mouldy rye bread Mira had so carefully prepared for her. She could've done with some of this medicine herself, but she only had enough for one, and Rozalia needed it more than her.

THE SOUND OF SILENCE

Still hiding in the haystack, Mira watches the gathered crowd with a combing glance, but Elina isn't in the village square. The bright russet of her squirrel furs would stand out amongst the dull rags of the peasants. Something or someone must have stopped her from coming. Has her health turned for the worse or has her father locked her up at the manor?

Whilst the elders nestle the firewood at the stake, the black-robed priest circles Rozalia with the hunger of a raven eager for his carrion. He preaches against heresy, his voice catching in his throat with anger as he points at Rozalia, calling her a witch who will burn in hell for all eternity.

Without any warning, he grabs her hair, twisting it around his wrist, and pulls out a pair of shears from the folds of his robe. He snips away at her locks with quick, sharp moves, the dark coils quivering in the snow like a bed of distressed eels.

When the priest is done with his sermon, the elders push Rozalia towards the stake where they tie her left foot – Satan's favoured side – both hands and neck. Only after checking the knots a second time does one of them give a grave nod while another lights the torch. Despite the elders' efforts, the damp wood smokes and smoulders for some time before it catches fire, and judging by Rozalia's tilted head, Mira knows she has fulfilled the old woman's wish. The fumes have lulled her into a deep sleep to be spared the pain of her melting flesh.

The smell of bacon is so convincing that for a moment, Mira thinks it's not Rozalia but a pig the villagers are roasting. She hasn't eaten in two days, her belly too tight for food. But instead of stirring her hunger, the whiff of pork crackling makes her want to throw up. Her body thrusts forward, but nothing comes up, save for a mouthful of briny bile.

Tears are slow to fill her eyes and she wonders if they've dried up during the past week, as she burned sage day and night, pleading with the Old Gods to save Rozalia. She had cried because she believed Rozalia could be saved, that she *would* be saved. But now she doesn't mourn Rozalia's death, for they don't believe in death or hell as the priest tells them to. She mourns her teacher's untimely departure, the injustice of it all, and the aching void she's left in Mira's heart.

She digs herself out of the haystack and joins the crowd in the village square, elbowing her way right to the front. The flames, leaping high into the sky, have bewitched the peasants and the priest alike, with everyone watching on, their mouths agape. Mira takes advantage of the momentary spell and shuffles from side to side, using her feet to gather as many of Rozalia's locks as she can reach. She squats as if to brush the snow off her boots and, stuffing the hair inside her sheepskin, she squeezes her way out before anyone can notice it. The priest will be looking for Rozalia's hair, to throw it in the fire and destroy every bit of the woman who has challenged his authority and faith.

Mira can't let that happen, for hair doesn't only preserve the memory and wisdom of its owner – it's also a mighty tool for those who know how to use it, a powerful link to someone's soul.

She stops briefly at the far end of the crowd to make sure no one is following her. Two elders are talking in hushed voices.

'I always knew the droughts were her fault,' one of them says. 'Just wait and see how rich the next harvest will be now that the witch is dead. Can't wait for the day I 'ave a full belly again.'

'We shoulda done this a lon' time ago. Before the witch could put her wicked spell on the boyar's daughter, poor thing—'

'She'll be a'right. They'll cast the devil outta her at the nunnery, you hear my word, they will.'

The nunnery? The words rumble around in Mira's mind.

The nunnery!

She wheezes white puffs of breath in the crispy air, the frost turning them into shards of ice, chiming as they fall to the ground.

She spends the afternoon in Rozalia's cellar, meticulously picking all bits of straw and woodchips out of the chopped hair before plaiting it into a tight braid. It's not to be washed or incensed, so that Rozalia's presence can be kept as strong as possible.

When Mira leaves, she sees the earlier snow clouds have peeled away. The unforgiving glare of the moon spreads a sheen on the frozen snow, making the entire village glitter and sparkle as though it's been encrusted with broken glass.

And the silence of it all! The hush of a world smothered by snow. Closing her eyes, Mira kneels and listens to it, for silence is an altogether different sound.

INN OF INIQUITY

Elina is leaving for the Blessed Virgin convent, a day's ride away from the manor. No amount of pleading with her father has made any difference. 'The sooner you atone for your sins, the sooner you can return home,' he has told her, without explaining what that means, or how long it will take.

She watches her father give Stefan, the priest's apprentice and her sleigh driver on this journey, a scroll with strict instructions to be handed to Mother Superior. Stefan tucks it carefully in the pouch hanging from his sash. How much is her father offering to pay? she wonders. She must find a way to get rid of the scroll before they reach the convent. That way the nuns won't take her in, and she will come back home.

Elina is helped into the sleigh by Ana, who carries her bag, and who now, due to Stefan's presence, is to act as her chaperone as well as her maid until she arrives at the convent.

Her father turns his back and closes the gate before the sleigh has even pulled away. Tears prick Elina's eyes, but the sharp easterly wind stops them from rolling down her cheeks.

The sleigh glides through the wintry woods, only the sweep of the runner blades audible on the crisp snow, and the tinkle of the bells. The sky is heavy with the burden of more snow. Is there a blizzard on its way?

Ana, who sits at Elina's feet, starts humming to herself.

'Keeps me warm, miss,' she says. It strikes Elina how young the maid really is, despite being a mother many times over.

'Come up here.' Elina taps the spot next to her on the bench.

'Oh no, miss, I'm a'right,' the maid says, looking over her shoulder at Stefan.

She can't be alright, not in that tattered sheepskin, when Elina is bundled up in a squirrel fur coat and muffs and with a bearskin over her lap and can still feel the frost biting into her flesh.

'Sitting next to each other will keep me warmer too.'

Ana hesitates.

'Come now, I'm freezing.' Elina exaggerates the admonishing in her voice.

Ana makes to stand up, but her legs give way and Elina helps her crawl onto the bench. She shifts closer to the maid and tucks the other end of the bearskin tight under her slight frame.

They pass by a couple of sleepy villages, separated by long stretches of woods. The maid's humming helps to soothe Elina's anguish as her mind churns with questions. When will she see Mira again? What will happen to Rozalia? Could she run away from the convent if they don't let her out?

The whistle of the wind grows louder and the trees sway to its song.

'How much longer?' she asks. 'The sky will burst open at any moment.'

'Before nightfall, with any luck,' Stefan says, flogging the horses harder.

'They haven't got wings, you know,' Elina snaps, questioning the compassion of this future priest. Though Stefan doesn't acknowledge her words, he lowers his whip.

The trees are thinning out ahead and, as they pass a roadside inn, Elina notices Stefan crossing himself three times and saying a prayer in his beard. She thinks he's observing the evening hour of the *vecernie*, but something in Stefan's eyes, as he turns to look back at the inn, tells her his prayers aren't to do with the church service.

'Why don't we stop for a break at the inn?' she asks, watching him closely. 'We could all do with warming up and getting a little rest.'

Stefan says something, but his words are blasted over her head. The wind is wailing now, the trees shaking and rocking like distressed mourners.

'Looks like the blizzard is upon us. We better go back to the inn.' Elina has to shout to make sure he can hear her.

'It's not an inn, but a devil's den, miss. Seething with vices.'

'How's that?'

'Gypsy harlots. Snaking their hips to pagan tunes… Ripping honest men out of their coins… Not right for the eyes and ears of—'

'I don't care, so long as the place has a roof and a fire to take the chill out of my bones.'

'We're not far from the convent now.'

The words have hardly left Stefan's lips when the sky bursts open and snowflakes the size of goose feathers fall thick and fast, wiping out the world around them.

'We'll get lost.' Elina stands up.

'The convent is very close.'

'You're even closer and I can hardly see you. I think my father would rather I lodged in a devil's den than die in a snowstorm. If your common sense has frozen, I will take the reins myself.' She leans forward and pulls at his sleeve.

Stefan, crossing himself fervently, turns the horses around. By the time they make it to the inn, the blizzard is whipping at them without mercy.

As the stablehand meets them to receive the horses, Elina is already on her way into the inn, not waiting for Stefan, who has stopped on the porch to whisper more prayers. She pushes the door open and halts as loud music smacks her in the face. The room is crowded with men of all ages, some with daggers hanging off their hips, or axes resting by their feet like loyal pets. A few lightly dressed women, their hair loose around their shoulders, glide about the room, sweet-talking the bearded brutes or perching on their laps around the fire. Smoke, sweat, and something that reminds Elina of her uncle, clogs her nose, and she breathes through her mouth to stop from retching.

The clamour in the inn dips as all eyes turn to her and Ana. Even the fiddler and the flute player pause mid-song. The men's stares are wild and hungry, while the women's flash with a glint of rivalry and threatened pride.

'This is the daughter of Boyar Constantin Pogor.' Stefan barges in and steps in front of Elina, as though to protect her from a pack of wild dogs. 'I expect you to treat her with all due respect, or you'll encounter the wrath of her father's sword,' he says and, dropping a few coins on the counter, he ushers Elina up a rickety staircase.

'How come you know the layout of the inn so well?' she asks.

His hesitation is brief, but enough to tell Elina what his words won't. 'I saw the stairs and took a guess.'

The attic is dark and even more stuffy than the room below. The hay-covered floor is strewn with the tattered mantles and coats marking the bedding of those who arrived at the inn earlier, their oily filth catching the low flicker of the *opaiț*.

Ana gets busy, unfurling Elina's bearskin in the furthest corner of the room, and next to it, she spreads her own sheepskin.

'Go get some supper for you and your mistress,' Stefan instructs the maid, 'but I'm not to be disturbed in my prayers. Goodnight.' With that, he turns his back on them and kneels by the icon of Jesus, hanging precariously on the eastern wall and framed with an embroidered cloth that once would have been white.

Ana returns with two bowls of cabbage broth and stale bread. Elina hardly touches her food even when the maid has finished hers.

'You can have mine too,' Elina says. 'I'm not hungry.'

Ana doesn't wait to be asked twice, slurping away and wiping the two bowls clean with the last of the bread.

They both lie down, and judging by Ana's breath, she must have fallen asleep the moment she closed her eyes – a miracle really, given the jollity downstairs. Elina waits for Stefan to follow suit when he's done with his prayers. Then she can finally reach for that scroll in the leather pouch.

The musicians change from a traditional folk song to an exuberant Turkish *pestref*. This must be what Stefan meant earlier by pagan tunes, because anything foreign, especially coming from the Turks, is seen as a threat to Christianity. As though to confirm this, the young priest, still facing the wall with the icon, increases the speed and urgency of his prayers.

There's another sound she picks up on. Barely audible at first but growing ever bolder with each stroke of the fiddle. It's the unmistakable clicking of coins. However, it's too harmonious and in tune with the music, too measured to be a random pouring of money. Elina tiptoes towards the hatch of the attic, where she kneels to peek into the room below her.

At first, she glimpses a pair of bare feet – tiny and delicate, yet skilful in their movement. As the dancer glides forward, Elina realises what the mysterious sound is. Save for the dark *şalvari* tightened at her ankles and the cropped scarlet blouse revealing her tiny waist, the slave woman is covered in gold. Three strands of coins are wrapped around her hips and another one adorns her forehead, her slithering arms glittering with bracelets elbow-high. The dancer moves with an enchanting jingle as she loops and twirls amongst the tables, thrusting her hips with a precision and grace that only years of practice could achieve.

None of the men make any attempts to touch the dancer, and soon Elina finds out why. The drunken merchant who throws his fat purse at her feet and tries to grope her is dragged outside by two burly men, who take their time to come back.

The dancer carries on unaffected. While her hips are fiery with a life of their own, her eyes – circled with thick kohl – watch the world from a far-off place.

When she flicks her eyes up suddenly and their gazes meet

over the lip of the hatch, a cold arrow shoots through Elina's shoulders, and she pushes herself away from the edge, her heart pounding like she's done something wrong. She immediately regrets it – a boyar's daughter can't be intimidated by a slave – but it's too late to undo it.

When the music stops, Elina, who is now back peering over the edge of the opening, can see the dancer walking slowly, fluidly towards the side of the bar, disappearing through the exit with a blanket for a door.

The noise and clatter resume, and Stefan raises his voice: 'Walk in the Spirit, and you shall not fulfil the lust of the flesh… For he who sows to his flesh, will of the flesh reap corruption, but he who sows to the Spirit, will of the Spirit reap everlasting life… Resist the devil and he will flee from you. Draw near to God and He will draw near to you. Cleanse your hands, you sinners; and purify your hearts…' The rest of his words are drowned in men's laughter and hooting.

Wishing for some quiet, Elina wonders if there are any rooms beyond the blanketed doorway the dancer slipped through earlier. Checking that Stefan still has his back to her, she climbs down from the attic, and under the stare of the more sober men, she approaches the innkeeper, who is lining up tumblers brimming with frothy beer. She whispers to him that she can't sleep and is looking for a quiet corner. But he shrugs, and without asking for his permission, she walks past him, straight to the door that's so inviting. She pulls the blanket aside and slips through, entering a pitch-dark hallway, save for the weak glow at the other end. Hands stretched out for balance, she tiptoes ahead, but when she hears men's voices coming out of the room where the candle is burning, Elina swivels on her heels and turns back.

'They are leaving,' a woman calls out in a sing-song voice. 'You may come in.'

Elina freezes to the spot. Is that the slave woman talking to her? Must be, for all the inn women are busy with customers. But how does she know? Elina hasn't made any noise…

Two shadows grow out of the open door – the burly men, who dealt with the drunken merchant earlier, open the door wide to let her in.

'Don't get on the wrong side of her.' One of them winks at Elina. 'Her curse is sharper than an axe's blade.'

Elina squeezes against the wall to let them pass and waits a few moments to steady her breath before walking into the room.

The slave dancer is sitting cross-legged on a pile of cushions on the floor, sipping from a silver cup.

'So… Why is the daughter of a boyar seeking out a slave like me?'

'I can't sleep. It's too noisy in the attic.'

The woman stares at her. 'Just like the rest of them, aren't you? Eager to flaunt your freedom and power to someone like me.'

'Not at all… it's just… you dance beautifully,' Elina says. 'It's hard to believe you're forced to do it.'

'I'm dancing from the heart – true – but that's because I've never had a choice to start with. It's all been decided at my birth. A gypsy is a slave, and slaves are at their owners' whim.'

'You're not like any slave I've ever seen.' Elina takes in the dancer's hands and feet, so well looked after that she could easily pass as someone from her own class.

'There's obvious slavery, and then there's cunning slavery.' The woman takes another sip from her cup. 'Anyway, I don't envy you your freedom. One cannot miss what one never had.' She pours herself another drink and, as an afterthought, she decants a second cup, handing it to Elina, who recognises the smell at once. It's the drink her father praises for its power to "summon happiness".

'I'm alright, thank you,' she says.

'It's a miraculous drink. The secret is to know when to stop.'

'Really, I'm—'

'Talking of freedom… maybe I'm the one who's got more of it. I do what I love doing – dancing and stirring men's passions, bathing in their mad adoration for me. I hold all the power, for they can never touch me. What about you? How much say do you have in what happens to you?'

Elina accepts the silver cup and sits on the cushions next to the slave. She's right – despite their class differences, their circumstances aren't that much different.

One tiny sip sends an arrow of fire down her throat, burning her misery as well as her gut.

'I'm Elina. What's your name?'

'Dafina.' The dancer raises her cup. 'Here's to good health and a full belly. Freedom is secondary and only as important as we make it to be.'

But after a few more sips, Dafina's assurance dwindles. The earlier pride Elina saw in her eyes is gradually replaced by a sorrow, old and deep, which she tries to drown with another cupful.

'You can kip here, if it's too noisy out there.'

'I think I better go back. The priest may notice my absence,' Elina says, even though she hopes Stefan is fast asleep by now so she can get that scroll from him.

'Ah, I know his kind. The pious ones are the most rotten,' Dafina says. 'He knows the moment he stops praying, he'll end up in the arms of those loving women you saw earlier. What he doesn't know is that he's fighting a losing battle. The demands of the flesh break the mind of even the strongest of men. But he's young. He'll live and learn.'

'You're not so much older yourself.'

'Some of us live by the count of years, others by our trials.'

The dancer's pithy comment reminds Elina of Rozalia, and with a twinge of sadness, she gets up from the cushions.

'Wait.' Dafina stops her. 'You can't visit a gypsy and not have your fortune told. Give me your left hand.'

Elina offers her palm and Dafina takes it close to her face. A smile flutters on her lips.

'Something funny?' Elina asks.

'Life is,' the slave says as she turns Elina's palm one way and another, the better to catch the glow of the oil lamp.

'What do you see?'

'Good news. You'll have a quiverful of children.'

This is certainly *not* good news. It's great to know that she won't end up a nun for the rest of her life, but the thought of marrying and having 'a quiverful of children' makes her teeter with its weight. What about Mira? Won't they get to run away together like they've planned? But she knows better than to ask a gypsy such questions.

'Thank you,' Elina says and turns to leave.

'Thanks are good, but words don't fill my belly. Nor do they keep me warm in winter.'

Elina gets the drift. 'I've been banished to a nunnery. I have no valuables on me.'

'You heard about the power of my curse.'

Fearing any more bad luck, Elina hastens to pull the amber charm Rozalia gave her to ward off evil and which Mira not only tied around her neck, but begged Elina not to remove. It hasn't worked against her uncle, but Dafina doesn't know that.

'Here, you can have this,' she says, tugging at the gem.

Dafina's eyes shine at the sight of the precious stone, but as she comes closer for a better look, she shakes her head. 'I'm no gypsy for nothing. I know a spell when I see one. A lucky charm for you, I must say, but harmful to anyone else who may touch it, or – God forbid – wear it. You're one very fortunate soul,' Dafina says, taking Elina's hands into hers and giving them a light squeeze.

First, she read her palm wrong – all those children she mentioned earlier. Now this. *Lucky charm, my eye*, Elina thinks. Dafina is as much a fortune teller as Elina is lucky. But she keeps her mouth shut – the gypsy curse may still be real, if nothing else is.

'Go in peace, sister.' Dafina bows. She didn't do it when they met. It's probably that fiery drink getting the best of her judgement, yet Elina returns the gesture just as earnestly.

Walking back to the attic, she treads carefully, so as not to step on the arms or legs of those lying about, drunk or asleep. The earlier music has been replaced with snoring and heavy wheezing. A man grunts somewhere in the dark and a woman moans. A few others huddle by the counter, talking over each other and arguing over something they won't remember in the morning.

In the attic, Stefan is so still that Elina thinks he's finally fallen asleep, even though he's kneeling. Perhaps he can sleep upright, like horses. She makes her way towards him, and just as she leans in to check, he stirs and stretches his back, resuming his prayers.

Elina breaks into an angry whisper. 'Those men are all asleep. Listen to their peaceful snores. They've all forgotten about their sins, but you… You're still holding on to them in your mind.'

'In my prayers.'

'Same thing.'

'It's not befitting a boyar's daughter to talk like that. I've sinned just bringing you here. 'Tis an evil place, and the nature of evil is such that it goes straight for the soul of the innocent.'

Doesn't he know why her father has sent her to the nunnery?

'An inn of iniquity. A demons' den. A pit of snakes.' Stefan makes the sign of the cross and commences the Lord's Prayer. Again.

The fool is going to stay up all night – there's no way she can retrieve the scroll from him. And once the nuns see it tomorrow – a promise of generous remuneration, no doubt – Elina won't be going home any time soon. She'll have to find a way to escape before Mira is married off to Barbu. She must do everything she can to avoid the fate the gypsy has glimpsed in her palm.

A quiverful of children, a quiverful of children…

The floor is too hard, the air too heavy – with unwashed bodies, with snores, with groans and giggles – and the dawn finds Elina staring at the beams in the ceiling, a pounding headache splitting her skull.

ARRIVAL

The following morning there are many puffy, hung-over faces shuffling about the inn, but none as weary and tormented as Stefan's.

As soon as the innkeeper and a few men claim the door from the mound of snow burying it from the other side, people start leaving, most of them by foot, others riding, or in sleighs. Elina looks around, but there's no sight of Dafina. She has either left or is still asleep, or else Elina has dreamt her up.

Once in the sleigh, only the maid chats away, but sensing the gloomy mood, Ana soon falls silent too. The blizzard has swept drifts of snow all over the woods, making them look like stooped huts where fairies may live. The snow is too soft and thick to allow for any speed, and the horses struggle to make headway.

Elina kicks her feet together to get some life into them, but they hurt more than they warm up. Stefan's cry startles her.

'There it is.' He indicates somewhere ahead, but Elina can see nothing except more snow-laden trees.

Ana points out a sooty smudge in the sky. 'A chimney is puffing nearby, miss. It'll be warm where you're going.'

The sleigh bells must have alerted the nuns to their arrival. When they reach the convent's imposing wooden gate, two nuns in long habits are ready to greet them. Stefan has a quick word with the older one – who Elina guesses is the abbess, judging by her round, stiff head cover – and hands her the scroll from his leather pouch. The abbess nods as soon as she lays her eyes on it.

'Send my gratitude to Boyar Constantin and assure him his daughter will be well looked after.'

Stefan bows and jumps back into the sleigh. Elina says goodbye to Ana, who whispers in her ear. 'Don't worry, miss. Your father loves you more than he loves his horses and that says something. He'll come for you soon enough, you'll see.'

Elina watches the sleigh wind its way back into the woods, with Ana waving, until it disappears over the hillock. Her father has sent her far from home to punish her, as if the abuse she has endured has been her fault. She feels worthless, discarded like a broken pot. The injustice of it all feeds the rage sweeping through her, and she's about to break into a sprint after the sleigh when the abbess steps in front of her.

'That way, young lady.' She points behind Elina, towards the convent. Her voice is kind and unhurried, reminding Elina of Rozalia, whose gaze cradled the same unbounded patience. What have they done with Rozalia? she wonders but doesn't dare follow her thoughts. Rozalia's fate is a burden she'll have to carry for the rest of her days.

'Do you need a hand with your bag?' asks the younger nun.

Elina squeezes her belongings closer to her chest. The few changes of clothes and her mother's *cobză* are the only things to remind her of home.

The younger nun bolts the gate as soon as they are on the other side. The abbess turns to Elina. 'This is a holy place you've come to. It's the outcome of a vision I had as a sixteen-year-old girl, when our Lord Jesus Christ poured His light onto this piece of land, calling for a monastery to be built. I hope you appreciate what a privilege it is to be here.' The abbess pauses, no doubt growing impatient with Elina's reticence. But her eyes are too heavy with unspilled tears to raise and meet the nun's gaze.

'I am Mother Superior. You can call me Reverend

Mother.' She turns to the younger nun. 'Sister Alexandra will show you around now. Meet me at the refectory when you're done.' The abbess walks away, one end of the scroll peeking out of her sleeve.

As soon as the abbess is out of earshot, Elina, who is already thinking about how to escape this place, asks Sister Alexandra in a small voice:

'Why all the bolts and latches on the gate? I didn't think nuns had anyone to fear.'

'It's not to stop people from coming in,' the nun says, confirming Elina's fears.

They walk down a path guarded by a straight line of trees on each side.

'Aren't you here of your own will?' Elina asks.

'I am. Many of us are. But some aren't. Like you, for example.'

Elina is startled by the nun's keen observation. 'What makes you think I'm not?'

'A hunch.' Sister Alexandra looks at her sideways.

'I'm not here to stay. It's just a temporary—'

'Things change—'

'Not in my case.'

'And they don't always change with our own accord. Unknown are the works of the Holy Spirit. These are the sisters' cells.' The nun points to a cluster of whitewashed huts on the left, with tiny doors and slits for windows.

'How many sisters live here?' she asks, wanting to know how many pairs of eyes will be watching her every move.

'Twenty-six. The youngest is thirteen and the oldest eighty-seven. And see that hut over there' – the nun waves to the right – 'that's the priest's abode.'

'But this is a—'

'Every convent requires the services of a priest to celebrate the Divine Liturgy. And Father Arcady was here from the start. He helped Mother Superior, herself a boyar's daughter once, to build this place.'

The nun takes Elina to the other side of the church to show her where the kitchen, laundry and refectory are. 'And over there, behind everything else, is the *bolniță*, for any injuries or medicine.'

A familiar scent tingles Elina's nostrils. Worn leather and manure – the unmistakable smell of a stable. She takes a deep breath for the first time since she's arrived.

'Where are the horses?'

The nun stops. 'How did you know?'

'A hunch,' Elina says with a knowing look. 'I'd like to see them.'

'After Mother Superior inspects your bag. She's waiting for us at the refectory.'

They pass a small cemetery strewn with a handful of graves. The enclosed space at the top end, surrounded by shrubs, looks much bigger and better tended than the rest of the graves.

'It's Mother Superior's lot for when her soul departs this world,' Sister Alexandra says as if guessing her unvoiced question.

Elina stops, frowning in confusion at the nun.

'I know it must seem strange to you,' Sister Alexandra says. 'Our life is just a preparation for death, but not many people want to see the truth. They much prefer to fool themselves.'

Elina thinks this must be a very boring place if planning for death and tending to their future graves is how they choose to spend their time. This is no place for her. She'll run away at the first opportunity.

They enter a shed with a long wooden table in the middle and two rows of benches on each side. The abbess is sitting at the top end of the table, underneath a huge icon of the Virgin Mary.

'Welcome to our community,' she says.

She's right. The nunnery is a community, like a village almost. It's got everything a self-contained *obște* may need: a church for worship, land to grow food and keep animals, a couple of wells for fresh water, a nearby stream for fishing, large orchards stretching out at the back, and even a cemetery. But like all communities, surely this too must have its secrets. Elina wonders what they might be.

'This is where you say, *Thank you, Reverend Mother*,' the abbess prompts her.

'Thank you, Reverend Mother.'

'Before you're shown to your cell, I have to check your bag. I know what boyars' daughters are like. I was one myself a long time ago,' she says and unties the rope to Elina's bag.

The abbess tuts as she pulls out the *cobză*. 'Now, this I did not expect. Mirrors, jewellery – yes – but not this. Where did you think you were coming to?'

'It was my mother's.'

'This is a convent, not an inn. I'll keep it for you—'

'I won't play it, I promise. I just want to hold it—'

'This might be the first lesson you need to learn. Detachment from all worldly possessions. Your devotion to our Lord is all you should be thinking about while you're here. No distractions.'

'Reverend Mother… please…'

'Lesson number two – you don't haggle or question my decisions. You nod and do what you're told. Show me you understand.'

Elina hesitates, but something tells her that getting on the wrong side of the abbess won't make things easy for her.

'I do, Reverend Mother.'

'Excellent!' She rummages through the rest of Elina's bag. 'I see you've been sensible enough to bring austere clothes. You can keep the dark-coloured garments, but I'll take your fur coat and muffs. They're out of place here.'

'Coldest winter in five years—'

'Then you'll have to pray harder. The more intense the fire of your devotion, the warmer you'll keep.' The abbess holds her arms out, prompting Elina to remove her warm garments. In return, she's given a black habit and a headscarf.

'That'll be all for now. Make sure you have an early night tonight. The days here start at the crack of dawn.' The abbess gathers the things she's robbed Elina of and glides out of the refectory, her own habit swaying to reveal a trim of sable fur on the hem of her underskirt.

The hermit cell Elina is shown to is half the size of a servant's room at home. Judging by the two wooden benches lining the opposite walls, she is to share this cramped space with the young nun praying in the corner of the room. She doesn't acknowledge Elina, who's standing in the doorway, unsure what to do with herself.

The narrow window hardly allows any daylight in. A weak *opaiț* flickers on the windowsill, guttering occasionally from the wind blowing in through the cracks. The straw on the floor has been raked over to the other side, leaving only a handful to cover the clay by Elina's bed. She notices two grooves in the ground. Marks from prolonged kneeling. She wonders whose they are. Two wicker baskets are propped against the bottom of the beds, one of them with some folded clothes.

The nun stirs in the corner and stands up too quickly, causing her legs to fold under her.

'Rock back and forth a couple of times, then rest a little on your heels,' Elina says, sharing the helpful tip she learned from Rozalia. 'It helps to avoid pins and needles.'

The nun tries it. 'It works. Thank you.' She sounds surprised. 'You must be a devout Christian who prays a lot. Thank you, Lord, for sending me a pious soul this time.' She brings her palms together in praise.

'This time?' Elina asks.

'I'm Sister Katerina. What's your name?'

'Elina—' she says, shivering with cold.

The nun reaches for the two ragged sheepskins hanging on a nail by the door and hands one to Elina. 'Don't worry, Mother Superior isn't as harsh as she seems. She gives us *cojoace* and woolly socks,' she says, putting on the second coat. 'I'm off to the *cuhnia*. It's my turn to cook supper this evening. Hope you like beetroot soup.'

'Whose knee marks are these?' Elina points to the two small dips in the ground.

Sister Katerina clears her throat. 'The previous sister's.'

'Where is she now?'

'She's with our Lord.'

The words are spoken lightly, but their meaning spills dread in her heart: people don't get to leave this place. They die here.

'What happened to her?' she asks, trying to keep her voice steady.

'A tormented soul, but she's at peace now.'

'How did she die?'

Sister Katerina makes the sign of the cross three times and walks out, the wind slamming the door behind her.

With a flutter in her heart, Elina looks about the room, turning round and round, dreading that she might spot the dead woman's ghost lurking in the shadows.

She has to get out of this spooky cell. And she knows exactly where she wants to go.

Elina glances out the window to make sure there's nobody about. She doesn't fancy bumping into anyone. Hopefully, the frost will keep the nuns indoors, wherever they are. Looking at the snow, Elina wonders how they are expected to keep warm, since she can't see a fireplace anywhere in the room. The huts belonging to the priest and the abbess are the only ones with smoking chimneys. And the kitchen. That's a little relief. She'll heat up beets on the hearth, like she's seen Rozalia and Mira do, and sneak them out to keep her warm at night.

She pulls the wick of the *opaiț* further out to increase the flame and rubs her hands above it.

Taking advantage of the empty courtyard, Elina leaves the cell and hurries towards the place that's calling her. The stable.

The wooden enclosure is not just for horses. It's shared with five cows, a dozen sheep and a flock of chickens.

She approaches the three horses from the side, to alert them to her presence, and lets them sniff her hands before she pets them. The auburn mare takes the longest to warm up to Elina, but when she blows gently at the mare's nostrils, she seems pleased, sealing their friendship by nuzzling Elina's hair.

This affectionate touch – its warmth and tenderness – unravels Elina. She slides to the ground, kneeling, as the tears she's been holding back finally push through her eyes, washing down her cheeks. She brings her hands to her face to soften the sobs rising in her throat. The deep shame of her uncle's abuse and her father's unfairness on top of that, his brutal banishment, have built a wild fire scorching her insides.

The mare leans in with a gentle nudge and Elina looks up through blurry eyes.

'Thank you,' she says. 'I'll stop crying now. I'll stop crying and start thinking. I have to get away from here, and very soon.'

The mare brings her face closer to Elina's, and she knows – in sharing their breath, the mare shows support for her decision.

Remembering her earlier exchange with Sister Katerina, Elina thinks how much easier it is to communicate with animals. They perceive the world in silence, and they're never wrong.

Words are useless tools if you're digging for truth, she thinks. They lie, deceive and distort. Only in the absence of words can there be truth.

That's why people talk, because they have something to hide.

JOURNEYS

Since the blizzard before Elina's arrival at the nunnery three days ago, the weather has been stable. This means the snow still bears the marks of the sleigh which brought her here. All she needs to do is follow the road back to the inn and ask for help there. She needs to act before the next snowfall because even though she could still follow the road in fresh snow, it would be a lot harder and much more time consuming.

However, Elina has the unmistakable feeling she's being watched. At all times.

Sister Katerina stays up praying until Elina falls asleep and when she opens her eyes in the morning, the nun is already awake. She never finds herself alone for a moment. The nuns seek to keep her company, to ease her into life at the convent and help her settle here.

All this attention is not only smothering, but it's interfering with her exploration of the grounds and any potential ways to escape they might hide.

To succeed with her plan, Elina realises she must make the nuns believe that she is settling in smoothly, that she enjoys being here. She must pretend so well and so convincingly that she could almost believe it herself. Only then will the nuns drop their guard and stop following her every move.

Life at the convent runs by a rigid routine. Each day starts with solitary prayers at the crack of dawn, when one of the nuns rings the tower bell loud enough to raise the dead, never mind the living. They all gather in the chapel for the morning service, after which the day is spent in a flurry of hard work: cooking, baking, cleaning, sewing, doing the laundry and looking after the animals. They are not allowed back to their cells until after the evening service, again followed by lengthy prayers.

'This is such a busy place in winter. I can only imagine what it must be like the rest of the year,' Elina says to Sister Katerina one evening as they get ready for bed.

'The nunnery's estate has a dozen gypsy slaves who live just beyond the apple orchard,' the nun says, 'but we've all got to roll up our sleeves and contribute to our community. Working together not only strengthens the spirit of our sisterhood, but it helps to blunt our horns too, for we all have caprices of our own.'

The way the nun looks at Elina when she says *caprices* reminds her how much effort is required to fool the nuns.

'I'm an only child and I've always missed not having siblings. The sisterhood I've found here is the answer to my prayers,' Elina says, her eyes watering from a supressed yawn. Perhaps taking this as a sign of upset, Sister Katerina softens.

'Mighty is the Lord and His love for us. I'm glad to hear you've learned the wonders of faith and devotion.'

'Praise the Lord,' Elina says and tucks into bed, pulling the sheepskin coat over the blanket for added warmth.

Facing the wall, she lies wide awake. Sister Katerina will certainly report their conversation to the abbess, which Elina hopes will help strengthen the lie she lives outwardly each day. She has identified the gate as the best way of getting out of the convent, because the number of bolts would make it easier to scale and climb over than the fortress-like walls surrounding the grounds. Now she just needs the nuns to stop watching her.

Elina does her best to blend in. She reads from the book of Psalms, attends each service and mucks in with chores. The nights, however, are riddled with sleepless hours when the guilt about Rozalia tears her to pieces.

The only respite in this place is when she thinks of Mira. She likes to indulge in details of how they are going to make a home together in a town where nobody will know them. Pretending to be orphan sisters, as Mira suggested, will provide them with the necessary cover to be together the way they want.

The promise of such a future is what keeps Elina warm at night – alongside the hot beets she steals from the kitchen – and what gives her strength to get through the day.

Until one dawn when, during her ablutions, Elina realises the glaring fault of their plan: two young women living on their own will lead to unwanted attention, depriving them of the peace and secrecy required to live their love unhindered.

She must think of something else. There must be another way.

The first time Elina meets Father Arcady, she takes him for a shepherd from the mountains, like the ones she's seen at the Sunday bazaars – tall and weathered, the skin on his friendly face tanned by the four winds. He wears a long *cojoc* and a pointy hat made of lambskin. Only when he enters the church and approaches the altar does she realise he's the priest she's been told about.

'Bless us, Father,' the nuns call in unison at the morning service.

'God bless you.' The priest's voice is soft, yet resonant. Almost like the voice of God himself, she would have thought had she still believed in one.

She cannot reconcile the thin man standing in front of her with the priests she's met before, whose big bellies usually open the doors for them. Such quiet charm and humility exude from him that Elina finds herself engaged with the *utrenie* service, and not on the verge of dozing off, as was often the case at the church in her village. There's something about this priest's eyes, small and deep, watching the world with an immense kindness from under the eaves of his bushy brows. Here is someone at peace with himself and everyone around him.

After the service, the abbess gives a short speech.

'Life is nothing but shadows and dreams, sisters. Shadows and dreams. Our Lord and our devotion for Him is the only reality. And death. When we return to His everlasting Kingdom.

'Your oath of a life of poverty, chastity and holy obedience means this is your chance to prove your love for our Lord Jesus Christ and His teachings. Your worldly possessions and riches are of no consequence. Your spiritual life – that's the real treasure you must look after, and nurture. The search for salvation, this is our purpose.'

'Amen,' the nuns reply in chorus.

'Your love for our Lord should be such that neither hunger nor cold should bother you…'

The rest of the abbess's words are lost on Elina as she focuses on the nun's mouth. What's that white bit stuck in her left canine? Surely it can't be *slănină*, the cured fatback, or pork belly – that's forbidden on Wednesdays and Fridays when the nuns fast to commemorate, respectively, Christ's betrayal by Judas and His Crucifixion.

The abbess has stopped in front of Elina, stressing each and every word of her sermon: 'Sisters, your devotion to the Holy Spirit should be so complete that the boundless love for our Lord is all that fills your hearts. Amen.'

'Amen.' The nuns make the sign of the cross and disperse, each in a hurry to fulfil their chores for the day.

Elina heads to the *bolniță*, where she has offered her service. Having seen Sister Alexandra's skin so badly chapped from the frost that her fingers were bleeding, Elina has prepared an ointment of beeswax and pine resin – it's what she saw Rozalia do when she healed the cracked hands of the maids at the manor.

She stops briefly by the stable. The auburn mare immediately turns around to greet her with a soft blow in her face.

'Good morning to you too, beautiful.' Elina returns the soft blow into the mare's muzzle and feeds her a small beetroot, a treat she brings with her each time she comes to say hello.

Sister Alexandra is already waiting by the time Elina walks into the *bolniță*. 'Do the horses have names?' she asks as she washes her hands.

The nun gives her an odd look. 'The old mare, the young one and the stallion. No need for names.'

'The auburn one is such a graceful horse. I'll call her Castana in honour of her colour.'

'All things are equally beautiful in the Lord's kingdom.'

'Of course they are.' Elina warms up the ointment with a candle, the easier to spread it on the nun's hands. 'How did she die?'

'Who?'

'The nun whose bed I'm sleeping in.'

Sister Alexandra hesitates, as if she's trying to remember something she would rather not. Elina applies the balm on the nun's hand, blowing gently to relieve the sting.

'She was a muddled soul. Young and foolish. Her father had sent her here to make her forget the unsuitable man she was in love with. But instead of seeing the light, the silly child was irritable and insulted the abbess by calling her a hypocrite.'

'Why would she say that?'

'She challenged Mother Superior about why only rich women were allowed to join the convent. In vain did we try to explain that the church required decent resources so that we had the means to do our work and help the poor. As I said, she was a confused young woman, may her soul rest in peace.' Sister Alexandra crosses herself.

Maybe not so confused, Elina thinks. Perhaps that young woman too had noticed the abbess's weakness for sable fur and *slănină*.

'What happened to her?' Elina asks. She keeps her eyes on her work, smearing the balm on the nun's hands and wrapping them with strips of linen.

'Mother Superior had her restrained in the cellar for

prolonged prayer in penitence. We brought her food and water, but she refused to take any.'

'Did she starve herself to death?' Elina asks.

Sister Alexandra shakes her head. 'She lost weight… the knots around her wrists and ankles loosened. She got out of the cellar one night. God only knows how she climbed over that tall gate, but she must have fallen on the other side. She broke her leg. We found her frozen body in the woods the next day. Lucky no beast had got to her.'

An involuntary shudder runs through Elina. The gate clearly isn't going to be as easy to tackle as she had imagined, especially given it is winter and it will be slippery with ice. This, and the realisation that the nuns are likely to watch the gate closely given the previous attempt, makes her light-headed as though she's tottering on the edge of a precipice.

'Oh, dear, you're trembling. I'm sorry this is so upsetting. I'll shut my mouth.'

'No, it's the cold,' Elina says, eager to keep the nun talking. 'Did the priest… did Father Arcady know about this?'

'He had retreated into one of his regular spells of silent worship at the time. We couldn't interrupt his devotion.'

'Her family must have been devastated.'

'They should have brought her to us sooner, before that amorous folly had poisoned her heart,' Sister Alexandra says, appraising her swathed hands. 'They feel so much better already… How come you know so much about healing?'

'The privilege of being a boyar's daughter. Learning from the best *vraci* my father knew.'

'Quite right. In other circumstances, you'd be punished for such knowledge.'

Elina cannot tell if the edge in the nun's voice is an accusation or regret at the truth of her statement. She wants to gauge the nun's stance on this matter. 'Working with nature isn't against our Lord.'

'Not if you're His follower. Thank you for your help,' Sister Alexandra says and rushes out.

Elina tidies up in a frenzy, as if this might delay or stall the thought that circles her mind. She keeps pushing it away, but this only makes it stronger until it fills her whole head and she can no longer ignore it: she won't be escaping the convent any time soon. There's no choice but to wait until the worst of winter is over. Her best chance of getting out is in spring, when she's less likely to break a bone while climbing over the gate. This means she won't see Mira as soon as she'd hoped, but it's better she waits and does it right rather than hurry and ruin it all.

Elina steels herself for what she knows is going to be the longest winter of her life.

GLIMPSING GOD

After Rozalia's murder, Mira has been coming to her cellar night after night, hoping to find Elina waiting there, ready to run away and start a new life together, as they'd planned. Why hasn't she turned up? Has she really been sent to the convent? Or has she changed her mind at the thought of giving up her comfortable life and status?

It's been over two full moons and Mira still leaves twigs on the cellar's trapdoor to tell her if anyone comes here in her absence, but she finds them untouched each time.

Mira has thought about asking Barbu, who – as her betrothed – visits them almost every day now. Surely he knows enough to help her pick the truth from all those rumours about Elina. But she worries her questions may rouse his suspicions. The way he looks at her sometimes – into her – as though he knows she's hiding something which he's determined to ferret out.

Mira will find the answers to her questions this evening at the spring fair. If Elina is there by her father's side, it means she's changed her mind about running away with Mira but hasn't had the guts to tell her. And if she isn't next to Boyar Constantin… then maybe she has really been sent to live with the nuns.

The fair will start in the evening with the kindling of the ritual fires. Like all the *old* holidays, this one too has been claimed by the church. What was once used to mark the end of winter and the beginning of spring, and therefore the beginning of a new farming year, has acquired a Christian name – the Fires of the Saints. The priest tells them this is to celebrate the saints who are praying for the victory of Light over Darkness, but she has learned the truth from Rozalia: it's the time of the year when the night and day are equal.

Mira doesn't want to go to the village square too early and agonise over her guesses as to whether Elina will turn up or not. She takes her time to finish sorting through a basket of shallots to be planted soon, peeling the dry layers, chopping off the rot like Rozalia taught her.

Her father has gone ahead to help with getting the fires ready, and when Mira spots the glow in the sky, she too sets off towards the square.

She can hear the fair before she sees it. Cries of excitement soar in the air as children, no doubt, are already leaping over the flames for good health and good luck; women's singing rises above the smell of baking bread and pies; men laugh raucously with cheer that can only be fuelled by barley beer and wine – Boyar Constantin must be there already, bearing gifts. He, no doubt, has heard the rumours from the travelling merchants about peasants rebelling against landowners in other villages. He would want to keep his farmhands sweet, and he knows nothing will work better than roast game and wine.

When Mira turns the corner, she finds the square abustle just as she imagined. She holds her breath while sweeping the crowd with a quick glance, searching for the one person she longs to see.

Elina isn't here.

She looks again, combing the square with a steady squint, as if just by sheer will, she can conjure up the woman she loves. So absorbed is she that someone's greeting, though softly spoken, makes her jump.

'A maiden like you shouldn't be lurking in the shadows,' Barbu says. 'Why not join in the *horă*?' He nods towards the bunch of people dancing in a circle, their bare feet not only keeping up with the rhythm of the pipe music but challenging it with their speed.

Mira recovers quickly. 'I wasn't sure my betrothed would approve of that.'

'Oh, I don't mind at all,' Barbu says, but the swell in his chest tells Mira how pleased he is with her answer.

She takes advantage of this sweet moment and asks the question sitting heavy on her mind without really asking it.

'Boyar Constantin looks sad. He must be missing his daughter terribly,' she says.

'The convent will do her good. The longer she stays there, the better, if you ask me.'

So the rumours are true, Mira thinks, and blinks to bring the world back into focus.

'Don't be concerned about her—'

'Oh.' Mira is taken aback by Barbu's keen observation. 'I'm not. It's the smoke from all those roasting hares and quails—'

'You should stay away from her,' Barbu says. 'In fact, stay away from all rich people. They aren't to be trusted.'

'You aren't exactly poor yourself,' Mira says.

'But I wasn't born rich. There's a big difference. I've climbed the scaffolds of buildings long before those of high society. I know what it's like to be so hungry and cold that death would be a relief. But I've also come to taste things you couldn't dream of. That's why I'm telling you, the rich don't have friends – only allies and servants.'

Barbu's words send a skewer through her heart. What if he's right? What if Elina has used her and Rozalia in order to get rid of the shameful pregnancy, and now that she's safe and has been spared a public disgrace, she doesn't want to see Mira again? Well, her father had warned her, hadn't he, when he said that wolves didn't befriend sheep.

A part of her is angry, embarrassed, feeling dim and gullible, while another laughs, saying – *So what?*

She rolls her shoulders back. 'It's strange that Boyar Constantin would send his daughter away. People say he loves her more than anything.'

But Barbu isn't falling for her trick to get him to say more. He smiles and proffers his hand. 'Shall we dance?'

'Aren't you tired, my lord? Lugging stone and mortar every day. Can't be easy.'

He laughs. 'It's not work if you love it. Masonry – skilled masonry – is a gift from God and it's His glory that I sweat for. Some people call it passion. Even obsession.'

'What do you call it?' She takes his hand, and they start spinning with the music.

'Glimpsing God,' he whispers in her ear. 'My buildings will see centuries come and go. They will outlive us all… What we're doing here is far bigger than ourselves.' A wild glint flashes in his dark eyes. Excitement? Ambition? Insanity? Whatever it is, it sends a shiver up her spine and Mira jerks involuntarily.

'We?' she asks.

Barbu frowns. Is he annoyed at her question?

'Yes, we. You're soon to be my wife. Together we'll attain what I could never do on my own.'

Despite the pride Mira feels in her heart to hear such praise, and astonishment – for she's never witnessed any man hold his woman in such high regard – she's also startled by his groundless certainty that just because she was promised to him, she would also aid him in his work. If only he knew what truly lay in her heart.

'What do I know of masonry?' She shrugs.

'Your presence in my life, and your love, is all that's required. Together we will meet God on our own terms.' There it is again, the fierce glint in Barbu's eyes when he speaks of his work, suggesting a devotion so consummate that Mira wonders what it would take to impede such earnest purpose.

As soon as the music stops, he pulls her away from the crowd. 'Come, I want to show you something.'

They sit on the ground on the other side of the fire, and Barbu takes out a scroll from the leather pouch hanging from his belt. Is this the drawing Elina told her about? Is he about to confess his love for her? Mira's heart is thrashing in her throat.

Barbu's fingers quiver as he unfurls the scroll. It reveals a miracle. The structure is so lifelike and precise in all its details, as though a real church has been shrunk by a wizard to fit on this small parchment.

She brings it closer to her face, searching for the image Elina said resembled Mira perfectly, but she can't see it here. It's not on this scroll.

'So? What do you think?' Barbu asks.

'It's beautiful. But why such a grand structure? This is a small village—'

'Only when reminded about his own smallness would a man's heart open to the glory and the wonder of the Gospel.'

Mira looks up at the starry dome above her. She can't imagine how any church in this world could come close to the magnificence of a sky at night. But she and Barbu are talking about different things. She bows in awe to the creation all around her, whilst he upholds the authority and power of the church.

'Do you have any more sketches?' she asks.

'This is all I need to build the church.'

'So you don't have another?'

'Why would I have another one?' Barbu smiles, but something in his eyes tells Mira he's rattled.

She smiles back. It tickles her that a strong, worldly man like the master mason could be so easily embarrassed. He doesn't want her to see the other scroll, the one where he's sketched her amongst his building plans. He's too proud to admit his feelings for her.

'Why me?' she asks. She's been wondering about this ever since he asked for her hand. Why has he chosen her – a poor, crippled peasant – over, say, the beautiful sisters of the wool merchant or the priest's daughters? Any one of them would be a far better marriage arrangement for Barbu than her. 'There are many healthy, rich young women—'

'It's virtue I'm looking for, not money.'

How do you know I'm virtuous? she wants to ask. Instead she says, 'How do you know they are not virtuous?'

'Now I know you're a pest, I may change my mind about marrying you,' he says lightly, but his voice falters. He's clearly unnerved, despite his efforts to hide it. Could she have so much power over him? Because if he's in love with her, maybe she can persuade him to give up on building the church.

It won't be easy, knowing how much he loves his work, but she must try.

HOLES IN THE BUCKET

The bittersweet scent of catkins reassures Elina that spring has settled in. Immediately after *utrenie* and the morning prayers, she goes to pick nettles at the edge of the orchard. They remind her of Mira and Rozalia and their happy times together. She wraps her hands in burdock leaves to avoid the nettle stings and fills up two baskets. Even so, it won't be enough because she's learned that, when cooked, nettles reduce to less than half. She'll use Rozalia's tip and thicken them with flour. Elina chuckles to herself. Women of her kind know everything about eating and nothing about cooking. Whatever happened to her?

The sisters give her an odd look when she returns with the unusual crop. They will change their mind when they taste it. Elina goes straight to the *cuhnia*, where she starts her preparations. It's not a difficult meal to prepare but a fiddly one.

While her hands are busy with separating the leaves from the stalks, washing, soaking, chopping, her mind is free to wonder. The nuns have finally stopped watching her every move and no longer check on her when she takes her time working in the gardens, or the stable, or when she pretends to be praying in a far corner of the church so she can be left alone with her thoughts.

The time has come to run away from here. She'll do it next Friday, towards the end of the working week, when the nuns will be the most tired and sleeping most soundly. She feels light, as if part of her has already fled this place and has joined Mira. From this vantage point, it's easy to see her stay here as a little less miserable. Despite the hard work, the long, cold winter months, the simple food and plain clothes, her stay at the convent has been good training for what she imagines her life ahead as a runaway is going to be.

Life here has paradoxically given her a kind of freedom: to be somebody other than a boyar's daughter. She's been stripped not only of her warm clothes, but also of the comforts and pleasures of the rich which she's known since her birth, of her identity as it's been imposed on her by society and her own family. In the absence of these layers, Elina has received a glimpse of her true nature. The fireball burning in her chest, the force coursing in her blood has nothing to do with privilege or status – it's the uninhibited, uncoerced expression of who she is at heart. This will come in useful when she runs away and is no longer under her father's protection.

Elina hums to herself as she tastes the nettles. Add a little more salt and savory and maybe a sprinkle of—

The daylight in the kitchen dims as someone walks in. There are only two people Elina knows who can move so noiselessly: Mira and Rozalia. But neither of them could possibly…

And yet…

Elina swings around so fast that she stumbles over the stool behind her. The abbess leans in the doorway, a twinkle of amusement in her round eyes.

'Good day, Reverend Mother.' Elina bows and moves the stool out of the way.

'You're out of breath, dear.'

'Just a silly fright, I—'

'The truly devout never fear, for God is always within.'

'Yes, Reverend Mother.'

'What's for lunch?' The abbess walks towards the bubbling cauldron.

That's why she's here, Elina thinks. Someone must have complained about the unconventional meal she's putting together. But to her surprise, the old nun is pleased with her foraging.

'Ah! The joy of spring,' Mother Superior says. 'Fresh nourishment after the long, cold months. A healthy body means a healthy mind and a healthy spirit. Make sure you don't overcook it. We want to retain as much goodness as taste.'

Elina thinks how much the abbess sounds like Rozalia right now. She wonders how the nun would react if she told her she reminded her of a heathen woman. It's an entertaining thought.

'And don't forget: a bowl per soul!'

She's been told off previously when asking for, or offering, seconds. 'Our body is a vessel,' the abbess preaches, 'and if you fill it up with food, you leave no space for God. A full belly summons sleep, not the Holy Spirit.'

Mother Superior looks around, brushing her hands along her sides, smoothing out her habit. Elina senses it's not food she has come to talk about.

'I know we haven't talked about it yet,' the abbess says. 'It's still early days for such decisions to be made, but… Have you had any more thoughts about it?'

Elina guesses where Mother Superior is headed with this, but she remains silent.

'About crossing the bridge. You'll be glad you did it. So much life gets wasted when decisions aren't being made. They're like holes in a bucket – you'll never fetch water from the well until you plug those holes. What is there to wait for? Make up your mind and peace shall be yours forever.'

The abbess's speech feels rehearsed. Is this what she's told all the other nuns before her? Is this what she preached to the young woman who died trying to escape this place? The thing is that the abbess's words are in contradiction with her actions. So much is clear to anyone who has eyes to see past her habit and the golden cross hanging on her neck. Mother Superior is more interested in Elina's dowry than saving her soul. The dead woman, no doubt, felt the same frustration. The word 'hypocrite' tingles Elina's tongue. She enjoys its taste silently, and just as silently, she swallows it.

Mother Superior clears her throat, impatient with Elina's hesitation.

'Yes, Reverend Mother, I pray for clarity and guidance every day. I hope the answer will come to me soon, God willing.'

With a sharp nod, the abbess retreats to the door but swings around just as she's about to reach it. 'I almost forgot. Your father is coming to visit in a fortnight.'

Elina draws a quick breath and wants to scream her delight. Her father is finally coming to take her home. She won't have to climb over the tall gate in the middle of the night in order to get out of here.

She wills her body to be still. Excitement, like many other good things, is viewed as a weakness in this place.

'You think about what we've discussed today, child,' says the abbess. 'I'm always here if... when you need my counsel.'

'God willing, Reverend Mother.'

SHADOW-THIEVES

Having always shied away from the village gossip, now Mira plans to take advantage of it. Inciting the villagers against Barbu may be her best chance of stopping him.

She goes to fetch water from the well in the early morning when it's at its busiest. When she arrives, there's already a long queue of women chatting away, doing their best to challenge the dawn chorus for merit.

'You all,' Mira whispers like she's seen them do when there's an especially juicy bit of gossip. 'Make sure you stay away from those scaffolds, especially your children.'

The women draw closer around Mira.

'The masons are shadow-thieves. I saw two of them idling with the knot-rope in their hands, watching the road like predators in waiting.'

The lore has it that masons steal people's shadows by measuring them with a rope, which they bury into the floor of their building. The man, woman or child whose shadow has so been trapped dies within forty days, their sacrifice propitiating the Spirit of the Land who will protect the new structure.

'They can't be doing this. They're with our Lord Jesus Christ.' The shepherd's daughter crosses herself.

'And Christians don't believe in black magic.' The carpenter's wife shakes her head. 'Our children are safe.'

'I wouldn't be so sure,' Mira says. 'They're not from around here and who's to say what lies in their hearts?'

'But yer betrothed is the master mason himself,' Vera, the broom-maker's wife, says. 'He's in charge, isn't he?'

'He may not know about it,' Mira says.

'Aren't you goin' to tell him?' Vera rolls her eyes at the other women.

'Don't be stupid.' Nastasia, an elder, frowns at Vera, waving her away. 'It's not for us to meddle in our men's work.' She turns to Mira. 'Don't listen to her. She's just a stirrer.'

Mira can hear the kindness in the old woman's voice more that she can see it, given her face is so wrinkled and wrung out from a lifetime of toil.

Mira brings food to her husband-to-be every day, not so much out of duty as his betrothed as to keep an eye on how the works are progressing. Up here – among the hard-working masons calling instructions to each other, hammering away, or carrying stone and mortar – she's hardly noticed. Sweet invisibility.

Contrary to her hopes, the walls are growing taller by the day. It looks like Barbu is going to achieve what two previous masons have failed to do.

Her heart skips with joy when, a week after she's started the rumours, she can hear children singing in the road:

'Beware of the lurking foe,

Who lies in wait to steal thy shadow.'

Mira doesn't mention this to Barbu, but she knows he must have heard them too, seeing how sad he is one evening when he comes to visit them, bearing a gift of two grouse. The generous man he is, Barbu never comes empty-handed.

She wants to find out how worried he is. 'Don't listen to those rascals, my lord,' she says as she grinds herbs for the meat. 'They don't know what they're saying.'

'Come again?'

'Those children singing silly—'

'Ha! I'm not bothered about it at all.' Barbu's eyes brighten up for a moment.

'You're not? What if these rumours reach the ears of the priest? Or the boyar?' Mira does her best to sound concerned.

'They know it's all gossip. Besides, they don't care how I do it, as long as I do it.'

If this isn't why Barbu is upset, then what's troubling him? But she knows better than to ask, and goes about cooking the meal, casting glances at him now and again. He sits in the corner of the hut, watching the flickering flame of the *opaiț* as if he's learning secrets from the fire.

Her own heart is heavy with brooding. Her plan of discrediting Barbu and his men hasn't worked. It calls for a different measure, the truth of which curdles the blood in her heart.

Did Rozalia know it would come to this? Is that why she'd taught Mira about plants and potions?

Her head is spinning like she's trapped in a river rapid – swirled and tumbled and rolled, not quite knowing which side of the banks the waters will spit her out.

THE HOUR

Given how well Barbu treats her – his courtesy and kindness – Mira's heart shrinks with guilt each time she ponders her intent. She could try to talk him out of his pursuit to spare him his fate, but she knows how much his work means to him. Teasing a hungry bear would be safer than hurting a man's pride.

Still, she must fulfil her duty to the Old Gods and stop the false faith from growing deeper roots in their village.

Yesterday he brought them a chunk of wild boar from his hunting with Boyar Constantin. Today Mira is going to cook his last meal. Her husband-to-be was more thoughtful than usual before he left, and she wondered if he could smell the air like Rozalia used to, sensing the woe ordained for him.

Mira goes to Rozalia's cellar at dawn to avoid anyone seeing her. She gathers what she needs: a fistful of banewort nuggets, a pinch of henbane seeds and the powder whose name should not be said out loud. She rolls everything in a cloth and ties it around her belly under her dress.

Back home, Mira makes a fire in the courtyard on the opposite side to where her father is kneading a batch of clay. She goes about preparing the meal in absolute silence, each move a deliberate, focused action. She closes her eyes, praising the Old Gods, the ancient wisdom and the sacred knowledge she's acquired to fight the lie which seeks to subjugate the spirit. If she can stop this church from being built, it's one less dungeon for the soul.

'Odd time and place to be praying,' her father says.

'Live and breathe God. Isn't that what the priest teaches us?'

'When was the last time you went to church?' her father asks. 'People will start talking if you keep finding excuses.'

There's more of God in our courtyard than in the church, she wants to say, but instead she nods. 'You're right, Father.' She knows she has to keep up appearances. Going to church will provide the cover she needs to carry on Rozalia's work and pass on the ancient teachings she's been entrusted with. She won't make Rozalia's mistake. She won't challenge the church in the open.

Mira skewers the joints of wild boar and props them above the fire, but the first whiff of roasting pork sends her retching. Memories of Rozalia going up in flames swim in her mind. The melting flesh, the unbearable smell that clung to the inside of her nostrils for weeks after that.

She grabs the sizzling chops and with her nose in her armpit, she scurries to the far end of the garden where she buries the meat. She'll tell Barbu that a stray dog has run off with it. He'll be disappointed, of course, but she'd rather bear his wrath a hundred times over than have to smell cooked pork again. Or worse – have to cook it herself.

When she returns to the courtyard, there are two white doves ambling about, the male plumping up his feathers and cooing softly as he struts in circles around the female. The hen ignores his efforts as if he's not even there. There's nobody putting pressure on her to acknowledge his presence or give in to his advances, and Mira envies this small-brained bird her freedom.

They'll do, she thinks of the meal she's yet to cook, and entices the two birds into the hut with a handful of grains. The male dodges her trap and gets away. The female isn't so lucky.

Mira grinds the special herbs from Rozalia's cellar and mixes them with spices before stirring them into the dove stew.

When all is ready, she bundles the pot into a shawl and takes it to Barbu before the food gets cold.

OFFERING

Mira stops in the shade of a tree before she begins climbing the hill. They've been blessed with a warm spring and the midday sun is merciless. Her skin itches from the woolly shawl on her back, to which she's tied the pot, the easier to carry it.

She brings her hand to her eyes and looks up the hill. The masons are all perched on the unfinished walls like a line of roosting crows. She's certain Barbu isn't there. His men wouldn't be idling like this if he was.

Mira can hear someone behind her, but when she glances over her shoulder, there's no one there. Still, she can sense a presence – that charge in the air that tells you you're not alone.

She takes her time walking up the hill, not wishing to arrive at the top until Barbu returns. He's probably gone to see the boyar about one thing or another and will be back soon. Mira won't tell him his men are slacking behind his back. She wants him to be in a good mood so that he enjoys the food and eats it to the last mouthful.

There – she hears it again – a light step barely audible, but present nonetheless.

'Who's there?' she calls out, but no one answers.

She won't be easily spooked, and instead of hurrying up to get away from whoever is following her, Mira sits down facing the way she has come. And waits.

Trees in bloom have draped the length of the hill, their sticky-sweet scent filling the air. The bounty of blossom and the myriads of swallows that have returned to the village this year foretell rich crops. They are due a change of fortune after years of drought. Watching the bees and the ants and the birds, all so earnestly engaged with their lives, Mira wonders about her own purpose, about her task ahead.

She notices the fields below the woods are empty. They were teeming with peasants yesterday and the day before, dragging their harrows and hand-sowing the boyar's lands. Where have they all gone today?

As Mira stands to resume her journey, she spots a shadow lurking behind a tree, and she laughs. The stealthy pursuer is one of the scrawny stray dogs who roam the village. 'Trust me,' she tells the dog, 'you don't want to eat the food you can smell.'

When she reaches the hilltop, the masons look hard at work. Of course they are. Barbu is back amongst them now, lugging stones and dripping with sweat.

Where are all the serfs? She looks around, but none of the usual village men are here today. It's just Barbu and his builders. Mira notices his eyes are red and puffy, as if he's been crying, but of course that can't be true. She's never seen any men cry, other than when they are drunk.

'The serfs are at the quarry today, doing *corvoadă*,' Barbu informs Mira before she even asks the question. 'We need more stone for our works.'

'I did wonder why there was nobody working in the fields today.'

'Besides,' Barbu scratches his head, 'we've reached a point where we can't go on. We were going to consecrate the statue of Virgin Mary, but it isn't ready. The stone carver won't bring it for at least another week and that's going to delay our works.'

Mira arranges her face to look like she's sorry to hear the bad news, but in her heart, she hopes the idol never makes it up here. She hopes it gets struck by lightning and turned to dust.

'I'm so sorry to hear this, my lord,' she says to him. 'I know how much this means to you… Anything I can help with?'

'Thank you, but I don't think so. It's just a matter of… In fact, there may be a way you can help us.'

Mira hasn't expected this answer, but she must play on. 'Tell me how and I will.'

'Yes, I think you could certainly help us, and I'll be forever grateful to you. All you have to do is stand in the statue's place so we can mark the spot and know how much space to leave for when the real thing turns up.'

Some of the builders nod while others look away, surely appalled by Barbu's audacity to have her, a mere mortal, stand in for their revered saint.

Mira knows it doesn't matter whether she helps him or not. This church will never be finished. After he eats his lunch today, Barbu will be gone within a week. She looks at him and all she sees is a dying man, whose pain she will ease with special brews, fooling him about his healing as she waits for the bane to turn his blood to rot.

'Of course I'll help, my lord,' she says and hands him the food bundle.

The builders hurry to kindle a fire. Mira guesses it's a ceremonial fire – why else are the men holding hands and circling the flames, all the while singing a prayer of some sort? Scraps of their words reach her, a long-lasting edifice… to survive calamities be they at the hand of man or God… no earthquake will loosen its stones, no fire will burn it down, no battle will destroy its walls… accept our faith and offering… You, the one and only Deity… and us Your faithful worshippers…

They each jump through the fire and Barbu leads Mira to jump through it too.

The Great Purifier.

She's not surprised by the cleansing ritual before undertaking an important job, but she's puzzled to see these men do it.

What would the priest say if he knew about their unorthodox practice? Would he burn them at the stake too, like he did with Rozalia?

Is that why the masons have done it? Because there are no village men here today to witness their heresy and report it to the priest? Aren't they worried Mira could tell on them? They know she won't, of course. It's her word against theirs.

With the fire ceremony over, Barbu takes Mira's hand and leads her to an alcove in the corner of some unfinished walls. His thirteen masons gather around to start the work, carrying heavy buckets and pushing wheelbarrows heaped with large rocks.

'Mira, sweetheart, take off the amber from your neck,' Barbu tells her.

'Why?' She lifts her hand to protect the talisman Rozalia gave her.

'Stones tend to have a soul of their own,' he says. 'It may hinder our work.'

Mira can't be seen to disobey her husband-to-be in public, but equally she's not going to part with her amulet. Removing it from her neck or letting someone else touch it could disturb the powers Rozalia has blessed it with.

'Don't worry, I'll keep it safe.' Barbu is waiting with his hand stretched out, but Mira clasps her fist around her talisman and shakes her head.

Being humiliated in front of everyone can't be easy for Barbu, but he nods anyway, and his men carry on without forcing her to remove it.

She watches the wall rise to her knees, thighs, hips, as the men work quickly and in total silence, as though they've done this many times before and there's no need for words. Or else, their hands speak a language she doesn't understand.

When the wall reaches her chest, Mira tells Barbu she's helped enough. 'That'll do,' she says. 'You've got the space you need for your saint now.'

But neither he, nor the rest of his men, can hear her. Mira calls to them again, raising her voice.

And again.

But they all seem to have gone deaf and their busy hands are a blur. She tries pulling herself up, but the wall is too high to climb out of without any help.

'Alright, you've scared me enough.' She looks at Barbu. 'This isn't amusing any more.'

'It's not what it looks like,' he says. 'You must trust me.'

The reassuring words bring a lump to Mira's throat. 'I do, I do, my lord, but I just want to go home now. I've brought you your meal and I'm yet to cook my father's—'

'The lowly life of a peasant is beneath you. You've been born for bigger things.'

Mira wishes he would stop talking and just pull her out of this chilly pit.

'A man's life is short and insignificant. We must raise above our limitations and make it count. Our flesh and blood are earth-born and bound, but our imagination is of the Divine.' Barbu's voice is so tender. Why are his words making her shiver? 'What we're doing here will outlive us far beyond—'

'I'm sure it will be a beautiful church, but I've done my bit to help you… you've got your space… please…' Mira stretches her hands up towards Barbu. His strong arms could get her out in a blink. Then she'll bolt it down the hill all the way home and will never come anywhere near him ever again. She'll run away, far away, where she won't see this man with honey on his tongue and mortar in his heart…

Mortar! This is the smell from her nightmares.

A thought starts rattling around her head. Surely they can't be doing what she… But it appears that they are. It's not just the smell. Mira recognises this place too – the grave-like alcove she dreamed about being trapped in so many a night, and which jolted her awake drenched in sweat, gasping for air each time.

Except this time she isn't dreaming.

'Get me out! Someone help me! Help!' She kicks and throws her body against the wall, but the rocks are too heavy, and the mortar is setting fast. She tries clawing her way out, shredding her fingers and staining the white of the entombing stone a rabid red.

'Don't hurt yourself, Mira,' says Barbu. The softness of his voice is so discordant with his callous heart that she thinks he has gone mad. Or is it she who's losing her mind?

Mira cradles her bleeding fingers to her chest, but there's no pain. How is it possible, given all this torn flesh? Her brain must be busy with other things than to register pain.

'You planned this…' she stammers, seeking Barbu's eyes.

'It may be hard to believe, but I love you more than you can imagine—'

'Don't speak of love.' Her words come out in a choking cry. 'You don't love anyone but yourself, and I've learned this a little too late.'

A memory flashes in her mind – Barbu's embarrassment at the spring fair. When she mentioned the second scroll which contained her image, he didn't pale because he was shy to talk about his feelings for her – as she foolishly believed at the time – but because he was frightened she'd guess his motives.

'That's why you chose me, as opposed to anyone else in the village. Motherless, poor and crippled, I'm the perfect prey, aren't I? A disappointment to my own father because I can't make pots any more, I won't be a loss to anyone if I just disappear—'

'Don't fear death, sweetheart. We all—'

'I haven't lived yet.'

'You haven't sinned yet. Your maiden blood is the magic this church needs. Your soul will keep it vibrant for centuries to come. Aren't you honoured?'

The glint in Barbu's eyes convinces Mira that insanity lies on his side, not on hers.

She turns to the rest of the men. 'Someone help me, please,

I beg you, please get me out.' She looks from one man to another, but none of them meet her eye, save for the swarthy young mason who suddenly kneels at the edge of the wall and offers her his hand. A wide, callused hand that should belong to someone twice his age.

Mira raises both arms towards this kind soul who's taken pity on her, but the young man's glance slides off her face, towards her chest. His hand pushes past hers, reaching for her neck…

Her talisman.

But before the brash builder can yank it from her neck, Mira sinks her teeth in his arm, and he lets go at once, spitting swear words her way.

Her pleadings go unheard as the men continue to work in devout silence, their hands steady and fast.

'Waste of a young woman,' one of them says suddenly.

'You say this every time,' another one replies.

Mira starts screaming cries and curses that fly out of her mouth, perching themselves on the men's shoulders like birds of doom.

Barbu walks away. He picks up the food bundle and seeks the shadow of the old oak, right in front of the eastern wall, beyond which Mira is slowly disappearing. However, instead of tucking into his lunch, he leans against the gnarled tree trunk, his arms wrapped around his knees. Mira stands on the tip of her toes, lifting her head as high as she can, willing him to get the food out and take the first bite. If only she could see him eat a mouthful, then she'd know he wouldn't be far behind in dying.

She keeps jumping, straining her neck to see over the wall which is now above her eyeline. The bricks are piling up, shutting her off from the world. Soon, even her jumps aren't high enough to see over the edge any more. Mira squats low to boost her one last jump.

She sees Barbu in the same spot, face buried in his hands,

and a dog – the stray who followed her up the hill – scuttling away, the food bundle swinging wildly in its jaws.

Mira's heart sinks to her heels as it catches up with her brain.

The image of the male pigeon eluding her trap earlier flashes in her mind, and she lets out a cry that rips the air above her.

THE VISIT

'You've grown thinner,' her father says, remaining seated at the far end of the table in the refectory.

You've grown older, Elina wants to say, noticing the hole in his beard, where he picks at it, has widened. Instead she asks, 'How are things at home?'

'Uprisings everywhere. Peasants calling for lower tithes and such nonsense.' He flicks his wrist as if to say the news is negligible. 'Let's not talk about that when I'm full of good news for you. Let's start with Fulger. He's so restless, nickering at night, calling for you.'

'I miss him too. I miss all of you. What happened to Rozalia?'

'Water under the bridge. She got what she deserved.'

'She's not guilty. You know the truth.'

'She had plenty of other sins to pay for.'

'Had?'

'You have too much trust in people. It's not befitting a boyar's daughter. A boyar's wife soon.'

'Pardon me? You can't expect me to marry my cousin after what his father did—'

'Not at all. I've heard your cousin Mihnea is marrying the *ciohodar*'s daughter, while you, my angel – and this is the second piece of good news – you're betrothed to Dragos Calmasu—'

'I don't know him. Wait, what happened to Rozalia?'

'The stake was where she was headed all along. All you need to know about Dragos is that he comes from a high-ranking boyar family up north. His father is one of the voivode's treasurers.'

They killed Rozalia.

And all because of her.

She shouldn't have gone to Rozalia's that night. If only she hadn't…

'Trust me, my angel. I know what I'm doing. God, your cheeks are flushing just like your mother's when she was upset,' he says. 'But more wealth is not something to get angry about. Marrying Dragos won't be just an honour for us, but a very useful allegiance too.'

He hasn't got a clue. Though her hatred of him is burning her chest right now, the mention of her mother reminds Elina how much he had done for his wife. He must have really loved her to have put his life in danger by letting her embellish the church books, and pretending it was him all along. Given this, surely he'd understand why she wouldn't want to marry a stranger.

'I don't know him. How can I love him?'

'Is that what they teach in convents these days?'

Elina drops her voice. 'I know about the church books… Who really painted them. You must know something about love yourself.'

Though the refectory is empty, her father looks around and his fingers start picking at his beard.

'I see we didn't kill that witch soon enough.' He takes a long breath. 'Love will come with time. Your mother and I hadn't met before the wedding day. And you know the rest.'

'And I thought you came to visit because you missed me.'

'You can return home at the end of summer if you agree to marry Dragos. Don't you see? I want the best for you. It's what keeps me awake at night. Your welfare—'

'You care about my purse, not happiness.'

'Talking about your purse – that's the third piece of good

news. Barbu has almost finished building the church. The walls are up finally. They'll be starting on the roof soon. Once that's done and we fulfil the ruler's whim, your full rights of inheritance are assured.'

How has Barbu managed to get so far with his work? Two previous masters failed in their efforts, and Barbu himself struggled for months. What's changed? Something flashes in her mind but so quickly and elusively she can't catch it. Maybe it will come back to her later.

Her father's wide grin angers her.

'If my enhanced status is as good as confirmed, then I don't have to marry. I can be my own master like you, be free to—'

'There are two things wrong with that, dearest. First, you'll be viewed as a son on paper only, for inheritance purposes. In reality, you're a still woman and cannot compare yourself to a man – society's rules, not mine. Second, even I'm not as free as you imagine. Nobody is. We all do what's required of us. By our family and loved ones, and by our supreme ruler, the voivode.'

There's no point in arguing with her father. He has gone to great lengths to craft her future for the best practical and societal outcome. She gets that. But her heart doesn't.

Her heart longs for the day she'll be out of the convent and see Mira again. For the day they can live their forbidden love somewhere where nobody knows them.

But first she must lay the groundwork, a plan already budding in her mind.

'Mother Superior has been very kind to me,' she says. 'I would like to gift her something special. Could you ask the potter's daughter to make another colourful vessel, like the one she made for me?'

'I'll certainly ask her father to do it. His daughter disappeared. Word is she went to the woods and never returned. Probably attacked by a beast. Are you alright, my angel?' Her father is by her side in an instant, pulling the bench from under the table so she can sit. 'I see you're faint with hunger as ever. When are you going to start eating properly? What's your future husband going to think when he sees you like this, thin as a sapling? You can't embarrass me, looking worse than a serf.'

'When… when did she disappear?' Elina's chest is heaving.

'I'm not sure. A few weeks back. More or less. Who cares? Poor Barbu, their wedding was supposed to take place in the autumn. Shall I get you some water? You've gone very pale.'

Her father is calling for help and searching for water in the refectory and talking to her at the same time, but his words slide off her brain.

Mira has disappeared. Attacked by a beast? Is she dead? Something about her disappearance at the same time as Barbu's change of fortune with building the church doesn't sit well with Elina, but for a few moments, she cannot think why.

Then it comes back to her. The flash of recognition she had earlier and couldn't remember. It's the image of Mira she'd spied on the side of Barbu's parchment with the construction plans.

Why would he do that? Did he link her image to his work for a reason?

Something dark and unnerving niggles at her. She's heard the rumours of dubious masons who were shadow-thieves, or who sacrificed animals in their structures. What if…

Elina suddenly recalls that Rozalia had said Barbu had a darkness about him she didn't trust. And that if he succeeded in building the church, there'd be a dear price to pay, and she didn't mean just money.

Did Rozalia know about his plans?

That's why the wise old woman was against the building of this church right from the beginning. That's why she'd wanted to hide the voivode's arrow before anyone found it and marked the spot for the future church. But Elina had got in the way. With the ignorance and the arrogance of her younger self, she'd accused Rozalia of being a thief, instead of trusting her, as Rozalia had pleaded – *You're too young to understand the wrong that's being done. One day you will, but it may be too late by then.*

It is too late.

Mira disappeared a few weeks back.

Mira is dead.

The sinking-in of this news roils Elina's stomach and she vomits just as her father brings her a jug of water. Her half-digested beetroot soup splashes all over his blue velvet boots, leaving shreds of cabbage hanging off them.

'Are you ill, my angel?'

All their plans of running away… Mira is dead. A world without Mira…

'What's wrong? Why are you shaking so?' Her father's hand touches her cheeks and forehead, checking for fever.

'Father,' she whispers. 'I think Mira has been… murdered.'

'What are you saying, child?'

Elina tells him about Barbu's secret scroll with Mira's image on it.

'So what? The man was in love. They were going to marry—'

'Do you remember what he called the other masons who failed to build the church?'

'Why does that matter?'

'He called them bumblers, not proper masons because they used animals as sacrifice – roosters and wild boars. He mocked them for it as if animals weren't a big enough sacrifice. What if he'd been planning it all along? What if he wasn't in love but only grooming Mira for—'

'It must be a terribly boring place, this convent, for you to come up with such wild stories,' her father says, holding her hand.

Elina pulls away.

'Say you're right and things have happened as you think. It's sad and unfortunate, but there's nothing we can do about it. The poor girl must be dead by now—'

'But we can't leave her walled up in those cursed walls.'

‘What do you mean? You’re not—’

‘Father, a young woman may have been killed—’

‘And we can’t bring her back, may her soul rest in peace.’ Her father makes the sign of the cross.

‘As God-fearing Christians, we owe her a proper burial.’

‘Don’t do anything stupid. Now that we’re so close to confirming your special status—’

‘I don’t want it if it’s paid for with Mira’s blood.’

‘You have everything to lose and nothing to gain.’

Elina shrugs. She can’t imagine a world without Mira. Without her, it’s empty. Useless, and painful, and ugly. She might as well become a nun. At least that way she won’t be forced to marry anyone.

‘I’ll do what’s right by Mira, then I’ll return to the convent.’

‘We both know you’re not made for the convent. It was meant to be temporary—’

‘Maybe you don’t know me at all, Father.’ Their eyes lock and she is not going to be the first to look away.

‘If you leave here without permission, they won’t take you back.’

‘A genuine seeker will always find a home.’

‘You’re a good liar, but you can’t fool me.’

‘I’ve made up my mind, Father. I will take the monastic vows. And if you know me so well, you’ll know I mean it.’

Mother Superior has just walked through the door. She must have heard Elina’s firm statement. Her smile is just about discernible, but it’s unmistakably there.

Haughty, satisfied, victorious.

CONFINEMENT

Mira knows this place so well. Its chill has crept into her bone marrow from all those times it trapped her in her dreams. What had Rozalia once said about dreams? *They are capricious harbingers who tell you everything if only you're versed in their language.*

This time Mira is confined for real, inside a square column, her feet at foundation level, and the column built up around and above her. She can't tell how many days she's been walled up for, but she's past the dizziness, head rushes, shakes and stomach cramps – the effects of the first few days of fasting. It may be closer to a week now. Or even longer. But there isn't much difference after a certain point, except that her body is getting weaker and thinner. She can clasp her waist with her hands. It has started to eat itself up, burning through her sinews, judging by the awful stink she catches of herself.

Her previous fasts under Rozalia's guidance didn't deprive Mira of water completely. This is different. And her urine has become too strong to drink any more. She has to diminish the flame that's consuming her life. She has to lower her heartbeat just as Rozalia taught her, or she won't survive much longer.

Performing the special practice might prolong her life, but why bother? It's only going to delay her death and extend her pain. It's not as if Barbu, or his men, will change their mind and come to dig her up. And nobody else knows she's been confined to a hidden alcove within the walls of the new church. It would be easier to let nature take its course, let her body chew on itself until there's nothing left of her.

But thoughts of Elina won't let her give up. Not yet.

Mira alters her breath to the secret pattern she's been taught and trained in. An increased lightness spreads over her, so sweet and compelling it could easily be death. She folds her legs beneath her, hands gently clasped together, fingers entwined in a certain order. She doesn't have to remember what to do – the body has a memory of its own. The only thing she has to handle is her breath, and the rest will happen. *It has to happen*, Rozalia had assured her. *It has no choice in the same way a flower doesn't choose to bloom – if the conditions are right, it just opens up.*

Watching her breath isn't easy though. Thoughts get in the way. The lack of food in her body has slowed down their endless stream. It's a trickle now, but they still meddle with what needs to be done.

Mira has to fool her mind, put it to sleep with a chant. But chanting is such an effort right now. The words are heavy, and her tongue is sticky and too weak to say them. She hums the rhythm instead.

Reaching the invisible passage within her, the one that leads to freedom, is a slow and painstaking process, but Mira isn't going anywhere in a hurry, so she keeps at it with everything she's got left in her. Rozalia had warned her that it wouldn't be easy to do it on her own. *But it's not impossible. It all depends on how much you want it, like with most things.*

Mira follows her breath in and out, steadily, relentlessly – like a predator in pursuit of its prey – until she recognises the familiar shiver which she knows will lead her out of the prison of her body and into the unbounded nothingness which props up the world. She's on her way there…

Mira sees herself on the breezy porch of a grand manor house, sitting on a pile of coloured cushions and watching her half-dozen children frolic about the green gardens surrounding the house.

And there is her husband, chasing after them as they scream with excitement and joy. He looks familiar. He is what Elina would look like had she been born a man. Or perhaps this is a glimpse into a future lifetime when Elina *will* be born a man and the two of them will be husband and wife. That's why Mira is not appalled at the sight of her mothering so many children. Perhaps in a future life, with Elina as her husband, Mira won't be so against bearing children as she has been in this life.

Mira enjoys the contentment she sees on her own face. It's a blessed future life, and it no longer matters if she dies.

FUGITIVE

In the millet field, Elina finds herself nudged by the nuns, who tell her she's being slow in pulling out the weeds.

'You're preoccupied, sister,' one of them says. 'What's the matter?'

'Dreaming is done at night. No time for idling now,' another one chips in.

'You look a little wan. Why don't you take a short break?'

Elina presses her lips together. It takes everything she has not to shout at them, *Don't you know Mira is dead?*

How can everyone carry on as normal? How can the world keep going when hers has been destroyed? They were so close to carving a future together, so close… To think that she'll never see her Froglet again, ever…

Elina grabs a fistful of thistle and crumples it in her hand. The sharp thorns give her a good reason to let out the raging ache in her chest.

Her cry brings Father Arcady running from the edge of the orchard where he is smoking the trees with vine prunings and frankincense to protect them from pests.

'It's only a little scratch,' Sister Alexandra says, as though to admonish Elina for her exaggerated reaction. 'Hardly bleeding at all.'

'Blood isn't always present where there's pain, sister,'

Father Arcady says. He places a handful of freshly plucked burdock in Elina's palm. 'This will help.' He looks her straight in the eye. 'With your hand.'

Elina mumbles a quick thank you and turns away, resuming her weeding, fearful that the priest's searching gaze will dig up the root of her anguish. She shouldn't be causing any fuss if she wants to succeed with her plan.

If she's right about what happened to Mira, she has to find her body before tomorrow. Her father will be lodging at the convent tonight and won't return to the village until the following day, when he most certainly will alert Barbu to her suspicion. She shouldn't have told him anything. She should have kept her mouth shut, but the blow of the news had clouded her judgement.

When she returns to the convent, hopefully in a couple of days, she will blame her running off on a spell of madness. After all, her mother's *cobză* is still here, kept safe by the abbess. Elina would never leave it behind if she intended to leave this place for good.

In the evening, after the longest day Elina has ever had to live through, she blows out the *opaiț*. But Sister Katerina is in the mood for talking. 'I've heard the wonderful news. That you'll be taking the vows soon.'

'Aren't you tired, sister?' Elina feigns a loud yawn. 'Toiling in the fields is hard work. I can barely keep my eyes open.'

'Yes, it can be arduous. You know, I was thinking' – Sister Katerina props herself up on her elbow – 'this weeding that we do… how very telling it is of our condition, don't you think?'

Elina rolls her eyes in the dark. 'It's been a long day. We need to rest.'

'I mean, it's like weeding out our sins through prayers and devout living, giving the Holy Spirit a chance to grow and bear fruit. Our sinful thoughts aren't that different to the stubborn thistle and clover that's choking our millet, our sustenance.'

Elina knows better than to get into an argument with the nun, but she's too riled up to stop herself.

'All herbs are useful,' she says, quoting Rozalia. 'It's just that we're ignorant of their benefits.'

Sister Katerina sits up. 'The weeds absorb twice as much water as the millet. Why else do you think we pull them out?'

Realising that any pursuit of this argument will only delay her plan, Elina bids the nun goodnight a second time and turns her face to the wall. She can hear Sister Katerina tossing and turning in the next bed, probably thinking of the best way to inform the abbess about Elina's unorthodox views. She'll deal with it when she returns to the convent. Right now she has a more pressing matter and time is running out. While a part of her brain is feverish with planning and anticipating difficulties she may encounter in the hours ahead, another part of her is seeking a different kind of answer.

Three of the people closest to her have died in her short lifetime. First her mother, then Rozalia, and now Mira. It's like a bad spell has been cast on her. Wasn't the talisman Rozalia gave her, and which Elina has worn ever since Mira tied it around her neck – wasn't it supposed to protect her?

Elina pulls out the charm, which she wears in secret, and studies it in the cold gleam of the moon pervading their cell. The dark flecks trapped on the inside shine red, making the gem look like it's been sprinkled with blood. What if it's cursed and not blessed, as Rozalia claimed? What if Rozalia got it wrong, or made a mistake? Surely nobody can be right all the time. But then Dafina – the gypsy dancer at the inn – assured her it carried a good spell. And if Elina remembers right, Rozalia told her it would protect her against harm, not pain. But it doesn't even do that. It hasn't worked for Mira – it hasn't protected her against Barbu's malice and his evil plot.

Elina pulls at her talisman to yank it away, but the thread is strong, and it only burns the flesh on her neck. It will have to wait until she can get her hands on something sharp…

In fact, she may just wait a little longer before she gets rid of this dubious gem. For if there's any truth to it, any at all, let it prove its worth on the journey she's about to take. Though she knows she owes it to Mira to find her body and expose the mason's crime, Elina is numb at the thought of having to see the woman she loves dead, rotting away, eaten by worms and beetles… Will she have the strength to face it all?

The moment Sister Katerina's breathing falls deep and steady, Elina sneaks out of the cell. She sidles up against walls and trees to avoid the waxing moon, which will be a blessing once she's in the woods.

As soon as Elina passes the abbess's hut and then the priest's, she breaks into a run all the way to the gate, where she stops to catch her breath and appraise which side will be less challenging to climb. If someone else managed to do it before, there's a good chance she too—

'Going somewhere?'

The voice, though soft and kind, startles her. While her brain flashes with a hundred thoughts at once – deny, run, plead, confess, lie, persuade – her legs have given up on her and she wobbles as she turns around.

Father Arcady is sitting on a tree stump to the left of the gate.

'I'm sorry, Holy Father, I… This is not what it looks like—'

'Do you know something strange? When you watch a storm from a quiet place, you can see where it has come from and where it's headed.'

'It's not what you think, Father. I'm not running away… Just something I have to take care of before sunrise. I'll be back as soon as—'

'If there's one thing I've learned in my many years, it's that it's easier to protect people from wild beasts than from themselves.'

He doesn't believe her and that's unfair, Elina thinks. She's never given him any reason to doubt her.

She balls her hands into fists to stop them from shaking.

'I'll tell you the truth, Father – where I'm going and why. It may sound a little… but God is my witness—'

'I gather your truth may be quite a story to tell and I have a feeling you're in a hurry. I'll open the gate, child. You go get yourself a horse from the stable. You won't get far on foot.'

Elina doesn't move. Surely the priest is tricking her. He is tempting her to go ahead with her plan, only to summon the abbess, and probably her father too, the moment she puts a foot wrong. In fact, they may be hiding in the shadows already. Elina looks about her, bracing herself to hear her father's angry, disappointed voice at any moment.

'Serving God is by choice, not force,' the priest says. 'Now go and be well! But if it's the horse you're worried about… Your father has paid enough for your upkeep here to replace it with two others.'

He still doesn't believe that she'll be back. Elina bites her tongue – well, she'll prove him wrong when she returns to the convent as soon as she's done right by Mira.

She sprints towards the stable, thinking that she's either the most fortunate being alive, or a wretched fool about to be shamed and disgraced.

It wouldn't be the first time.

RACING AGAINST TIME

Though she rides at full gallop through the open gate, Elina still looks over her shoulder, half expecting to see her father or the priest chasing after her. Unable to rely on her hearing, with her ears full of wind, she keeps glancing back until she's certain that if anyone wanted to catch up with her and force her back to the convent, they would've done so by now. This thought must lift some weight off her, because Castana suddenly picks up speed when it seemed they were already flying through the woods.

The moon's glow reveals a well-trodden path, but it doesn't mean that it will take her home. If only Elina knew the way back to her village, she wouldn't need to stop at the inn to ask for help. It's a long shot, but Dafina, the gypsy dancer, is her only hope.

Riding through the dark woods makes her skin prickle and she wishes she had her bow with her. Castana, however, is at ease and that's reassuring. The mare would spook if she smelled wolves nearby.

When she glimpses a weak light ahead, Elina comes off the path. She circles the inn and dismounts at the back, where she hooks Castana's reins on to a tree out of sight. Because who has ever seen a nun riding bareback?

The inn is as full as it was last time. The expectant presence of so many men under one roof makes her hopeful. The *lăutari* stop playing their fiddles when she walks in and the men's hungry eyes appraise her body up and down, despite her nun's habit. She doesn't have anyone to speak for her this time, so she musters her most commanding voice.

'I'm the daughter of Boyar Constantin Pogor and I seek to speak to the innkeeper.'

A red-bearded man grumbles from behind the counter, and she makes her way towards him. The *lăutari* resume their music.

'This is no place for a nun…' He watches her with a muddled frown.

'It's not rest I'm after,' Elina says and asks to see the dancer. She speaks like she *knows* that Dafina is here.

The innkeeper breaks into a laugh. 'Don't waste your efforts, sister. The gypsy is beyond redemption—'

'A little blessing has never hurt anyone.'

'Look, sister—'

'You can't turn away a servant of God. I'll be gone in the time it takes you to pour another sinful drink, poisoning another soul.' Elina stares at the innkeeper, directing all her grief and anger into her glare.

The man mumbles an apology and disappears through the entrance that had been covered by a woollen blanket in winter.

Moments later, he returns and waves Elina through. Dafina is in the same room, cross-legged on a floor of cushions, circling her eyes with kohl.

'I hear you're concerned for my salvation.' The mocking in Dafina's voice tells Elina she's been recognised despite the dimness of the room.

'I can't believe my luck to find you here again. What are the chances of that?'

'Quite high.' There isn't a trace of humour on Dafina's face. 'You forget I'm a slave. To what do I owe this honour? Somehow I don't think you're here because you're worried for my soul.'

The unfair words cut deep. In other circumstances, Elina would spend more time with Dafina, prove to her that she doesn't care about their class differences. Perhaps even tell her how much in love she is – was – with a peasant woman. But every passing moment that she isn't on her way home is a moment that could make all the difference in finding Mira's body before morning, when the masons return to work.

'I sense some gloom about you,' Dafina says. 'How can I help?'

'I need to get to Pasareasca village before dawn.' The words tumble out of her mouth in one breath.

'Such haste?' Dafina has finished painting her face and looks up at Elina. 'Something on fire?'

The two of them lock eyes without blinking, in the way of conveying urgency without embroiling it with words.

'What do you need?' Dafina asks.

'Someone to show me the quickest way back to the village.'

'I have just the man for you,' she says. 'My servant. He used to live in these woods as a young man, ambushing and robbing the wealthy when they travelled. No one knows the woods better than him.'

Elina doesn't let the fact that she's to be guided by a robber worry her. She has no choice. Instead, she thinks how strange it is for a slave to have a servant.

Dafina whistles and a skinny man in an oversized cape appears in the doorway. A drooping hood obscures his eyes, leaving only a scar visible, slicing his left cheek from ear to mouth.

He doesn't say a word all the time he's being instructed, only sharply nods his head. Dafina warns Elina to make sure she keeps pace with him: 'He's faster than the wind.'

'Thank you. I'm very grateful—'

Dafina touches her lips with her forefinger. 'Be on your way now. May you get there in time.'

'I'll reward you when I see you next. I hope I can find you again.'

'And if you can't find me – reward my people.'

Her words don't make sense, but Elina doesn't have time to ask for an explanation.

When she slips out of the inn, the thief is waiting in the shadows, his horse pawing the ground. She leads him into the woods where her own horse is, and before she's barely astride, he charges ahead without warning, ignoring the main path and cutting through trees and shrubbery as though following a trail only he can see.

Elina wonders if he has heard the destination right. Or, what if… With all the uprisings against boyars happening up and down the country, what if he's abducting her for ransom? Or worse…

It's too late to worry about it now. She's in his hands and she better focus on keeping up with him. Elina thought she was an excellent rider, but she's falling behind him. His oversized cape flaps in the wind like the wings of a giant bat steadily out of her reach. Just like she used to think of her mother being one with her *cobză* when she played it, so is this man part of his horse in riding.

They've travelled so fast that it feels they've met time halfway. It can hardly have been a few hours when Elina recognises the hill of the Three Springs ahead of them. *It can't be right*, she thinks. It took them a whole day to reach the inn back in winter. Of course there's no snow, or blizzard, to impede their journey now, but even so.

She thinks her eyes and mind are playing tricks on her and waits a little longer, but when they pass the familiar crossroads where her father's estate leads towards the vineyards, she has no doubt they are on home ground.

Eager to be rid of the thief, she calls out to him. 'Hey you.' It strikes her she doesn't even know his name.

He slows down and she catches up with him. 'I know where I am now. You can go. Thank you… What are you called?'

'Murgu.'

'Isn't that a horse name?'

'My father called me after his favourite steed.'

'Is that why you ride so well?'

'I was born in a stable and mare's milk was often my only food.'

Elina smiles and relaxes for the first time since they left. 'Thank you. You brought me back a lot quicker than I thought.'

'The way the crow flies,' he says.

'I'm very grateful… but I'm afraid I don't have anything to pay you—'

'Pray for me, sister. That'll be enough,' he says and turns around, dashing spurs into his horse.

Elina matches his galloping but in the opposite direction, towards home. This is not how she imagined her return. It was supposed to be filled with high hopes and happiness for her future with Mira.

Instead, she has to dig for her body.

A RIDDLE

A heap of rubble lies where, only a few months back, Rozalia's hut stood. Elina circles the yard, her feet tripping and sinking in the overgrown grass. She leads Castana to the stream running alongside Rozalia's garden to quench the mare's thirst, and unexpectedly finds herself kneeling too, scooping fistfuls of water she brings to her mouth and face. A bracing chill trickles down her neck and back, soothing her feverish skin.

The two boulders to her right gleam white in the moonlight: the entrance to the secret cellar. What if… Could Mira be hiding here from Barbu? It's possible… Unlikely… Still…

Her heart lurches, slamming into her ribs, and she can't reach the trapdoor quick enough. She shoves the boulder aside and feels her way down the bumpy steps.

'Mira?' she calls into the darkness. 'Mira, are you here?'

The flint rock and the *iască* are at the bottom of the stairs where she remembers Mira coaxing fire last time. She strikes the rocks repeatedly but manages only to catch her fingers and would give up if it wasn't for the promising smoky whiff rising from her hands. When a tiny spark finally lands on the *iască*, Elina holds her breath for fear of snuffing it out. The pinprick glow quickly blossoms into a flame, and she lights the *opaiț*.

She takes in the cellar with a searching look. It's empty now, but someone lives here. Or maybe – lived.

The bench serving as bed is covered by a frayed blanket, twisted and jumbled as though the occupant has left it in a hurry. Elina touches it instinctively. It's cold.

She's about to blow out the *opaiț* and dash out when she notices a pair of large boots by the stairs, tangled in a pile of clothing.

Male clothing.

She picks up the first garment to convince herself they are a pair of trousers. Underneath there's a sheepskin, a hefty hat and a large shirt, which seem to carry the faint trace of Mira's herby scent. Has she worn them? Why on earth would she have dressed as a man?

Gazing at the puzzling items, Elina has an idea. She discards her nun's habit in one breath and pulls on the *ițari*, tightening them with the piece of string someone has already threaded through the waist. Even so, they hang loose on her. The shirt falls to her knees like a dress, and she tucks it into the trousers. As far as she can tell, she looks like any other young man. Though she didn't inherit her mother's abundant chest, there's enough of it that could spoil her cover. She finds a piece of linen and straps her breasts.

There's one more thing. Her long hair won't fit in the hat. She has to get rid of it. They won't know about it when she returns to the convent – all the sisters wear headscarves there anyway.

With a twinge in her heart, Elina gathers her hair and chops it short with a knife she finds on the table. The thick strands fall to the ground, clinging to her feet as though asking for mercy.

She feels exposed and vulnerable, as if her hair was a shield protecting her against the world. But she draws courage from the male clothing she's wearing. It feels good, empowering. Is this how all men feel?

She pulls on the oversized boots, dons the hat and blows out the *opaiț*.

Castana sprints up the hill despite being kept at the gallop since the previous evening. When they are close to the summit where the church is being built, Elina slows the mare down. Better to be cautious in case someone is up there. She alights before they're out of the woods and creeps on foot towards the high walls.

There's a stillness in the air that you can only find in the first hours of the morning – ripe and boundless, yet full of life. The peaceful purl of the Third Spring nearby is overcome by the hooting of a Little Owl – the same old bearer of bad news – whose ghastly call is an unnecessary reminder of Elina's unspeakable loss, shattering her heart anew.

She walks around the building site, thinking that if she stumbles upon anyone, she'll say she's lost. The glow of the moon helps her avoid tripping on the various tools lying about – ropes, hammers, trowels, paddles, chisels, wheels and other unfamiliar objects.

When she's certain there's nobody there, Elina picks up an iron rod and starts knocking on the walls as she circles the scaffolds. Neculai has taught her how to determine the amount of wine in a barrel by tapping on its head and side stave. Given her gift of the ear, she wasn't only able to tell when the barrel was full or empty, but she could guess the exact spot where the wine filled the vessel. The twig Neculai immersed into the barrel to verify her guess came out stained with wine exactly where she'd pointed.

The sound of her thumping on the newly built walls is consistent, mostly, and when it isn't, she looks for a reason. Is it because of gaps in the wall left for doors and windows? Is it an outer wall or an inner one? She hopes she'll know it when she finds the telltale spot.

She's soon back where she started without having found any dubious walls. What if she's wrong and Barbu is innocent? What if her suspicions are misguided? It's possible, but right now she doesn't have any other idea about what could have happened to Mira. Her getting lost in the woods, being attacked by a wild beast – these are stories she'd be tempted to believe about anyone else. But Mira knows how to see and treat nature for what it is – a sanctuary, not a deathtrap.

'I know you must be somewhere in there, I just know it,' she says under her breath. 'Why can't I find you?'

Her nails dig into her palms, and she props herself against a wall, closing her eyes, trying to focus like Rozalia taught her when she went hunting – slowing down her breath by counting to a certain rhythm. Gradually, her hands unclench and the sting in her flesh eases.

She catches a soft whisper in her ear, akin to the flutter of butterfly wings. But who's heard of butterflies at night-time? Whether in her head or outside it, the word she's heard makes her sprint to the other side of the building.

She doesn't know where exactly the altar is going to be set up, but like all altars, it will face the sunrise. Having appraised the most eastern wall, Elina starts knocking on it again, taking her time listening to its echo. However, each section sounds the same, and when she reaches the end of the wall without detecting anything suspicious, her heart sinks heavy.

She's about to move on to the next wall, but something niggles at her. Something doesn't feel right with this wall and so she circles it again.

And again.

This is it.

The steps don't add up.

She counts them twice inside and outside the building to make sure she isn't imagining things. There are at least three steps missing. Enough to hide a small alcove between the walls.

Elina lifts the rod as high as she can and strikes at the wall. Not a scratch. She hammers away with all her might, but it's obvious she doesn't have the strength to break it open. Her knees give in, and she buries her face into her hands, unable to tell if the bite of salt on her lips is from sweat or tears.

Feverish and furious, she whistles for Castana and spurs the horse into a race towards the village.

SEEK AND YOU SHALL FIND

Elina leaves Castana at the edge of the woods and sneaks on foot towards the potter's house. Riding through the village would agitate the dogs.

Despite her best efforts to be quiet, the moment she pushes Pavel's gate open, a mongrel charges at her out of nowhere, barking like mad. She could try going in through the garden, but she'll never make it to the door in time. Other dogs in the neighbourhood join in the barking and though she crouches behind a fence pole, the dogs aren't fooled.

There's a squeak and a scrape as a door opens and a gruff voice calls out: '*Țâbă*, Suru. Be quiet!'

The barking stops for a moment and Elina immediately pops her head above the twig gate.

'Pavel!'

The dog starts barking again.

'*Țâbă*, Suru! Who's there?'

'Pavel, I need to talk to you.'

The old man stomps his foot and the dog skulks away. Elina pushes the gate open and walks into the courtyard.

'Who are you, young man? What's your need at this ungodly hour? If robbing me is what you're after, I have nothing—'

'I come in peace. Can we go inside? The night has unseen eyes and ears.'

The old man watches Elina a moment longer before letting her into his house.

As soon as the door is shut behind them, she says, 'I'm so sorry… about Mira.' Her throat tightens.

'Who are you and what do you want?' It's too dark in the hut to see Pavel's face, but the distrust in his voice is obvious.

'I think I know what happened to your daughter.'

Pavel moves closer to the window, where the moon's glow shines on half his face. He's blinking like he has trouble understanding what Elina has said.

'You know where she is?'

'I'm almost certain.'

'Is she alive?' he asks, his whispering words pleading for a miracle.

Elina tells him about her suspicion, but as she speaks, she can see a frown pressing on the old man's forehead.

'What you're claiming, young man… is murder. You're a stranger to our village. Let me tell you – the master mason is a man of God. I see him in church every Sunday. He's kind and generous and—'

'He has fooled us all.'

'I don't know what your gripe is with the mason, but I want no part in it. Please, it's very late and I—'

'Pavel, look at me.' Elina wasn't going to reveal her identity, but she has to if she wants to win his trust. 'Don't you recognise me?'

'I know you from somewhere, but my memory isn't… Hang on, your voice. I know your voice.' He narrows his eyes. 'No, you can't be…'

'Yes, it's me, Elina, the boyar's daughter. I'm in disguise because I shouldn't be here.'

'Is this how the rich amuse themselves? Playing games with our misfortunes?'

The moonlight softens everything in the room, except his

eyes, whose fierceness is not only exposed but enhanced. Elina catches a glimpse of his turmoil. A hurt deeply rooted in his heart from a lifetime of disappointments with the rich.

'I'd never do that. Your daughter and I were friends. You must trust me.'

'When people like you say they want to help, it's because they want something in return. What are you after?'

Elina is bewildered by his stubbornness and the anger flashing in his eyes. 'I want to dig Mira out of those cursed walls and give her a proper burial. Don't you want to have a grave for her? A place where you can grieve your daughter?'

The old man stares at her. The hostility in his eyes eases off a little and she presses on. 'We need to get going, Pavel. I've left the convent without permission after my father came to visit and told me the news about Mira's disappearance. I've come to ask for your help so we can dig Mira out before my father returns and alerts Barbu. I've made the mistake of telling him what I thought happened to your daughter, but like you, he dismissed my hypothesis—'

'Your what?'

'My suspicion. Look, Pavel, we better hurry. If you're not coming, I'll find help somewhere else.' Elina steps towards the door.

'Wait.' He stops her. Despite his age, his fingers are nimble as he ties up his *opinci* in a haste. 'Shall I bring a hammer with us?'

'There're plenty of tools up on the hill. We just need enough strength to break the wall.'

The two of them sneak into the night, making their way towards the woods. An oil lamp is burning at the shepherd's hut and two people move about the courtyard.

'Lambing,' Pavel says.

'He looks strong.' Elina points at the young man who seems familiar. 'Isn't he the one who wins all the wrestling games at the harvest fair?'

'Andrei, the shepherd's son. A bear of a man. Wouldn't want to get an ill-meant hug off 'im. And that's his mother, Lisaveta, a big mouth. Don't ever get into an argument with her.'

'We may need his help to break the wall,' Elina says. 'Is he trustworthy?'

'He is, but—'

'The wall is at least six bricks deep,' Elina exaggerates. She's suddenly worried that the two of them won't be enough. 'I'll go speak to him.'

'Leave it to me.' Pavel waves her back and goes to greet the two peasants. He takes Andrei to the side, where they speak in low voices. The old woman scowls at them, eavesdropping, and Elina approaches to distract her.

'Newly born, are they?' She nods to the two lambs struggling to find their legs.

Lisaveta grunts without taking her eyes off the men.

'What's that?' Elina points to the messy blob discarded on the side.

'That one didn't make it,' Lisaveta says.

The sight of the lifeless ball of mucus and bloodied flesh fills Elina with unpleasant memories from the night she almost bled to death. Bile rises in her throat. She swallows it down, but not quickly enough, and a burning at the back of her mouth brings on a coughing fit. She makes it as loud as she can and Lisaveta is clearly annoyed with her.

'Are you trying to spit your guts out, young man?'

'I'd be grateful for a cup of water.'

'There's a well down the road,' Lisaveta says, her eyes staying fixed on the whispering men.

Andrei comes back and looks at his mother. 'The potter needs my help with something. I won't be long.'

Lisaveta bars their way, her hands planted on her hips like a protective mother hen. 'Where are you taking my son at this hour?'

'The sooner we go, the sooner he'll be back.' Pavel's voice is soft and reassuring.

'He's the only man left in our family. If something happens to him, I'll curse you for the rest of your days,' she says and steps aside reluctantly.

Noticing Pavel's laboured walk, Elina suggests he rides the mare ahead of them.

'Andrei and I will take a shortcut and meet you at the top.'

Swift as a hare, Elina cuts through gorse and bracken, following her nose up the hill.

'You're not from around here,' Andrei says. 'How come you know these grounds so well?'

'I used to work for the boyar, but I've learned better,' she says, and to deflect attention from her, she thanks him for coming to help.

'I owe Mira. She came to comfort my sister when our father was dying. She was so kind. It's hard to believe what's happened to her.' Andrei shakes his head.

Elina walks ahead, in part to show the way, but mostly to hide her face, lest he notices her sadness.

When they reach the building site, Pavel is already holding a club hammer and a crowbar in his hands.

'Which wall is it?' he asks.

She leads the two men to the eastern side, pointing to where she believes Mira is walled up. Andrei looks at her and she guesses his unease, but she can't tell him that all she's relying on are scraps of observation, a wisp of intuition and the little knowledge about numbers her mother has taught her.

Pavel too regards her with eyes brimming with doubt.

'Listen to the birds waking up,' she says. 'The dawn will break soon.'

Pavel lifts the hammer above his head and strikes the wall, but the tool springs back at him. 'Stubborn rocks,' he says.

Andrei joins in with another hammer, his steady blows setting off sparks in places. Sweat trickles down his face and neck and he takes off his tunic.

'I won't stand in your way,' Pavel says and moves aside, clasping his hands in prayer.

Elina goes to fetch the ladder and the coil of rope she spotted earlier. They'll need them to retrieve Mira's body – if she's right about the whole thing.

By the time Andrei makes a dent in the stone, his back is awash with sweat, glistening in the light of the paling moon. This little conquest reinforces his strength, and he hammers away until a chunk of stone breaks and falls silently on the other side.

'You're right,' he says, looking at Elina. 'It's a hollow wall.'

'Hurry up,' she says. 'I'll climb through as soon as the gap is big enough.'

Andrei's efforts are helped by Pavel who, using the crowbar, pulls at the rocks with the ferocity of a mother bear whose cubs are trapped.

'That'll do,' Elina says.

Andrei scratches his head. 'Hardly a fox could squeeze through.'

Elina ties the rope around her waist. 'I don't know how deep it is, or if you can hear me from the other side. Watch the rope. I'll tug it when I'm ready to come out.'

Andrei shakes his head. 'No, lad. These knots won't do.' He undoes her work and starts again by securing her with double loops, threading the rope under her armpits – she's glad she's strapped her breasts – around her waist and between her legs.

Andrei must have sensed her tension. 'No bother, I won't catch your balls,' he says and ties a final knot.

There's a glint of amusement in Pavel's eyes and Elina is glad to see his face soften a little, however briefly.

'Here, lad.' Andrei clasps his hands together, the way her father used to do when she was little and needed a leg-up to boost her into the saddle.

She clambers up the wall and crawls through the hole to the other side, comfortable in the knowledge that Andrei is holding on to the other end of the rope.

The darkness here is of a pitch that sends her skin tingling. Despite the dogged chill digging its fangs into her flesh, her hands are damp, and she struggles to keep hold of the rope.

Stale air and limestone are all Elina can smell. No rotting flesh as she expected. What if she is wrong after all and Mira isn't here?

Elina's eyes sting with the effort of trying to see something, anything, but it makes no difference whether her eyes are open or closed. She crawls, groping her way around and wincing each time a sharp pebble jabs her palms or knees. One arm stretched out, she dreads, yet hopes, to find Mira's body at any moment. She fights the sickening thought that she may have asked the men to wreck the wall for nothing. Or worse, the wrong wall.

When she touches something other than cold stone, she yelps and pulls back, pressing on her heaving chest to tame her heartbeat, but it only increases, rising into her throat, her ears, her head. She reaches for the body again, tracing her fingers across what she's certain is human flesh, making out a pair of small feet and thin ankles locked together. A singeing bolt shoots through her.

It's not Mira, but a child!

She was right about the wall, but wrong about Mira. She feels blindly about the stiff body propped up against the wall, face turned up, hands in the lap—

Hands!

She picks up the child's right hand and counts the fingers. Four. A missing forefinger. Elina touches the slim, cold neck. She finds the amulet and feels it in her fingers, recognising its crescent shape.

It is her! Barbu didn't kill Mira. He buried her alive and she has starved to death, hence her shrivelled body.

Elina clasps both of Mira's wrists, but there is no throb of life in them. What did she expect? Mira has been here for weeks. But now that Elina is facing her worst fear – seeing Mira dead – she can't believe it. Maybe that's why she does what she saw Rozalia do to her mother on that fateful day, not that it helped, but if Rozalia thought there was a slight chance it could, then Elina has to try it too. She starts moving Mira's arms up and down and side to side, up and down and side to side…

The body is limp and lifeless.

'Oh, my Froglet, I'm so sorry.' Elina hugs Mira close to her chest, feeling the jolts of her sobbing pass through the shrunken body.

'Have you found her?' a voice calls from above. 'Is she there?'

'Take down the rest of the wall,' Elina calls back.

The hammers are at work once more. The men's ferocious strikes send stone chips and rocks falling on their side. Elina covers Mira with her own body as though she could still feel the pain.

There's a soft moan.

'Mira? Mira!' Elina shakes Mira's body, but there isn't the slightest reaction. She's overheard their servants at the manor say that dead bodies can make noises as they rot away. But Mira's body isn't rotting, or maybe it's just that she can't smell the decay due to the chill down here. Perhaps she has just imagined the moan.

Still, she keeps a close ear to Mira's face, praying that she hears it again, the—

There it is again – the sound of life.

'You're alive, oh heavens, you're alive… Mira? Talk to me. Can you hear me?'

Could this really be true? She remembers Mira telling her about the fasting Rozalia made her do in the name of her teachings. Is there any way it could have helped to keep her alive all this time?

'Hurry up with the wall, and come give me a hand,' Elina calls at the top of her voice, not only to urge the men on, but also to shut up the Little Owl still hooting above. Of course, it doesn't mean Mira is out of danger, but it feels good to claim this small victory over the bird, who once had called just as eagerly for her mother's death. 'You're wrong, you horrible, stupid, ugly bird, you're wrong.' Elina's sobs rock her body.

The gap in the wall above them grows bigger with each stone the two men rip out with their hammers. The fuzzy glow of the moon reaches them in the pit and Elina sees Mira's face shining with the tears she has wept on her.

Mira's lips stir as though she wants to say something, when Elina realises she's after the moisture she can feel on her skin.

'They will only increase your thirst, my Froglet. Hang on just a little bit longer and I'll brush your mouth with fresh water from the spring.' She strokes Mira's face and kisses her lips, which feel like cracked clay.

When the opening in the wall is big enough, Andrei slides the ladder in and comes down too fast for someone his size. 'Oh Lord! Mighty and merciful Lord. All skin and bone, poor thing,' he says, picking Mira up and slinging her over his shoulder like she's a dry pelt.

Elina holds the bottom of the ladder, waiting for Andrei to climb out before she steps on it. The thought of it crushing under their weight, trapping them all there, breaks cold sweat on her back.

When Andrei is on the other side and she can hear Pavel's cries of anger, relief and disbelief at the sight of his daughter, Elina starts crawling her way up, worried her damp hands will slip or that she may put a foot wrong. Why is it taking so long to reach the top?

Fresh air has never smelled sweeter. Fallen into a pile on the ground to catch her breath, Elina sees Mira stretched out on a patch of grass glistening with dew in moonlight, groaning softly, and her father kneeling beside her, stroking her face.

'My child, my soul… You're safe now… I've got you… It'll be alright…' Pavel's words are lost in his sobs. 'Thank the Lord for His mercy… Our Saviour…' The old man wipes his face with his sleeve and launches into a string of curses directed at Barbu. If they were to come true, the mason would be struck by lightning, catch the plague, die a leper and burn forever in the flames of hell.

'Hear that?' Elina says, putting her ear to the ground.

The two men look at her in confusion. 'What is it?' Andrei asks.

'Galloping horses coming this way,' Elina says. 'At least three.'

Andrei jumps to his feet. 'My mother must've alerted the priest or the village elders when she realised I wasn't back yet.'

'We must get away before they arrive,' Pavel says.

'It could be Barbu,' Elina says. 'And if it's him, we won't get away in time.' She looks from one man to the other. 'I know a safe place for Mira where they won't find her. But one of you has to stay behind to delay and distract Barbu.'

'I'll do it,' Andrei says.

'No.' Pavel shakes his head. 'He buried *my* daughter alive. *I* will stay.'

Elina whistles for Castana and jumps on her back before the mare comes to a complete halt. Andrei lifts Mira on the horse, propping her into Elina's arms.

'Look after her, will you?' Pavel doesn't take his eyes off his daughter.

'I will, I promise.'

'You're a wo… You're a man of your word. Please forgive me for doubting you—'

'I'll come visit you later with news of how she's doing,' Elina calls over her shoulder. She leads Castana in the opposite direction, away from the sound of the horses tearing the ground.

The wind rushes in her ears, filling them with the trills and warbles of the skylarks cheering the new dawn.

PAYING DEBTS

Back at Rozalia's cellar, Elina wraps Mira in a sheepskin and gives her regular sips of warm water laced with honey to get her stomach working again. Her breath is laboured, and her eyes are still glazed with bafflement and exhaustion.

'You'll feel better soon, my love, I promise.'

She stays by Mira's side, holding her hand and talking to her about what's happened since that fateful night at Rozalia's.

'I'm so sorry I couldn't protect her from my father's fury. I still have nightmares about it. If only I hadn't stolen that tansy… I should've asked for her help instead.'

Mira's head rolls to the side. Is she disagreeing with Elina or is it just her weak body doing its own thing?

Elina tells Mira how she had to reveal to her father the truth about her uncle, and how she took revenge on him by spearing his balls. Mira's lips move, but there's no sound coming out, only a weak smile. Or perhaps it's a grimace of pain.

Elina caresses Mira's face, kissing her lips softly. 'We'll run away as soon as you recover. Nothing is going to stop us this time.'

When Mira dozes off, Elina checks the throb in her wrist to make sure she's only asleep. Relieved, she stands up to stretch her legs and to start thinking about food for herself. She could go out hunting, but she doesn't want to leave Mira on her own. She sweeps the cellar with a glance – rows of pots and bundles line the shelves, but knowing Rozalia, what could look like food could just as easily be poison.

What about the trunk in the far corner? What's in that?

She approaches it with caution as though it could really be concealing a dead body, as she'd teased Mira last time. She opens it and laughs. More herbs and potions stacked up from one end to the—

The other end is filled with scrolls. Her mother's scrolls! She'd recognise them anywhere.

So this is where Rozalia has been keeping them safe all this time. But there are so many more here than what the old woman has shown her.

The same drawings of her younger self she's already seen, the scenes from the Bible, the skylark singing its silent song, the mysterious eyes… Why can't she remember where she's seen them before? It's definitely a man, judging by the wild brows, but it's not her father's blue-eyed, self-assured gaze. This is a youthful look – intense, with a deep, sorrowful kind of longing… Never mind, it'll come to her.

The next scrolls depict a woman holding a long brush in her hand dripping with paint, variously crouched over an open book, or looking out of a barred window. Even though the woman's face is obscured in all the drawings, and they don't have barred windows at the manor, Elina recognises her mother – the pointed slippers, stitched with squirrel belly fur, are distinctly hers.

The vivid sketches act as a magic window into the past when her mother was still alive, and a torrent of happy memories flood her mind. She sinks her hands to the bottom of the trunk, bringing up an armful of scrolls, one of which slips to the ground, half unfurling as it rolls under the table. She picks it up and gasps, looking at the mysterious eyes, this time drawn on the face they belong to.

His hair is the shiny black of a raven's wing, and not the hoary curls Elina remembers from when she met him, but his dimples are unmistakable. Her mother has captured them perfectly.

The Old Cobzar!

Elina goes through the rest of the unopened scrolls. Most of them feature the Old Cobzar – grooming a horse, playing the *cobză* in front of a fire, resting against a haystack, swimming in the lake… *This can't be right*, she thinks. Why are there none of her father? Oh, she's such a fool – of course her mother would've given them to him as soon as they were finished, all those years ago. She must ask her father for one – she would love to have a drawing of him too.

Looking at her mother's work has stirred that old, bone-deep ache of missing her, a pain she knows can only be soothed by playing the *cobză*. But the instrument is still at the convent, where Elina thought she'd return after finding Mira's body. However, now that Mira has tricked Death and is recovering, Elina's place is in the world, not at the nunnery. Even so, she will have to set foot there one more time. As soon as Mira is well enough to be left alone for a day, Elina will go to bring the *cobză* back to where it belongs: in her arms.

On the second night after Mira's rescue, Elina brews tea with acacia flowers. Mira chokes on it as she gulps it down.

'Don't be greedy. There's plenty more.'

Mira's lips twist with effort as she whispers her first words. 'Most… delicious… thing… ever…'

Elina jumps to her feet, praising all gods – pagan and Christian – for bringing the woman she loves back to life.

'More…' Mira's gaze is fixed on the cup of tea.

'In a little while, my dearest. We have to be careful… God, I missed you so much, you will never know. I'll never leave you ever again.' Elina gathers Mira into a tight embrace, but seeing the terror in her eyes, she lets go at once.

'Air… Can't have enough of it…' Mira says, her eyes focusing on Elina for the first time. 'You're a sweet dream—'

'No, I'm not.' Elina squeezes Mira's hand. 'I'm real. Right by your side.'

'You're a handsome man.'

'Oh, my short hair,' Elina laughs. 'Don't you like it? Don't worry, it will grow back.'

'You're my future husband… from a future life… when you'll be born a man.'

'It's alright, you're safe. We're safe. Go back to sleep now. You need lots of rest.' Elina starts singing softly to help Mira drift away.

As soon as Mira's breath is peaceful again, Elina decides to take advantage of her slumber and visit Pavel quickly. She has promised to bring him news of his daughter.

She pulls down the wick of the *opaiț* so as to leave some light in the cellar, in case Mira wakes up while she's out. Finding herself in complete darkness again will no doubt frighten her.

The potter's house is abustle with villagers mingling in the courtyard. Judging by the brightness of the light, there must be a few candles burning. Anger heats up her blood. Isn't it a little too soon for celebrations?

She leans over the gate and skims the crowd for Pavel. Andrei approaches her with a quick step.

'We can't talk here,' he says in a low voice and walks her down the road.

'Where is Pavel?'

'Keep walking. I don't want anyone to overhear us.'

When they reach the meadow, Andrei drops into a squat, cradling his head.

'What's the matter?' Elina sits on the grass next to him.

'After you rode away with Mira, I hid in the bracken by the church, in case the old man needed help. But it all happened so quickly.'

'What happened quickly?'

'You were right. Barbu and his men were coming for us.

He was so mad with fury that he cried like a little boy when he saw the shattered wall, telling the potter that Mira wasn't his daughter any longer but that she belonged to God. While Pavel cursed, calling him a beastly man with the devil in his heart, Barbu sniffed the air, looking the way you rode into the woods, as if he could smell your scent. That's when Pavel grabbed at the reins of his horse.'

'He attacked Barbu?'

'Yes, but the mason kicked him in the chest and the old man stumbled and fell. He hit his head on this stone that was jutting out. Sounded like a ripe beetroot splitting.' Andrei shakes his head like he wants to shed the memory.

'Is that…' Elina's belly twists with dread. 'Is that a vigil at his house?'

'I leaped out of the bracken to help Pavel, but there was nothing to be done. I pleaded with Barbu to let me take the potter's body and give him a Christian burial like he deserved. But the mason's men jumped me. I said I was their witness that Pavel's death was an accident. They asked about Mira, and I lied, telling them the village elders took her away…'

Andrei's words swim in Elina's mind as she remembers the hooting of the Little Owl on the night they'd rescued Mira. The dutiful bird was warning them about the potter's imminent death. But Elina misunderstood it.

'When is his funeral?' she asks.

'Tomorrow, of course. It's the third day since his death,' Andrei says, somewhat annoyed.

'I'm sorry, I've hardly slept in the last few days.'

'How is Mira doing?'

'We got her out just in time,' Elina says.

'I don't even know your name, lad—'

'I'm Matei,' she says with such ease as though she's been called a male name her entire life.

'How did you even know about what happened to Mira?'

Elina has been expecting this question. 'Not all of Barbu's men shared his cruelty and evil. Some of them talked.'

'Too bad they didn't talk earlier. And he got away too, fled the village that same day. But Boyar Constantin is still here,' Andrei says, his voice raspy with menace.

'What? Wait…' Elina makes an effort to restrain her rising panic. 'What's the boyar got to do with—'

'He was the one who brought the evil mason to our village in the first place. And he's bleeding us dry of grains and livestock, the greedy pig. He's had it coming for a long time.'

Her cheeks are so hot she worries their heat will make her look like one of those beetles glowing in the dark.

'When are you planning—'

'Tomorrow. Straight after Pavel's funeral, while the peasants are still angry. Will you join us?'

Elina runs her hand through the cool grass as though searching for a hole in the ground she could fall through. 'Sure, I'll join you—'

'Bring an axe, or a garden fork.' Andrei stands up. 'See you tomorrow,' he says and leaves, the night swallowing him up at once.

Elina sits there, holding her head to stop it from spinning. She has to warn her father. Angry peasants armed with sharp tools and a lifetime of repression will be heading to the manor as soon as they bury Pavel tomorrow.

There's no one she can send word with. She must do it herself. This means facing her father's wrath sooner than she'd thought. He'll be utterly furious with her, for not only has she humiliated and disrespected him by running away from the convent, but she has also irrevocably ruined her future after he has worked so hard for it all these years.

Even so, this is no time to think about pride and reputation. Her father is in danger, and she must see him right away.

BURNED BRIDGES

Elina stops briefly at Rozalia's cellar to check on Mira, who – thankfully – is still in a deep sleep. She cannot help but check Mira's wrist once more and, happy with her finding, she darts out again.

The moon glides in and out of the clouds, one moment wrapping Elina in protective darkness, the next revealing her shadow with a haze of dust rising from Castana's hooves and trailing behind them.

The thought of facing her father right now, and dressed as a man too, makes her heart outpace the mare's sprint.

Neculai unbolts the gate, a torch in his hand and his face scrunched up. Will he recognise her?

'Who are you, young man, and what do you want?'

'I'm bringing urgent news for Boyar Constantin,' she says in her deepest voice.

His eyes open wide for a moment. If her disguise has fooled him, her voice may have just betrayed her. But Neculai doesn't say anything. Instead he lets her into the courtyard and goes to fetch his master.

Harsh, grating sounds emerge from the open window of the day room. It's the *cobză*. Her father must have brought it back from the convent, and she's grateful because it has spared her having to go there for it herself. She winces, however, at the abuse the instrument is being subjected to right now, as an angry, untrained hand is plucking at its strings, as though to punish it. The coarse scratching noise stops and, soon after, her father's belly peeks from behind the door before the rest of him appears. He has trimmed his beard, presumably to make the ever-growing bald patch under his lips less obvious. How can someone age so much in a few days?

'What's your news, young man?' he asks, the five words robbing him of his breath.

Elina looks at Neculai standing to her father's right, and thinks of the other servants who, no doubt, are lurking in the shadows. She says, 'My news is for your ears only.'

Her father scowls at her and Elina hopes the darkness and the oversized hat will keep her secret until they're out of anyone's earshot. Relief washes over her when he invites her inside the house.

His waddle is worse than ever. As they pass under the window of her mother's bedroom, there's a sharp pinching in her chest. Will this ache ever go away?

Her father shows her into the room with all the hunting tools, clearly wishing to impress the young man he sees in front of him. Warm delight bursts in her chest at the sight of her bow and arrows hanging on the wall.

'Depending on your message, I may offer you some wine,' her father says, reaching for the silver pitcher and pouring himself a cupful.

'The villagers are angry. There's going to be an uprising.'

Her father takes a few steps towards her. 'You look like my nephew Mihnea and sound just like my daughter,' he says. 'Let me guess, a bastard of my brother's, are you?'

'Closer to home, Father.'

His laugh turns into a cough. 'Nice try, lad, but you're not mine. I don't have any bastards—'

'I'm *not* out of wedlock.'

Her father's brows shoot up. 'Is it you, my angel?' He comes close and grabs her shoulder, turning her face towards the oil lamp. 'But it is you! I'll be damned. Well, you can forget about the wine, young lady. Now' – his face hardens as though he's just remembered his anger at her – 'you've disobeyed me, you've gone behind my back,' he says, taking a long slurp at his wine.

'I was right though. About Barbu's crime. I found her—'

Her father slams the table with his fist, his breath sending ripples in his wine. 'You've ruined your future—'

'I've saved a life.'

'All my efforts… All that hard work for nothing—'

'So what if she's poor? She's someone else's daughter too.' Elina's earlier fears and worry about this confrontation turn to anger.

But her father is oblivious to anything she says, blinded by his own reasons. 'We had a deal with the voivode. To build a church where his arrow had landed. That's never going to happen now after what you've done. You can say goodbye to your special status, to your independence…'

Elina watches her father gesticulate wildly, slashing the air with his arms to emphasise his words, which come as a torrent of accusations and remonstrations. When he's fuming, she's learned, it's best to let him run out of breath, which doesn't take long, especially with his latest weight gain.

Taking her silence as agreement, her father drops his voice. 'Why don't you go change out of these awful clothes. We'll have some food and think about how we can fix this.'

'I like them.' The words are out before she can stop them. Something on her father's face – perhaps his wide eyes, or the incredulity curling his lip – amuses her and she decides to tease him a little more. 'Wearing men's clothes makes me feel strong and powerful. I get to taste what it's like to be you.' She smiles, but her father isn't humoured.

'Stop this nonsense and go get changed.'

Perhaps if he had laughed or said it differently, she would have dropped it, but the dismissive wave and the impatience in his voice like she's still a silly little girl has rubbed her the wrong way.

'You've always wished I was a son.'

'I'll hear no more of this.' Her father turns away to refill his silver cup. The glugs of wine are all that can be heard in the ensuing silence, followed by a loud sigh as he sinks into a chair.

His stubbornness feeds her fire. What if…

Her trail of thoughts is interrupted suddenly by the memory of what Mira said to her earlier: *You're a sweet dream… You're my future husband… from a future life… when you'll be born a man.*

What if Mira has truly seen their future? And what if it's not from another lifetime, but this one? Elina isn't going back to the convent now that she's found Mira alive. And, thinking about it, she really does like wearing male clothes. They are more comfortable, for starters, easier to ride in. Certainly a better match to her spirit than the dresses she's had to wear her whole life.

But most important of all is that this arrangement would allow them to be together. Running away and pretending to be sisters wouldn't work because two women living on their own would never be safe. But as a couple – husband and wife – this is their only way.

It doesn't feel like a decision – it's almost a recognition of fate. Joy, fear, excitement – they are all tearing through her in a dizzying medley. Could this really be their chance? It would be her biggest secret yet. And what did Rozalia say about that? *The bigger the secret, the higher the danger and greater the loss if you're found out. But, sometimes, it's worth it.*

'There's a wild glint in your eye which gives me palpitations,' her father says. 'Talk to me. What are you plotting now?'

'You once told me that nobody was free. But I think freedom exists, only it's relative to sacrifice. How badly does one want it? How much is one willing to give up?'

Her father is sloshing the wine around his mouth, frowning like something is wrong with its taste. 'What's that supposed to mean?' he asks, his voice suspicious as though he's not sure he wants to hear the answer.

'I can be the son you've always wanted. This way we don't need the voivode and his favours.'

'I don't understand…' Her father starts picking at his beard.

'Like you said, the voivode won't forgive us our failure. He'll revoke my special status and I'll never come into your inheritance as a daughter. Given my prospects of a good marriage depend on Uncle Bogdan keeping quiet, we both know what that's worth. How confident are you that your brother isn't going to try and ruin the marriage you've arranged for me? And what's going to happen to me when you're no longer here to look after me? I'll end up a pauper, while our greedy ruler will benefit from all that's ours and has been for generations.'

'Surely you don't mean—'

'I do. I am… Let's see… Call me Matei. I am Matei Pogor, a bastard child you haven't recognised until now. Your daughter… Tell people she has become a nun. As Matei Pogor, I can be a real heir and look after all that's ours. Nobody will know—'

'Elina, my angel, you must be running a fever—'

'It's the best for both of us,' she says, hoping her father won't notice the clicks and pops of her dry mouth.

'How can that be? Say it works and you become my heir – then what? How are you going to give me the grandchildren I need to make it all worth the while if you dress like a man and have no intention of getting married?'

'I'll work it out, Father. One step at a time. Would you please sign a testimony to confirm—'

'You're the undoing of me, of our family.' The disappointment in her father's voice makes him sound a hundred years old.

It's clear she's asking the impossible of him. But so did her mother when she'd asked him to pretend he was the one painting the church books. He broke the rules once…

'If you change your mind and want to find me, look for

Matei Pogor. I hope you do. Didn't you once tell me that blood was thicker than water?' She walks to the other side of the room and picks her bow and arrows off the wall. 'I'll need this.'

'If you leave now, you'll never be welcome here ever again.'

'Father, you have to leave the manor yourself for a while. Ask Neculai to move everything of value in the cellars and be gone to our town house before dawn. There's no stopping those angry peasants. The tithes, the days of back-breaking *corvoadă*… And now they blame you for bringing the evil mason to the village too. Now he's run away, they will make you pay for it all.'

'It's not me you should be worried about.' Her father's face glistens with sweat.

'You're not hearing me. Well, I guess you can't reproach me for my stubbornness. I can see where I've got it from,' Elina says, tying the quiver with arrows around her waist and slipping the bow over her shoulder.

'You can't really mean what you're saying, for though you're ready to abandon me, you'll never abandon this place. It's where your mother's grave is.'

Of course. How has she not thought about that? But she won't let her father see her wavering.

'Talking about my mother, I would love to have one of the drawings she did of you.'

'What drawings? What do you mean?'

Judging by his frown, her father isn't playing up. He genuinely doesn't seem to know anything about her mother's *other* sketches.

'Rozalia has kept some of my mother's work in a safe place – quite a few drawings of me and I thought she must've done one or two of you.'

'Your mother loved you more than anything in the world; it makes sense that she'd paint you. But no' – he shakes his head – 'she wouldn't waste her precious pigments on her husband.'

What about the Old Cobzar? She wants to say. Why are

there so many sketches of this total stranger when there are none of her father? Her mind is clicking with questions as if a cloud of bats has just taken roost in her head.

To avoid blurting out something inappropriate which she may regret later, Elina diverts the conversation.

'By the way, thank you for bringing the *cobză* back from the convent. How did you know I wasn't going back there?'

'I didn't know. The abbess gave me your things the morning after you left. She said she wouldn't have you back even if you returned and begged her.'

'Did she return my fur coat and muffs too?'

'Don't know anything about that,' he says.

Elina smiles, nodding to herself, knowing she was right about the abbess all along.

'Alright, Father, take care and remember my name – Matei Pogor,' she says and heads for the door.

'Come off it, my angel.' Her father heaves himself out of the deep chair and steps towards her.

'If you call the servants to restrain me, I'll have no choice but to use this,' she says, pointing to the bow on her shoulder.

Her father's face flushes red, and his throat moves up and down as if he's choosing some words and discarding others. 'You will grow out of it. You're used to a certain way of life. When you see what living outside these walls is like, you *will* be back.'

'You can't treat me as a weak daughter when you've raised me like the son you've always wanted.' Elina bobs her head in a quick goodbye and scurries out of the room.

She stops by the day room where she picks up the *cobză*, and seeing her father's velvet mantles hanging by the door, she grabs one. He won't notice one missing.

Elina spots Fulger amongst the grazing horses in the fields behind the manor. The distinguished poise and raven shine of his hide makes him unmistakable. She crouches at the edge of the woods and lets out the high-pitched whistle the horse knows so well. Fulger pricks up his ears and stretches his neck, smelling the air. Elina whistles again and the horse bolts towards the line of acacia trees where she's lurking in the shadows.

'Hello, old boy.' She blows on his muzzle. 'I've missed you.'

The horse sniffs her like she's been away for a lifetime.

'I won't leave you again, I promise.' Elina removes the reins off Castana and places them on Fulger, whose neighing is less than convivial towards the other horse.

'Alright, Mr Grumpy, don't you get all fretful now. She looked after me when I didn't have you. And now she'll be looking after Mira. We're all one family now.'

There's no need to tie Castana. The mare is at their heels as they hurtle through the woods.

Before they reach the village, Elina stops for a little hunting. The villagers hardly have any food themselves to be able to contribute much towards the *praznic* for Pavel's funeral. Besides, her hands are itchy – she's missed her bow and arrows.

Nine dead pheasants later, Elina thinks that should be enough. She ties eight of them together with willow boughs and hauls them across Fulger's back. The last one she places on top – for Mira's dinner.

The village is aglow with flickering oil lamps. A cooking fire sends up sparks and smoke in the potter's courtyard, where women take turns in stirring pots and men pass around a cup they share a drink from. Wide-eyed children are huddled together, listening to stories of love and greed, of hardship and courage, of faith and fate.

Elina stays hidden behind a mulberry tree on the other side of the road. Unable to see Andrei in the yard, she hopes the young man will be coming soon so she can give him the game she's brought for the meal.

Two figures are walking up the road and though Elina moves around the tree trunk to avoid being spotted, Lisaveta has the eye of a hawk. She lifts the stick she's leaning on, pointing it at Elina.

'You're bad news, lad. Keep away from my son.'

'Leave him alone, Mother,' Andrei says, pushing a wheelbarrow heaped with logs.

Elina picks the bunch of pheasants and offers it to them. 'For Pavel's *praznic*,' she says, answering the unspoken question in Andrei's eyes. 'It's the least I can do.'

Still glaring, Lisaveta doesn't wait to be asked twice and carries the pheasants into the yard.

'Thank you for your gift,' Andrei says. 'You haven't changed your mind about joining us in the uprising tomorrow, have you?'

Elina is almost certain her father won't heed her warning. She has to be there to try and protect him from the villagers' wrath. More than that, she has to save her home. It's not her home any more, strictly speaking, but still. It's also her mother's resting place. She can't let it be desecrated. She won't.

Elina swallows hard. 'I will be there.'

The thin clouds veiling the moon are chased by darker ones, bearing the promise of a much-awaited rain. The thirsty land needs to drink soon, or the villagers will be heading into another hungry year. Living at the manor may have sheltered Elina from many truths, but her relationship with Rozalia and Mira has kept her feet firm on the ground.

As she approaches Rozalia's cellar, it strikes Elina that this is the only home she has now. There's a strange ripple in her chest. Is it regret, worry, excitement? She remembers her father's words – *When you see what living outside these walls is like, you* will *be back.*

Home isn't really someone's hut or manor, she thinks, but the place where your loved one is waiting for you. She hooks the limp pheasant on a tree and hurries down the stairs.

'I could tell you were coming from a long way away,' Mira whispers in the dimness of the cellar. 'The thuds of your horse's hooves.'

Elina lifts the wick of the *opaiț*, and the room instantly brightens up. Mira is propped up against the wall.

'Feeling much better, are we?' She kisses Mira and adjusts the blankets for more comfort. 'You'll be on your feet in no time. I've got a plump pheasant that's definitely going to help with that.'

'A boyar's daughter cooking for a peasant,' Mira says, her face twisting into a grin. Elina recognises the smile in her eyes. Though sunken, the glint in them is promising.

'You keep on giving me lip and you'll have to cook your own dinner,' Elina says as she starts getting things ready to prepare the meal.

Mira watches her as she potters about. 'This disguise suits you. You'd have made a handsome man. How much longer are you going to pretend?'

Elina leaves the fowl in the pot and comes to sit next to Mira. 'When you first opened your eyes and saw my short hair, you said I was your future husband, from a future life.'

'I had some beautiful dreams while trapped in that wall. We were husband and wife, and we had a big family with lots of children running around. Silly dreams, perhaps, but they kept me alive.'

'What if we can make it happen in this life? Except for the children, of course.'

'How?'

'We stand a better chance of living together by posing as husband and wife than orphan sisters. That's how we'll comply with the law – by fooling it.'

'You mean…'

'I won't ever wear another dress in my life.'

Mira's face is scrunched up in confusion, but then it relaxes into what once would have been her widest smile. 'Lovely. I'll get to wear all your dresses and be the pretty one.'

'And I won't complain if I don't ride side-saddle ever again,' says Elina, caressing Mira's hollow face. It's surprising Mira has accepted such a dangerous, unlawful proposition so readily. Perhaps in her fogginess, she hasn't really grasped it.

But what Mira says next proves she's more lucid than Elina has given her credit for.

'It runs in your family. Fearlessness on the verge of madness. You mother had it, painting all those church books in secret, and now you. Wanting to challenge the church and law all over again. She'd be very proud of you.'

'I think even my mother would have drawn the line at running away with another woman.'

'We'll never know.'

'Right, I better go and cook that meal or I may not have a bride to run away with.'

'See that small pot over there, nestled between the old pumpkin and the pitcher?' Mira points with her eyes to the shelf on the left. 'Take a fistful of powder and mix it with my meal. It will help me recover quicker.'

'What is it?' Elina asks.

'Do you think I'm stupid enough to fall for the same trick twice? I shouldn't have told you about the tansy last time,' Mira says, attempting another smile. 'You keep your nose out of my herbs. Rozalia was right when she said that a little knowledge was dangerous.'

'I see you're definitely on the mend.'

UPRISING

The following morning, Elina insists that Mira eats some meat and doesn't just drink the broth as she did the previous night.

'I'm not hungry,' Mira says.

'You need to eat. How else will you get better?'

'I miss the daylight more than food.'

'I'll take you out once you gain some strength, maybe in a couple of days if you start eating properly.'

'Could you crack open the trapdoor, please? I want to see the sky.'

Elina considers this for a moment. Though they are at the edge of the village, out of everyone's way – you never know. But she cannot ignore the pleading in Mira's eyes.

It takes a long time for Mira to finish what's in her bowl, though Elina has chopped everything into tiny pieces. Her mouth moves like it has forgotten how to chew, while her eyes are glued to the sliver of light framed by the opened trapdoor.

A faint sound drifts into the cellar.

'What's that?' Mira asks.

Elina chokes on a spoonful of broth. The tolling of the Passing Bell, its call long and mournful, sweeps the village, reaching all the way to their lair. Elina doesn't want to tell Mira about her father's death until she has grown stronger. It's not like she can attend her father's funeral anyway.

'Someone always dies,' Elina says, avoiding Mira's eyes, which are now fixed on her. Looking through her somehow. 'A little top-up?'

'How did he die? What happened?' Mira asks.

'Who? What do you mean?' Elina coughs to hide her embarrassment.

'You've lied to me once. If you do it twice, you'll never stop.'

'How did you know?'

'Words are not the only means of knowing.'

'I'm sorry, it was an accident,' Elina says, reaching for Mira's hand. 'The night we freed you from the church walls, Barbu was hot on our heels. Your father tried to stop him, but the mason kicked him in the chest, and he fell badly. Andrei said it was quick. He didn't suffer. I'm so sorry.'

Mira's eyes are glistening. It's good to see her body has gathered enough water to shed tears, but Elina worries this may hinder her healing. She's gone silent for much longer than Elina is comfortable with, and she kisses Mira's hand. 'I'll do everything I can to look after you.'

'He was a good father, despite our many disagreements,' Mira says finally. 'Gone too early, may he rest in peace.'

Though Elina doesn't want to see Mira too upset, her composure seems odd and unnatural. Since her rescue, Mira is somewhat different from her old self. As though a part of her did get buried in those walls for good.

'You're judging me, I can tell,' Mira says. 'Please forgive me if I'm not laughing hysterically as you did at your mother's funeral.'

'You're right, I'm sorry. We all show our grief in different ways.' Elina gives Mira a hug, but she wriggles out of it at once, gasping for air. Her aversion to tight spaces is becoming more apparent. Mira used to love hugs, but now she's uneasy every time Elina puts her arms around her. And she wants to keep the trapdoor open at all times, even during the night.

'What about Barbu? Has he been punished?' Mira asks.

'He got away.'

'Judging by how fast they worked, I wasn't the first woman they walled up. And as long as Barbu lives, I won't be the last one either. Let's hope his sins catch up with him before he can hurt someone else. Rozalia must've seen his dark side the moment she met him. That's why she did that warding ritual for us. That's why she taught me her secret.'

'What secret?'

'It's what kept me alive while trapped in those walls.'

'Does that mean you're immortal now?'

'Rozalia wasn't. I am not. But the ancient wisdom we're guardians to is.'

'Bless you. Whatever you're talking about, I'm just glad it worked. I'd press you for details, but I see you've turned into Rozalia – talking in riddles and saying nothing,' Elina says, kissing Mira on her lips and stroking her cheeks. Is her face filling out or is she just imagining it?

'I have to go to my father's grave to perform certain rites for his departed soul,' Mira says. 'I can't let his spirit be stuck between the two worlds.'

'Just what I said, you're making no sense.'

'There are certain things to be done – that must be done – for those who die an unnatural death. It's all I can say, I'm sorry, and no, don't worry, I wasn't going to do it right now. I know we have to be cautious. We'll wait till later, maybe this evening, when there's no one around.'

'The villagers will have an early night tonight, I hope, tired from the uprising.'

'Uprising?'

'They are angry with my father for bringing Barbu to the village.'

'You've warned him, I hope?'

'He's a stubborn old fool. I don't know if he'll leave the manor. That's why I'm going to join in the uprising, to try and protect him.'

'You can't stop the angry people on your own.'

'I have a plan.'

'It's dangerous. What if—'

'It'll be alright, I promise.'

'You can never promise the future.'

'I'll be careful. And if it gets out of control, remember – I've got the horse while the villagers are on foot.'

Mira looks away.

'I'll be back as soon as I can,' Elina says. 'In the meantime, you keep nibbling at the food even if you're not hungry.'

She pulls on her boots and clambers out of the cellar, taking the uneven stairs two at a time. Outside, the gathering clouds circle in the sky, as though searching for the best place to rest. If Rozalia were alive, she'd know how to make them linger above the village long enough to coax the rain out of their full bellies. Perhaps she's taught Mira this secret too? In fact, how much of Rozalia's unconventional wisdom and knowledge has Mira been entrusted with? Probably enough, judging by her miraculous survival.

Elina arrives at the cemetery just as Pavel's body, wrapped in a cloth, is lowered into the ground. The priest has finished his service and someone's impatient hand throws the first fistful of earth, followed by others, as people hurry back to the village, eager for the *praznic* of wild fowls. Andrei is left on his own to shovel the earth and mark the grave.

'Tough work for one man,' Elina says and attempts to give him a hand, though she has no idea what she's doing.

'I don't blame 'em. It's not often we're spoiled with pheasants.' Andrei is panting with effort.

Elina tries to copy his movements – scoop the soil, turn, shovel it into the grave – but he makes it look so easy.

She thinks of her mother's grave – the same shaped heap of soil marking her resting place. And of how the earth receives us all equally: boyars or peasants, it eats up our flesh just the same.

Andrei plants a wooden cross at the top end of the grave. 'There! May you rest in peace, old man.' He closes his eyes briefly, perhaps saying a prayer, and then turns to Elina.

'Keep hold of the spade, lad. You'll need it later. C'mon now, let's head back to the village, or there won't be any food left for us.'

People leave the table still chewing on their food. They make the sign of the cross, flicking their eyes towards the grey sky – *bogdaprosti*, thank you Lord and forgive us our sins – followed immediately by reaching for an axe, club or a garden fork.

Elina marvels at their ability to think of God at the same time as preparing to spill blood.

Andrei just about has time to grab a pheasant wing, which his mother has saved for him, before the mob gathers, village elders at the front, looking at him expectantly. They have unofficially made him their leader since he proved his courage by rescuing Mira and exposing Barbu's crime. At his sign, the thirty-something men follow him towards the hill of the manor house.

Elina slips to the back of the crowd and as soon as they enter the woods, she disappears through the trees to the side. Fulger shouldn't be too far away from here, but her sharp whistle fails to summon him. She whistles a second time and when the horse is still nowhere to be seen, she considers sprinting up the hill. She'd still make it to the manor before the mob does, but she may not have time to carry out her plan. Her ears pick up a faint neighing somewhere in the thick of the woods. Fulger is having trouble locating her and is asking for more clues. Elina imitates his whinnying, and moments later, the horse is threading through the trees, flying towards her.

They shoot up the hill, the pounding of her heart matching that of the horse's hooves, their breath one with the wild. Though it's only midday, the low-hanging clouds are making it look like evening. A little rain would be such a blessing to the parched ground. This year's dry summer is making everyone nervous, the memory of the long droughts from two years ago only too fresh in people's minds.

This was supposed to be a shortcut. Why is it taking so long? Elina thinks, staring at the never-ending hill.

When she finally arrives, out of breath and Fulger foaming at the mouth, a pair of eyes watch her through the gate wicket. Neculai was always the first to announce whenever they had visitors coming. Ear to the ground, he could tell how far the riders were and how long before they reached the manor.

'Good evening, Neculai. I'm Matei, the boyar's son—'

'Bastard son,' the old man corrects her from behind the gate. 'A mongrel. And a thief. You stole Miss Elina's horse.' He looks at Fulger.

Elina needs Neculai's help if she's to succeed with her plan. And in the absence of this trust – save for revealing her identity – she has one other option. She knows that servants respond to authority and so she musters her most commanding voice.

'A mongrel or not, I have my father's noble blood throbbing in my heart. And Miss Elina is my half-sister. Besides, she's at the convent and won't be needing her horse any time soon. Look, I've come to protect my father and there's no time... The peasants have revolted. They're on their way here, axes and all—'

'Boyar Constantin has left. The manor is empty and has been boarded up. There's nothing to loot.'

Thank God for that, she thinks, and out loud she says, 'The people are angry, and they may still try to gain entrance—'

'Over my dead body.'

'I don't think my father will appreciate that. He has entrusted you with looking after the estate and keeping him updated, hasn't he? Now listen – go gather all the servants quick and tell them their master isn't coming back and they can leave. Also, open the gates and release some of the cattle and sheep – the peasants are hungry, seeing so much food will distract them, I hope... You must also set fire to the furthest haystacks behind the stable—'

'Are you mad?'

'If we don't trick them, they'll want to burn down the

house themselves. You've heard what happened to other boyars. I'll go deal with the angry mob – you make sure the fire is contained to the haystacks.'

'They may be poor, but they aren't stupid. They'll be back to finish the job if—'

'It buys us time and that's all we can ask for right now. If you defy my orders, yes, they are orders, I'll take it upon myself to break in. Don't make us lose any more time – it can make all the difference—'

The wicket is slammed shut in her face. As she's trying to figure out if Neculai is obeying her instructions or has decided to ignore them, there's sudden clamour in the courtyard and the gates swing wide open. Animals pour out – sheep, cattle, pigs, geese – followed by a handful of servants who, as soon as they are outside the property, start chasing after the livestock.

While keeping an eye on the road, praying that the mob gets delayed, Elina watches the sky above the manor, willing Neculai to hurry up and set fire to the haystacks.

She bites three of her nails to the quick by the time she spots a thread of smoke billowing in the air. It's coming from the garden, but from here it looks like it's shooting right out of the roof of the main house. 'Well done, old man,' she whispers and sprints down the hill. The further away from the manor she meets the peasants, the easier it will be to sell them her lie. Well, half lie: her father has truly left the manor.

What happens next throws her at first, but it's a golden opportunity she could have never planned for or predicted.

The servants and peasants are pushing and shoving each other to catch the animals. Moos, bleats and honks are mixed with people's shouting, calling and scrambling about. All this chaos is momentarily suspended when drops of rain start to fall suddenly, plump and heavy, splashing onto trees, on the faded grass, on the many outstretched hands reaching for the sky. People sink to their knees, their faces upturned in gratitude at this heavenly gift. The spell, however, is soon broken by a fight between stray dogs and the hissing ganders who, to protect their flock, are charging fearlessly with their wings spread wide.

The peasants jump to their feet again, and though someone wisely suggests they should work together and herd the animals towards the village where they can divide them amongst all families, this sound advice is drowned in the commotion. Most of the men who joined the uprising are now disappearing into the woods in pursuit of the scared, fleeing food. Only a handful of them are facing Elina, with Andrei at the front.

'We are late, I'm afraid,' Elina says. 'The boyar has long been gone, the manor is empty and boarded up – well, not much of a manor at all soon,' she says and points over her shoulder, happy to see the plume of smoke floating in the air.

'How did you—'

'I told you, I used to work for the leeching boyar.' She hopes her language will please the peasants. 'I'm happy to say I've got my revenge on him now.'

The rain is growing heavier and Elina smiles at the sky, thanking the heavens for giving Neculai a hand with containing the fire. To the men she says, 'Just what the land needs, eh? We won't starve this winter after all.'

Andrei isn't convinced. 'It'll stop the house from burning down…' he says and breaks off, perhaps realising it's the wrong thing to say. He sounds ungrateful, blasphemous even. The silent, disapproving looks he's getting all round are a confirmation of that. Elina is quick to play it in her favour. It's cheap and disingenuous, but she'll do anything to save her home.

'We've been praying for this rain for ages. You can't—'

'That's not what I meant,' Andrei snaps.

'We've done our job here,' Elina says. 'We really have tried, but it seems God has other plans, and we'd be wise not to meddle with them. Now that He's finally bestowing His grace on us, let's show our devotion in prayer and goodwill for our friends as well as our enemies. But of course, I'm not stopping you. I just don't want to be the one who brings God's wrath upon us again.'

Elina starts walking down the hill, a brief fluttering tingling her chest as she wonders if the men will follow suit.

They do. All of them, including Andrei.

The rain is pelting sideways, whipping her face and stinging her eyes, and though her feet are sloshing through muddy streams, her heart is light as a sparrow's.

'You look like a soaked ferret,' Mira says the moment Elina walks in.

'The sky has split open. Do you still want to go to your father's grave?'

'The best time. There'll be nobody about in this weather. How did it go?'

'My father heeded my warning, surprisingly, and left for our town house. Let's hope things settle here before too long. Are you sure you're strong enough to go to the cemetery?'

'Yes, if you help me.'

With one hand around Mira's waist and the other offered for support, Elina eases Mira off the bed and together they shuffle slowly up the stairs.

'I don't remember these stairs being so long.' Mira looks up at the patch of sky gleaming above the trapdoor.

The rain has stopped, the dripping trees and bushes being the only proof of it, for the thirsty ground has gobbled it all up, looking dry as ever. Mira gasps. 'Air, and space, and endless sky… Just one moment longer, please.'

When Elina whistles and two horses come galloping out of the woods, Mira looks at her, puzzled.

'She's yours,' Elina says, pointing at Castana.

Now Mira laughs. 'She will be, when you teach me how to ride.'

Registering her erroneous assumption, Elina nods and helps Mira up on Fulger's back. She leaps on behind her, embracing Mira with one arm and holding the reins with the other. Castana trots behind them, whinnying, evidently showing her displeasure at being left out.

Despite the downpour earlier, the ground is hard, and the horses keep a steady pace.

'Look.' Mira points at the sky.

A faint red arc grows into a spectacular rainbow. One end of its perfect bow plunges right into the heart of the cemetery, as though acting like a bridge between the two worlds.

Something growls as they approach Pavel's grave. A ball of wet fur lies close to the fresh mound of earth.

'It's me, silly,' Mira calls out.

The dog springs up and runs towards Mira, doing circles around her, panting and jumping and whining with excitement.

'That's right, boy, I'm back.' Mira scratches the filthy mongrel. 'Here, Suru, meet my friend,' she says and holds Elina's hand out so he can sniff it.

'It's what I do with horses,' Elina says, not totally comfortable with the wild look in the dog's eyes. But Suru is friendlier than he looks, and they both pet and stroke him until he curls up once more, this time by Mira's feet.

Dog appeased, the two of them kneel by Pavel's grave, two scrawny figures, one of them burning herbs and singing unintelligible chants in order to bless a soul's journey into the beyond, the other watching silently.

A SECOND LIFE

The town of Galbena is seven villages down the river from Pasareasca and hosts a big bazaar every Sunday. Having dug up the treasure she'd buried by the lake the previous year, Elina travels to the market twice, selling her jewellery and gemstones. Only hers. What belongs to her mother, she'll never part with.

Galbena is a good town to settle in. With so many people mingling about, the two of them won't stick out. Also, it's far enough from their own village not to bump into anyone who may know them. Elina won't have any trouble – her own father didn't recognise her. It's Mira she's worried about.

The hut Elina has found to rent is one of the last at the edge of town. It's a hovel with two small rooms instead of twelve, as she was used to at the manor, but one more than she had at the convent. Besides, it has a decent cellar as per Mira's request.

It takes Elina an entire week to move the heaps of potions and herbs from Rozalia's cellar to the new one. And when all is done and the new home is ready to move into, Elina swallows hard to push down the knot that is clogging her throat. Though excited about the new life ahead, shared with the woman she loves, the new circumstances demand that she forgets her past completely and forges a new identity.

She isn't a boyar's daughter any longer, but the man of the household now.

'We'll leave here tomorrow,' Mira says, despite being too weak to travel.

'Why don't we wait another week or two?'

'Yesterday was the longest day of the year.'

'And?'

Mira shrugs. 'It's auspicious to follow the rhythm of life. Not as dictated by man, but nature.'

'You sound so much like her. As if she never died.'

Elina understands for the first time how the ancient wisdom Rozalia was so well versed in has survived all these centuries. It has been entrusted by master to a chosen student each time, with each generation. And if it has survived this long… Why, the church will never extirpate it. Elina has this vision of a deathly dance between truth and lie, light and shadow, twirling around each other for ever. Just like it has been, she guesses, from the mists of time. And everyone chooses their own light or shadow, their own truth.

She has made her pick. They both have. And despite the dangers and difficulties of their choice, it's also the only one that allows them to live as they wish.

Mira squeezes her hand. 'It's time.'

They get ready to leave before the crack of dawn to avoid running into any villagers. Having tied her mother's scrolls around her belly, Elina helps Mira sling Rozalia's badger-snout pouch across her body, and though it's crammed with seeds and herbs, Elina slips two rocks in it.

'To stop the wind blowing you off the horse.'

'Haven't I proved my tight grip on life already?' Mira says, lifting her face to meet Elina's kiss.

They shut the cellar's trapdoor behind them, concealing it with leaves and twigs.

'There's one more thing we must do before we leave this

place,' Elina says, taking Mira's hands into hers. 'Will you be my wife?'

Mira bursts into laughter, but seeing Elina's solemn eyes, she stops. 'You aren't joking.'

'We'll play by society's rules, but on *our* terms.'

Mira looks around. 'Are we going to do it here?'

Elina nods. 'Let them be our witnesses – Suru, the moon, our horses. Their blessing is far better than a priest's.'

Mira hugs Elina. 'I'm yours today and forever. May our bond last through this life and the ones yet to come. May our souls recognise each other again, in love and in all things eternal.' She kisses Elina with such tenderness as though her mouth was a snowflake and she was afraid it would melt.

Elina breaks away to dig something out of the bosom of her shirt. A gold ring burning with the glow of a polished garnet.

'It was my mother's,' she says, holding it close to her chest and then, as if remembering what she's supposed to do with it, Elina offers it to her bride.

Mira looks bewitched by the shiny token and all it entails. She doesn't move as Elina reaches for her hand and slides the ring on her finger.

'A little loose now, but it'll fit you better when you're fully recovered.' Elina wedges in a chip of wood to stop the ring from falling off.

A flock of honking geese flies above them and over the woods, their undulating wings beaconing at them to follow.

'Heard that?' Elina smiles. 'We're now husband and wife.'

'Yes, my lord,' Mira says, and they both laugh.

With one last look towards the village, the two of them mount their horses and head in the opposite direction, with Suru following closely behind.

GHOSTS FROM THE PAST

At the bazaar in Galbena town, they look a distinguished couple. Elina wears her father's velvet mantle, newly adjusted to fit her much slimmer frame, and Mira is dressed in one of Elina's best gowns.

'Looking rich helps,' Elina whispers in Mira's ear as they amble about the market, in search of well-heeled customers to whom they can sell the silver tray Elina carries under her mantle.

Men and women shout their goods over each other, making it impossible to hear who is selling what. Their voices mingle with clucking, bleating and mooing, filling up the air with an incessant clamour where bargains are sought and barters are made all the time.

'You're good at selling,' Mira says. 'You should become a merchant.'

'I *am* one. Haven't I traded enough of my trinkets to prove that—' Elina's words are cut short as she stops suddenly.

Something catches her eye.

Someone.

A slave, tied to four others, and two men haggling over his price. She knows this man, the plunging scar on his ashen face…

‘What is it?’ Mira asks, but her words are swimming in Elina’s head as she approaches the slave owner to join in the bargaining.

Mira pulls at her sleeve. ‘Are you mad? We’re here to sell, not to buy. And we don’t need a—’

‘Trust me.’ Elina squeezes Mira’s hand while sweeping the crowds with her glance. But of course the person she’s looking for isn’t there, for if she was, Murgu wouldn’t be up for sale.

The other buyer isn’t prepared to match Elina’s offer for the maimed slave, even though it isn’t much more than the price of a silver bangle. The whip-holding merchant is eager to seal the deal, and spitting into his right hand, he holds it out to shake Elina’s. She ignores his gesture and instead drops a coin in his open palm from so high up that it rolls out of his hand and falls to the ground. The merchant lunges after it, sifting through the dust of the road on his hands and knees. When he retrieves it, he immediately bites it to ascertain its worth and, happy with his finding, he tosses Elina one end of the rope, the other knotted around the slave’s wrists and ankles.

‘’Tis a stubborn dog, this one.’ He prods Murgu with his whip. ‘Keep ’im tethered, I say.’

Elina insists that the merchant unties the rope, and he does so reluctantly, mumbling warnings in his beard. ‘Don’t come asking for your coin back, sir, if the filthy dog takes to the hills.’

Elina ignores the merchant, her full attention on Murgu, who takes his time rubbing his hands and feet before he staggers up. How did he end up here? And where is Dafina? Questions about the dancer swirl in Elina’s head, but this is neither the place nor the time to talk to Murgu.

‘Let’s go,’ she tells Mira. ‘We’ll trade the silverware another time.’

Frowning with bewilderment, Mira nods and follows in silence. Murgu shuffles behind them, keeping the necessary distance between owners and their slaves. Is the gap stretching,

Elina wonders, or is she imagining it? Her fear that the slave could break into a run at any moment, and that she'd never find out what happened to Dafina, makes her stop as soon as they reach the open field behind the bazaar. Looking right and left to make sure there aren't any curious ears about, Elina sits by the side of the road and beckons Murgu over with her finger. He comes closer but not too close.

'I know your previous owner – Dafina. Where is she?'

One of his eyes is blue and swollen. He stares at her with his good eye, making Elina squirm. They only met once, and it was night-time. Surely he cannot recognise her.

'What happened to Dafina? I know you wouldn't be for sale if she was well,' Elina says, mustering her deepest voice. She wishes the slave would start talking and stop searching her face like he's trying to place it in his memory.

'A spurned lover threw an axe at her mid-dance,' Murgu says finally.

Elina's mouth moves, but no words come out.

'T'was quick,' he adds. 'She knew no pain.' Murgu has a strong lisp, which she doesn't remember from the last time she saw him. His eyes are lingering on Elina a little too long, making her uncomfortable, and she stands up, keen to have her back to him.

They start walking again, Elina doing everything she can to put one foot in front of the other. She listens to Mira talk about the change in the air, how there's more rain on the way and how they should remember to thatch the roof where it leaked last time. She's grateful for Mira's light chatter, knowing full well there's something else Mira would rather be discussing but that she won't ask any questions until they are alone.

Elina stops looking over her shoulder to check on Murgu. Now that she's learned of Dafina's fate, she hopes the slave will run away. Isn't that why she bought him in the first place? So that she could set him free?

They are about to reach the maple grove which leads to

their hut, and Murgu will definitely want to take this chance to escape. She's seen how at home he is in the woods.

Yet, when they are out on the other side of the grove, she can still hear Murgu shuffling behind them. Perhaps he's worried his injured leg won't get him far and has decided to wait for the cover of night. Elina hopes this is what he's planning on. He better be, because they have no need for a servant. Given their circumstances, it's not only unnecessary, but dangerous too. She knows how nosy servants are, having nothing better to do than pry into their owners' lives. If he uncovers their secret, she and Mira would no doubt suffer Rozalia's fate.

'What's this all about?' Mira asks as soon as they are home with the door firmly shut behind them.

Elina tells her all about the gypsy dancer, how crucial and timely Dafina and Murgu's help had been in rescuing her from the church walls before it was too late.

'She was like Rozalia, I swear, some of the things she said…'

'What kind of things?' Mira asks.

'I didn't have anything to give her for her help, and when I promised I'd do it next time we met, she said to reward her people if I couldn't find her. What's that supposed to mean?' Elina shrugs as if to answer her own question. 'And then she read my palm. A quiverful of children, she predicted.' Elina laughs. 'Maybe she was just a charlatan.'

Mira turns away.

'Did I say something wrong?' Elina steps in front of her.

'There may be something to her words. I had a dream about it too, when I was trapped in the walls. And I thought—'

'We both know that can't happen. Neither of us is the Virgin Mary to bear children out of thin air,' Elina says, but the look on Mira's face is one of concentration, like she's searching for something she knows is there but cannot see right away.

The following morning, when Elina finds Murgu tending to the horses in the courtyard, she's not just a little annoyed with him, but angry for his failure to disappear overnight. She stands there glaring at him, not knowing what to say.

'These horses are well looked after,' he says, pretending not to notice her fury.

'You're still here.'

'For people like me, fortune means having a kind owner. I'm a lucky gypsy.'

'I believe you might be too proud for that.'

'Comes a time when safety is sweeter 'an pride.'

'I think I know what you're after, but if you think you can take advantage of my kindness, well, let me tell you something – you're wrong. I paid dearly to buy you from that whip-brandishing brute. I'm not going to waste any more coins to purchase your freedom. That's what you're after, isn't it?'

'No bother.' He shakes his head in earnest. 'I know you would if you could.'

The ground shifts under Elina's feet. Has he recognised her? Is it all over for her and Mira?

'What insolence. I shouldn't have rescued you—'

'Your words are sharp, but they don't bite.' Murgu doesn't look at her as he carries on stroking the horses.

'I did what I did for you because of your previous owner. I don't really need a slave. You can go. I'm giving you a chance. The best you'll ever get.'

Elina takes a deep breath, expecting the slave to stop petting the horses, bob his head and take to the road. Murgu does stop fussing about the horses, but instead of leaving, he turns towards Elina and looks her squarely in the face.

'Thank you. But I'm used to making ma' own choices, when I can. Just as you are.'

Black spots swirl before her eyes and Elina makes to lean on the ash tree to her side.

He knows.

He has recognised her.

He has known all this time while she's been pretending in front of him.

Elina searches his face for signs of threat. His countenance, however, remains serene and humble.

'You 'ave nothing to fear… sir.' Murgu smiles, its awkwardness a clear proof he's not used to it. 'My lips are sealed. I'll take it to the grave with me,' he says, placing his hand on his heart.

He sounds sincere, but who knows…

'I hope you keep your oath. For your own sake,' she says.

'Took me most o' the night to trace the rich young fool who killed her. But when I did, neither he nor his servant lived to see the rising sun.'

He has told her his own dark secret as reassurance that he can be trusted, for his crime is also punishable by death.

'The horses are thirsty, sir,' Murgu says. 'They're getting restless. I'll go take 'em to the water 'ole.'

Elina watches him disappear down the road with Fulger and Castana by his side. Here is a man made so utterly powerless by his social status, yet so powerful by circumstance and personal choice. They are equals in that which matters, and he knows it as well as she does.

Elina turns to head back to the house and there's Mira, standing on the threshold. She must have heard their talk.

'I brought trouble to our house, didn't I?' Elina sighs. 'I'm sorry.'

'You paid a debt to someone who helped you once. If it wasn't for him, I might not be standing here.' Mira touches Elina's arm. Her gesture is warm, but her eyes are cool and calm and uninvolved. Since her rescue, Mira appears to have lost something of who she was. Or perhaps gained something. It's hard to tell if the new, unfamiliar glint in her eyes is a flash of wisdom or one of madness.

'You remember how Rozalia used to say that the night is the best counsellor?' Mira says. 'She was right. I couldn't sleep, thinking about what you told me last night.'

‘I’m sorry, I didn’t mean to worry you—’

‘I think I know what the dancer meant when she told you to reward her people.’ There is no mischief or teasing in Mira’s voice. Nothing but certainty. ‘We’ve got to go back to the bazaar next Sunday.’

THE NATURE OF THE SEED

They saunter through the crowded market, walking arm in arm. Whiffs of roast acorn float in the air, its sweet scent curling up from an open fire where a peasant, smeared in soot, tosses the nuts. Elina's mouth waters as she remembers Rozalia's delicious drink, a treat she craves not only for its bittersweet taste, but for the peace and unexplained joy it always filled her with. A bolt of fury strikes her every time she thinks of Rozalia's wasteful death. She hopes the unfortunate woman is with her late mother now. Their friendship had been a source of great jealousy for her younger, selfish self. How she begrudged Rozalia when she turned up with small bundles – dyes for her mother's secret endeavour – which at the time, Rozalia claimed was 'medicine for the lady's headaches'. The hours the two of them spent behind closed doors used to make Elina bite her nails until she drew blood.

What would they say about her love for Mira? How would her mother and Rozalia take it, seeing her stroll through the bazaar dressed as a man and with a woman on her arm? Would they approve of it? Condone it? Condemn it?

Someone steps on Elina's heels, berating her for stopping in the middle of the road. She turns around to see a pair of elderly nuns shaking their head at her. For a moment, Elina is back at the convent, and she almost bobs a curtsy, but Mira nudges her in time.

'Matei, dear, don't be so clumsy.' Mira's chiding of her husband seems to please the nuns, who approve with a sharp nod and walk away.

'That was close,' Mira whispers, squeezing Elina's arm.

'Was it that obvious?'

'Only to me. But you must wear your trousers better. I won't always be by your side to remind you that men don't curtsy.'

'You, on the other hand, are doing just fine,' Elina says. 'Already nagging like an old wife.'

Mira chuckles and is about to say something when she stops suddenly. She's staring at a wagon cart not too far ahead of them, ramshackle and filthy, a whiff of dung spreading out from it.

'What's the matter?' Elina asks. And then she sees the scrawny child tethered to the back wheel of the cart. It's what they've been looking for. The child's blue eyes and swarthy skin are the telltale signs of a shameful birth – the cross-breed of a gypsy mother and a boyar. These bastard offspring have the worst fate, for they are spurned not only by their noble fathers, but by the gypsy community too.

'Is it a boy or a girl?' Elina narrows her eyes against the sun.

'Hard to tell. All those tattered cloths and tangled hair.'

'Doesn't matter. He or she is coming home with us. Dafina can rest in peace now. I've kept my promise.'

A YEAR LATER

By the following harvest celebrations, Mira grows strong and bold enough to do what she's been wanting to do for a long time. She starts selling herbs and seeds at the bazaar for all sorts of ailments. Dressed in embroidered gowns and with a merchant for a husband, she's not in danger of being dragged to the stake, like she would have been if she was a peasant.

The poor queue up to seek her advice for their aches, the rich summon her to their manors. No matter their status, in sickness and in death, all people look the same: frightened, vulnerable, meek.

Despite the dangers of her practice – the church have stepped up their hunt for wise women they call witches – Mira will not be deterred from her purpose. She owes it to the woman who gave birth to her, and to the woman who saved her life. Twice. Without Rozalia's teachings, Mira would have never survived her near-drowning, nor her immurement.

To help people find her, Mira returns to the same spot in the bazaar each week, next to the willow tree at the far end of the market. She's known as 'the lady with the dog', for Suru never leaves her side. He likes to curl up next to her even at the height of a summer's day. The dog has become her shadow since they found him whimpering at her father's grave.

Mira spots Elina's head bobbing above the crowd, *cobză* on her shoulder and a wide smile on her face.

'It's been a good day.' Elina waves from afar. When she comes closer, she opens her tunic to reveal a heavy purse hanging on her belt. 'I've sold both deer pelts and the three grouse I hunted earlier.'

'Now you can rest for the rest of the week,' Mira says, greeting her husband with a kiss on the cheek.

Their three children, who've been playing in the dirt of the road like sparrows bathing in the dust, have suddenly caught a glimpse of their father and are all scrambling to their feet and running into Elina's open arms. She always brings treats for them, and this time she lets them ferret honey-glazed nuts out of the bag tied to her waist.

Squealing with delight, they squat by the stream on the other side of the willow tree where they share the tasty gift.

'This is all so close to those strange visions I had when trapped in the walls,' Mira says, watching the children over her shoulder. 'Almost like I saw our life as we're living it now, us as husband and wife, and our children... except there were a lot more than three in my dreams.'

'We'll buy as many as we can raise,' says Elina. 'There's no shortage of gypsy slaves at the market.'

'And our home was a manor house in the middle of a grand estate.'

Elina laughs. 'That, I'm afraid, I can't see happening. Not by selling pelts and fresh game at the market.'

'I already have everything I ever wished for.' Mira pinches Elina's arm affectionately and goes to deal with the old nun who has stopped by her makeshift stall crammed with herbs.

Though Elina can't hear their chat, the tenderness in Mira's voice reaches her like the gentle murmur of a spring. The joy on her face speaks of peace, contentment, purpose. Not taking her eyes off the woman she loves, Elina reaches for the *cobză*, letting it sing everything she cannot – must not – put into words.

'I see you've surpassed your tutor,' someone says in a quiet voice, and it takes Elina a few moments to realise the words are addressed to her. She looks up, but the midday sun blinds her, making her eyes water. The stranger guesses her trouble and takes a few steps to the side, limping as he does so.

An old man with a straw hat, his face obscured by a white beard, long and wispy, its tousled ends reaching his sunken chest. A memory flickers in her mind, but her heart beats too fast to let her grasp it. Someone from the past has recognised her… this is it… it's all over… her life and Mira's… what will happen to their children?

Cold sweat trickles down Elina's neck.

'I don't know you,' she says, looking around to make sure nobody is listening. 'You've mistaken me for someone else.'

Mira must have heard the fear in Elina's voice, for she concludes her exchange with the nun and rushes to Elina's side.

'You're right. My sight isn't what it used to be, but my ears – they never fail me. Best ears in the country.' The old man smiles, a familiar groove in his cheeks.

The Old Cobzar! Of course it's him. He has aged, but his dimples are just as deep, though slightly warped by his hollow face.

A wave of joy soars in her belly and Elina wants to jump to her feet and greet him, enquire about his health and perhaps even ask him to play the *cobză*. More than anything, she wants to ask him about the time when he knew her mother, and why she did so many drawings of him.

But none of this is possible, of course. The choice she's made has severed her from her past and all the people in it. It's a choice she must live with.

'You're Matei Pogor, aren't you?' the Old Cobzar asks, though it sounds more of a statement than a question.

Elina stands up and takes a step forward.

'Yes, I am,' she says, relieved that he's using her adopted name. But how does he—

'I knew it. The spit image of your father, I tell you. Well, I'm bringing you news, sir. Good and bad.'

Elina braces herself. Though he treats her like the man she pretends to be, the fact that he complimented her *cobză* playing instead of greeting her has made it plain that he knows her true identity.

She locks eyes with him. Not a trace of menace in them, or threat – only kindness and something else which makes her think she's safe.

'Your father has recognised your noble blood, despite your shameful birth. Despite you being out of wedlock.'

Elina is stunned into silence, her mind spinning with memories of the last time she saw her father, when she had told him about her decision to be a man for life and asked him to play along with her plan by pretending she was his bastard son. She recalls his unsteady voice, his words choking and his eyes swimming with disappointment, hatred even. Is it possible that he has forgiven her? That he has come to terms with her choice? It's unlikely. The Old Cobzar must be playing with her. But how can he know all these details she has only discussed with her father and no one else?

'I don't know if I believe you. My father refused to accept me as part of his family. What's made him change his mind?'

'You see' – the Old Cobzar removes his hat briefly to scratch his head – 'his only lawful child, his daughter, has gone and become a nun, and in the absence of any other heirs, he has bequeathed his entire estate to you. Blood is thicker than water – your father's exact words, sir, swear to God.'

The Old Cobzar is in earnest. He can't know all this, including her father's favourite saying, unless her dear father has truly sent him. Mira's quick breath on Elina's neck tells her that she too has grasped the magnitude of this news.

Elina watches the old man closely. 'Why you? Why did my father choose you, out of all people, to be his messenger?'

'I'm a traveller, remember? Wandering up and down the country. He knew I'd come across you sooner or later—'

'And why are you – a free and proud man – why are you doing a boyar's bidding?'

The Old Cobzar wavers and wobbles as he shifts his weight from one foot to the other. He then turns to Mira, as though silently asking for privacy.

'You can speak in her presence,' Elina says, reaching for Mira's hand. 'I have nothing to hide from my wife.'

'Alright. Well…' The old man watches Elina with a steady gaze, while his hands – straightening his tunic, readjusting his hat, back to his tunic – tell a different story. 'The thing is… I owe your father. I… I don't know how to say this, but… we have a history.'

'Has it got anything to do with my mother, by any chance?' Her words are a little sharper than she intended.

The old man looks around to make sure nobody has heard that. People swarm everywhere, the clamour of selling and buying and haggling floating in the air like an unbroken song.

'She painted an awful lot of you,' Elina says.

'So you know about her gift. What a remarkable woman she was.'

His use of the word 'remarkable' throws her a little, before she reminds herself he is an educated gypsy, whose fate and freedom had been blessed by her own grandfather.

'How come she never painted my father's portrait when she did so many of you?'

'Your mother had great respect and admiration for your father—'

'It's not the same as love.'

He studies the air beyond her shoulder, his eyes brimming with a mixture of pained joy, and guilt, and something else which Elina can't work out.

'Did he know? Did my father know about…'

'When he sent me to find you, he said – "I don't care what it takes, or how long, but you must find Matei Pogor and tell him I've made him my lawful heir. You owe me, and we both know it. Find Matei and I'll forgive you." It was very clear what he meant.'

It strikes Elina she doesn't know her father at all. He's done so much for her and her mother, despite all the hurt the two of them have caused him. He has risked his life by shunning the social norms, lying to the church, breaking the law – and all this in order to protect his wife and daughter. She must go see him at once, beg for his forgiveness, and if there's anything she can do for him, anything at all—

'Hold on…' Elina's heart suddenly pounds in her throat. 'Why hasn't my father summoned me to the manor to tell me the good news himself?'

Something in the Old Cobzar's hesitation – in his eyes pinned to the ground – makes her blood run cold.

'That's the bad news, sir… I'm very sorry.' He removes his hat in the too well-known means of paying respect to higher authority, women, or… the deceased.

There's suddenly not enough air. Her chest is heaving, the thumping in her ears grows loud and unbearable.

Mira's face swims into focus as she grips her arm, her nails digging into Elina's flesh. A pain she welcomes. This she can deal with, and Elina presses on Mira's hand to sink her nails even deeper. Scraps of talk reach her as though from underwater – on the run from a peasants' uprising… attacked in the woods by robbers… coach crashed and flipped over… flung down a rocky ravine… broken bones… barely alive… a night in agony… Neculai had sent word that the manor was safe thanks to you, your name on your father's last breath… he was proud of you… that you're stronger and braver than any sons he could've ever wished for…

The world is spinning and Elina's head with it, her mind awhirl with clashing thoughts and feelings, and what ifs. The relief of acquiring a lawful identity, the sweetness of this moment so embittered by the news of her father's death. Bestowed with a safe future, she's now racked with guilt about the past. She should've been kinder to her father, more trusting of him. Maybe if she'd tried harder to make a deal with him and not been so hasty in running away, maybe he'd still be…

'He did have one request, your father did.' The Old Cobzar looks to catch her eye. 'Forgiveness.'

Elina nods quickly, though something doesn't add up. Forgiveness? Her brain wades through thick confusion: there's nothing to forgive her father for. It's the other way round.

'Forgiving yourself as readily as you forgive him – that was his wish.' The old man pats her shoulder with surprising vigour.

Before she has time to say anything, the Old Cobzar bows in farewell. 'Wishing you both well. And I'll keep my ears pricked to catch your music again.' He looks at the *cobză* propped against the willow tree, his gaze tender yet fierce somehow, no doubt reliving a moment from their shared past.

'Until next time.' He tips his hat and walks away, his limping figure shimmering in the summer's heat.

GLOSSARY

Anteriu: long, elaborate tunic worn by boyars in the past
Bacşiş: a small gratuity to someone who provides a service
Bogdaprosti: a way of thanking someone who gives alms
Bolniţă: hospital, infirmary
Boyar: a member of aristocracy
Ciohodar: low-ranking boyar in charge of shoemakers and the voivode's footwear
Clacă: collective voluntary labour performed by peasants to help each other, often accompanied by storytelling and singing
Cobză: multi-stringed instrument of the lute family
Cobzar: musician who plays the cobză
Coconi: young men, sons of aristocratic families
Cojoc (singular); *Cojoace* (plural): sheepskin coat
Compot: a drink made from fresh or dry fruit boiled in water and sugar
Corvoadă: labour performed by serfs or free peasants for the benefit of landowners
Cotlet: a chop of meat
Cuhnia: kitchen
Iască: a type of dry mushroom used to kindle fire
Iţari: long, narrow trousers worn by peasants
Horă: a traditional folk dance where dancers hold each other's hands, forming a circle

Lăutari: admired musicians, traditionally of Roma origin, often engaged to perform at markets, fairs and festivities for the elite
Obște: community
Opaiț: inexpensive candle or lamp made with fat or grease
Opinci: peasant footwear made of a single rectangle of hide (usually cow) and gathered around the foot, tightened with strips of leather, strings, horsehair, etc.
Pestref: light music sang at parties, of Turkish origin
Posmag: a slice of dry bread
Praznic: the meal at a funeral wake
Slănină: cured fatback or pork belly
Șalvari: loose trousers narrowed at the ankles
Străchini: plates made from clay or wood
Țâbă: (informal, regional, phonetic spelling of țibă) word used to send a dog away or to quieten it
Tizic: cow dung and straws mixed and dried, used as fuel by peasants
Trântă: a form of traditional wrestling
Turtă: flat unleavened bread
Utrenie: morning church service
Vecernie: evening church service
Vizitiu: coachman, driver
Voivode: country's ruler
Vraci: doctor
Zacuscă: finger food served to accompany drinks
Zmei (plural): fantastic creatures of Romanian folklore and mythology, often portrayed as anthropomorphic dragons that can spit fire

ACKNOWLEDGEMENTS

Though I've written and re-written this book many times over the past five years, it would not have seen the light of day if it wasn't for Cari Rosen, the commissioning editor at Legend Press. Thank you for believing in this book and for bringing it to readers. Your guidance, generosity and patience have made me feel truly blessed.

I'm full of gratitude for the entire team at Legend Press, whose hard work and dedication have helped my publishing dream become a reality. For Ross Dickinson, whose sharp eye and brilliant editing have made this a better novel. For Rose Cooper, for the stunning cover design which reflects the story so well.

Boundless thanks to my peer writers - Karen Hudson, Ian Critchley, Johanna Cordery, Nancy Saunders and Rose Wilkinson - for your regular support and detailed, thoughtful feedback along the years. This book is far better thanks to you.

I'm also deeply thankful to Marina Sofia, Daniel Culver and Julie-Ann Corrigan, for your advice on an earlier draft, the stepping stone to the finished book.

Forever grateful to Sean O' Reilly, Claire Keegan, and the Stinging Fly, for your encouragement to be bold and brave in my writing. To Esther Freud for sharing your passion and wisdom in crafting stories. To Faber Academy for the opportunity to hone my skills and find my tribe.

To my family and friends, for your love and unwavering support, with my deepest debt to Paul - thank you for everything!

A lot of what has gone into this book, I owe it to the small community where I grew up, who instilled in me the love for nature, how to see and treat it as a sanctuary – with respect, with awe, with gratitude.

And above all, I want to thank the women of Moldova, who have taught me strength, resilience, faith, kindness, and the virtue and value of hard work. You are the unsung heroes of an eternally challenging country. This is to you!